KAPTARA

VOLUME ONE: FEAR NOT, TINY ALIEN

CHIP ZDARSKY

KAGAN McLEOD

BECKA KINZIE COLOR ASSIST

TOMMY K EDITING

DREW GILL PRODUCTION

IMAGE COMICS, INC.
Robert Kirkman – Chief Operating Officer
Erik Larsen – Chief Financial Officer
Todd McFarlane – President
Marc Silvestri – Chief Executive Officer
Jim Valentino – Vice-President

Eric Stephenson – Publisher
Corey Murphy – Director of Sales
Jeff Boison – Director of Publishing Planning & Book Trade Sales
Jeremy Sullivan – Director of Digital Sales
Kat Salazar – Director of PR & Marketing
Emily Miller – Director of Operations
Branwyn Bigglestone – Senior Accounts Manager
Sarah Mello – Accounts Manager
Drew Gill – Art Director
Jonathan Chan – Production Manager
Meredith Wallace – Print Manager
Briah Skelly – Publicity Assistant
Randy Okamura – Marketing Production Designer
David Brothers – Branding Manager
Ally Power – Content Manager
Sasha Head – Production Artist
Addison Duke – Production Artist
Vincent Kukua – Production Artist
Tricia Ramos – Production Artist
Jeff Stang – Direct Market Sales Representative
Emilio Bautista – Digital Sales Associate
Chloe Ramos-Peterson – Administrative Assistant
IMAGECOMICS.COM

image

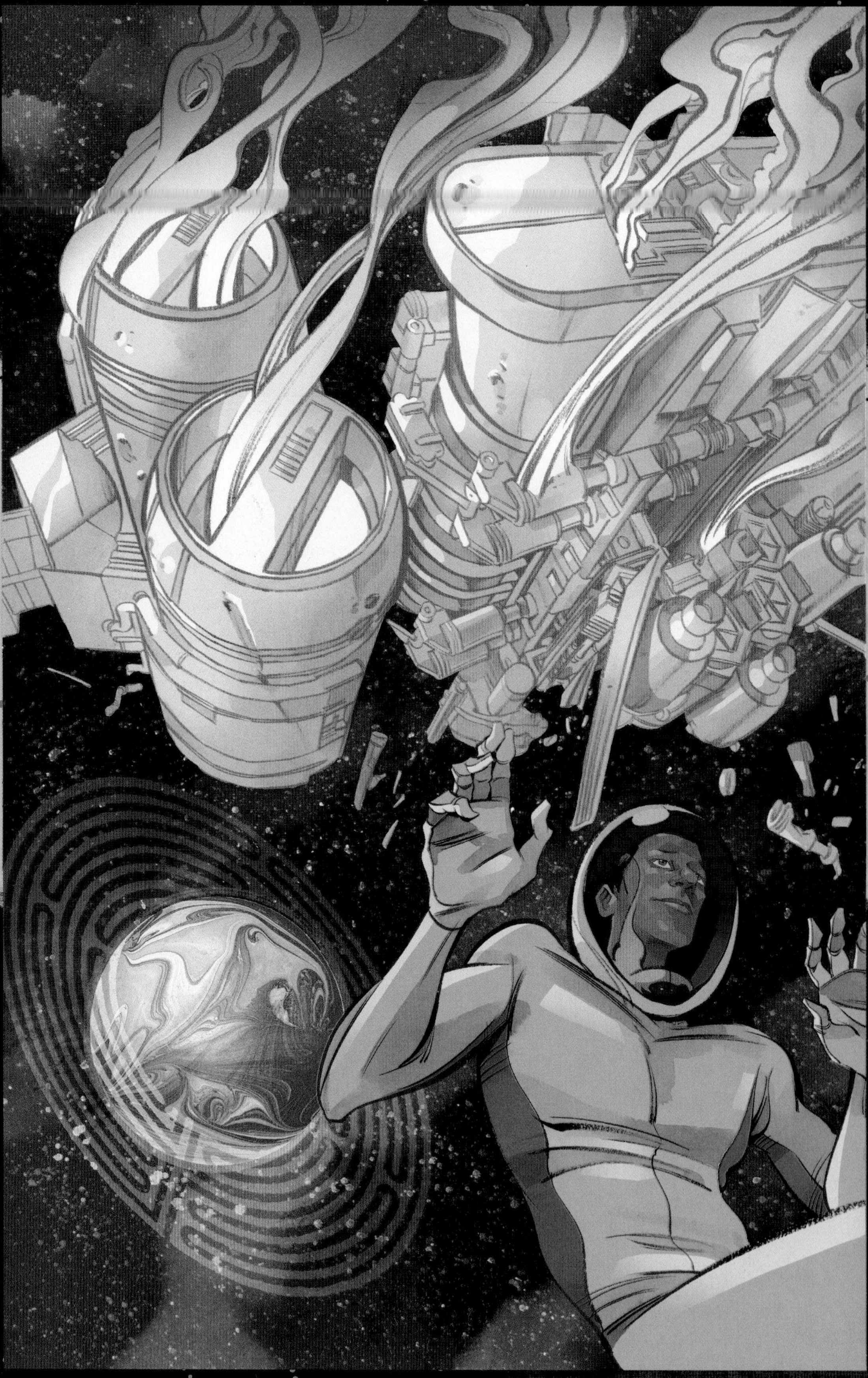

CHAPTER ONE

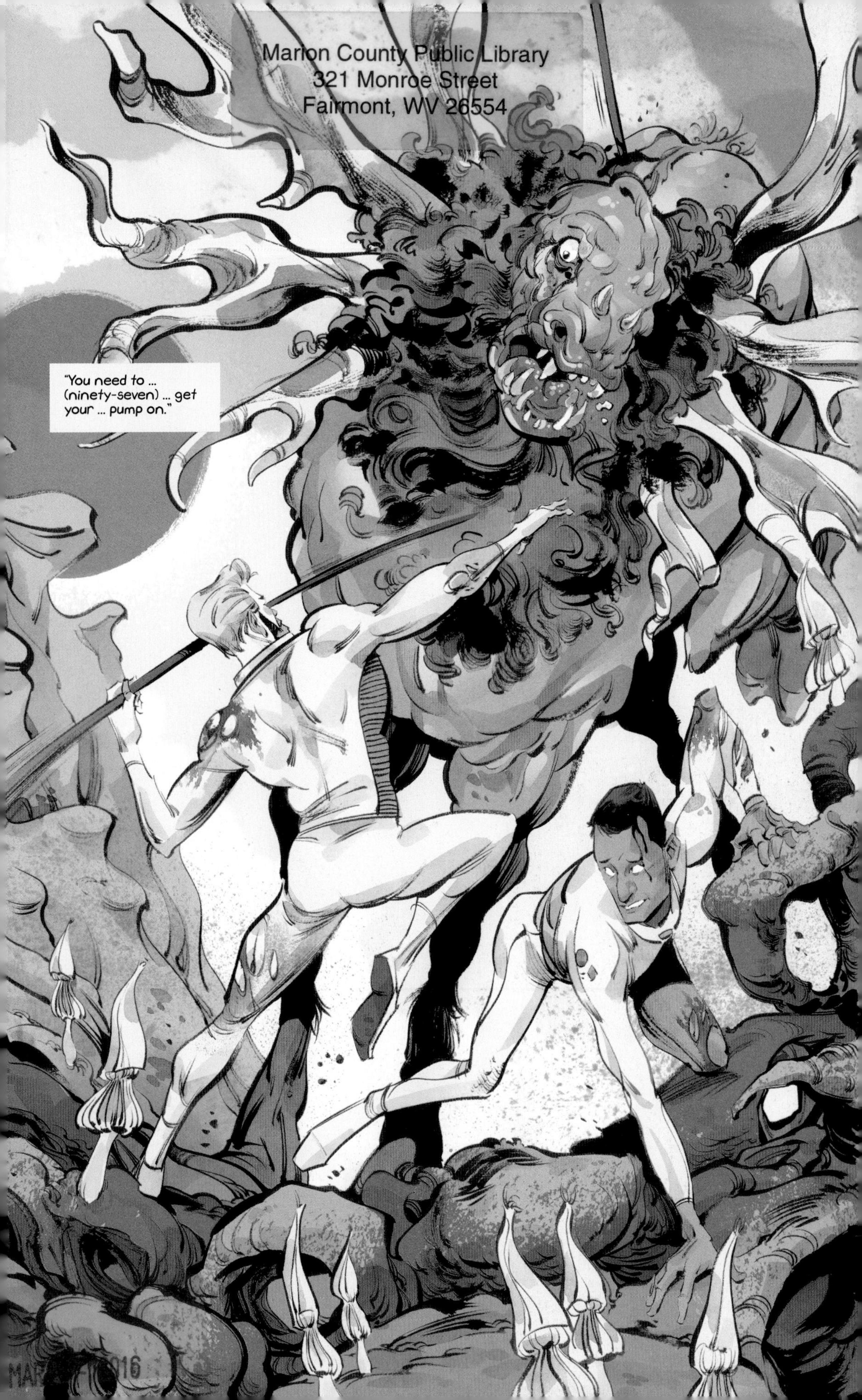
"You need to ... (ninety-seven) ... get your ... pump on."

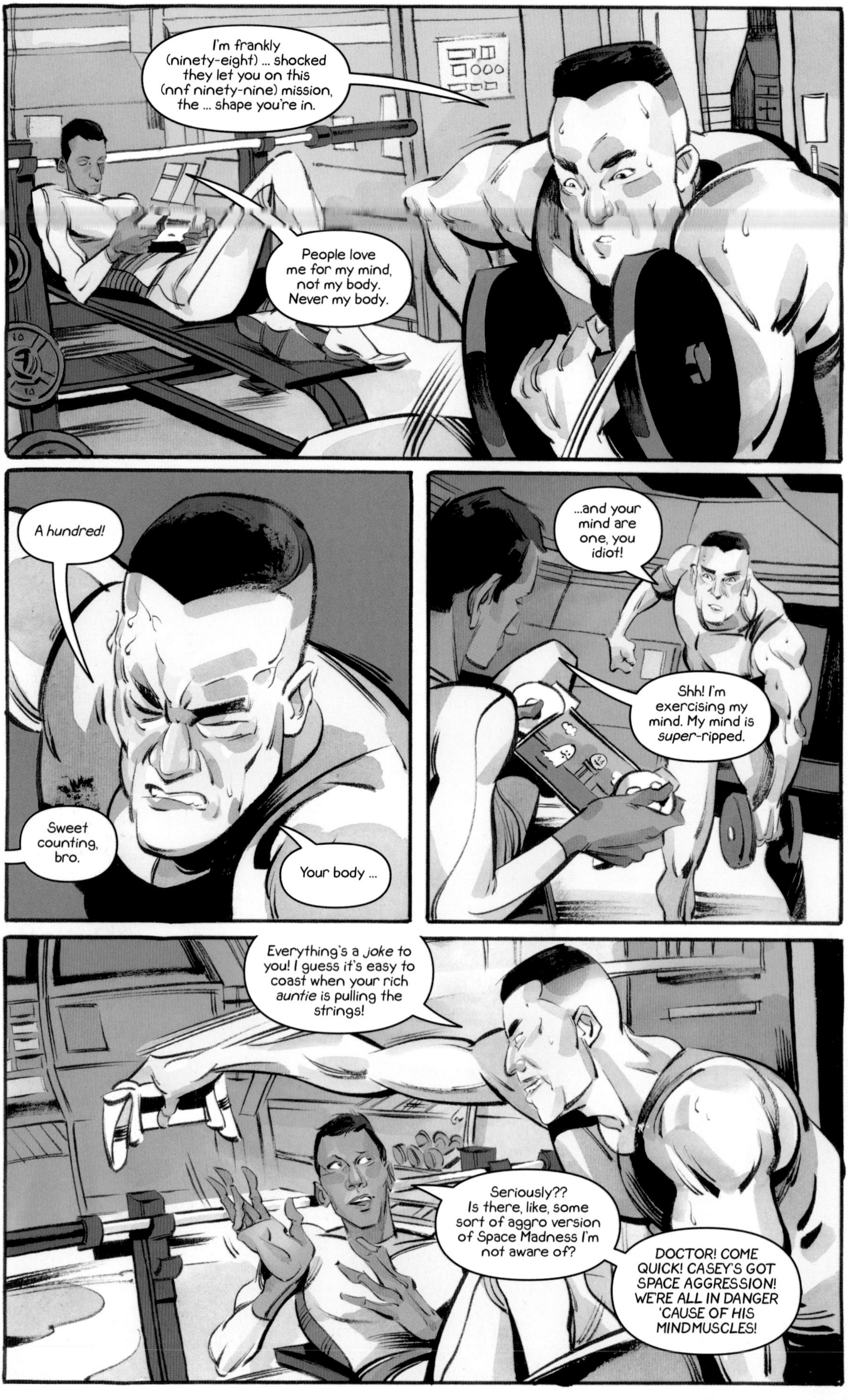
I'm frankly (ninety-eight) ... shocked they let you on this (nnf ninety-nine) mission, the ... shape you're in.
People love me for my mind, not my body. Never my body.
A *hundred!*
Sweet counting, bro.
Your body ...
...and your mind are one, you idiot!
Shh! I'm exercising my mind. My mind is *super*-ripped.
Everything's a *joke* to you! I guess it's easy to coast when your rich *auntie* is pulling the strings!
Seriously?? Is there, like, some sort of aggro version of Space Madness I'm not aware of?
DOCTOR! COME QUICK! CASEY'S GOT SPACE AGGRESSION! WE'RE ALL IN DANGER 'CAUSE OF HIS MINDMUSCLES!

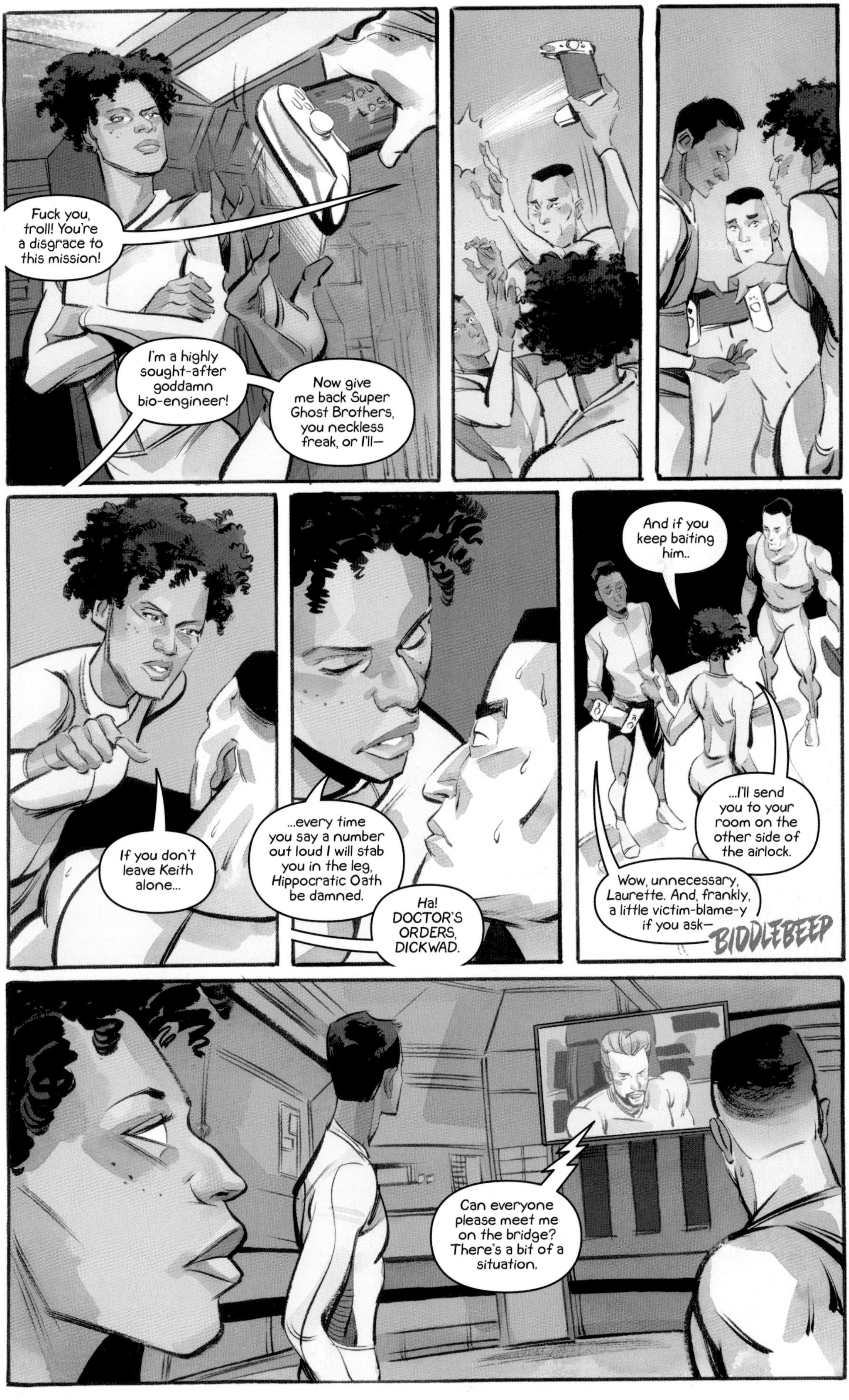
Fuck you, troll! You're a disgrace to this mission!
I'm a highly sought-after goddamn bio-engineer!
Now give me back Super Ghost Brothers, you neckless freak, or I'll—
If you don't leave Keith alone...
...every time you say a number out loud I will stab you in the leg, Hippocratic Oath be damned.
Ha! DOCTOR'S ORDERS, DICKWAD.
And if you keep baiting him..
...I'll send you to your room on the other side of the airlock.
Wow, unnecessary, Laurette. And, frankly, a little victim-blame-y if you ask—
BIDDLEBEEP
Can everyone please meet me on the bridge? There's a bit of a situation.

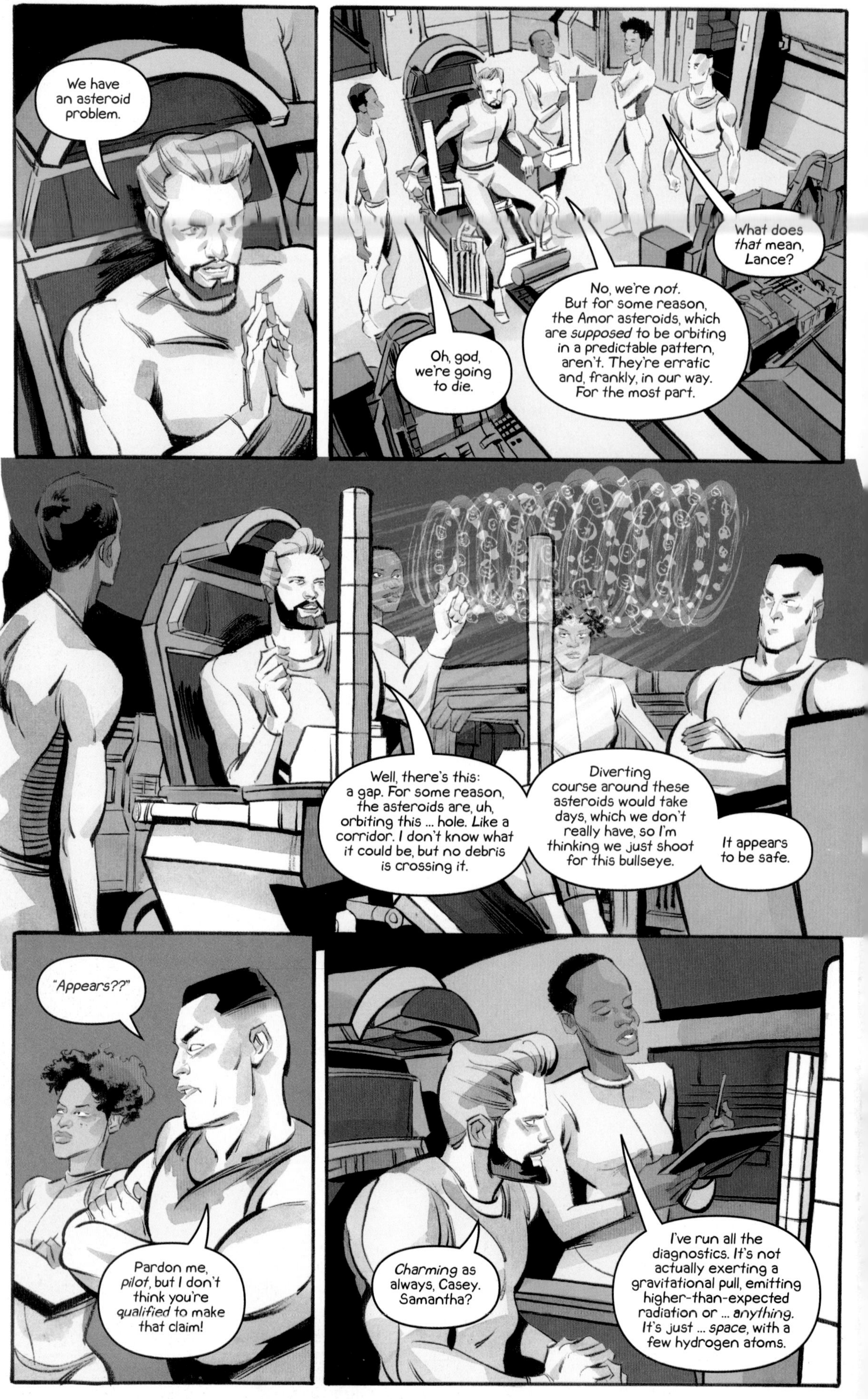
We have an asteroid problem.
What does *that* mean, Lance?
No, we're *not*. But for some reason, the Amor asteroids, which are *supposed* to be orbiting in a predictable pattern, aren't. They're erratic and, frankly, in our way. For the most part.
Oh, god, we're going to die.
Well, there's this: a gap. For some reason, the asteroids are, uh, orbiting this ... hole. Like a corridor. I don't know what it could be, but no debris is crossing it.
Diverting course around these asteroids would take days, which we don't really have, so I'm thinking we just shoot for this bullseye.
It appears to be safe.
"Appears??"
Pardon me, *pilot*, but I don't think you're *qualified* to make that claim!
Charming as always, Casey. Samantha?
I've run all the diagnostics. It's not actually exerting a gravitational pull, emitting higher-than-expected radiation or ... *anything*. It's just ... *space*, with a few hydrogen atoms.

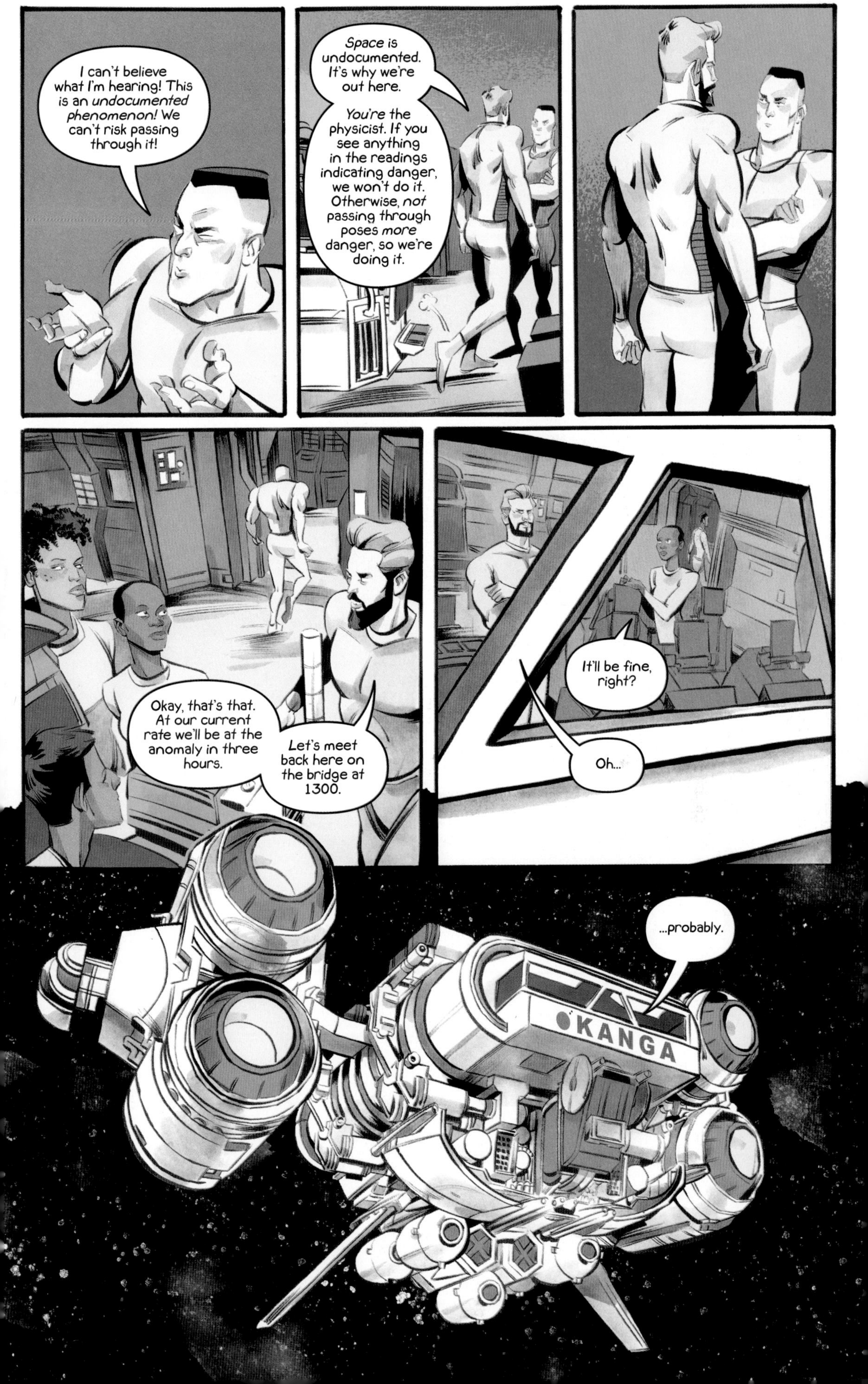
I can't believe what I'm hearing! This is an *undocumented phenomenon!* We can't risk passing through it!
Space is undocumented. It's why we're out here.
You're the physicist. If you see anything in the readings indicating danger, we won't do it. Otherwise, *not* passing through poses *more* danger, so we're doing it.
Okay, that's that. At our current rate we'll be at the anomaly in three hours.
Let's meet back here on the bridge at 1300.
It'll be fine, right?
Oh...
...probably.
KANGA

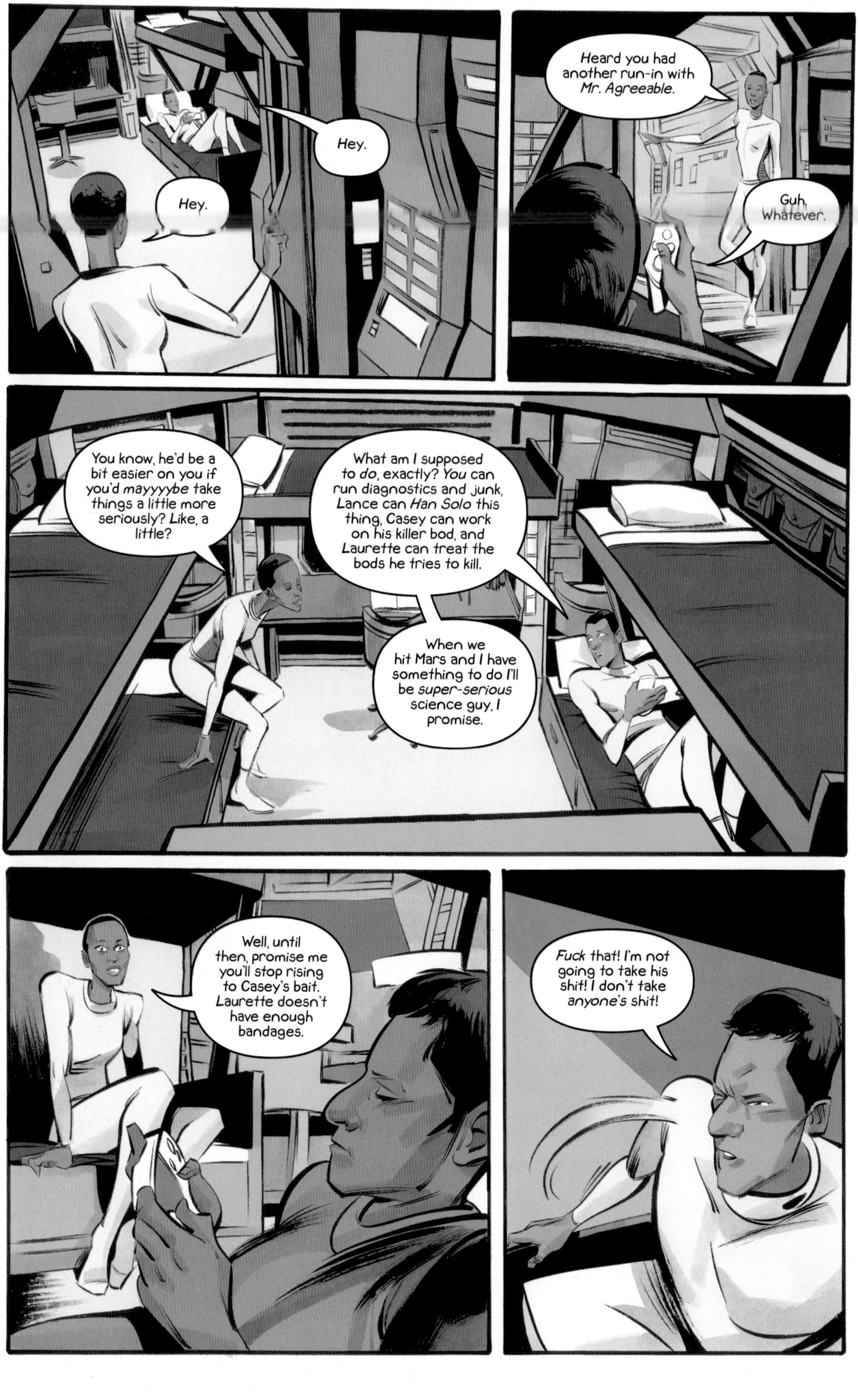
Hey.
Hey.
Heard you had another run-in with *Mr. Agreeable.*
Guh. Whatever.
You know, he'd be a bit easier on you if you'd *mayyyybe* take things a little more seriously? Like, a little?
What am I supposed to *do*, exactly? *You* can run diagnostics and junk, Lance can *Han Solo* this thing, Casey can work on his killer bod, and Laurette can treat the bods he tries to kill.
When we hit Mars and I have something to do I'll be *super-serious* science guy, I promise.
Well, until then, promise me you'll stop rising to Casey's bait. Laurette doesn't have enough bandages.
Fuck that! I'm not going to take his shit! I don't take *anyone's* shit!

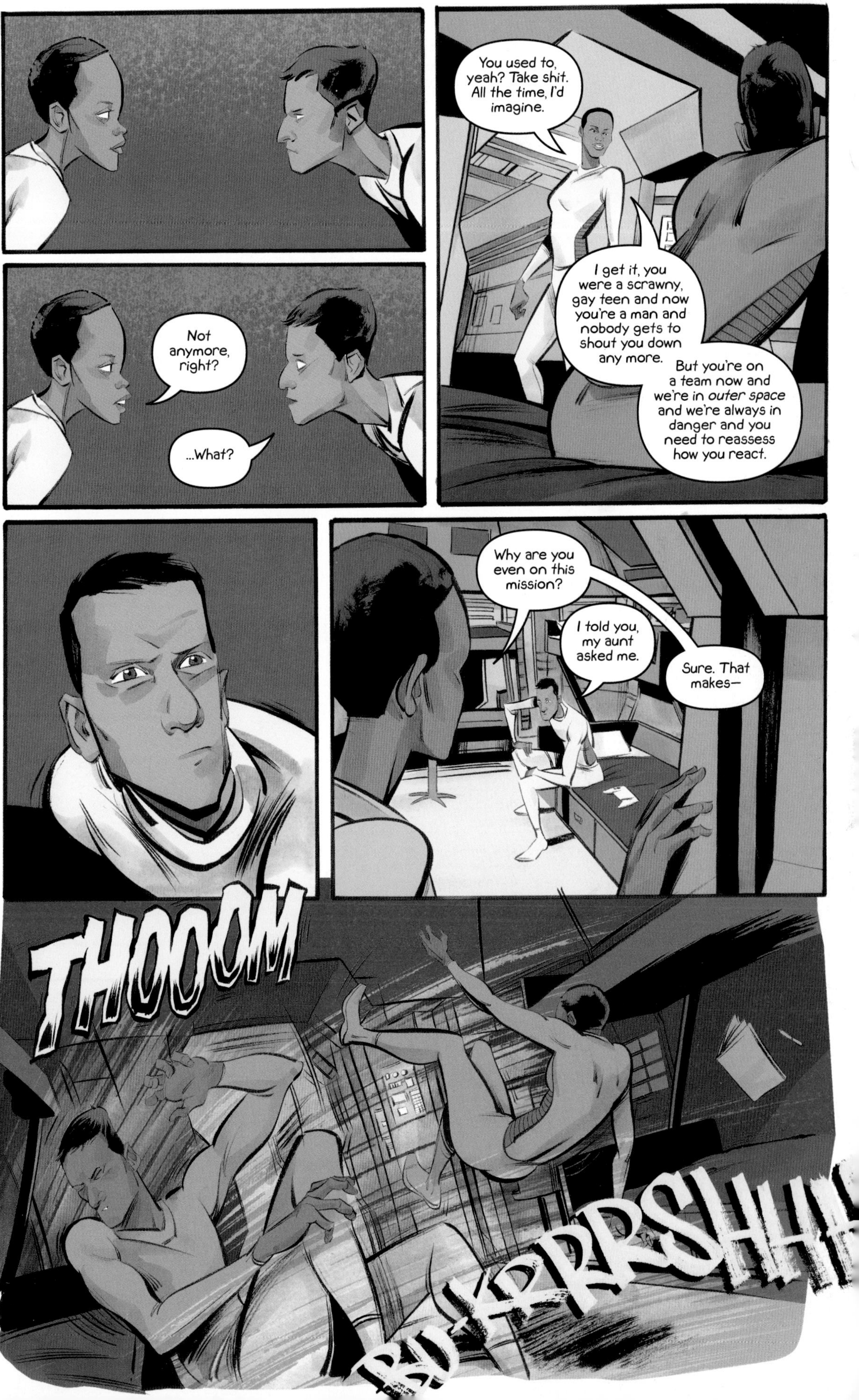

You used to, yeah? Take shit. All the time, I'd imagine.
Not anymore, right?
...What?
I get it, you were a scrawny, gay teen and now you're a man and nobody gets to shout you down any more.
But you're on a team now and we're in *outer space* and we're always in danger and you need to reassess how you react.
Why are you even on this mission?
I told you, my aunt asked me.
Sure. That makes—
THOOOM
BU-KRRRSHH

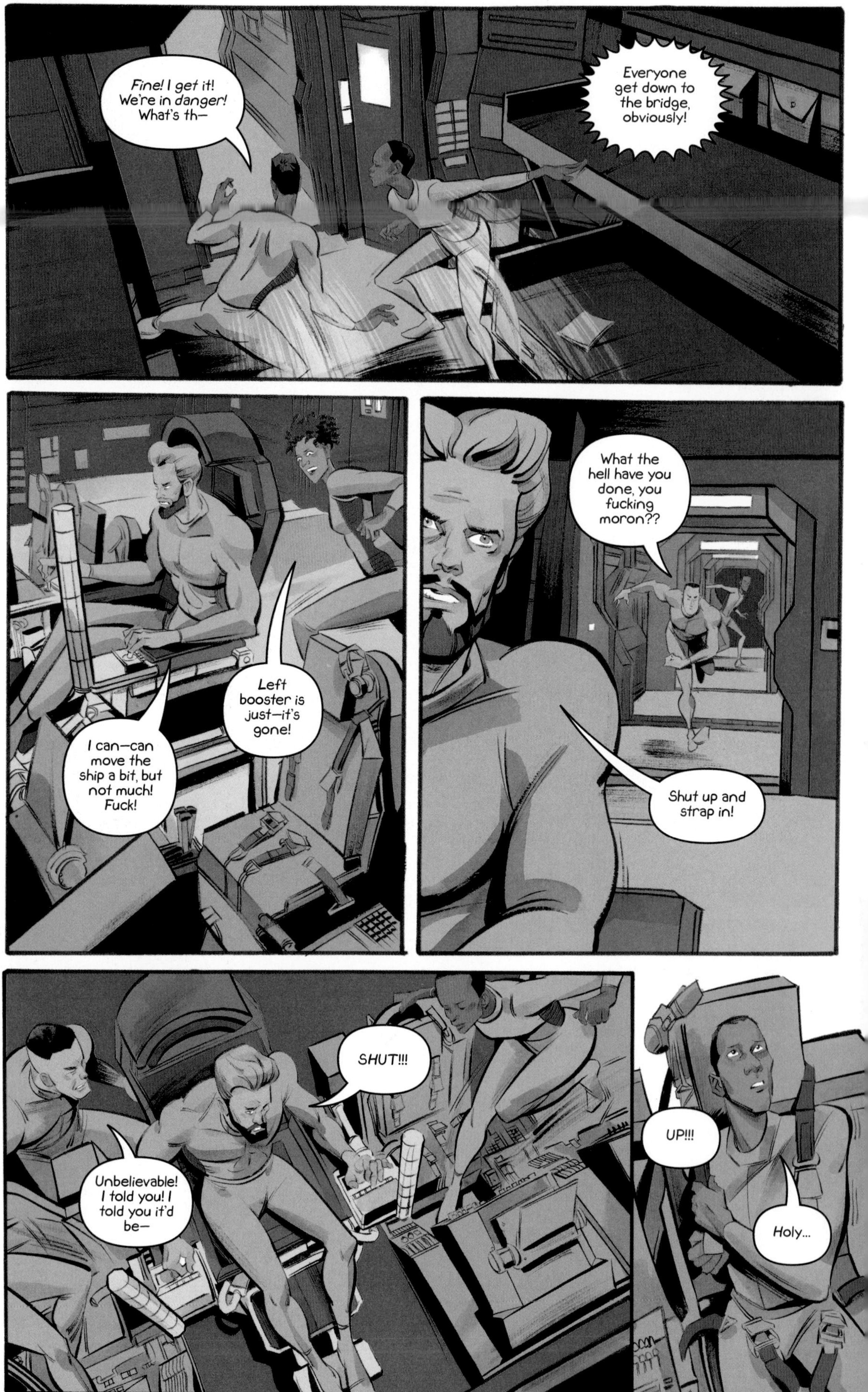
Fine! I get it! We're in danger! What's th—
Everyone get down to the bridge, obviously!
Left booster is just—it's gone!
I can—can move the ship a bit, but not much! Fuck!
What the hell have you done, you fucking moron??
Shut up and strap in!
Unbelievable! I told you! I told you it'd be—
SHUT!!!
UP!!!
Holy...

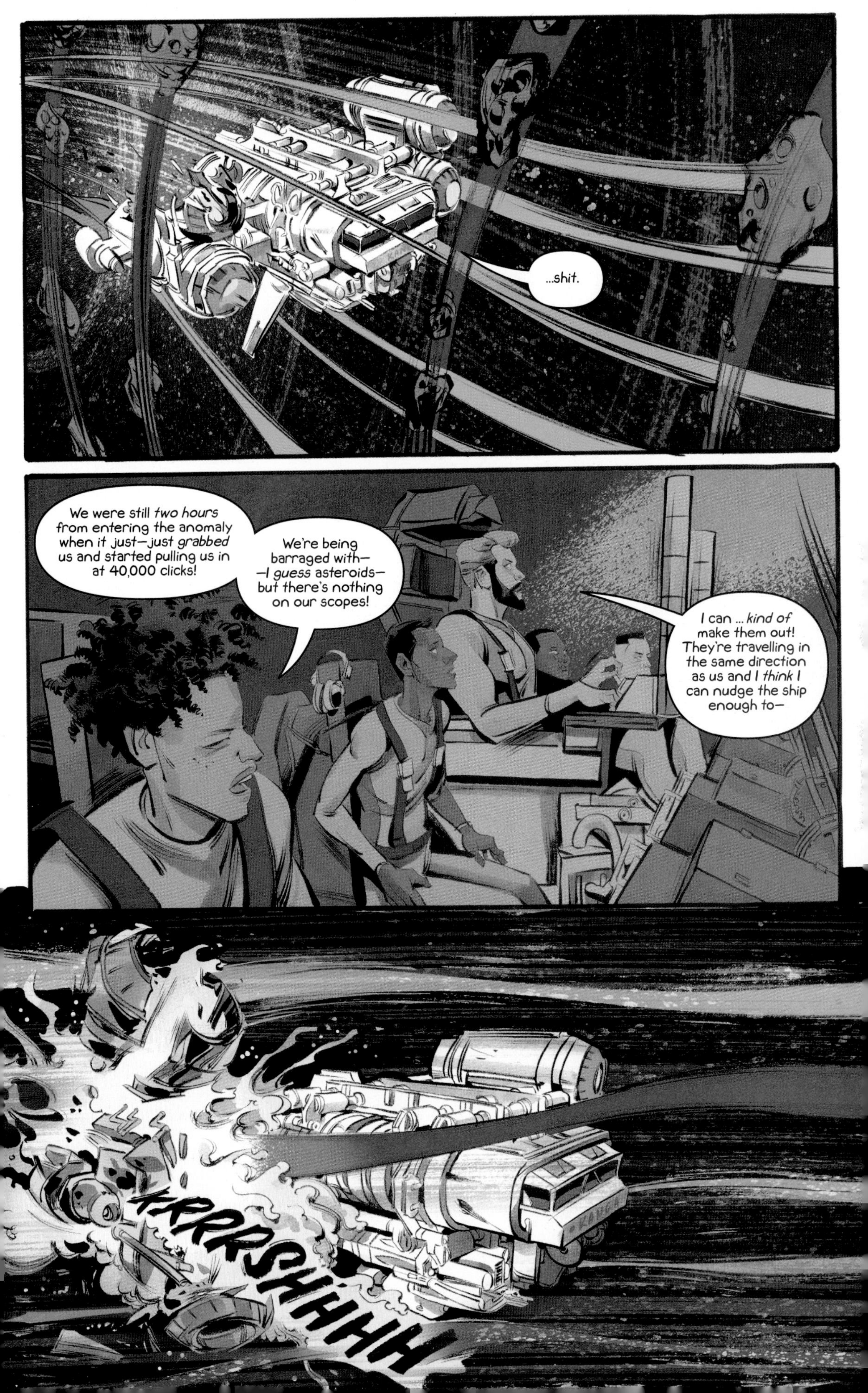
...shit.
We were still *two hours* from entering the anomaly when it just—just *grabbed* us and started pulling us in at 40,000 clicks!
We're being barraged with— —I *guess* asteroids— but there's nothing on our scopes!
I can ... *kind of* make them out! They're travelling in the same direction as us and I *think* I can nudge the ship enough to—
KRRSHHHHH

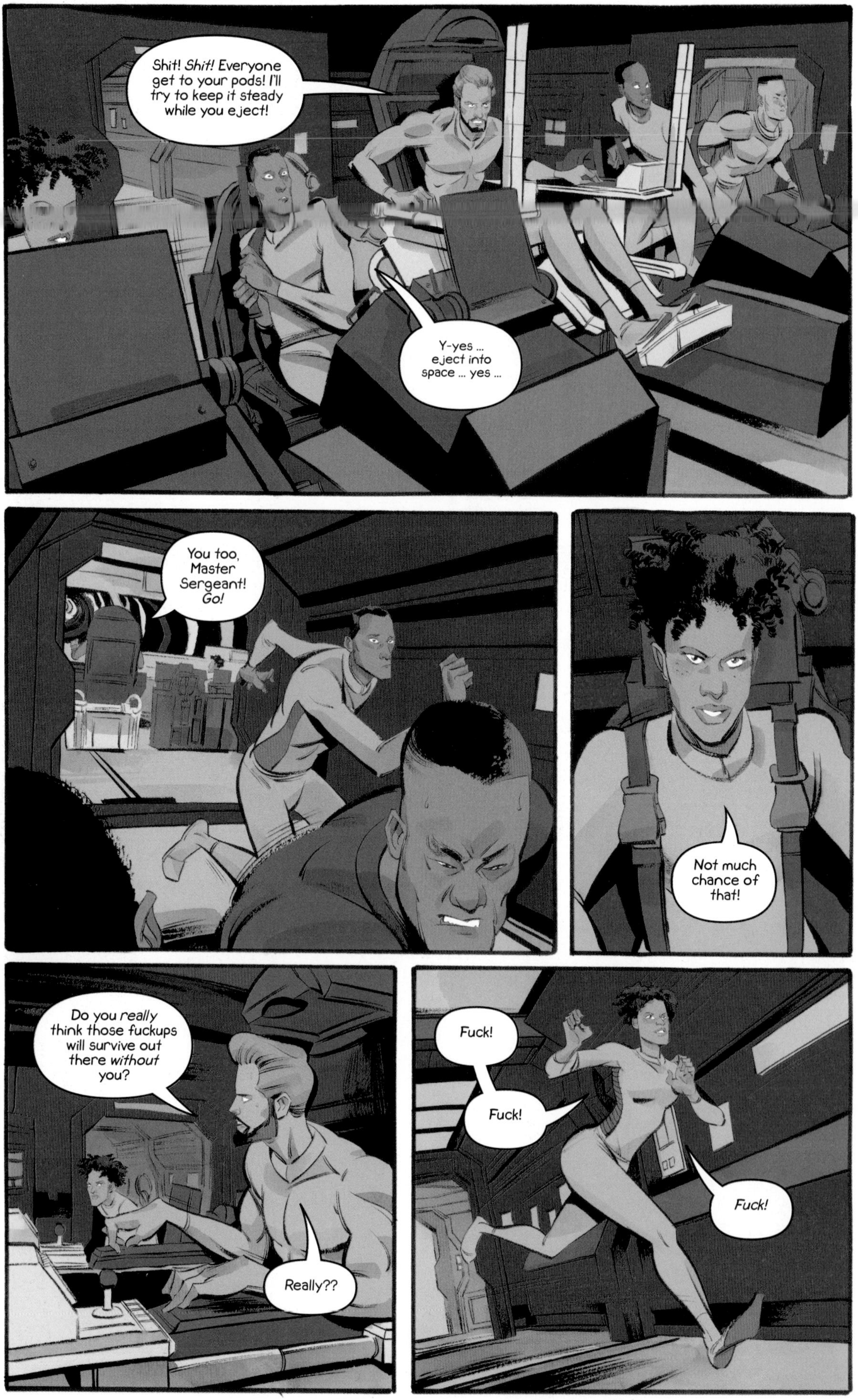
Shit! *Shit!* Everyone get to your pods! I'll try to keep it steady while you eject!
Y-yes ... eject into space ... yes ...
You too, Master Sergeant! *Go!*
Not much chance of that!
Do you *really* think those fuckups will survive out there *without* you?
Really??
Fuck!
Fuck!
Fuck!

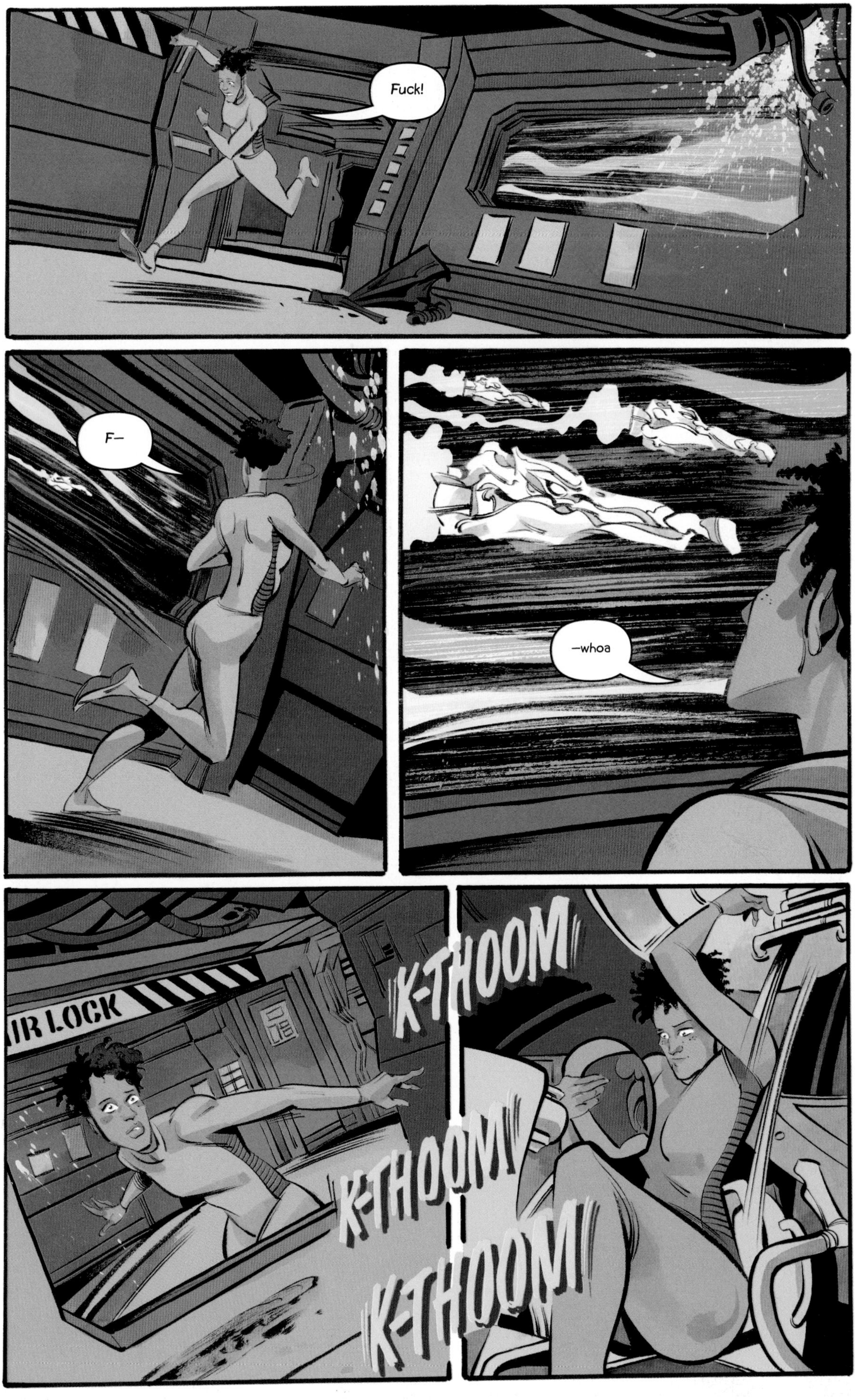

Fuck!
F—
—whoa
AIR LOCK
K-THOOM
K-THOOM
K-THOOM

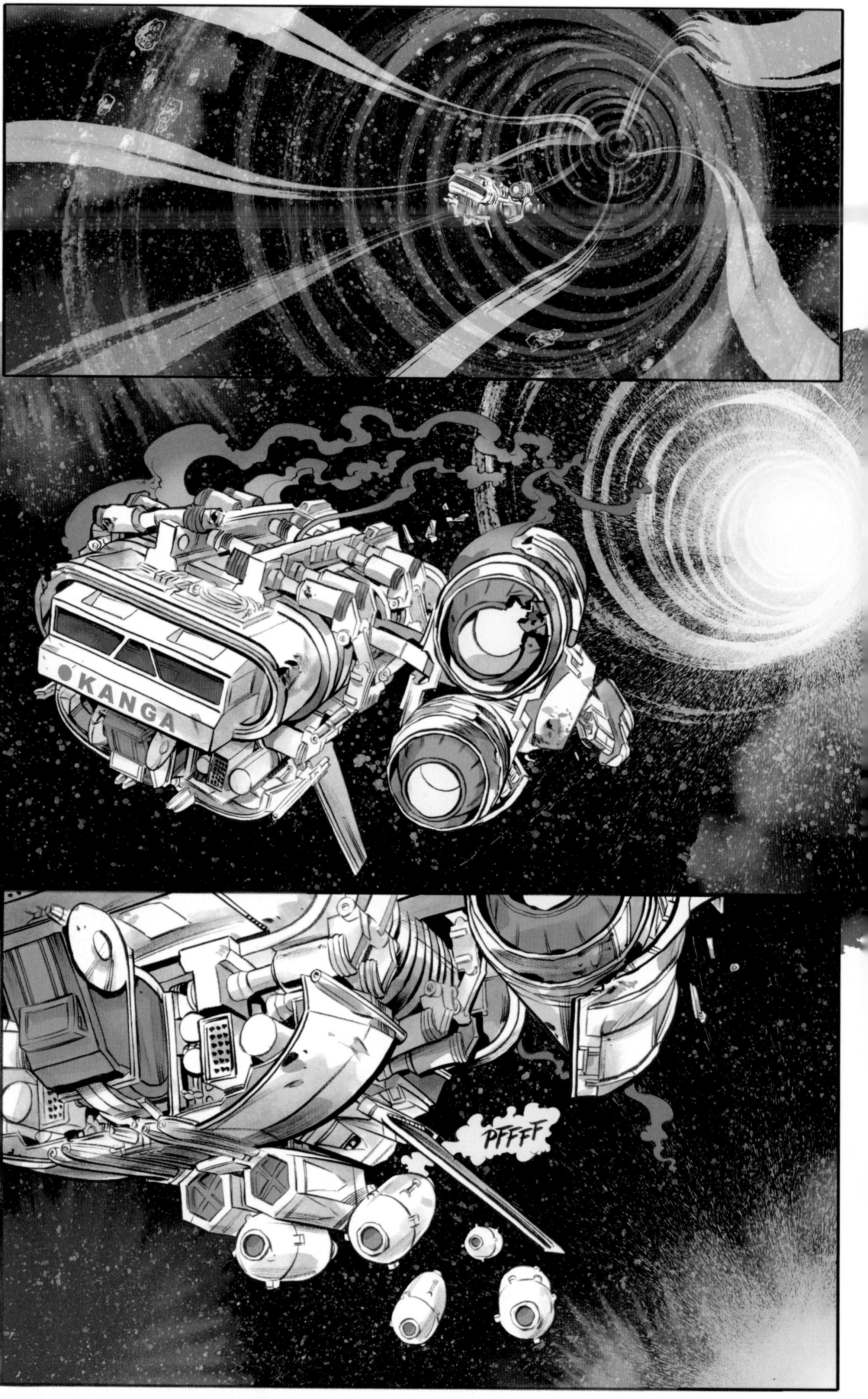
KANGA
PFFFF

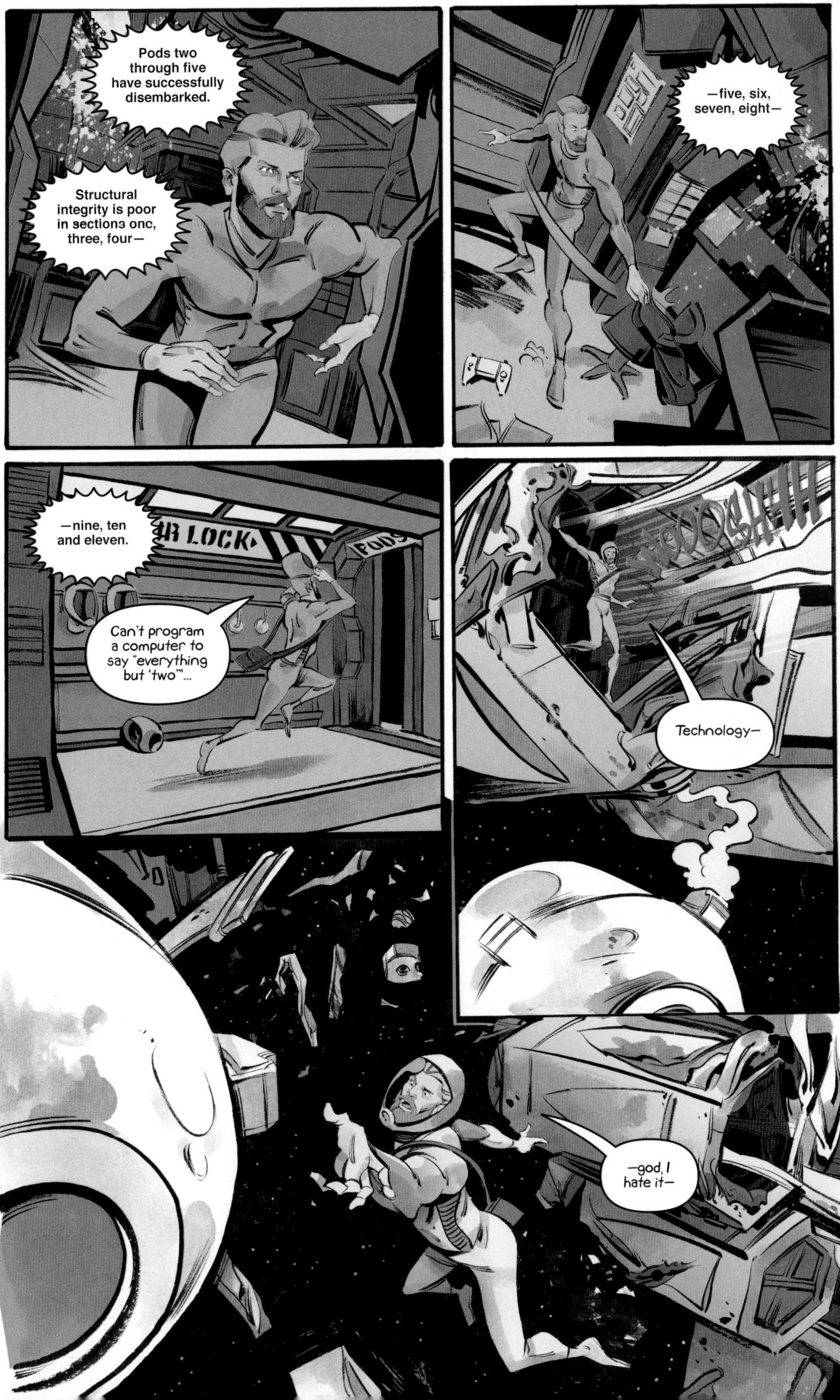
Pods two through five have successfully disembarked.
Structural integrity is poor in sections one, three, four—
—five, six, seven, eight—
—nine, ten and eleven.
Can't program a computer to say "everything but 'two'"...
Technology—
—god, I hate it—

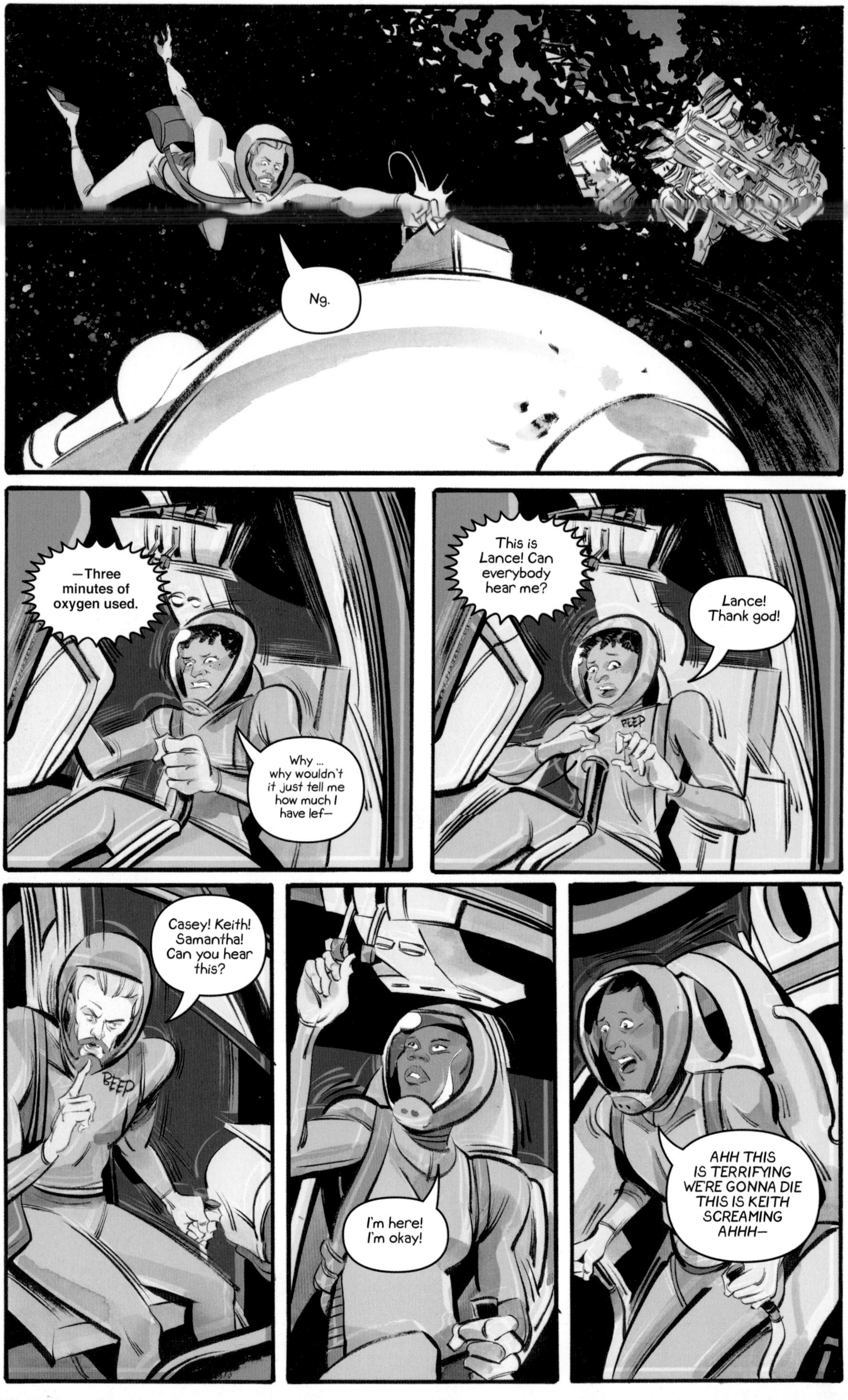
Ng.
—Three minutes of oxygen used.
Why ... why wouldn't it just tell me how much I have lef—
This is Lance! Can everybody hear me?
Lance! Thank god!
BEEP
Casey! Keith! Samantha! Can you hear this?
BEEP
I'm here! I'm okay!
AHH THIS IS TERRIFYING WE'RE GONNA DIE THIS IS KEITH SCREAMING AHHH—

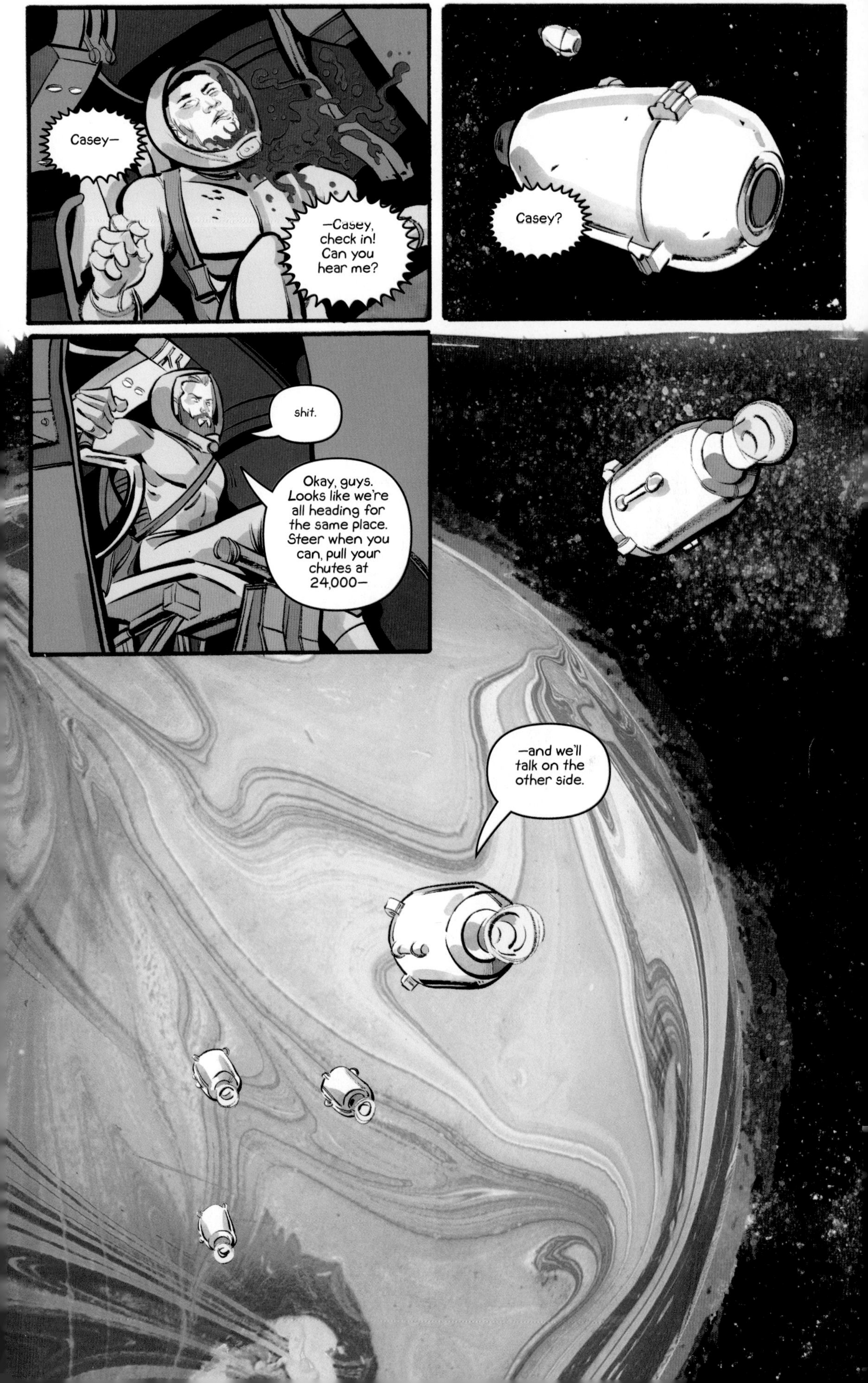
Casey—
—Casey, check in! Can you hear me?
Casey?
shit.
Okay, guys. Looks like we're all heading for the same place. Steer when you can, pull your chutes at 24,000—
—and we'll talk on the other side.

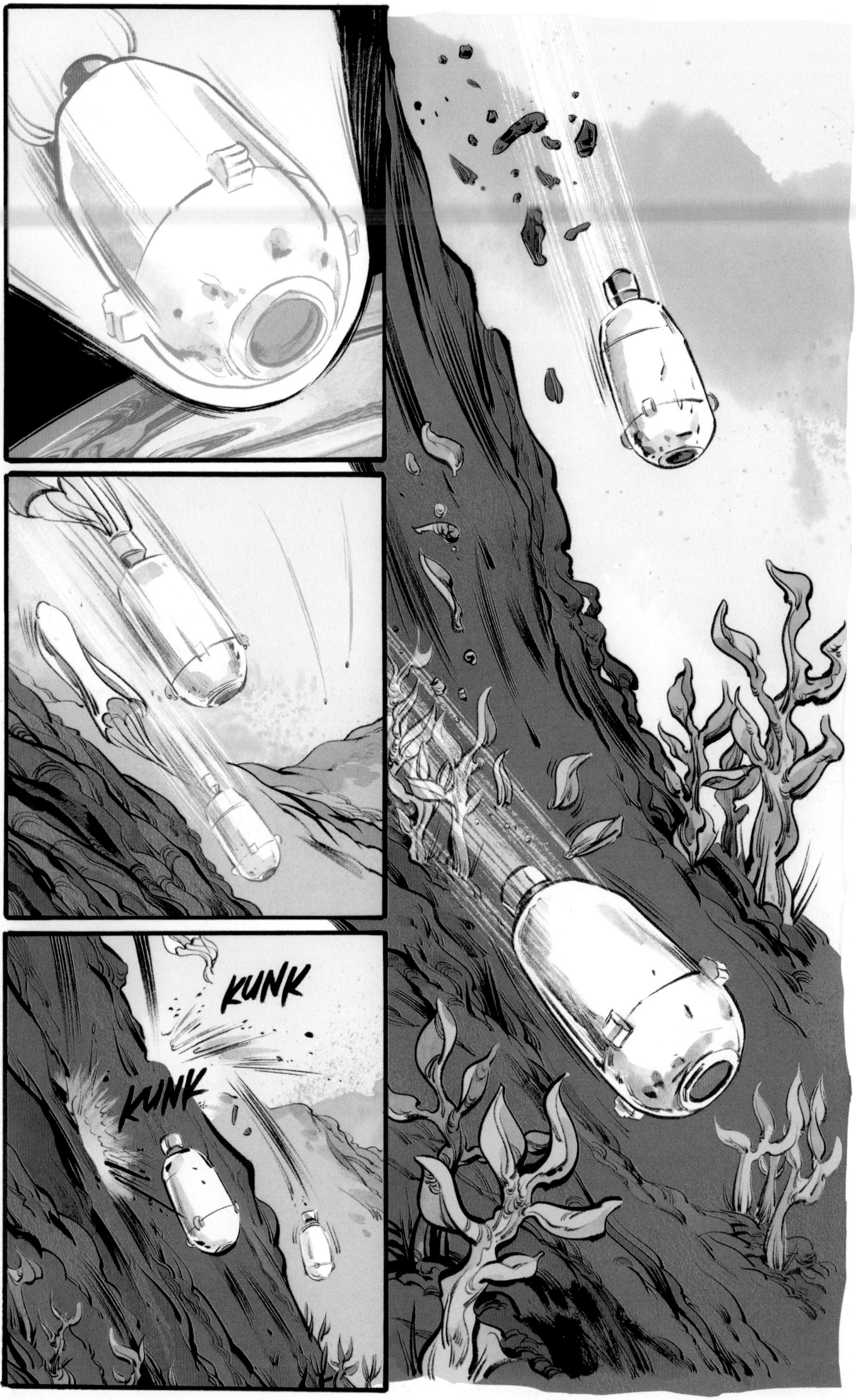
KUNK
KUNK

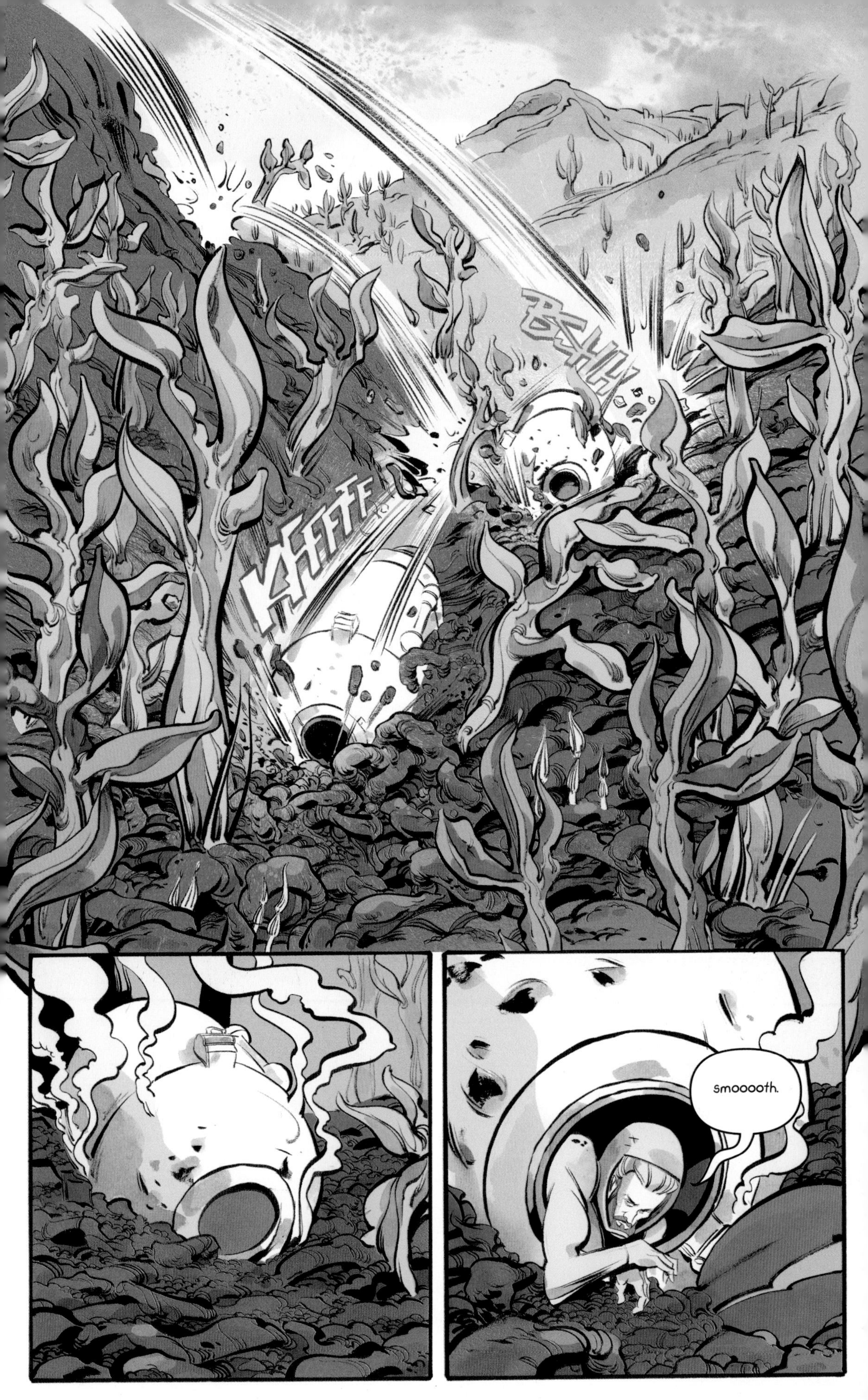
KFFFFF
smoooooth.

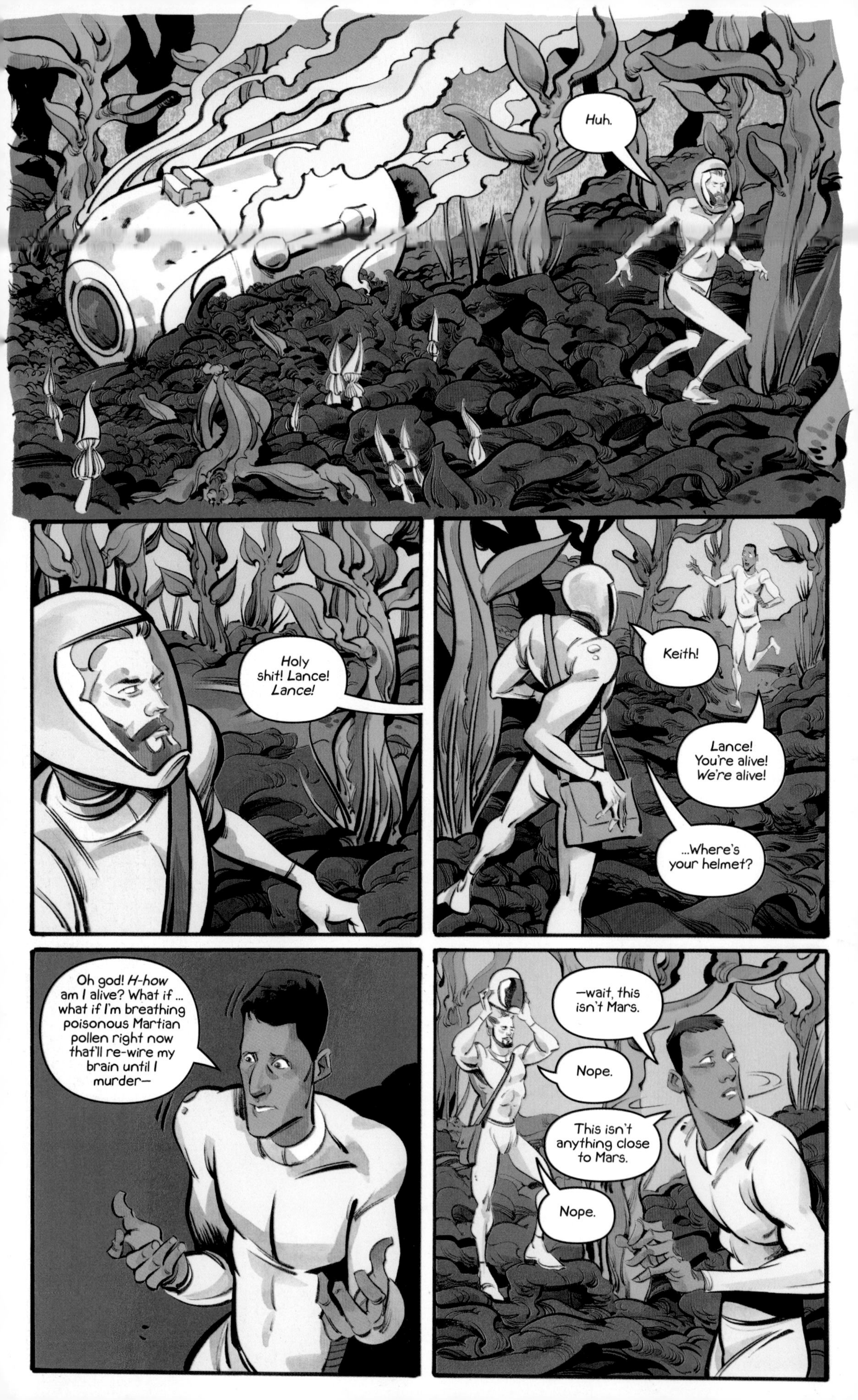
Huh.
Holy shit! Lance! *Lance!*
Keith!
Lance! You're alive! *We're* alive!
...Where's your helmet?
Oh god! *H-how* am I alive? What if ... what if I'm breathing poisonous Martian pollen right now that'll re-wire my brain until I murder—
—wait, this isn't Mars.
Nope.
This isn't anything close to Mars.
Nope.

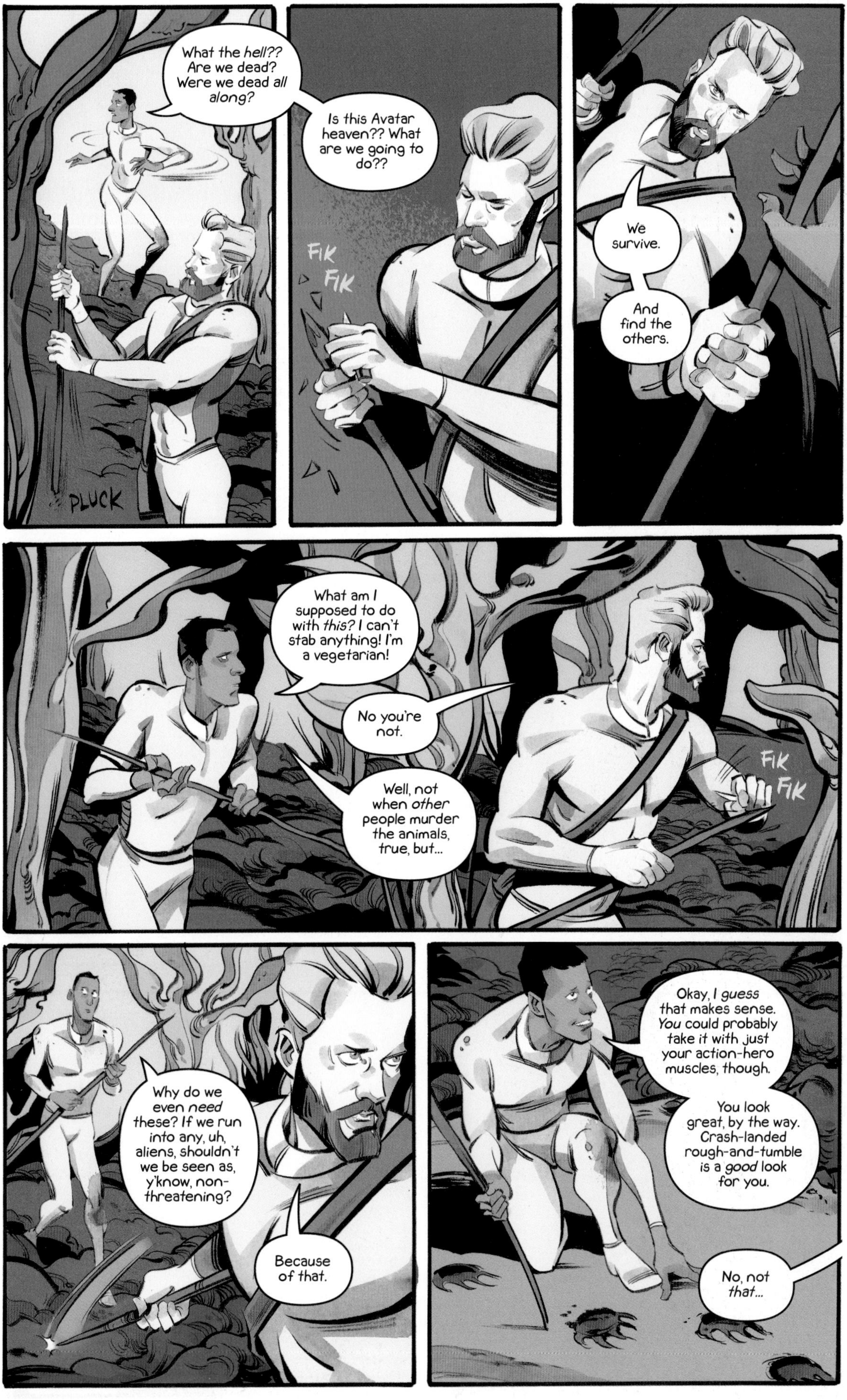
What the *hell??* Are we dead? Were we dead *all along?*
PLUCK
Is this Avatar heaven?? What are we going to do??
FIK FIK
We survive.
And find the others.
What am I supposed to do with *this?* I can't stab anything! I'm a vegetarian!
No you're not.
Well, not when *other* people murder the animals, true, but...
FIK FIK
Why do we even *need* these? If we run into any, uh, aliens, shouldn't we be seen as, y'know, non-threatening?
Because of that.
Okay, I *guess* that makes sense. *You* could probably take it with just your action-hero muscles, though.
You look great, by the way. Crash-landed rough-and-tumble is a *good* look for you.
No, not *that*...

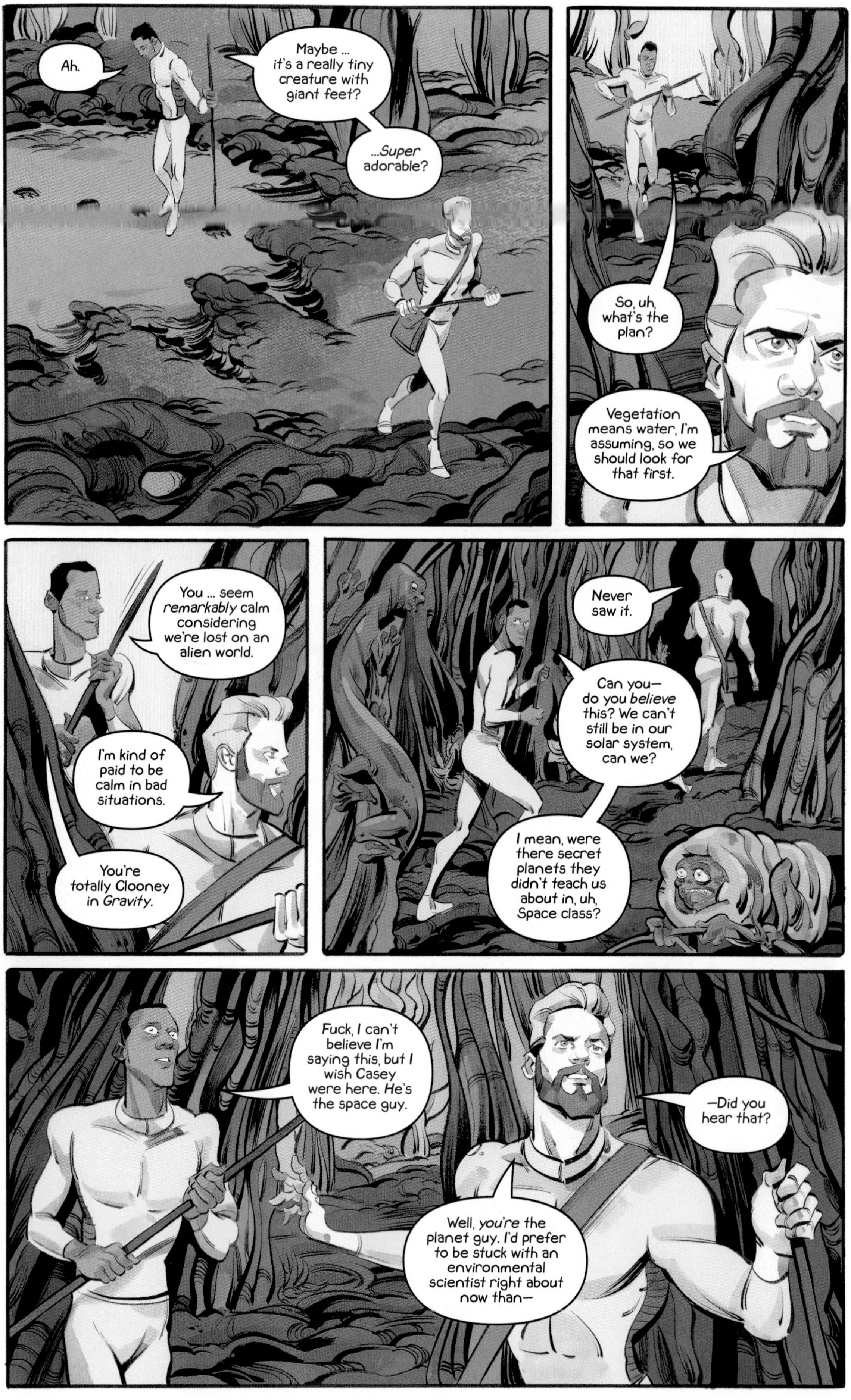
Ah.
Maybe ... it's a really tiny creature with giant feet?
...*Super* adorable?
So, uh, what's the plan?
Vegetation means water, I'm assuming, so we should look for that first.
You ... seem *remarkably* calm considering we're lost on an alien world.
I'm kind of paid to be calm in bad situations.
You're totally Clooney in *Gravity*.
Never saw it.
Can you— do you *believe* this? We can't still be in our solar system, can we?
I mean, were there secret planets they didn't teach us about in, uh, Space class?
Fuck, I can't believe I'm saying this, but I wish Casey were here. He's the space guy.
Well, *you're* the planet guy. I'd prefer to be stuck with an environmental scientist right about now than—
—Did you hear that?

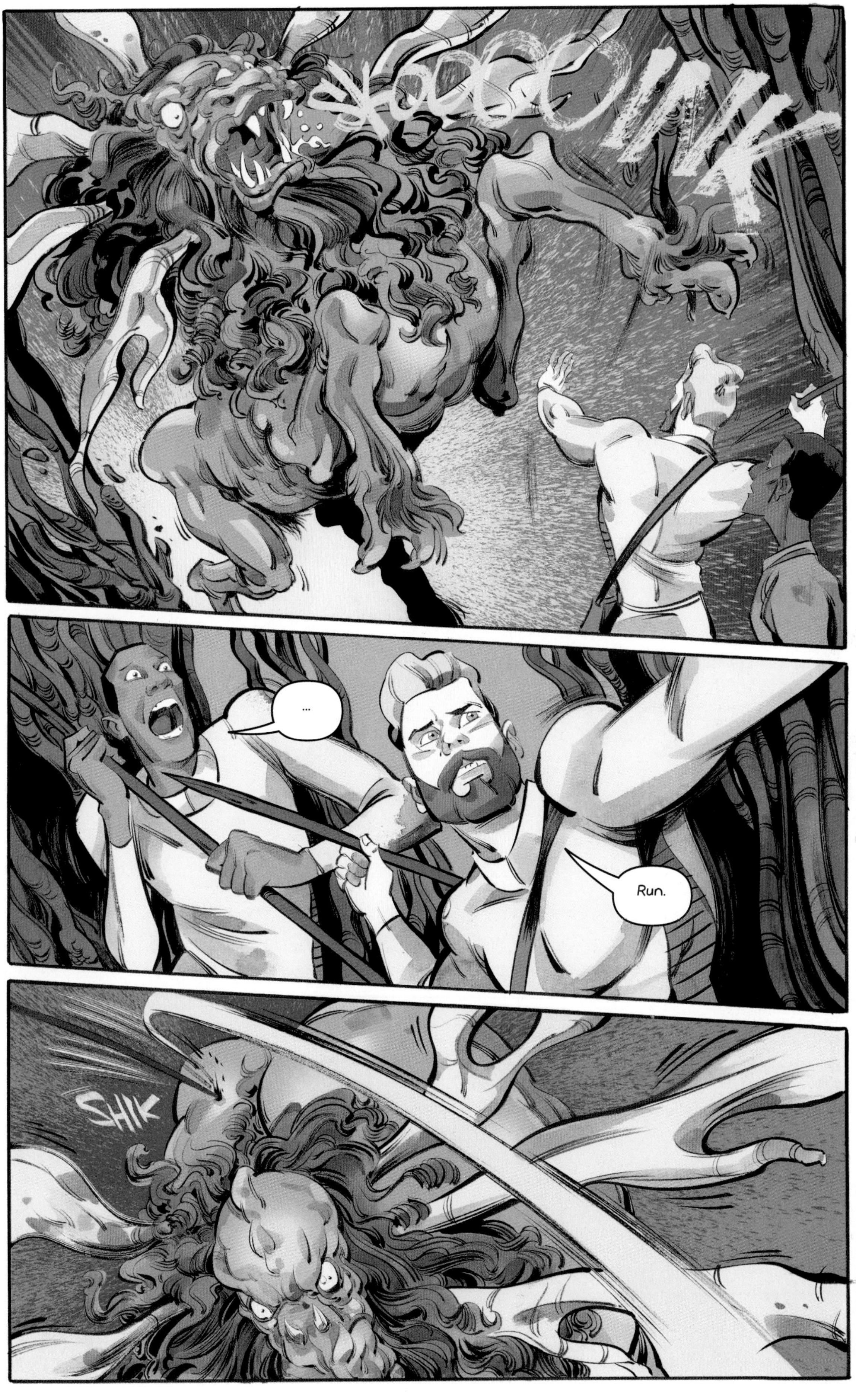
SKOOOONK
...
Run.
SHIK

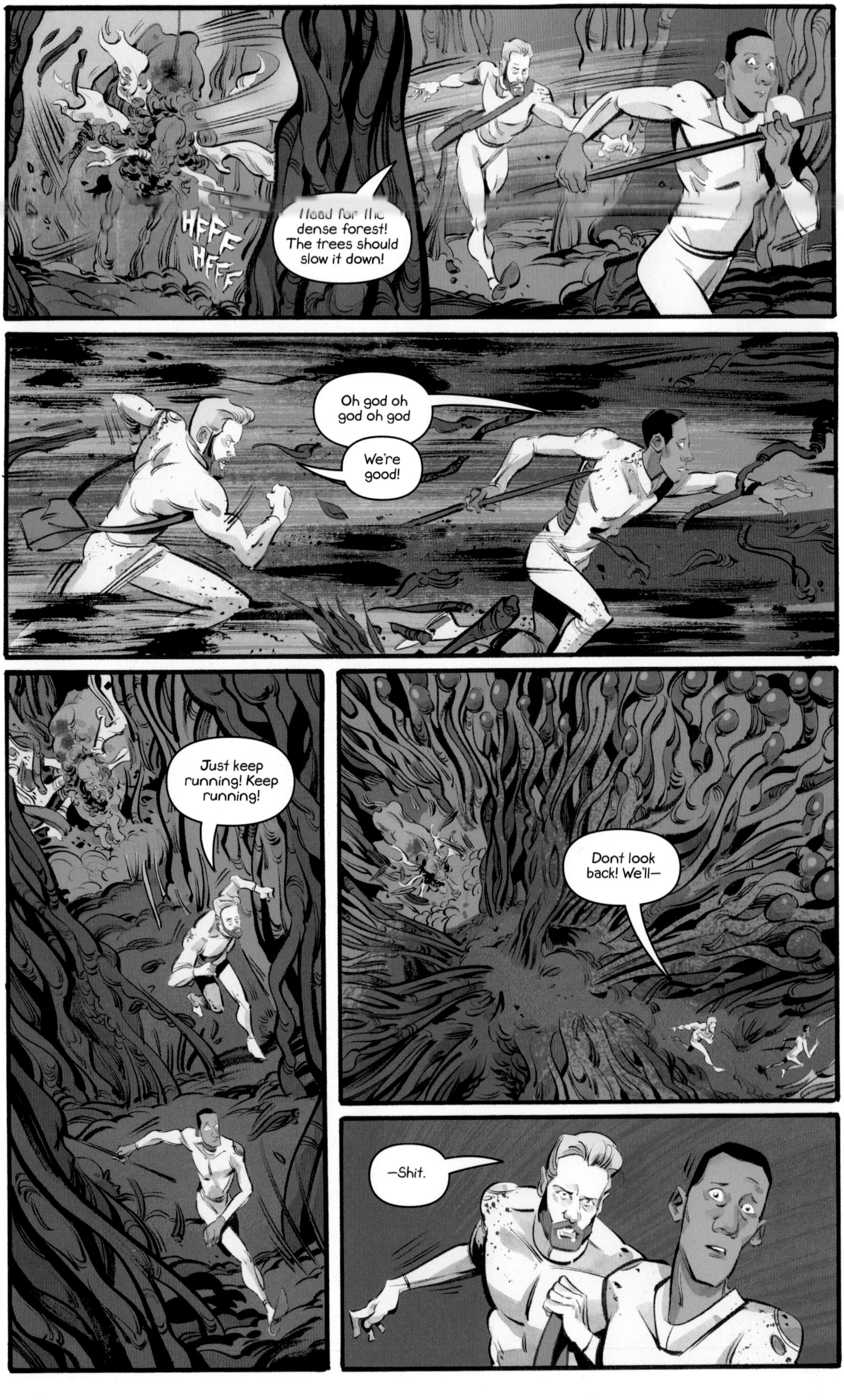
HFFF HFFF
Head for the dense forest! The trees should slow it down!
Oh god oh god oh god
We're good!
Just keep running! Keep running!
Dont look back! We'll—
—Shit.

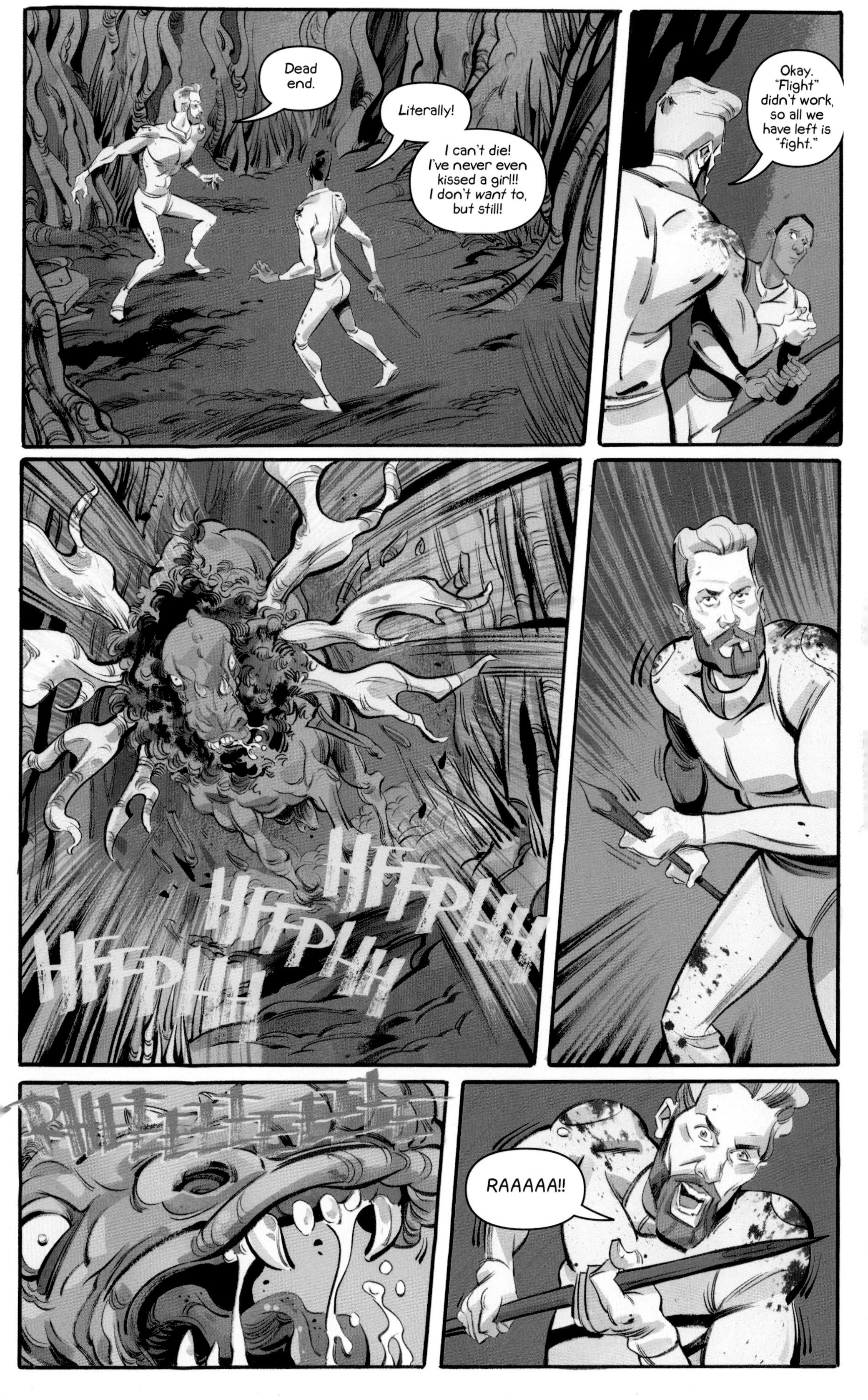
Dead end.
Literally!
I can't die! I've never even kissed a girl!! I don't *want* to, but still!
Okay. "Flight" didn't work, so all we have left is "fight."
HFFPHH
HFFPHH
HFFPHH
RAAAAA!!

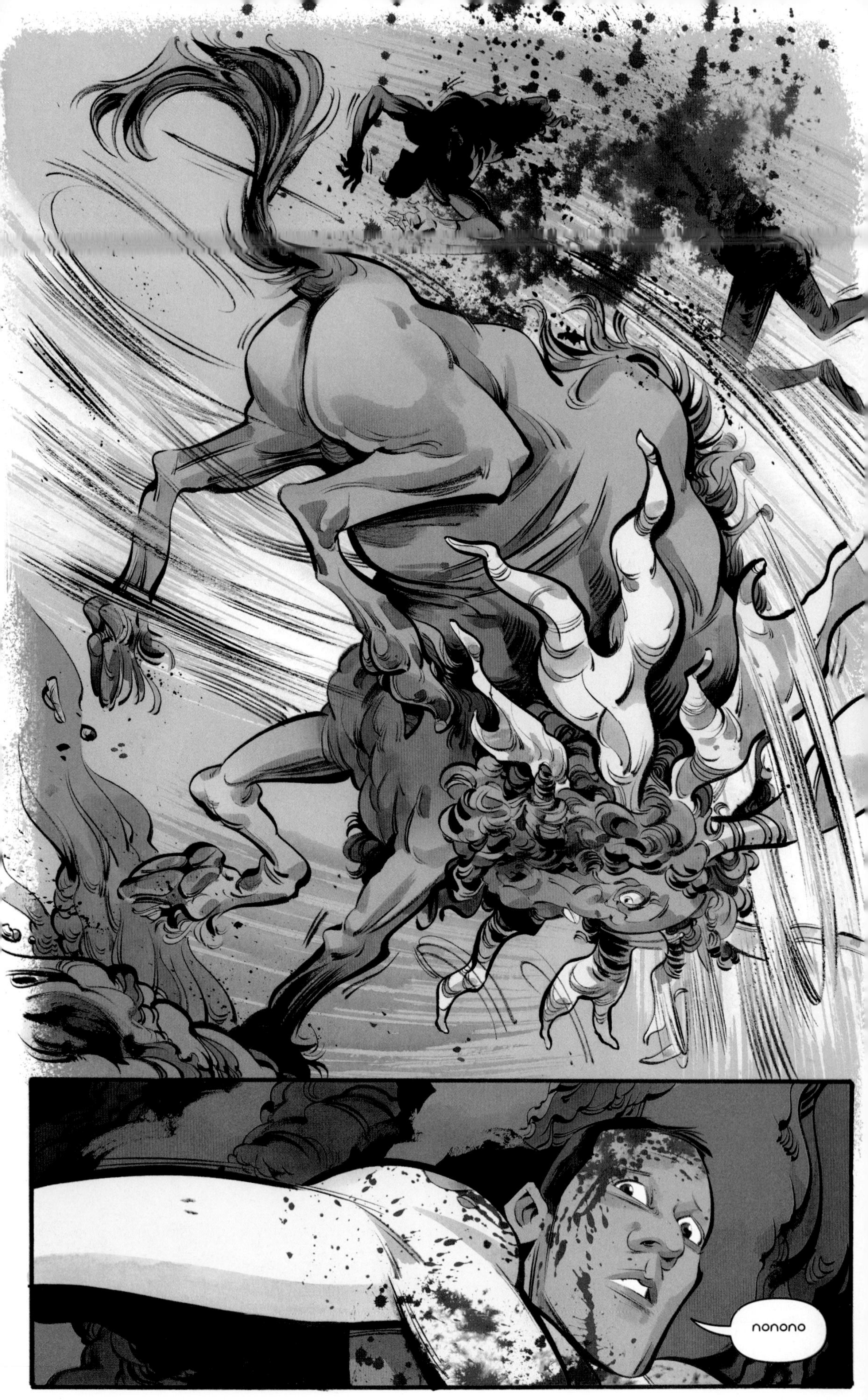
nonono

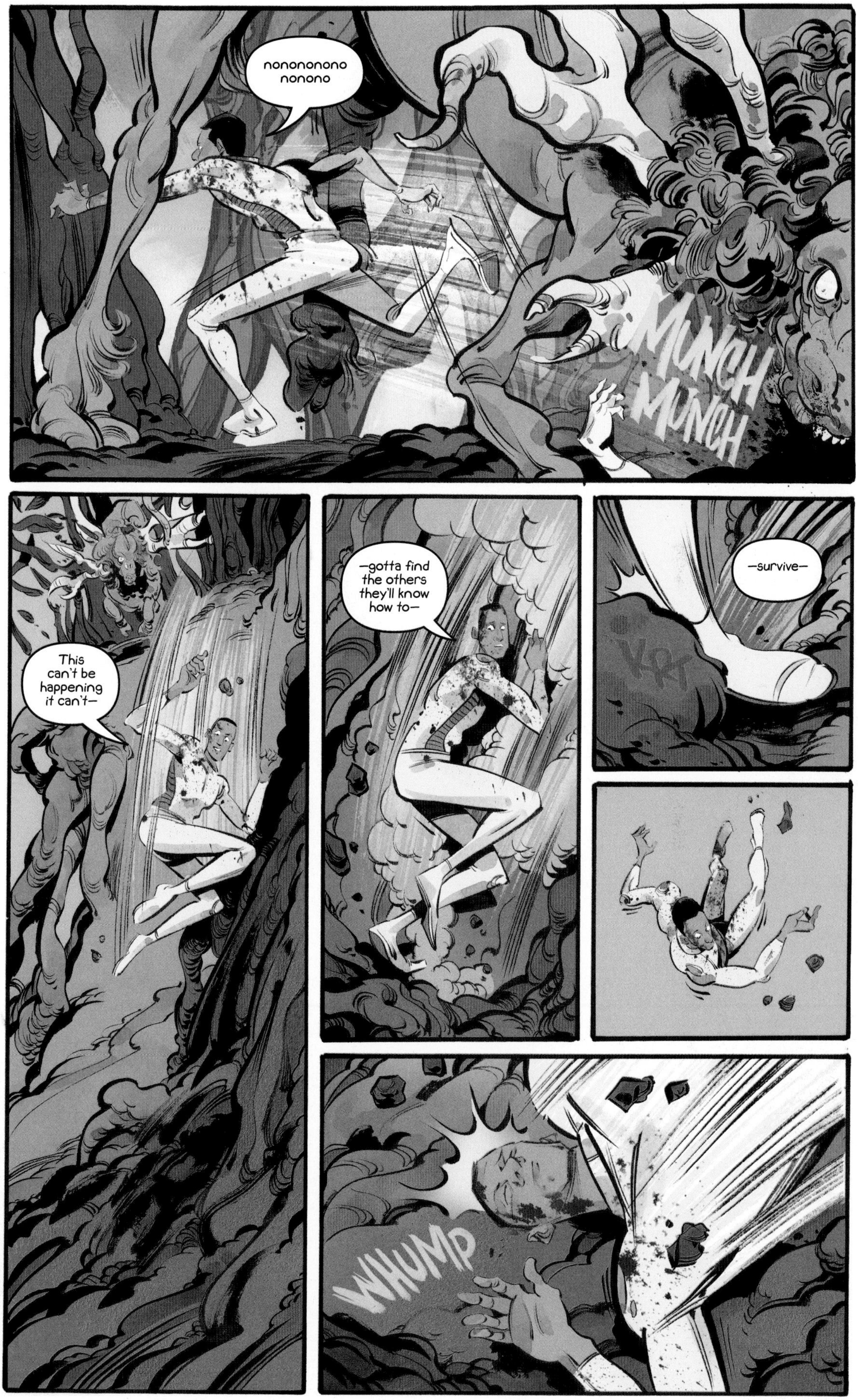
nonononono nonono
MUNCH
MUNCH
This can't be happening it can't—
—gotta find the others they'll know how to—
—survive—
WHUMP

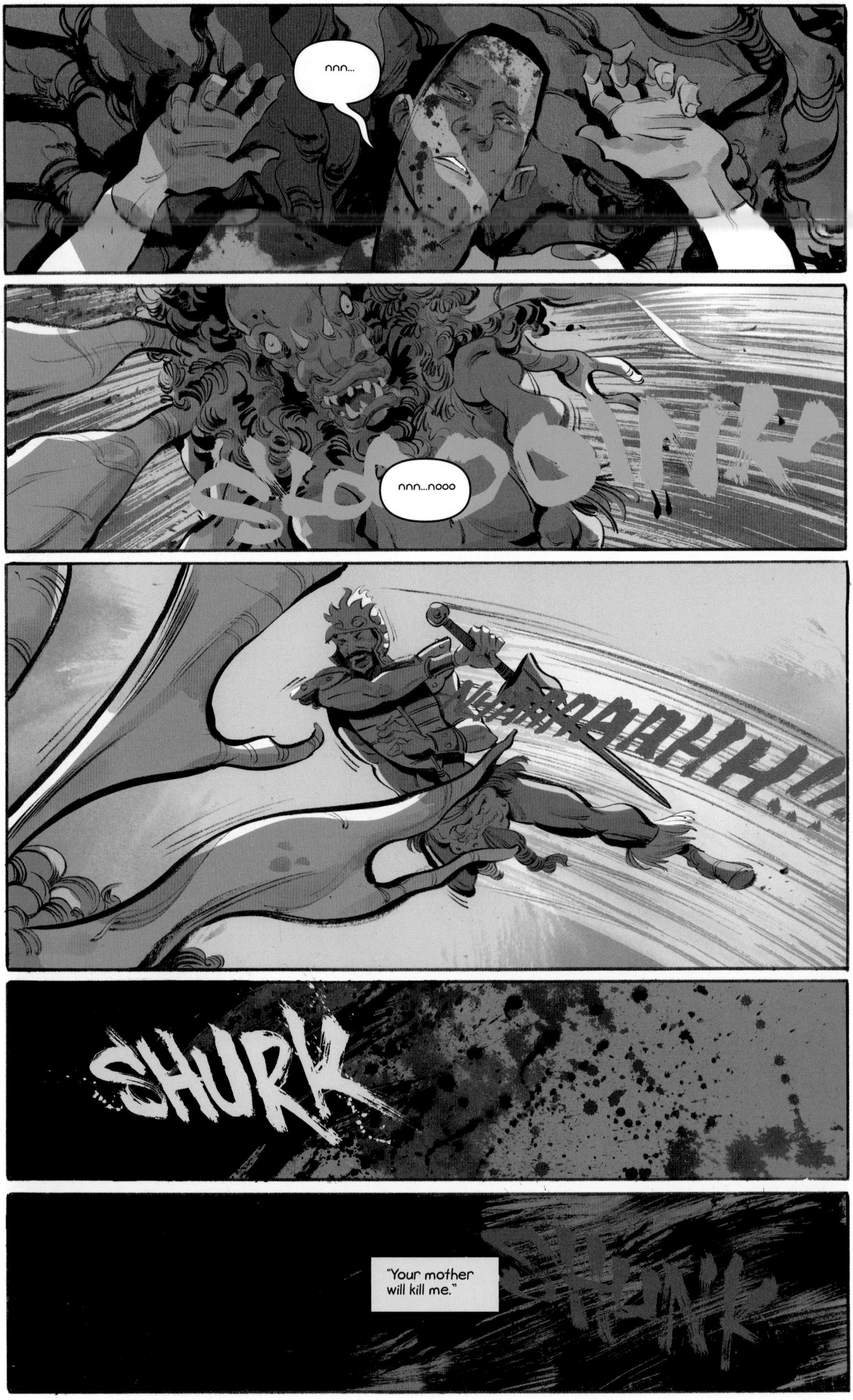
nnn...
nnn...nooo
SHURK
"Your mother will kill me."

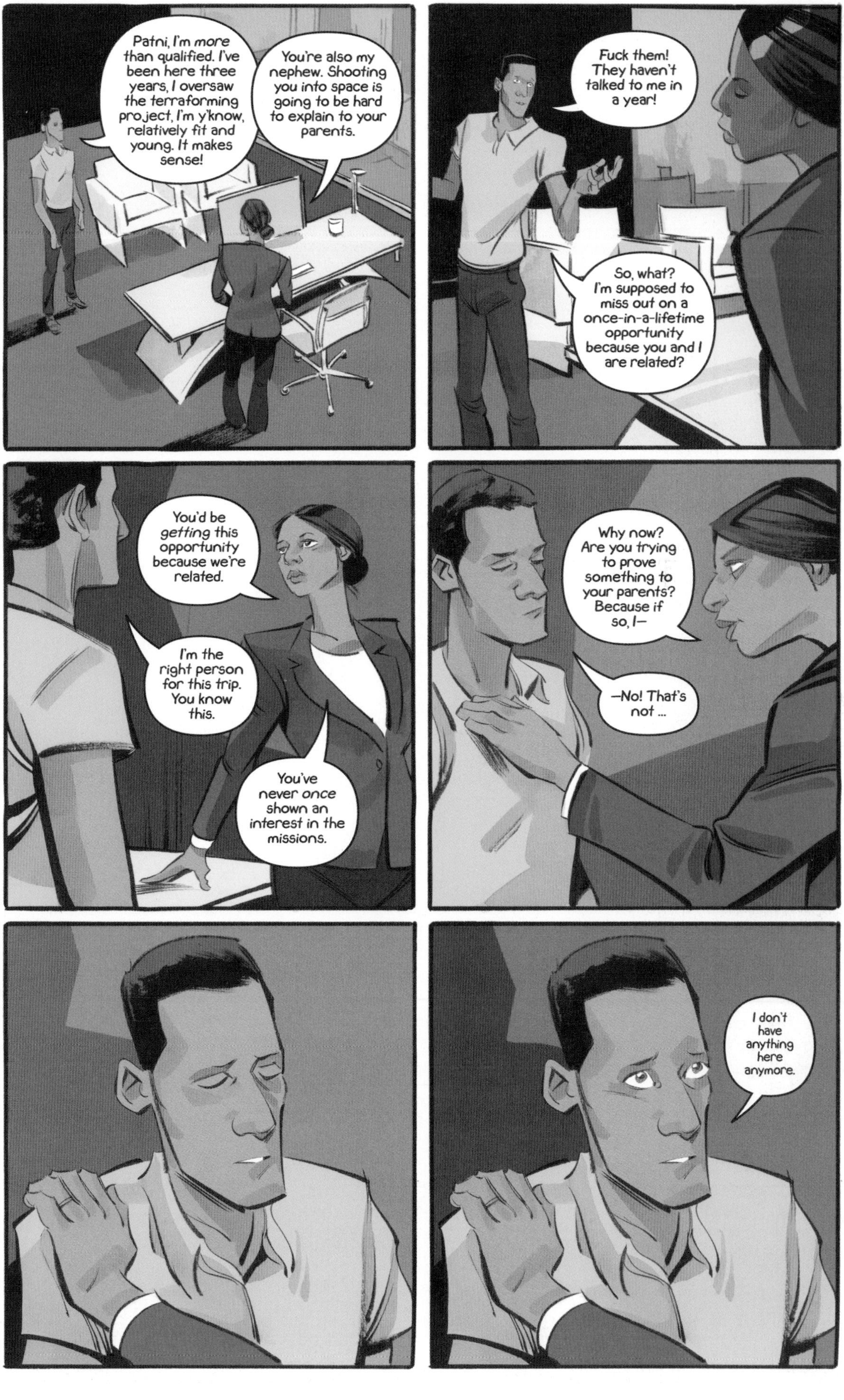
Patni, I'm *more* than qualified. I've been here three years, I oversaw the terraforming project, I'm y'know, relatively fit and young. It makes sense!
You're also my nephew. Shooting you into space is going to be hard to explain to your parents.
Fuck them! They haven't talked to me in a year!
So, what? I'm supposed to miss out on a once-in-a-lifetime opportunity because you and I are related?
You'd be *getting* this opportunity because we're related.
I'm the right person for this trip. You know this.
You've never *once* shown an interest in the missions.
Why now? Are you trying to prove something to your parents? Because if so, I—
—No! That's not ...
I don't have anything here anymore.

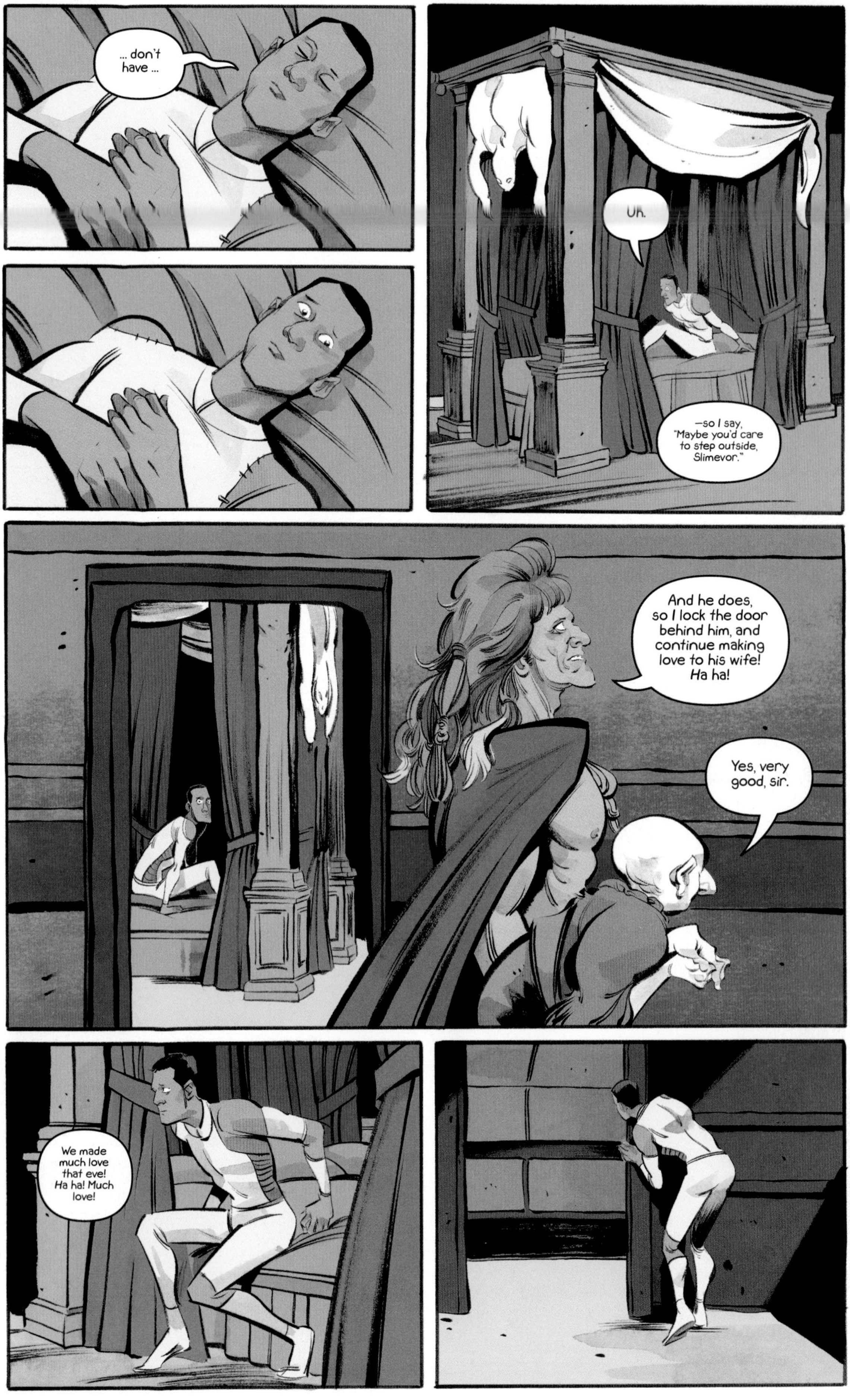
... don't have ...
UH.
—so I say, "Maybe you'd care to step outside, Slimevor."
And he does, so I lock the door behind him, and continue making love to his wife! Ha ha!
Yes, very good, sir.
We made much love that eve! Ha ha! Much love!

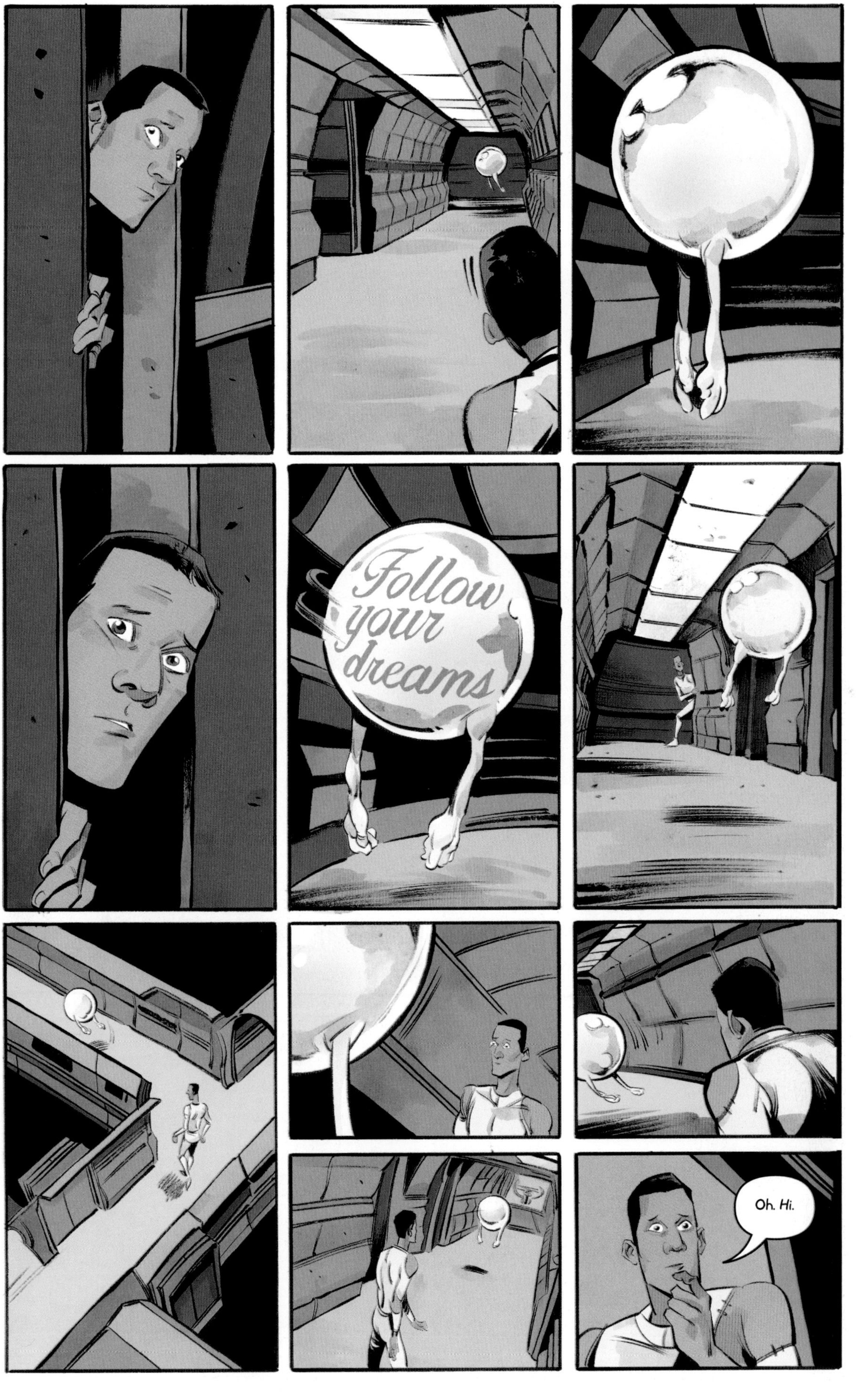
Follow your dreams
Oh. Hi.

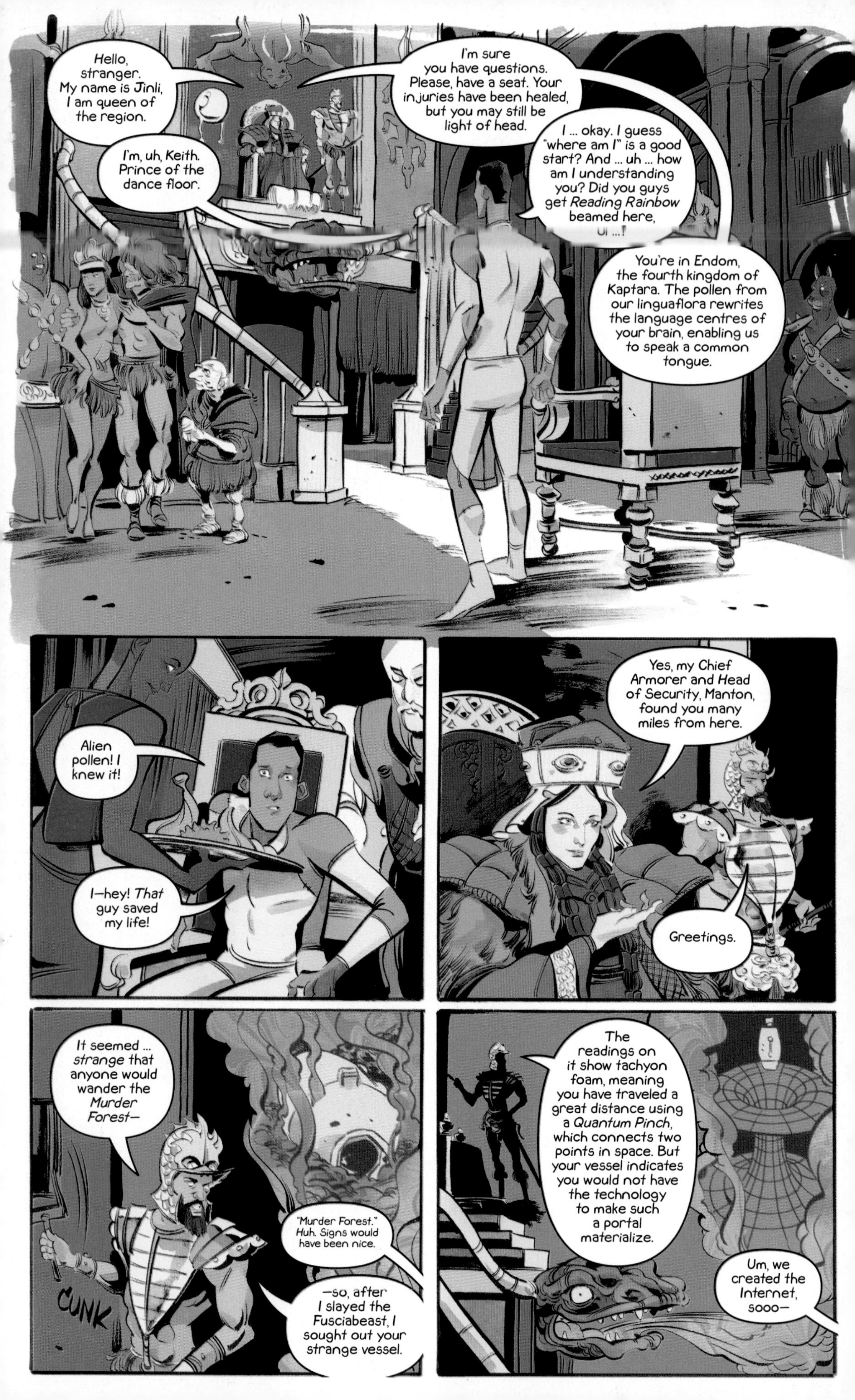

Hello, stranger. My name is Jinli, I am queen of the region.
I'm sure you have questions. Please, have a seat. Your injuries have been healed, but you may still be light of head.
I'm, uh, Keith. Prince of the dance floor.
I ... okay. I guess "where am I" is a good start? And ... uh ... how am I understanding you? Did you guys get *Reading Rainbow* beamed here,
You're in *Endom*, the fourth kingdom of Kaptara. The pollen from our linguaflora rewrites the language centres of your brain, enabling us to speak a common tongue.
Alien pollen! I knew it!
I—hey! *That* guy saved my life!
Yes, my Chief Armorer and Head of Security, Manton, found you many miles from here.
Greetings.
It seemed ... *strange* that anyone would wander the *Murder Forest*—
"Murder Forest." Huh. Signs would have been nice.
—so, after I slayed the Fusciabeast, I sought out your strange vessel.
CUNK
The readings on it show tachyon foam, meaning you have traveled a great distance using a *Quantum Pinch*, which connects two points in space. But your vessel indicates you would not have the technology to make such a portal materialize.
Um, we created the Internet, sooo—

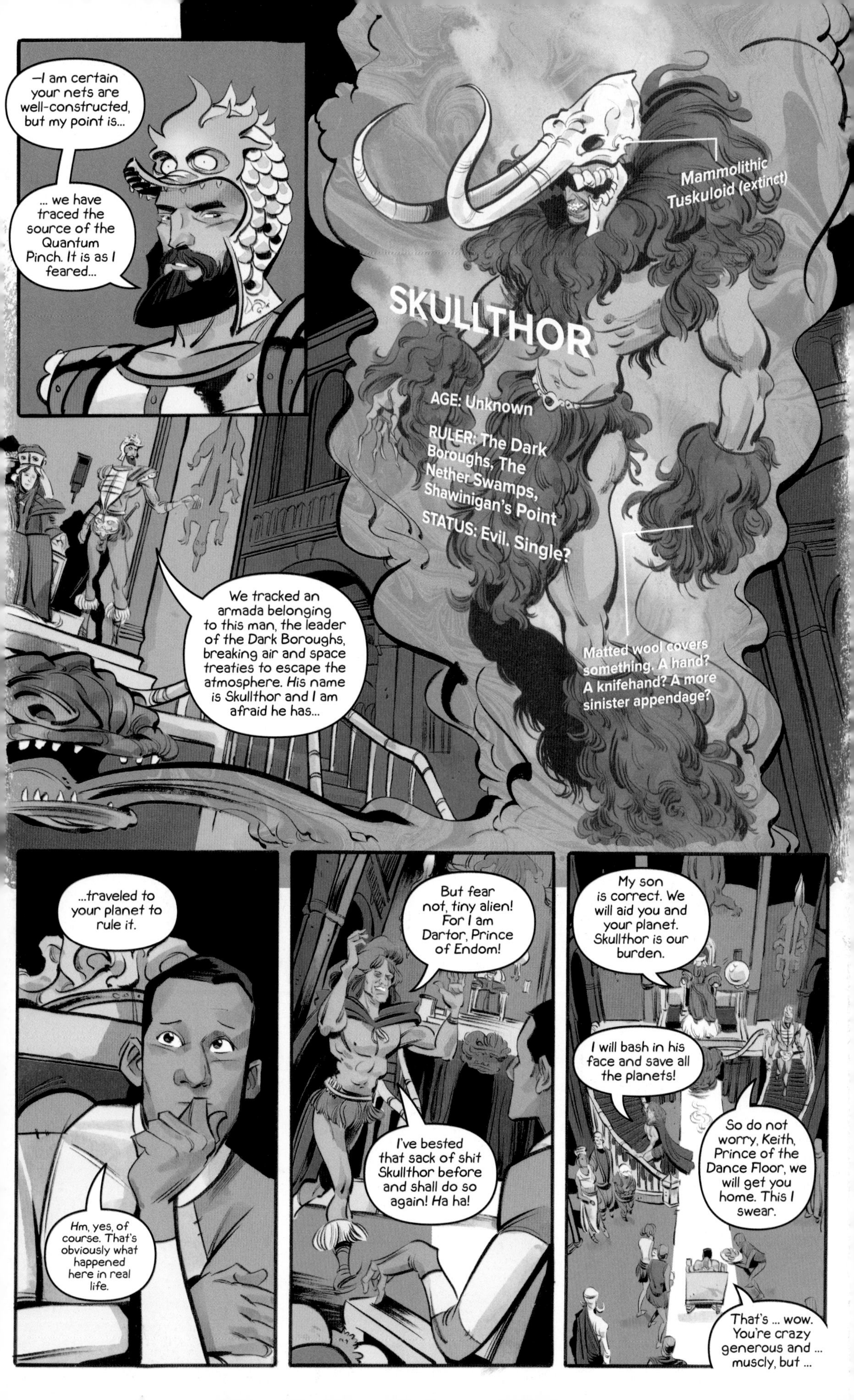
—I am certain your nets are well-constructed, but my point is...
... we have traced the source of the Quantum Pinch. It is as I feared...
SKULLTHOR
Mammolithic Tuskuloid (extinct)
AGE: Unknown
RULER: The Dark Boroughs, The Nether Swamps, Shawinigan's Point
STATUS: Evil. Single?
We tracked an armada belonging to this man, the leader of the Dark Boroughs, breaking air and space treaties to escape the atmosphere. His name is Skullthor and I am afraid he has...
Matted wool covers something. A hand? A knifehand? A more sinister appendage?
...traveled to your planet to rule it.
Hm, yes, of course. That's obviously what happened here in real life.
But fear not, tiny alien! For I am Dartor, Prince of Endom!
I've bested that sack of shit Skullthor before and shall do so again! Ha ha!
My son is correct. We will aid you and your planet. Skullthor is our burden.
I will bash in his face and save all the planets!
So do not worry, Keith, Prince of the Dance Floor, we will get you home. This I swear.
That's ... wow. You're crazy generous and ... muscly, but ...

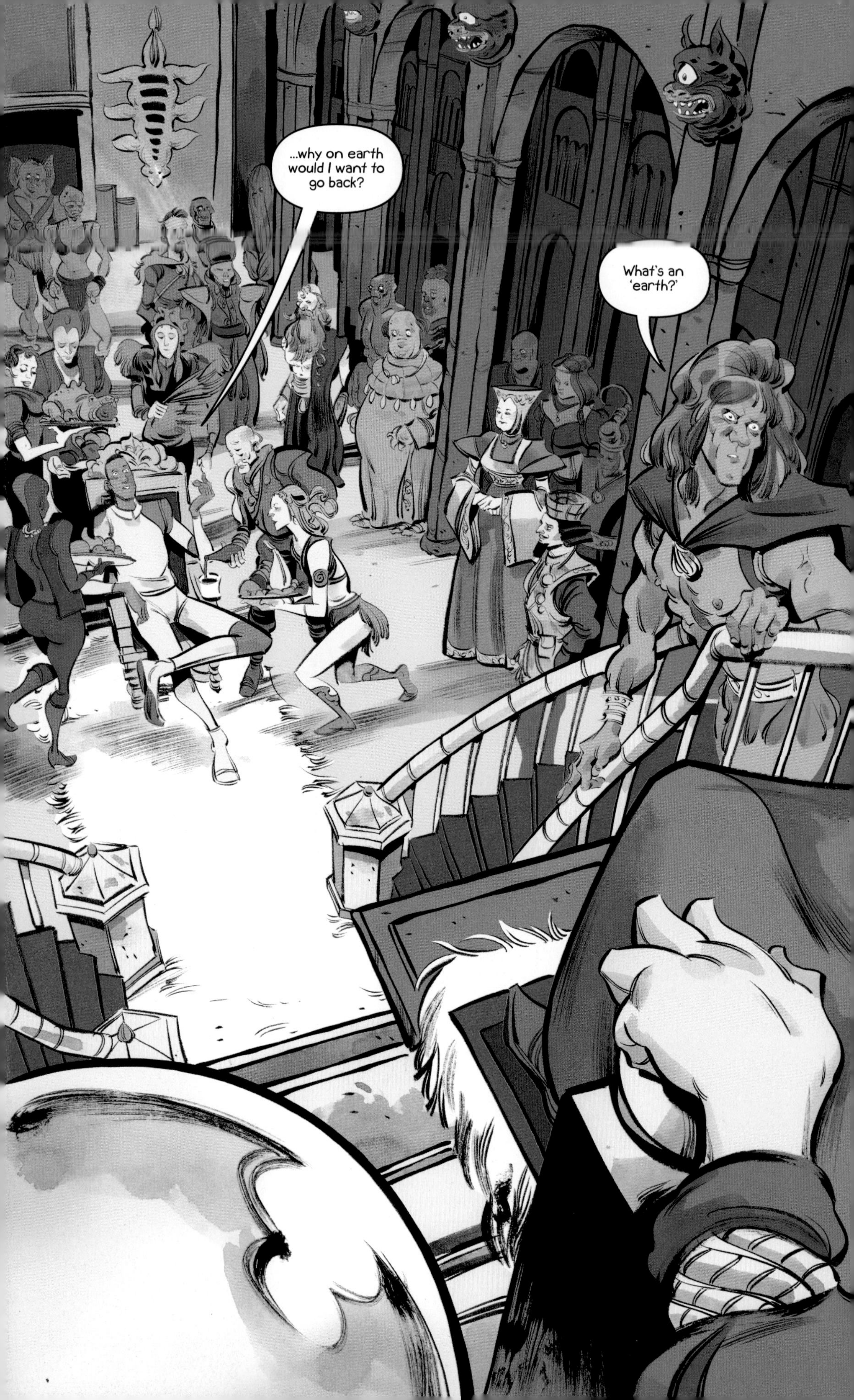
...why on earth would I want to go back?
What's an 'earth?'

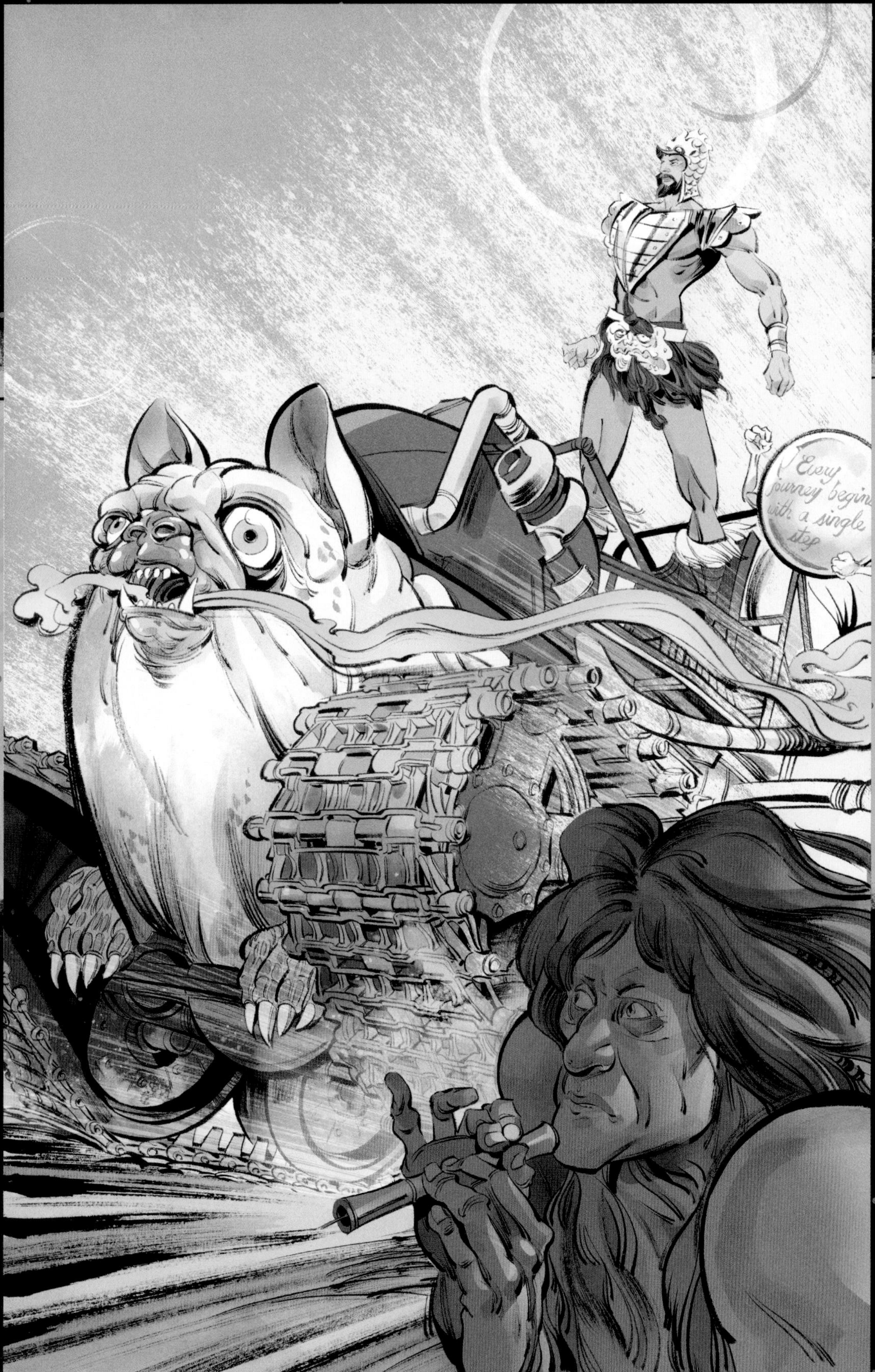
Every
journey begin
with a single
step

CHAPTER TWO

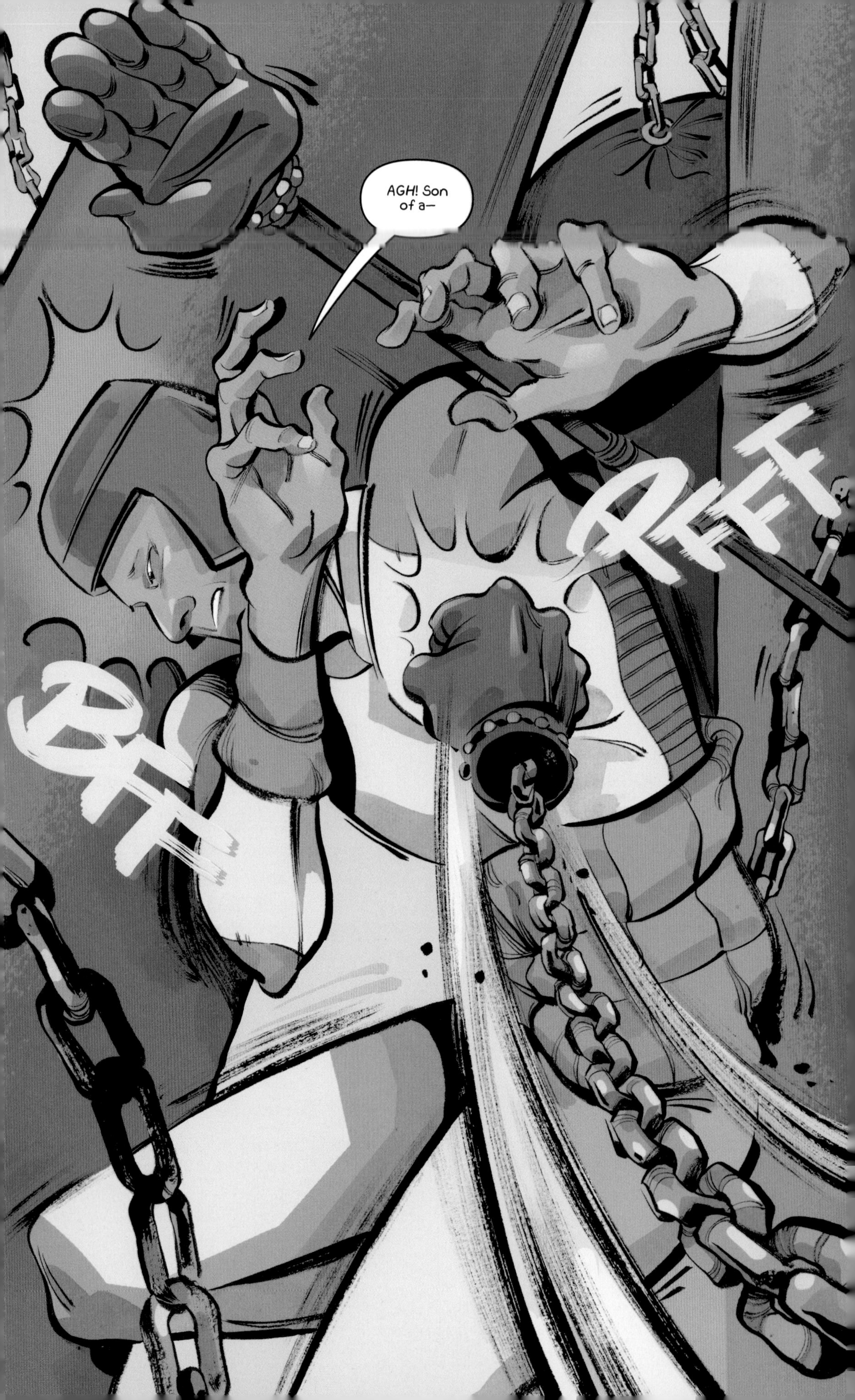
AGH! Son of a—
AFF
BFF

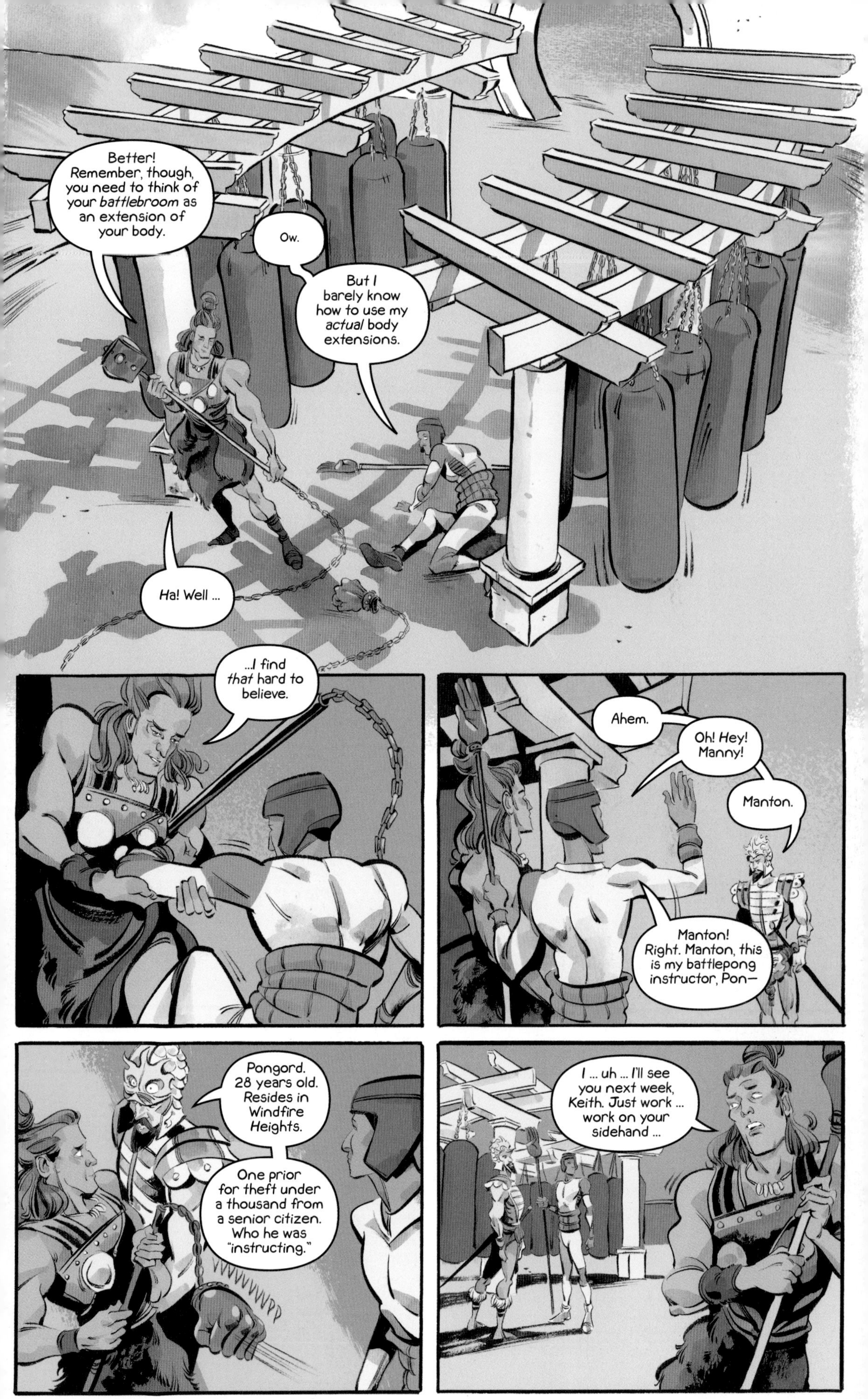

Better! Remember, though, you need to think of your *battlebroom* as an extension of your body.
Ow.
But I barely know how to use my *actual* body extensions.
Ha! Well ...
...I find *that* hard to believe.
Ahem.
Oh! Hey! Manny!
Manton.
Manton! Right. Manton, this is my battlepong instructor, Pon—
Pongord. 28 years old. Resides in Windfire Heights.
One prior for theft under a thousand from a senior citizen. Who he was "instructing."
VVVVVVVPP
I ... uh ... I'll see you next week, Keith. Just work ... work on your sidehand ...

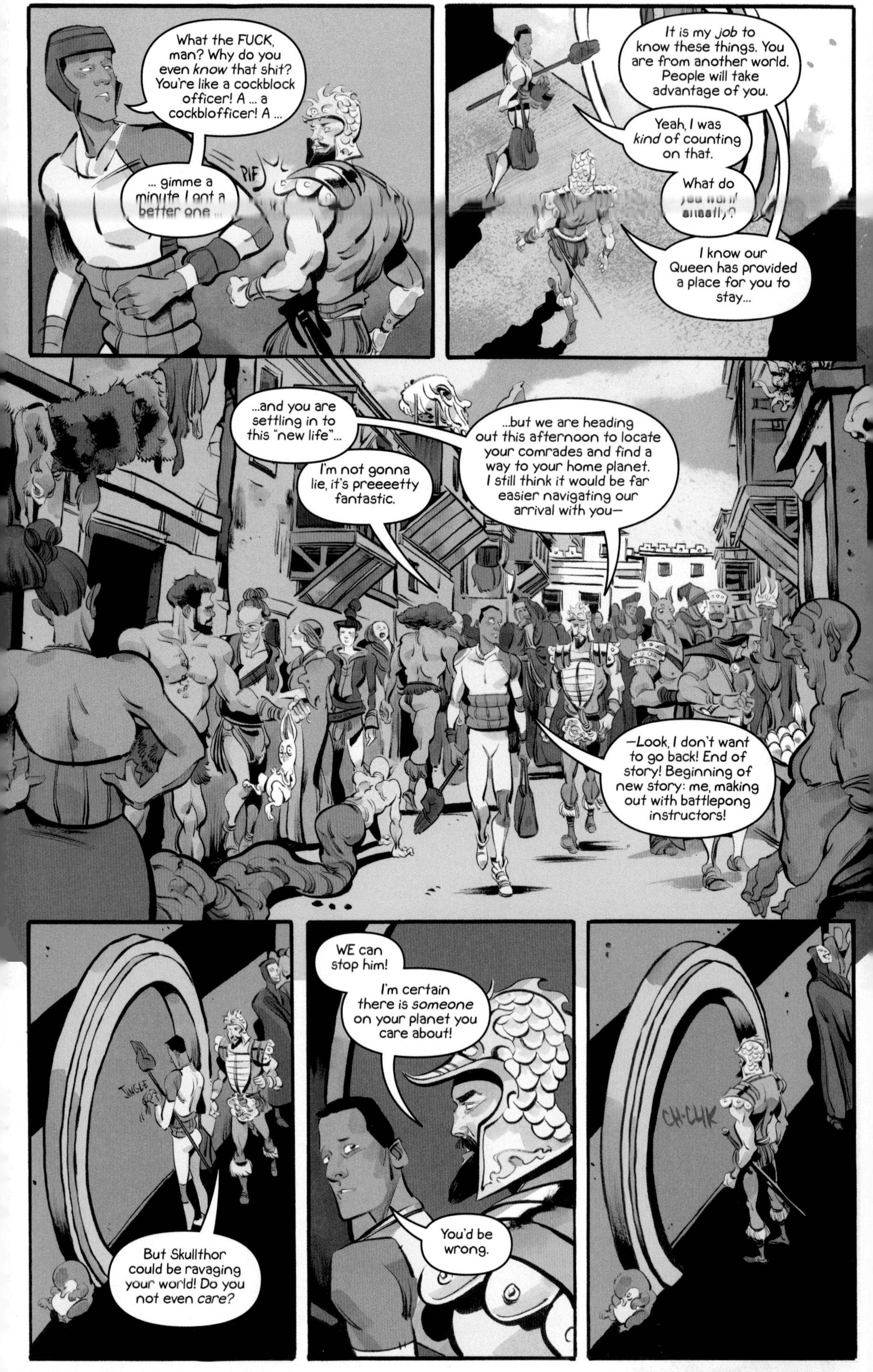
What the FUCK, man? Why do you even *know* that shit? You're like a cockblock officer! A ... a cockblofficer! A ...
PIF
... gimme a minute I got a better one ...
It is my *job* to know these things. You are from another world. People will take advantage of you.
Yeah, I was *kind* of counting on that.
What do
I know our Queen has provided a place for you to stay...
...and you are settling in to this "new life"...
I'm not gonna lie, it's preeeetty fantastic.
...but we are heading out this afternoon to locate your comrades and find a way to your home planet. I still think it would be far easier navigating our arrival with you—
—Look, I don't want to go back! End of story! Beginning of new story: me, making out with battlepong instructors!
JINGLE
But Skullthor could be ravaging your world! Do you not even *care*?
WE can stop him!
I'm certain there is *someone* on your planet you care about!
You'd be wrong.
CH-CLIK

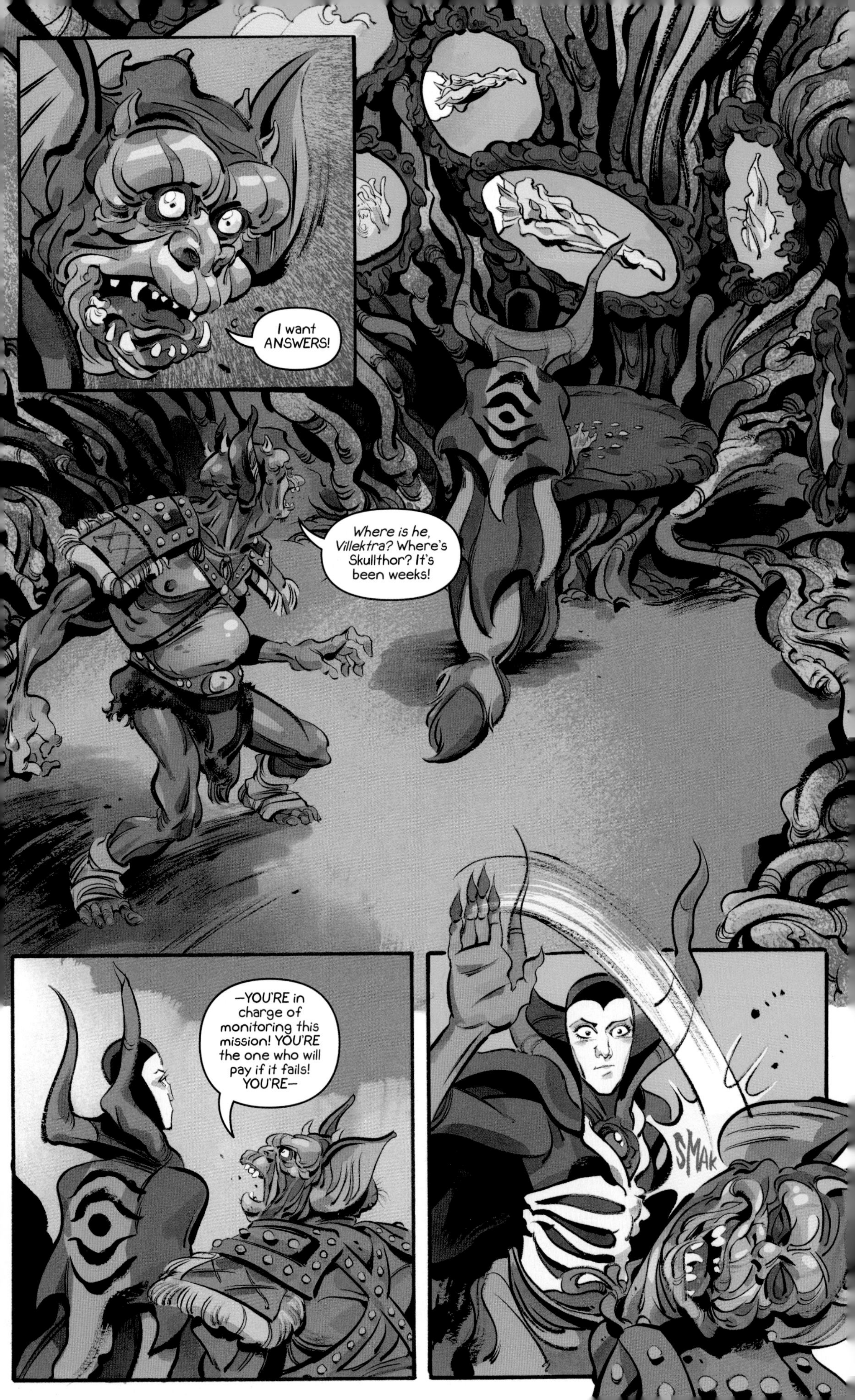
I want ANSWERS!
Where is he, Villektra? Where's Skullthor? It's been weeks!
—YOU'RE in charge of monitoring this mission! YOU'RE the one who will pay if it fails! YOU'RE—
SMAK

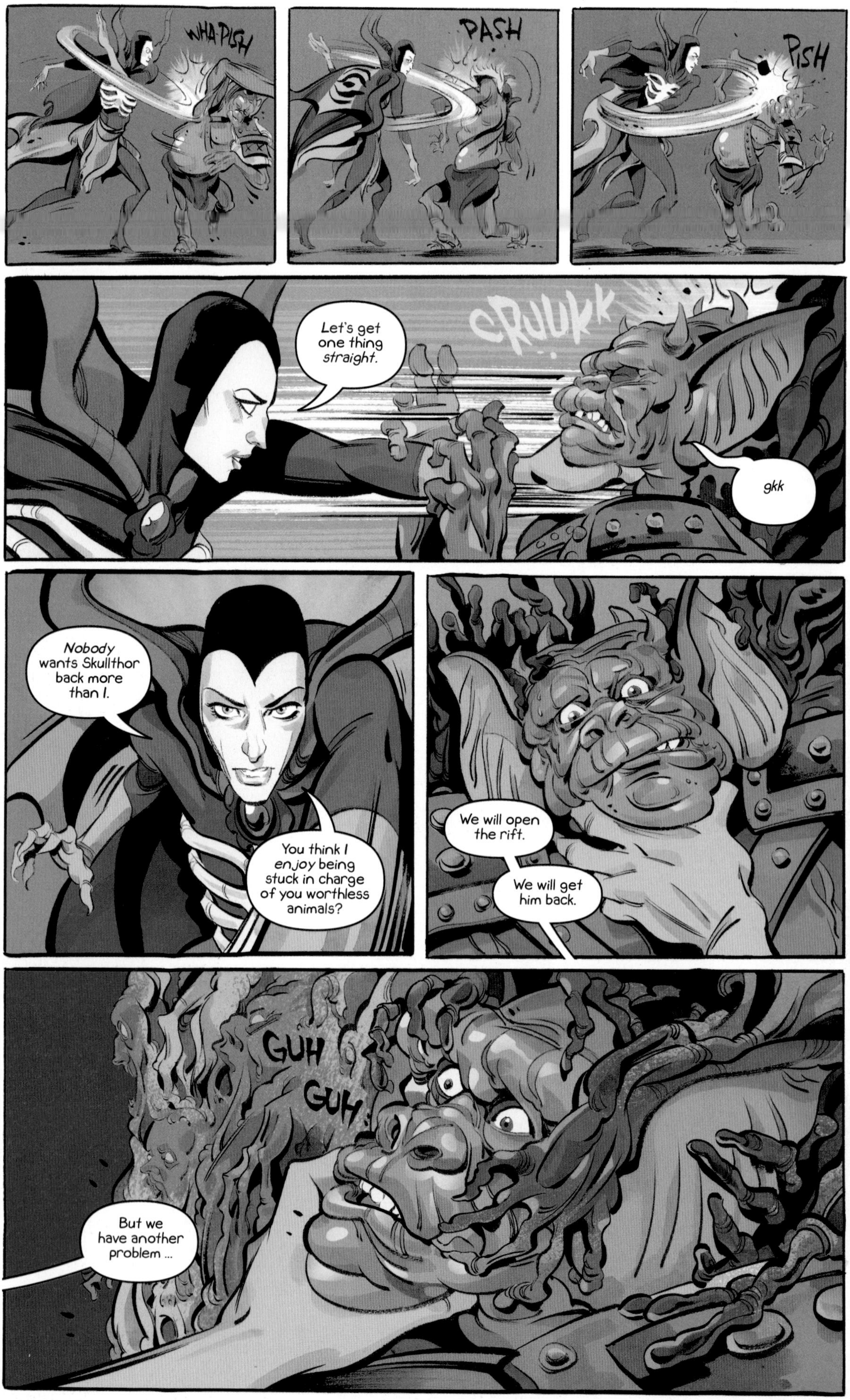
WHA-PISH
PASH
PISH
CRUUKK
Let's get one thing *straight.*
gkk
Nobody wants Skullthor back more than I.
You think I *enjoy* being stuck in charge of you worthless animals?
We will open the rift.
We will get him back.
GUH
GUH
But we have another problem ...

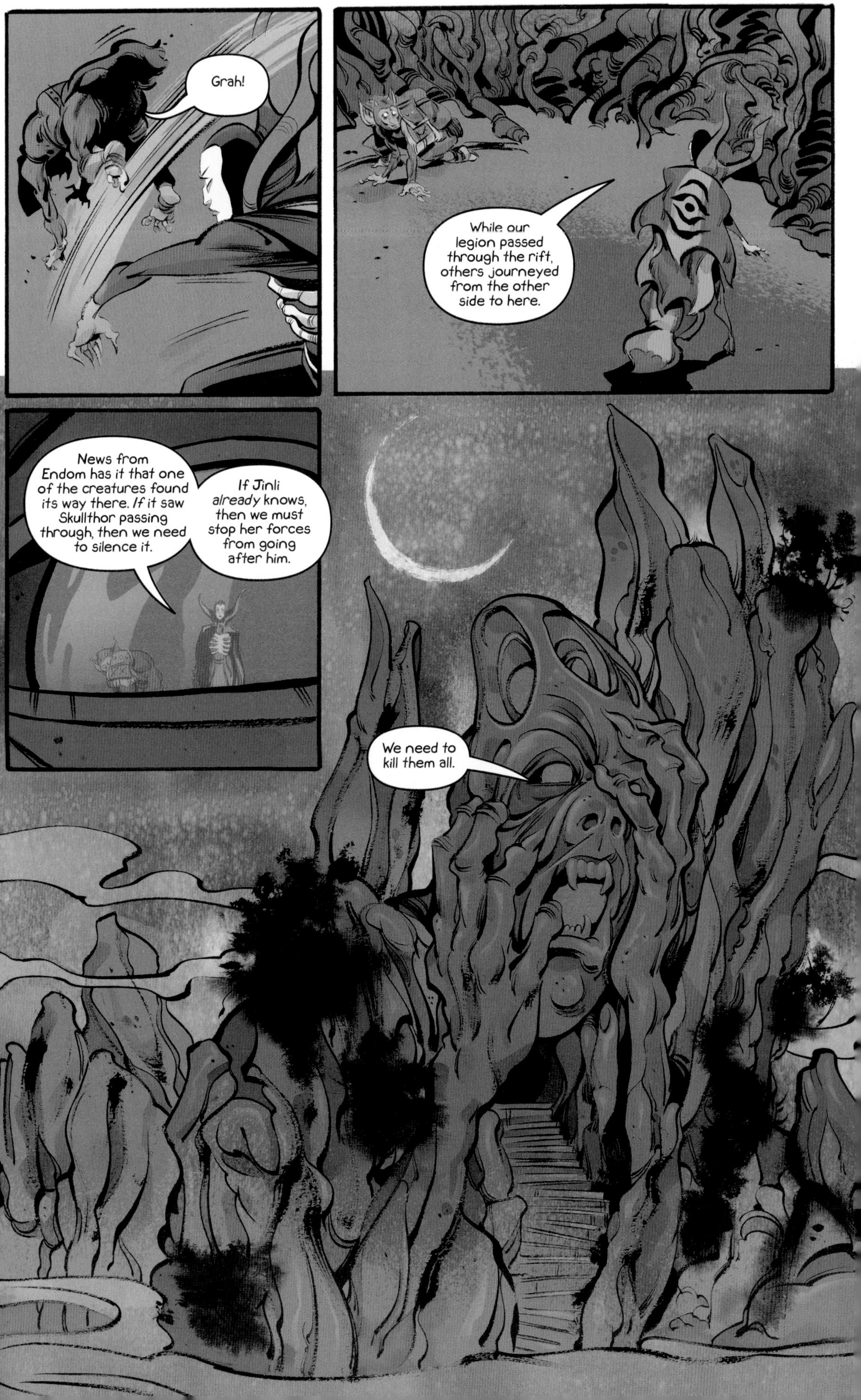
Grah!
While our legion passed through the rift, others journeyed from the other side to here.
News from Endom has *it* that one of the creatures found its way there. *If* it saw Skullthor passing through, then we need to silence it.
If Jinli *already* knows, then we must stop her forces from going after him.
We need to kill them all.

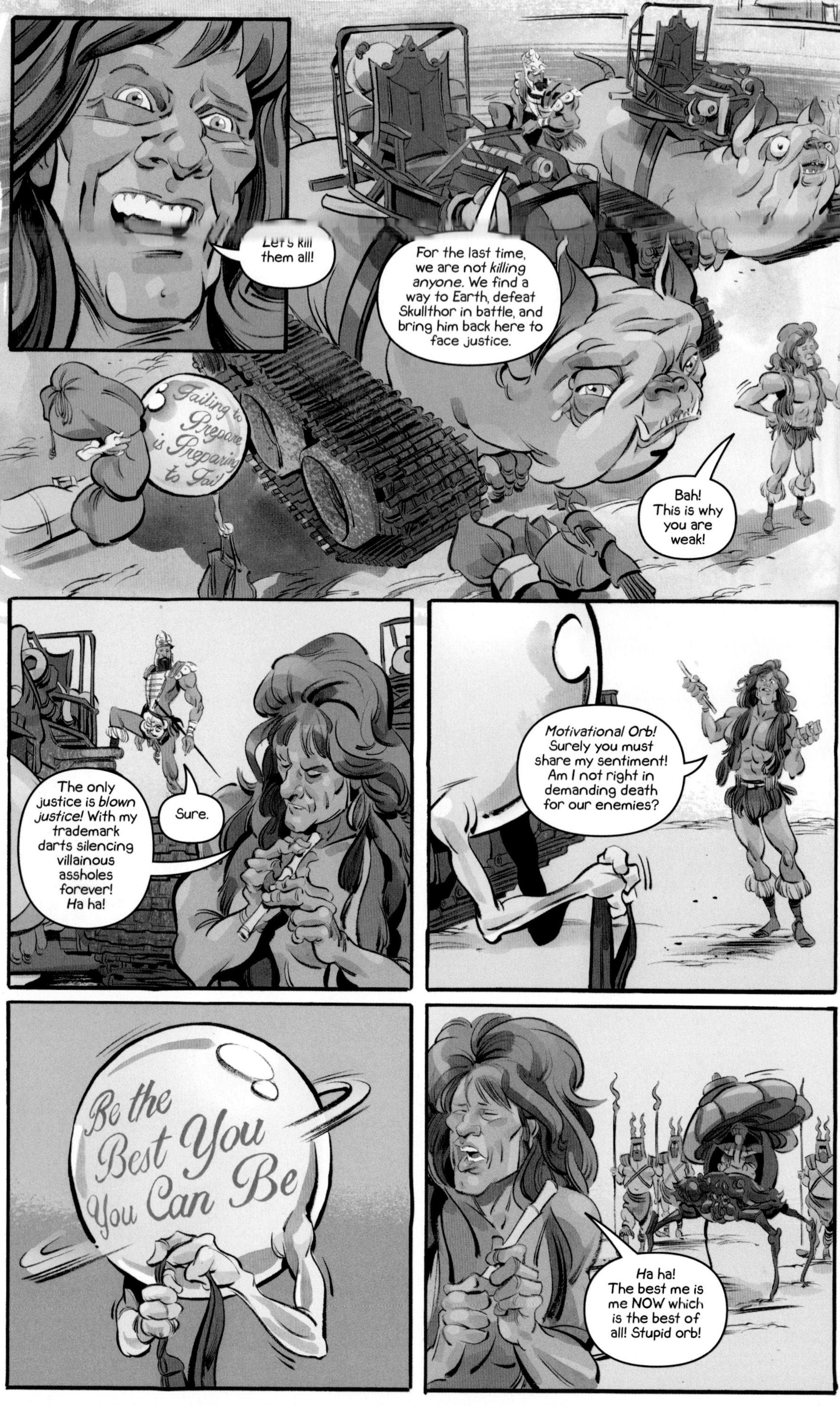
Let's kill them all!
For the last time, we are not *killing* *anyone*. We find a way to Earth, defeat Skullthor in battle, and bring him back here to face justice.
Failing to Prepare is Preparing to Fail
Bah! This is why you are weak!
The only justice is *blown justice!* With my trademark darts silencing villainous assholes forever! Ha ha!
Sure.
Motivational Orb! Surely you must share my sentiment! Am I not right in demanding death for our enemies?
Be the Best You You Can Be
Ha ha! The best me is me NOW which is the best of all! Stupid orb!

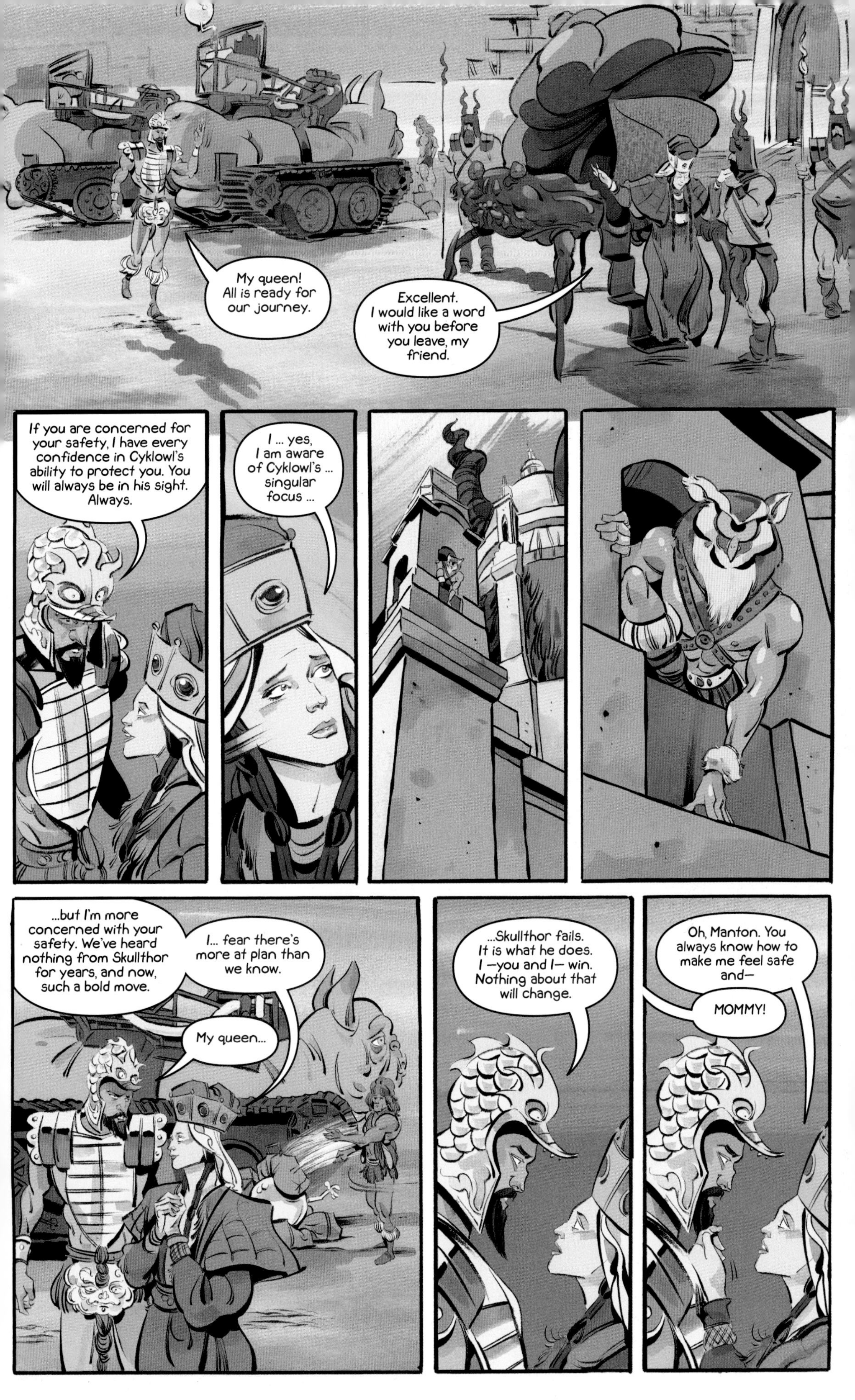
My queen! All is ready for our journey.
Excellent. I would like a word with you before you leave, my friend.
If you are concerned for your safety, I have every confidence in Cyklowl's ability to protect you. You will always be in his sight. Always.
I ... yes, I am aware of Cyklowl's ... singular focus ...
...but I'm more concerned with your safety. We've heard nothing from Skullthor for years, and now, such a bold move.
I... fear there's more at plan than we know.
My queen...
...Skullthor fails. It is what he does. I —you and I— win. Nothing about that will change.
Oh, Manton. You always know how to make me feel safe and—
MOMMY!

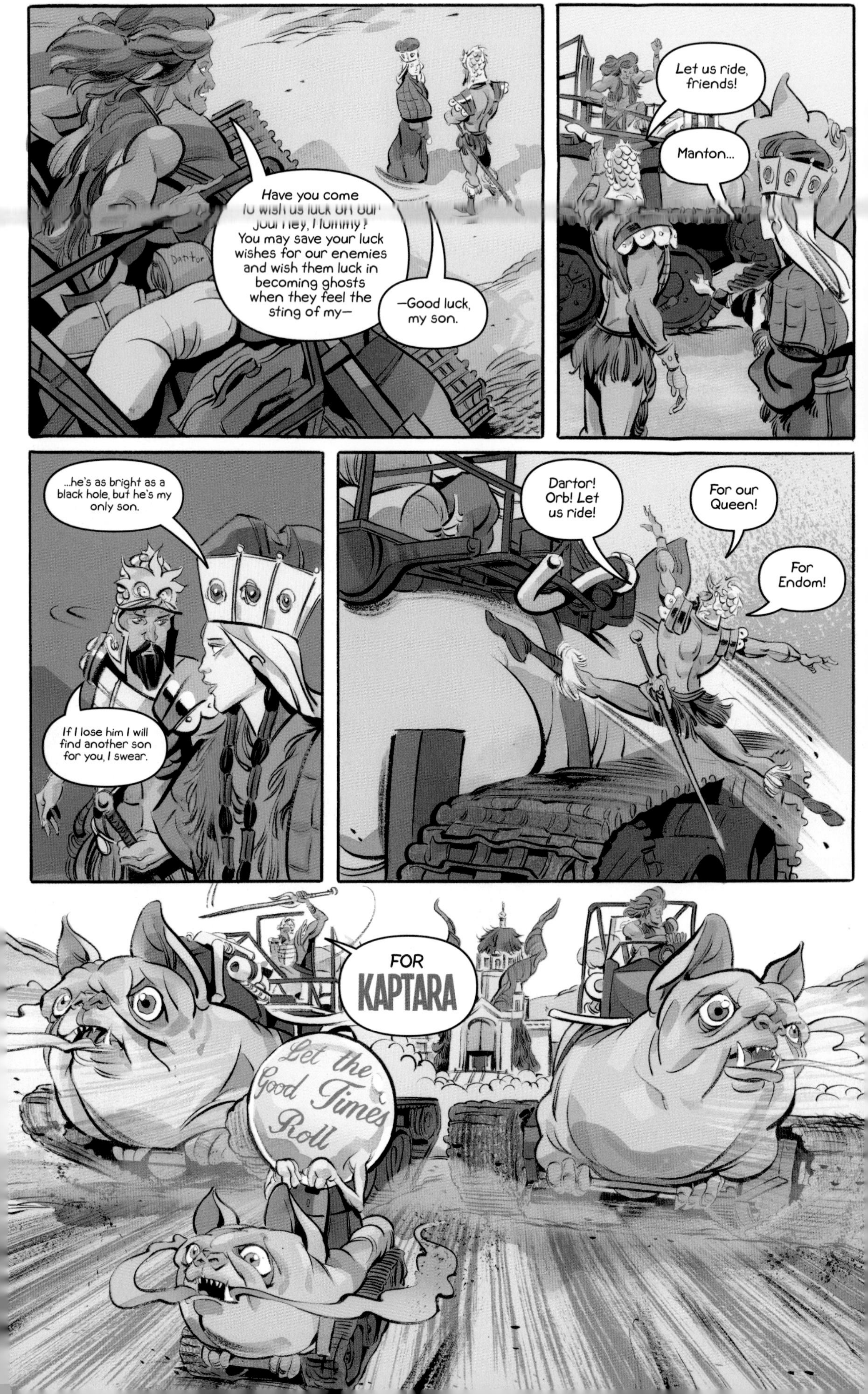
Have you come to wish us luck on our journey, Mommy? You may save your luck wishes for our enemies and wish them luck in becoming ghosts when they feel the sting of my—
—Good luck, my son.
Dartor
Let us ride, friends!
Manton...
...he's as bright as a black hole, but he's my only son.
If I lose him I will find another son for you, I swear.
Dartor! Orb! Let us ride!
For our Queen!
For Endom!
FOR KAPTARA
Let the Good Times Roll

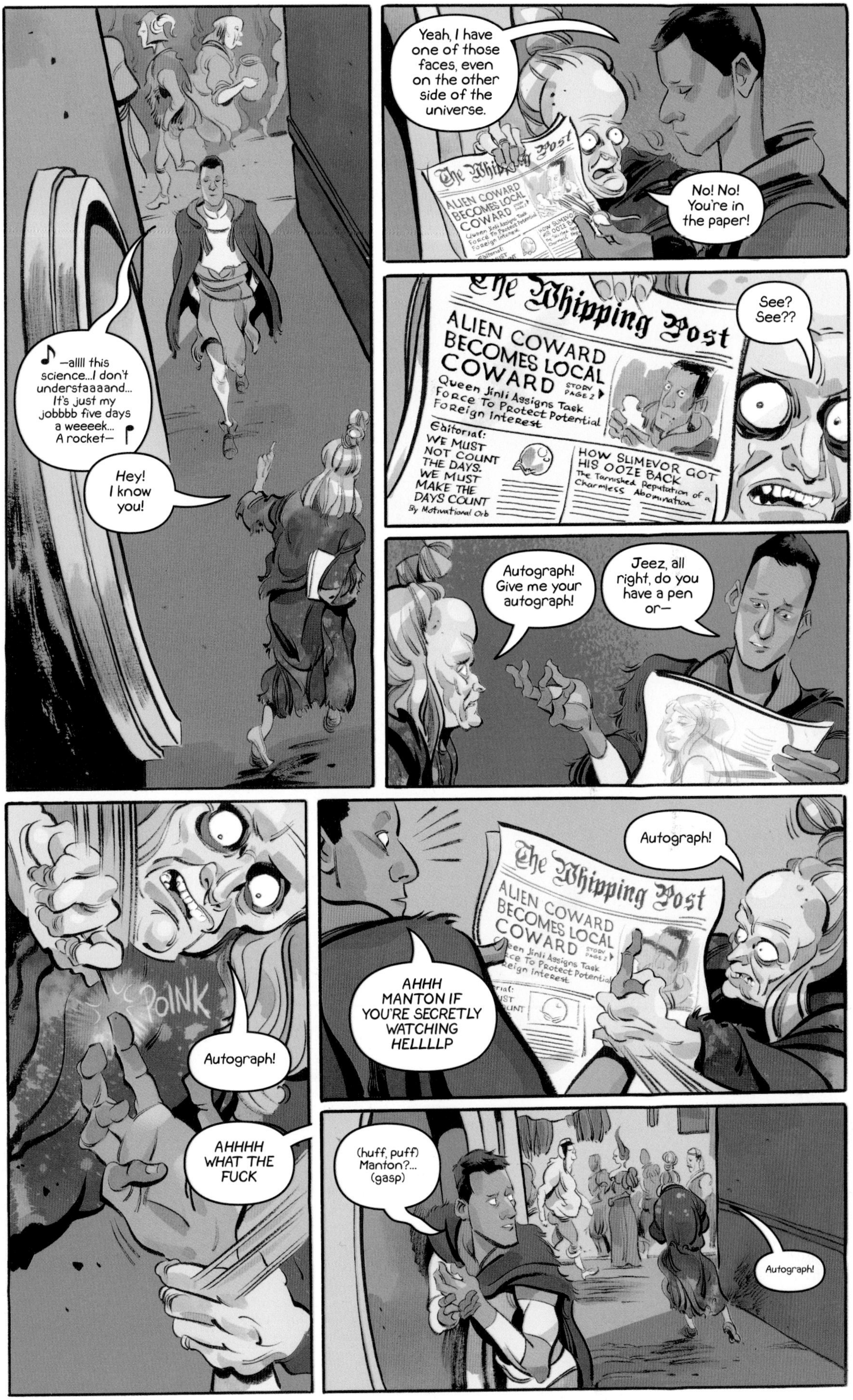
♪ —allll this science...I don't understaaaand... It's just my jobbbb five days a weeeek... A rocket— ♪
Hey! I know you!
Yeah, I have one of those faces, even on the other side of the universe.
No! No! You're in the paper!
The Whipping Post
ALIEN COWARD BECOMES LOCAL COWARD
STORY PAGE 2
Queen Jinli Assigns Task Force To Protect Potential Foreign Interest
Editorial: WE MUST NOT COUNT THE DAYS. WE MUST MAKE THE DAYS COUNT
By Motivational Orb
HOW SLIMEVOR GOT HIS OOZE BACK
The Tarnished Reputation of a Charmless Abomination
See? See??
Autograph! Give me your autograph!
Jeez, all right, do you have a pen or—
POINK
Autograph!
AHHHH WHAT THE FUCK
Autograph!
AHHH MANTON IF YOU'RE SECRETLY WATCHING HELLLLP
(huff, puff) Manton?... (gasp)
Autograph!

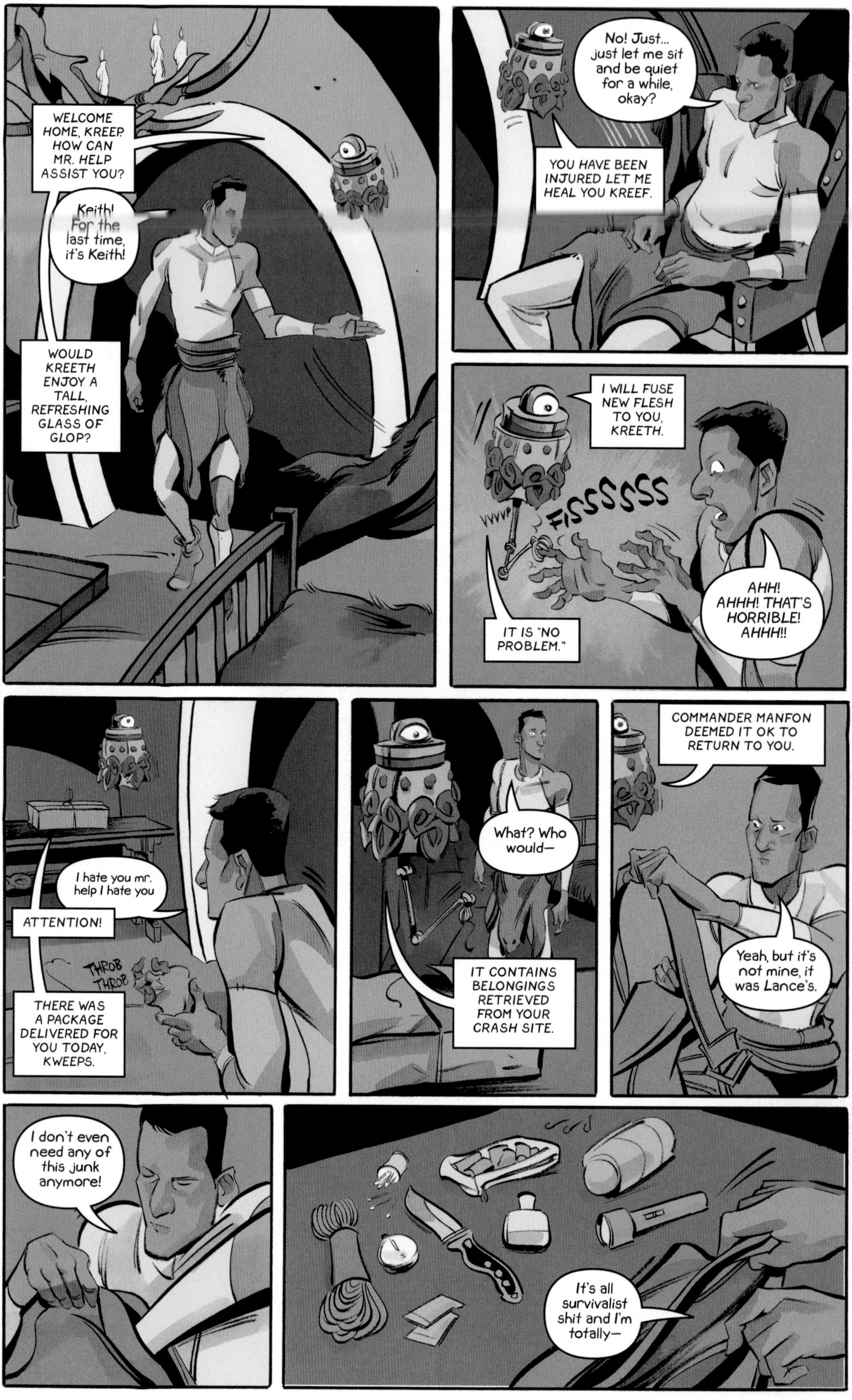

WELCOME HOME, KREEP. HOW CAN MR. HELP ASSIST YOU?
Keith! For the last time, it's Keith!
WOULD KREETH ENJOY A TALL, REFRESHING GLASS OF GLOP?
No! Just... just let me sit and be quiet for a while, okay?
YOU HAVE BEEN INJURED LET ME HEAL YOU KREEF.
I WILL FUSE NEW FLESH TO YOU, KREETH.
VVVVP
FISSSSSS
AHH! AHHH! THAT'S HORRIBLE! AHHH!!
IT IS "NO PROBLEM."
I hate you mr. help I hate you
ATTENTION!
THROB THROB
THERE WAS A PACKAGE DELIVERED FOR YOU TODAY, KWEEPS.
What? Who would—
IT CONTAINS BELONGINGS RETRIEVED FROM YOUR CRASH SITE.
COMMANDER MANFON DEEMED IT OK TO RETURN TO YOU.
Yeah, but it's not mine, it was Lance's.
I don't even need any of this junk anymore!
It's all survivalist shit and I'm totally—

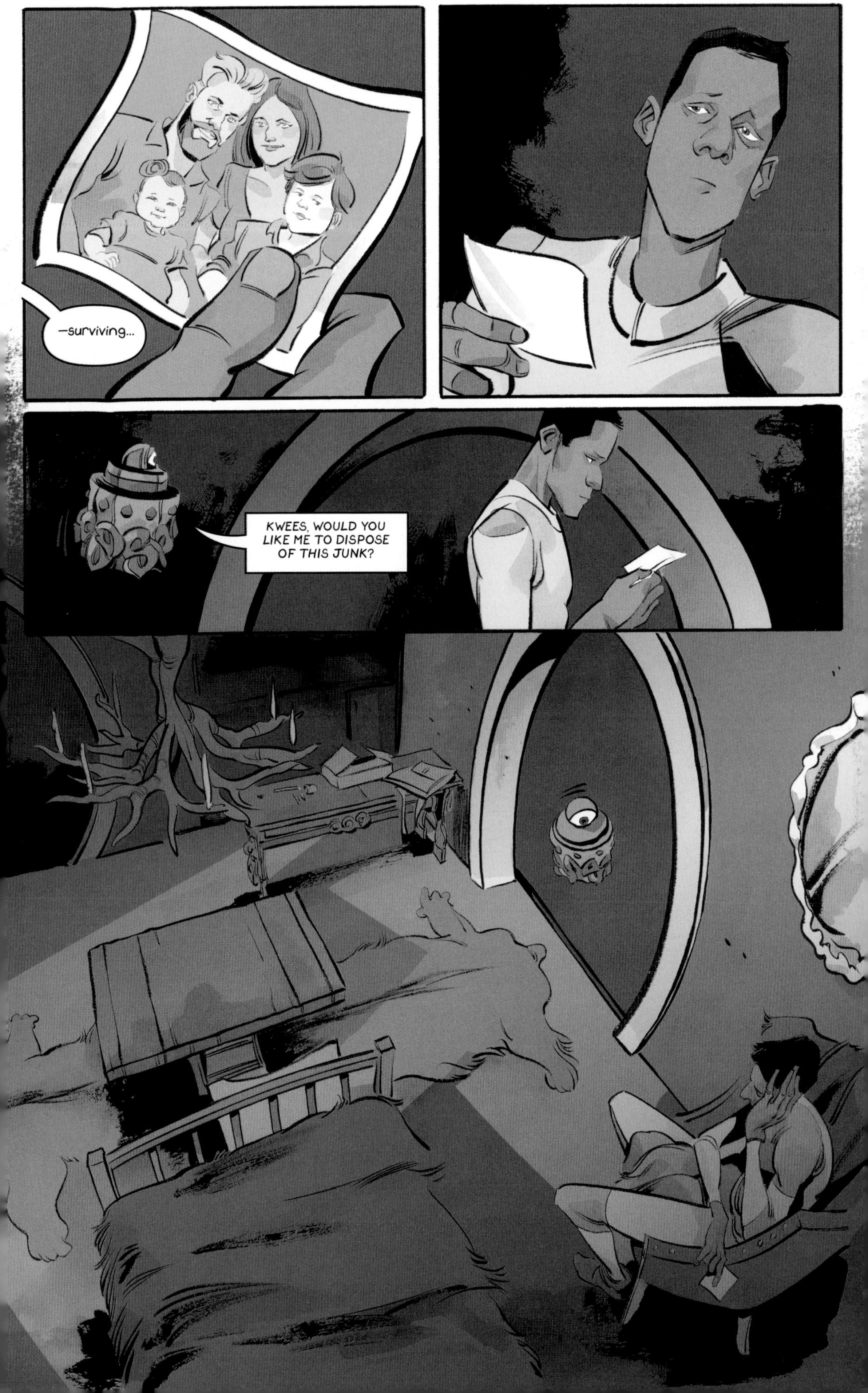
—surviving...
KWEES, WOULD YOU LIKE ME TO DISPOSE OF THIS JUNK?

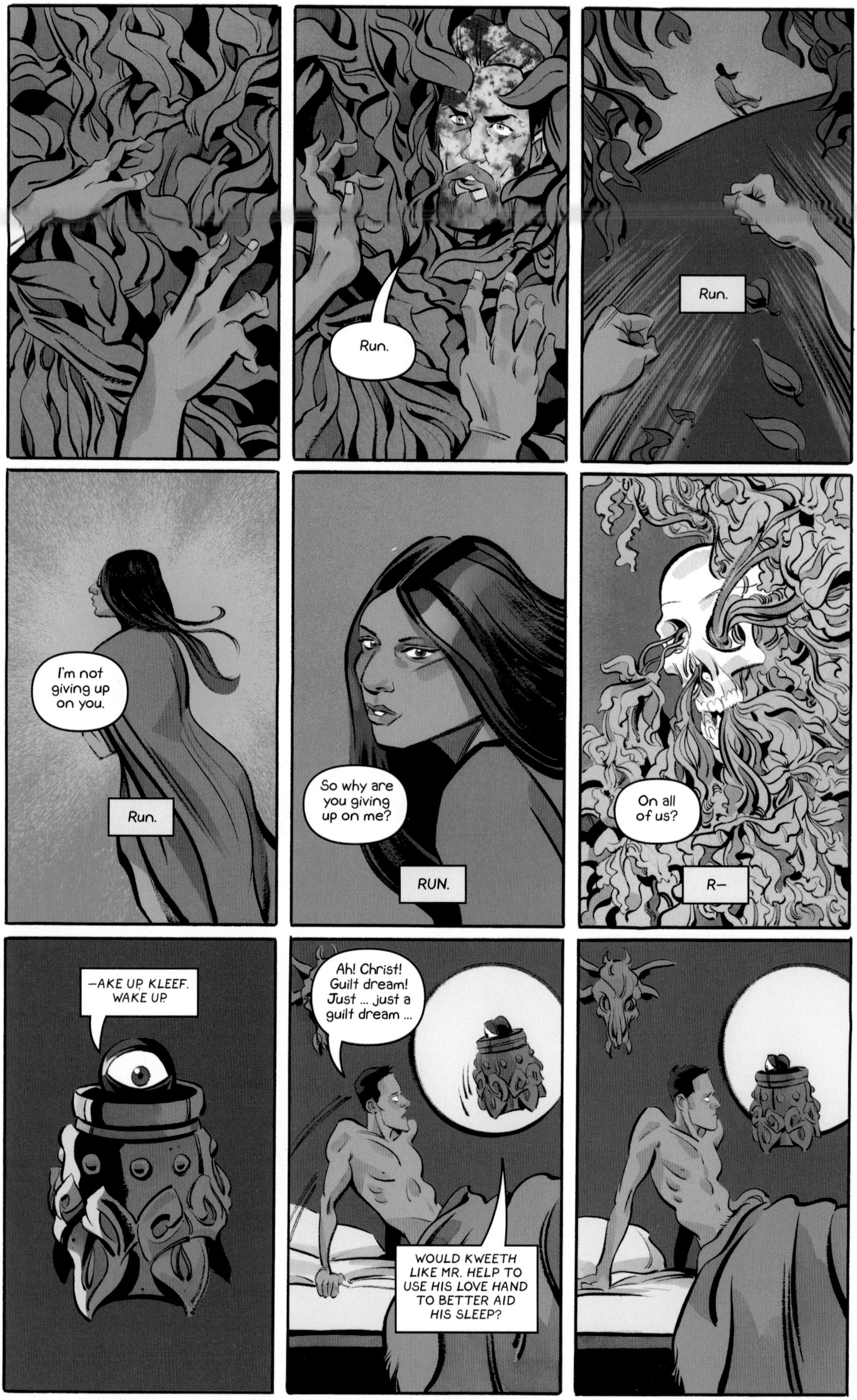
Run.
Run.
I'm not giving up on you.
Run.
So why are you giving up on me?
RUN.
On all of us?
R–
–AKE UP, KLEEF. WAKE UP.
Ah! Christ! Guilt dream! Just ... just a guilt dream ...
WOULD KWEETH LIKE MR. HELP TO USE HIS LOVE HAND TO BETTER AID HIS SLEEP?

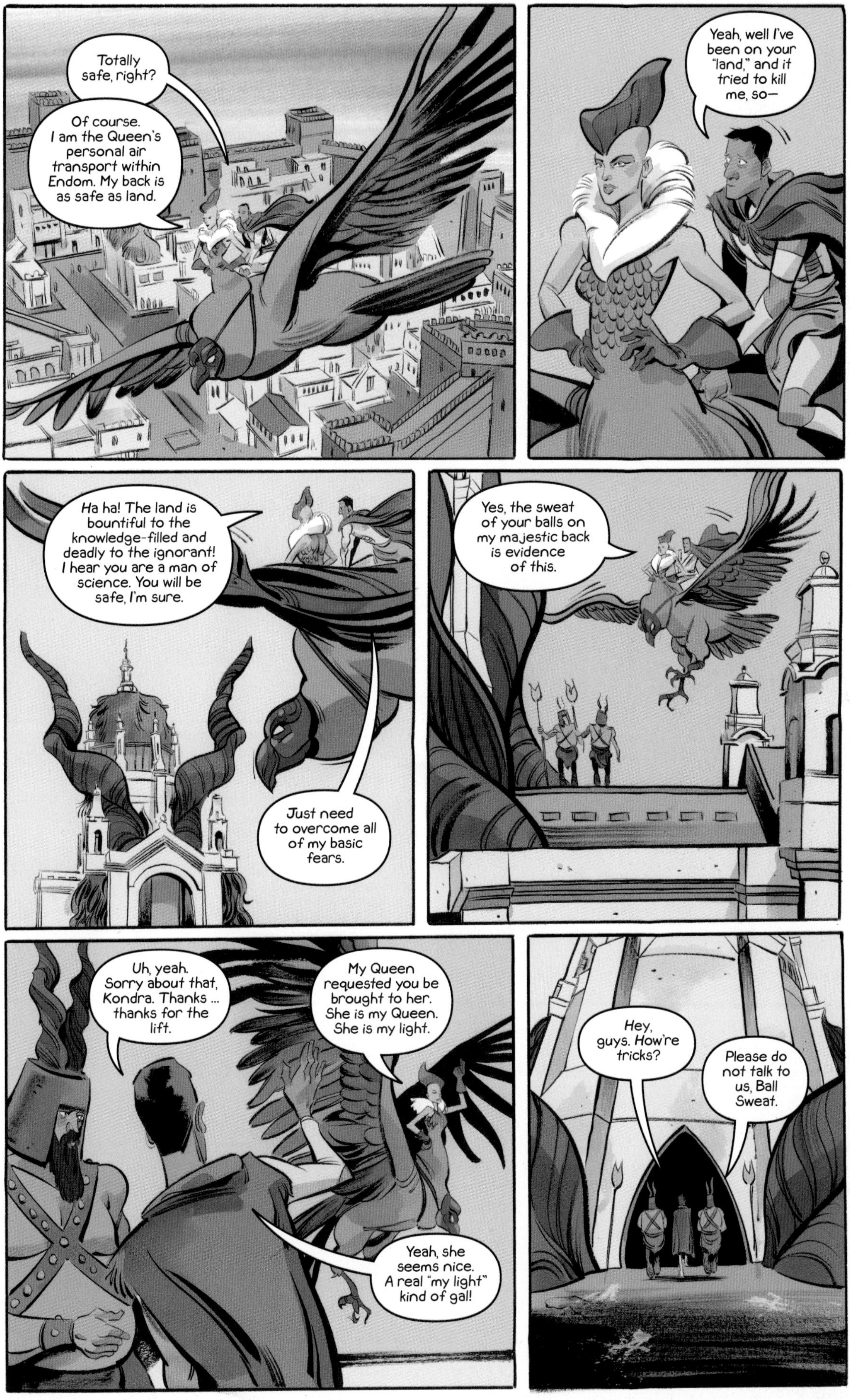
Totally safe, right?
Of course. I am the Queen's personal air transport within Endom. My back is as safe as land.
Yeah, well I've been on your "land," and it tried to kill me, so—
Ha ha! The land is bountiful to the knowledge-filled and deadly to the ignorant! I hear you are a man of science. You will be safe, I'm sure.
Just need to overcome all of my basic fears.
Yes, the sweat of your balls on my majestic back is evidence of this.
Uh, yeah. Sorry about that, Kondra. Thanks ... thanks for the lift.
My Queen requested you be brought to her. She is my Queen. She is my light.
Yeah, she seems nice. A real "my light" kind of gal!
Hey, guys. How're tricks?
Please do not talk to us, Ball Sweat.

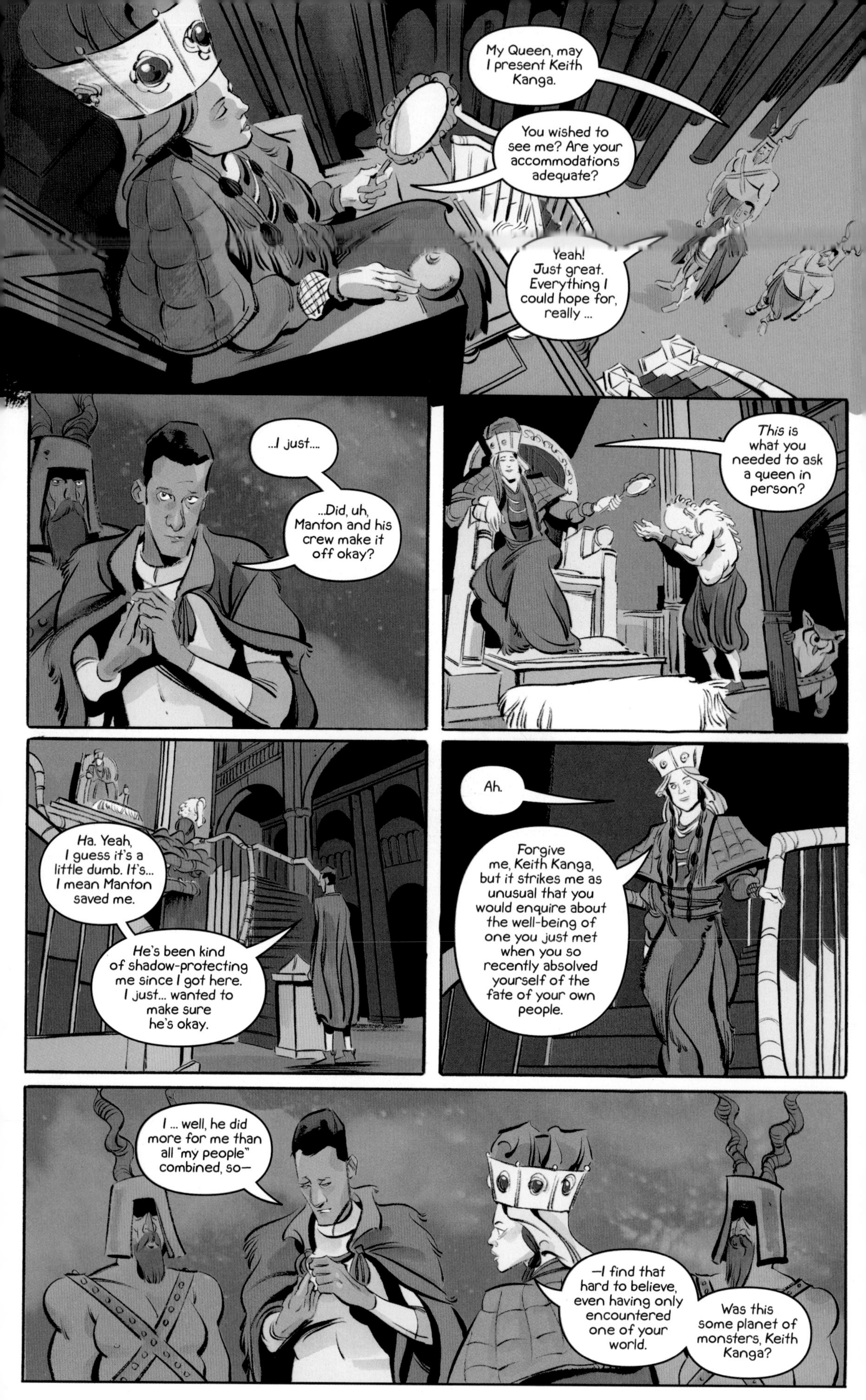
My Queen, may I present Keith Kanga.
You wished to see me? Are your accommodations adequate?
Yeah! Just great. Everything I could hope for, really ...
...I just....
...Did, uh, Manton and his crew make it off okay?
This is what you needed to ask a queen in person?
Ha. Yeah, I guess it's a little dumb. It's... I mean Manton saved me.
He's been kind of shadow-protecting me since I got here. I just... wanted to make sure he's okay.
Ah.
Forgive me, Keith Kanga, but it strikes me as unusual that you would enquire about the well-being of one you just met when you so recently absolved yourself of the fate of your own people.
I ... well, he did more for me than all "my people" combined, so—
—I find that hard to believe, even having only encountered one of your world.
Was this some planet of monsters, Keith Kanga?

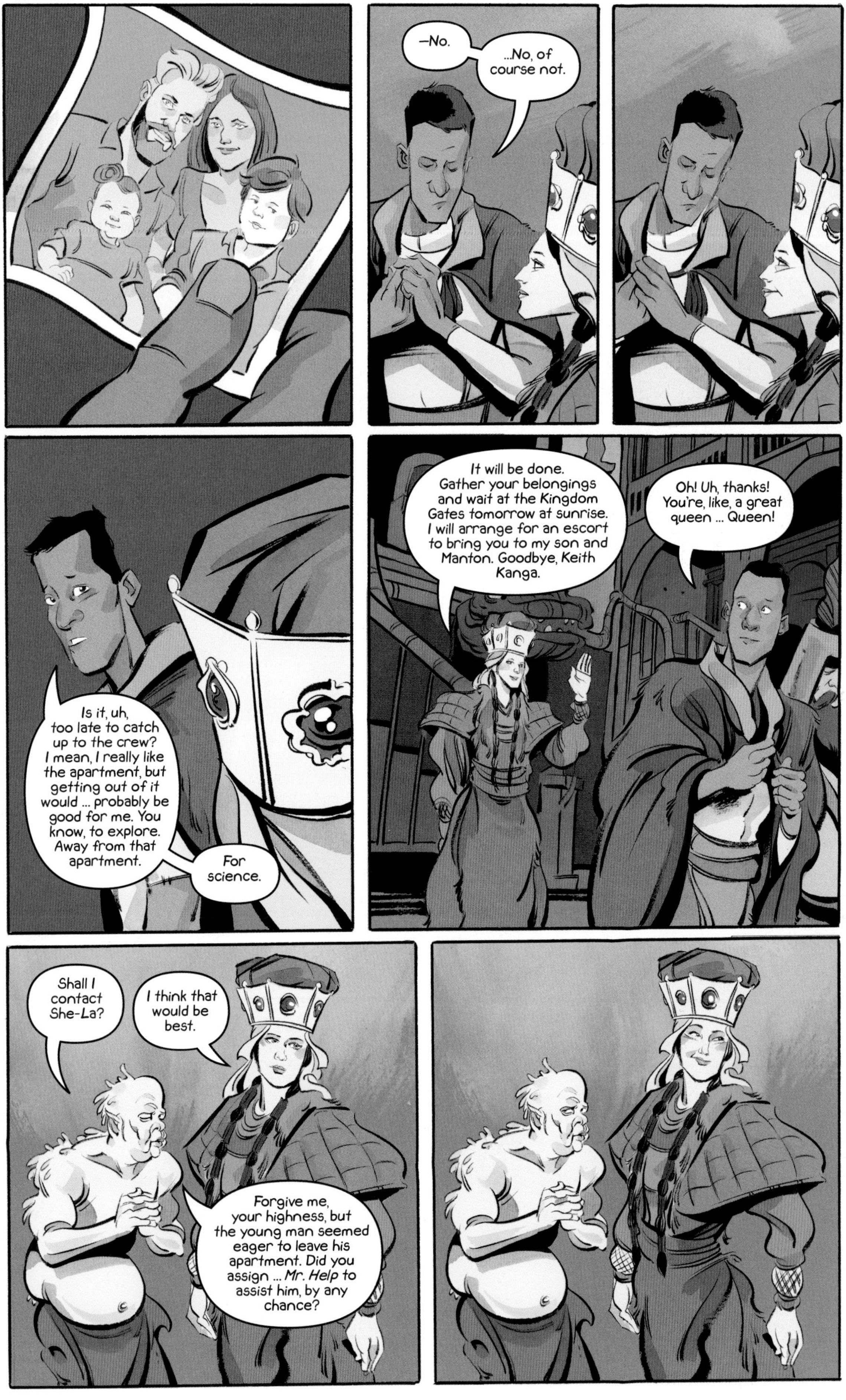
—No.
...No, of course not.
Is it, uh, too late to catch up to the crew? I mean, I really like the apartment, but getting out of it would ... probably be good for me. You know, to explore. Away from that apartment.
For science.
It will be done. Gather your belongings and wait at the Kingdom Gates tomorrow at sunrise. I will arrange for an escort to bring you to my son and Manton. Goodbye, Keith Kanga.
Oh! Uh, thanks! You're, like, a great queen ... Queen!
Shall I contact She-La?
I think that would be best.
Forgive me, your highness, but the young man seemed eager to leave his apartment. Did you assign ... *Mr. Help* to assist him, by any chance?

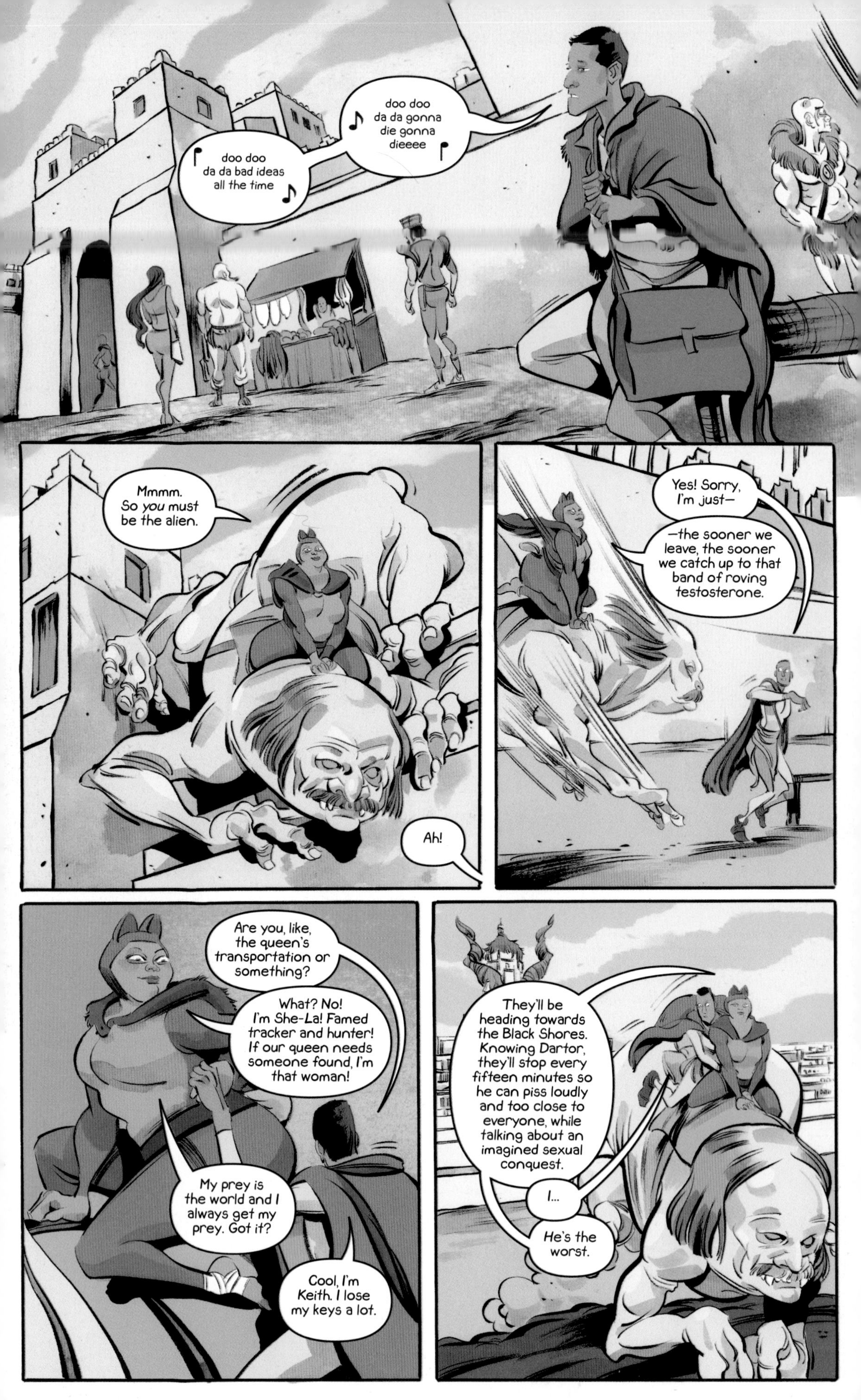
doo doo
da da bad ideas
all the time
doo doo
da da gonna
die gonna
dieeee
Mmmm.
So *you* must
be the alien.
Ah!
Yes! Sorry,
I'm just—
—the sooner we
leave, the sooner
we catch up to that
band of roving
testosterone.
Are you, like,
the queen's
transportation or
something?
What? No!
I'm She-La! Famed
tracker and hunter!
If our queen needs
someone found, I'm
that woman!
My prey is
the world and I
always get my
prey. Got it?
Cool, I'm
Keith. I lose
my keys a lot.
They'll be
heading towards
the Black Shores.
Knowing Dartor,
they'll stop every
fifteen minutes so
he can piss loudly
and too close to
everyone, while
talking about an
imagined sexual
conquest.
I...
He's the
worst.

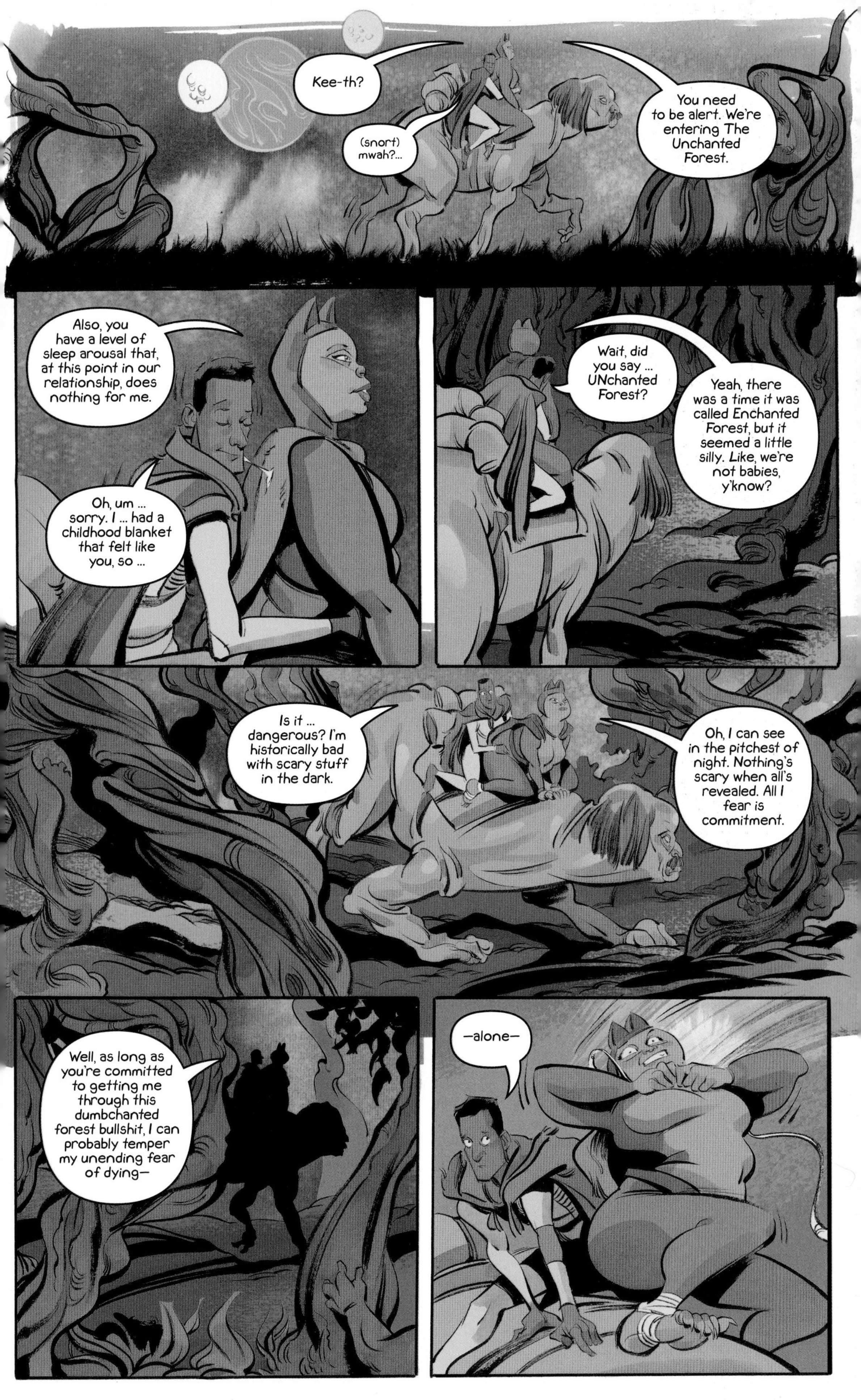
Kee-th?
(snort) mwah?...
You need to be alert. We're entering The Unchanted Forest.
Also, you have a level of sleep arousal that, at this point in our relationship, does nothing for me.
Oh, um ... sorry. I ... had a childhood blanket that felt like you, so ...
Wait, did you say ... UNchanted Forest?
Yeah, there was a time it was called Enchanted Forest, but it seemed a little silly. Like, we're not babies, y'know?
Is it ... dangerous? I'm historically bad with scary stuff in the dark.
Oh, I can see in the pitchest of night. Nothing's scary when all's revealed. All I fear is commitment.
Well, as long as you're committed to getting me through this dumbchanted forest bullshit, I can probably temper my unending fear of dying—
—alone—

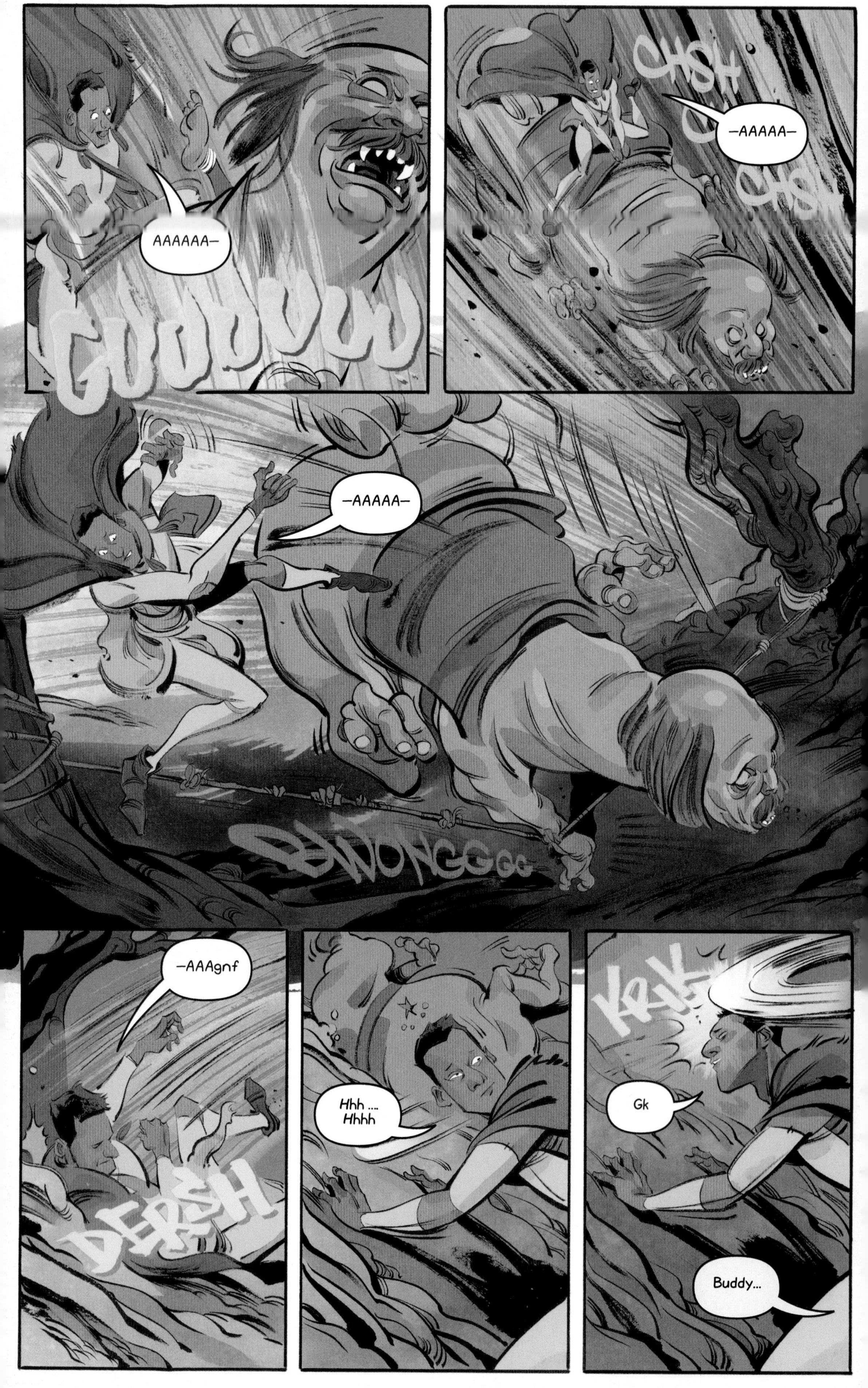
AAAAAA—
CHSH
—AAAAA—
CHSH
—AAAAA—
—AAAgnf
DERSH
Hhh ....
Hhhh
Gk
Buddy...

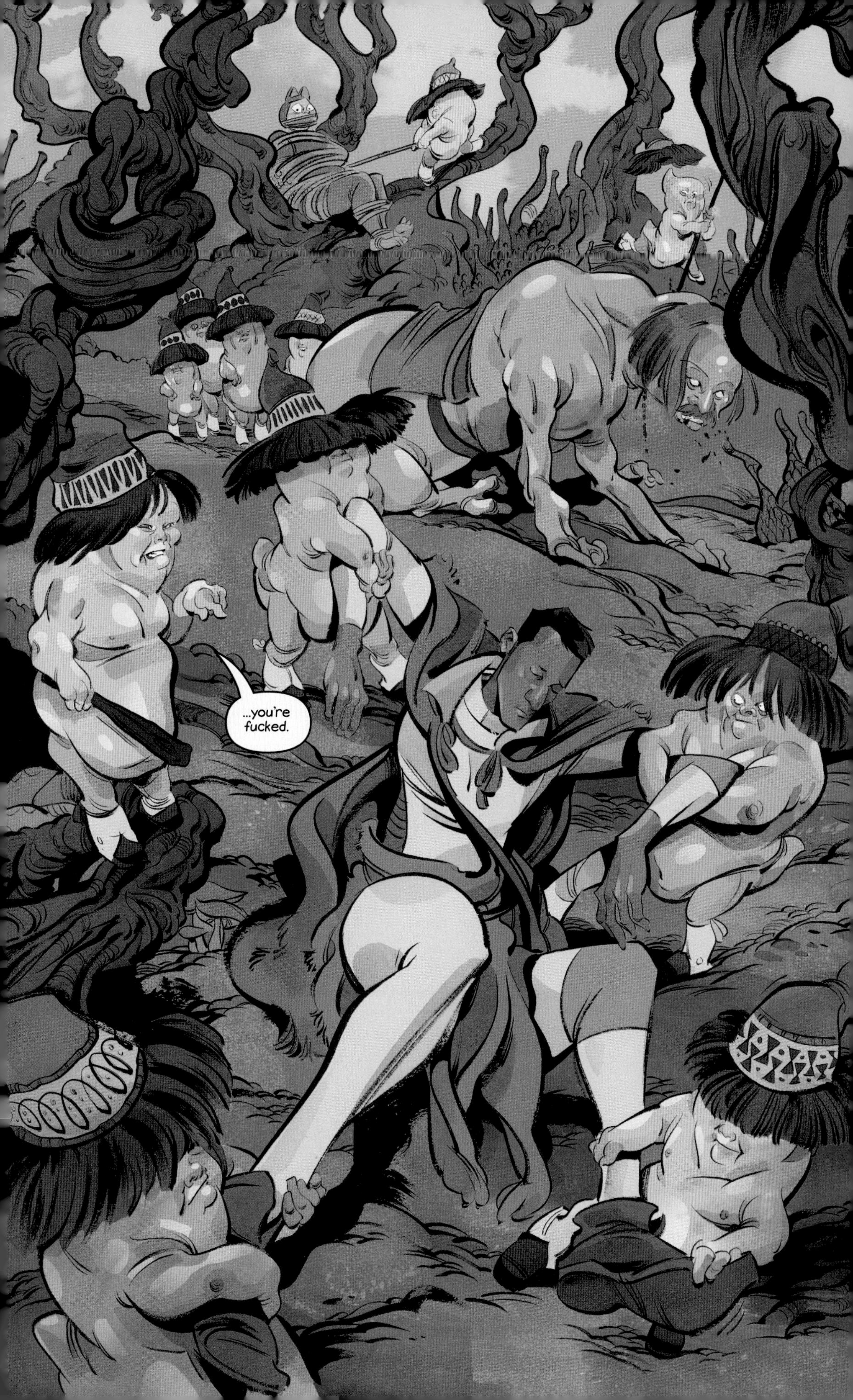
...you're fucked.

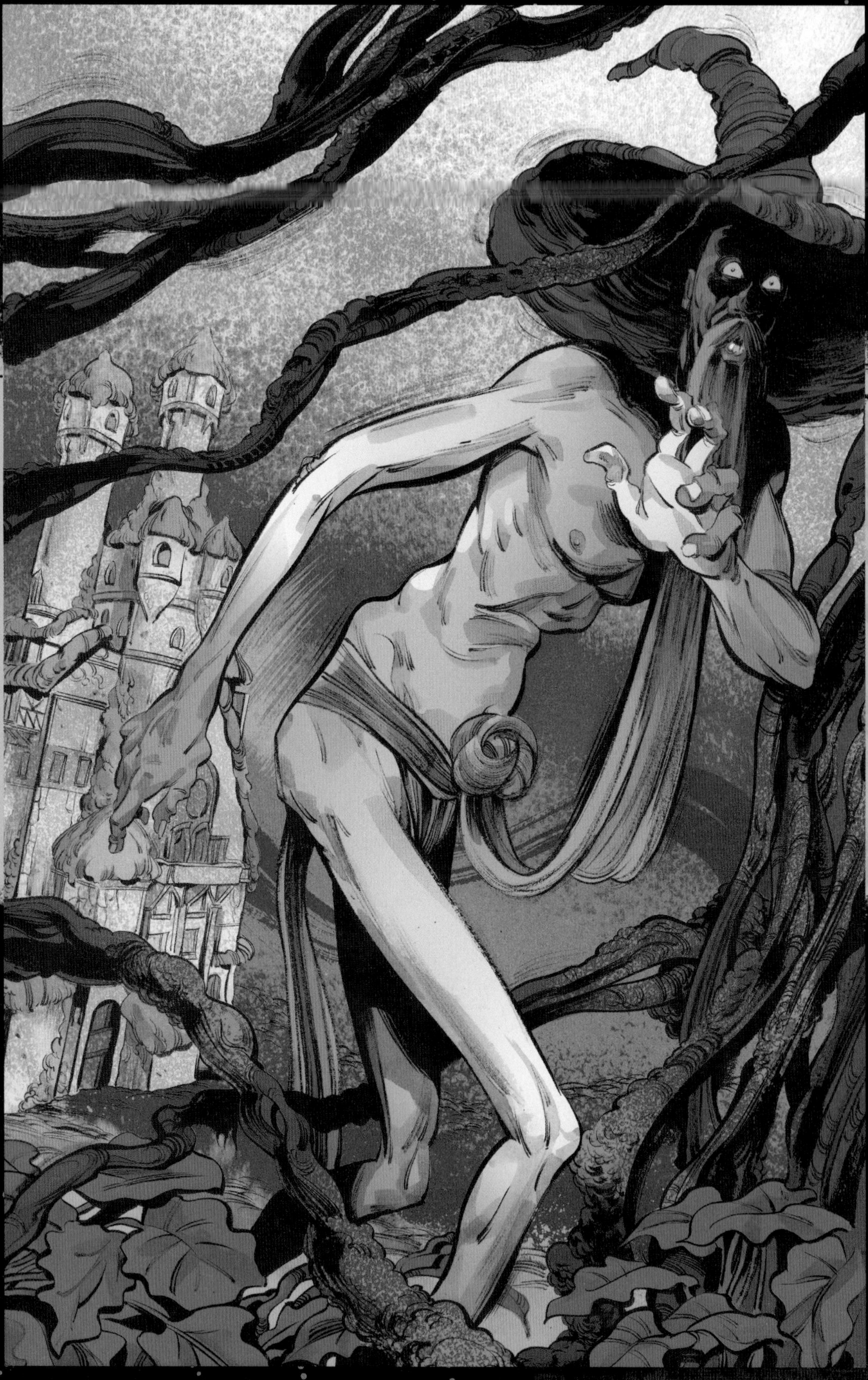

CHAPTER THREE

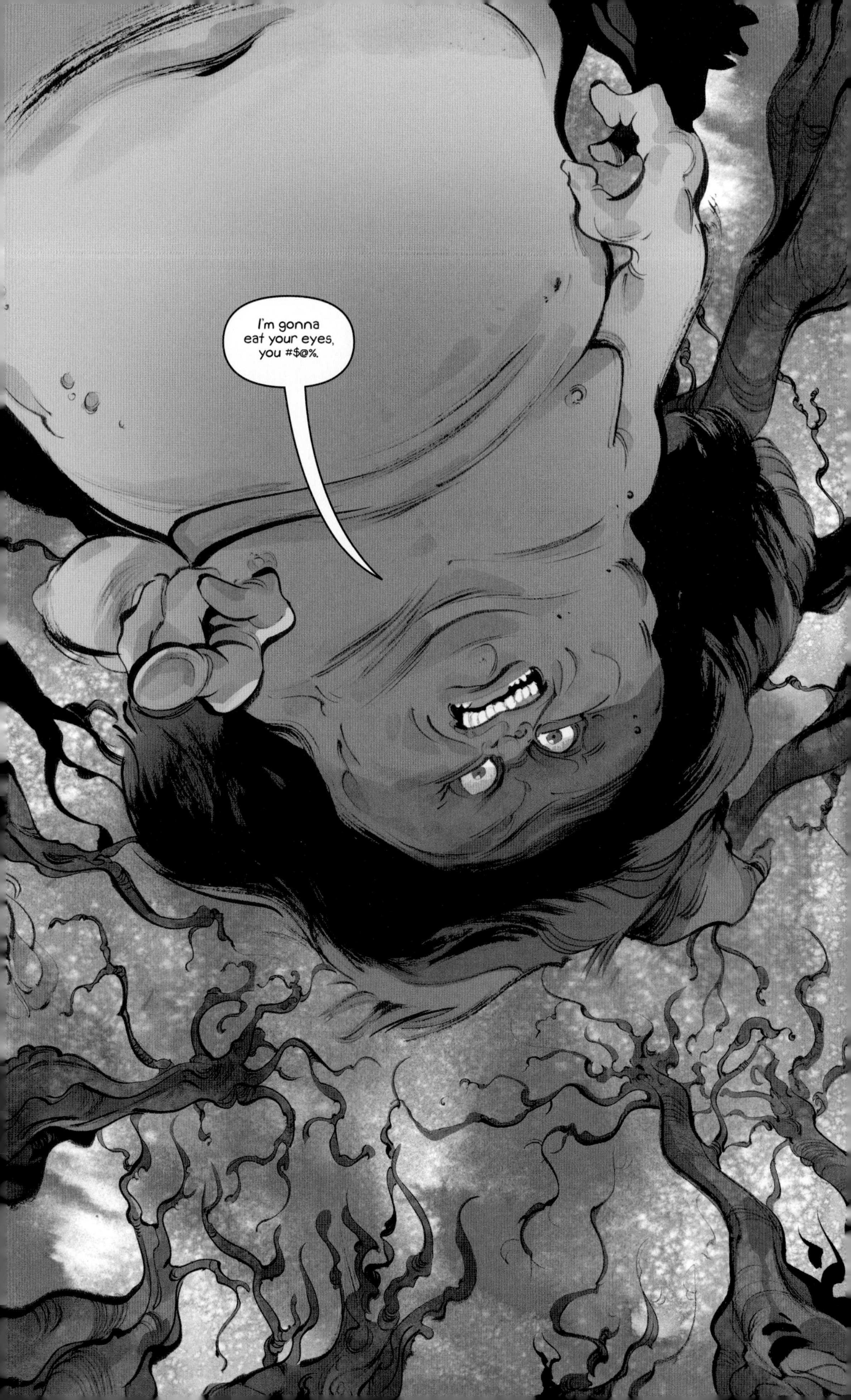
I'm gonna eat your eyes, you #$@%.

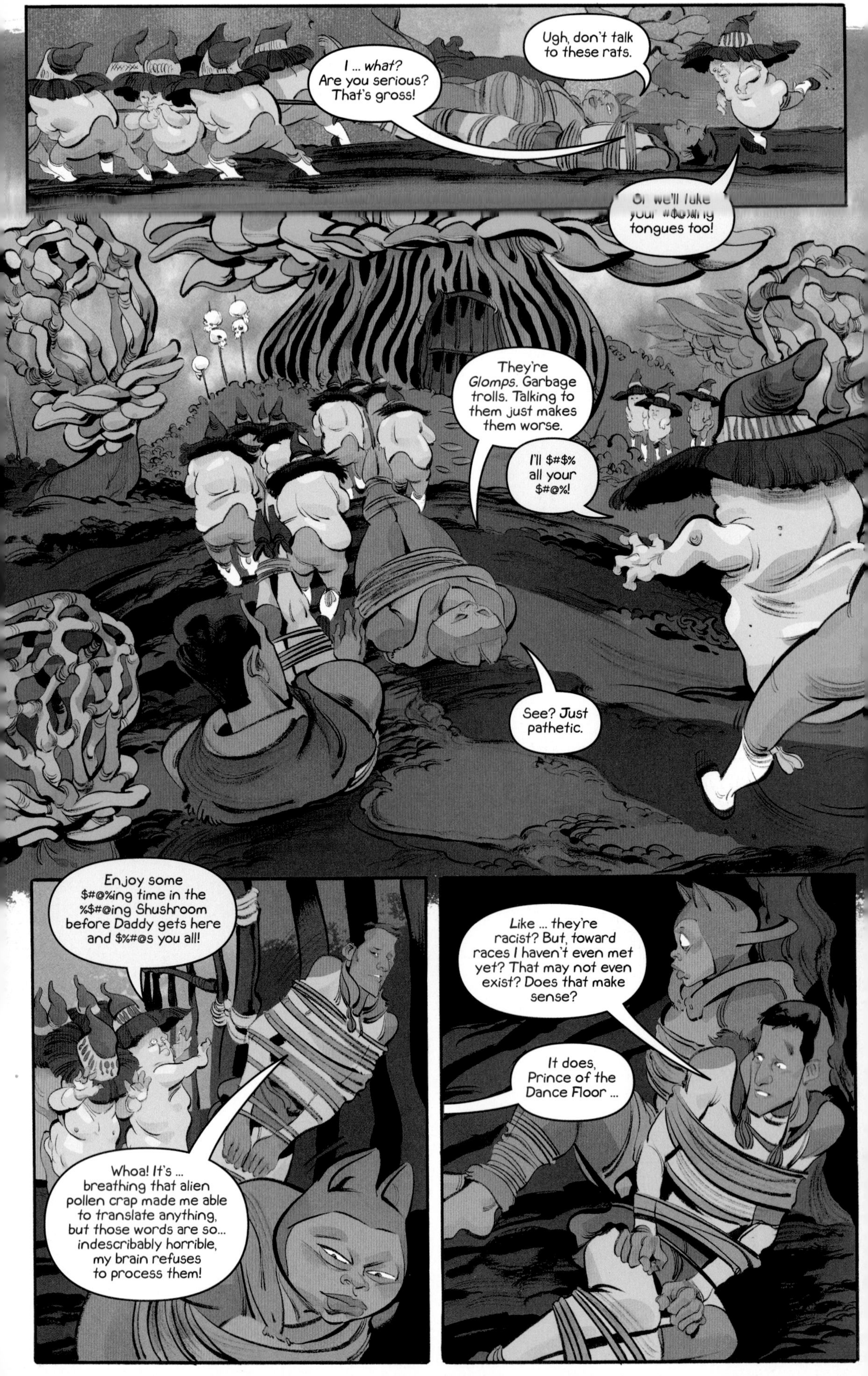
I ... what? Are you serious? That's gross!
Ugh, don't talk to these rats.
Or we'll take your
tongues too!
They're Glomps. Garbage trolls. Talking to them just makes them worse.
I'll $#$% all your $#@%!
See? Just pathetic.
Enjoy some $#@%ing time in the %$#@ing Shushroom before Daddy gets here and $%#@s you all!
Whoa! It's ... breathing that alien pollen crap made me able to translate anything, but those words are so... indescribably horrible, my brain refuses to process them!
Like ... they're racist? But, toward races I haven't even met yet? That may not even exist? Does that make sense?
It does, Prince of the Dance Floor ...

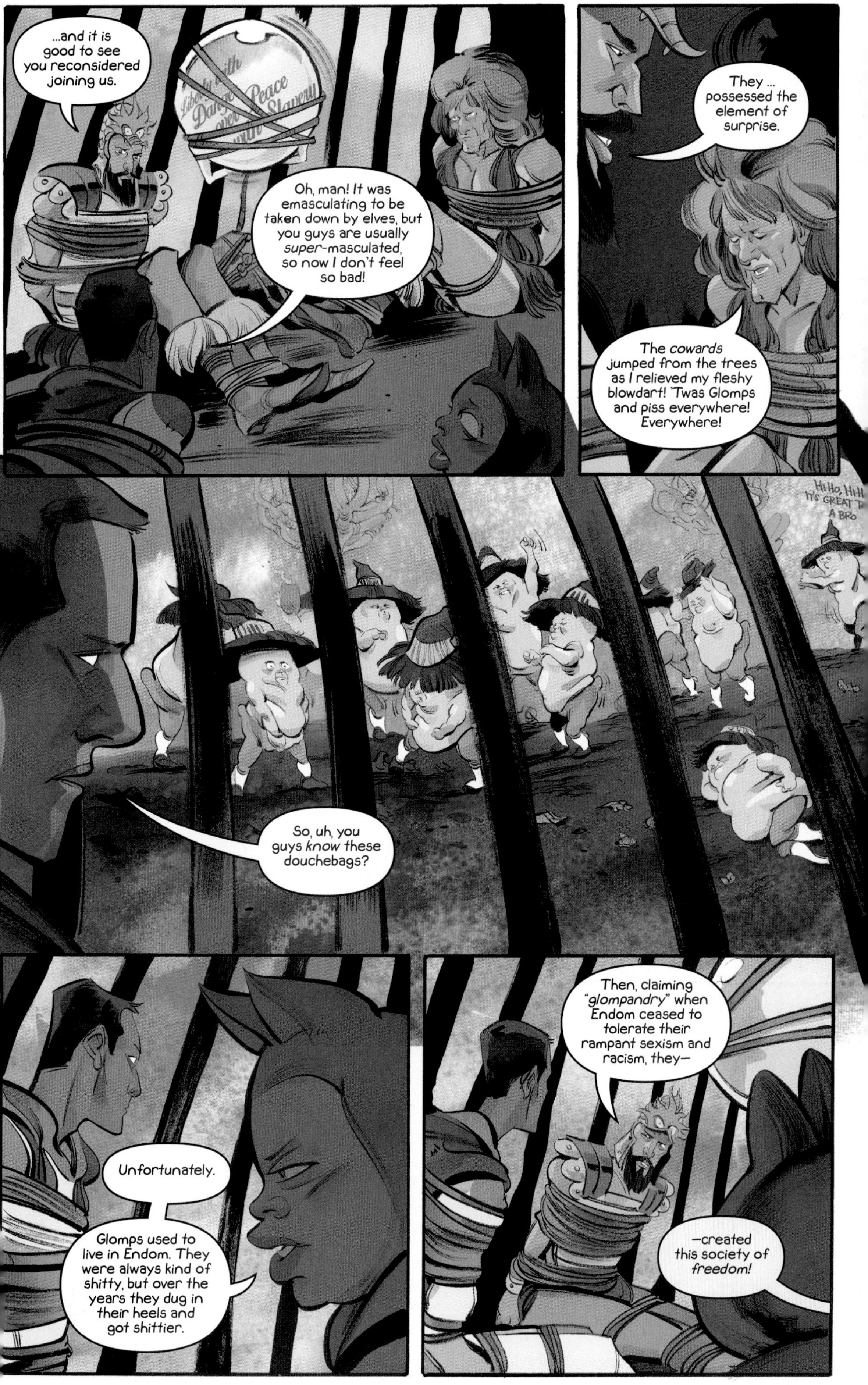
...and it is good to see you reconsidered joining us.
Oh, man! It was emasculating to be taken down by elves, but you guys are usually *super*-masculated, so now I don't feel so bad!
They ... possessed the element of surprise.
The *cowards* jumped from the trees as I relieved my fleshy blowdart! 'Twas Glomps and piss everywhere! Everywhere!
So, uh, you guys *know* these douchebags?
Unfortunately.
Glomps used to live in Endom. They were always kind of shitty, but over the years they dug in their heels and got shittier.
Then, claiming "*glompandry*" when Endom ceased to tolerate their rampant sexism and racism, they—
—created this society of *freedom!*

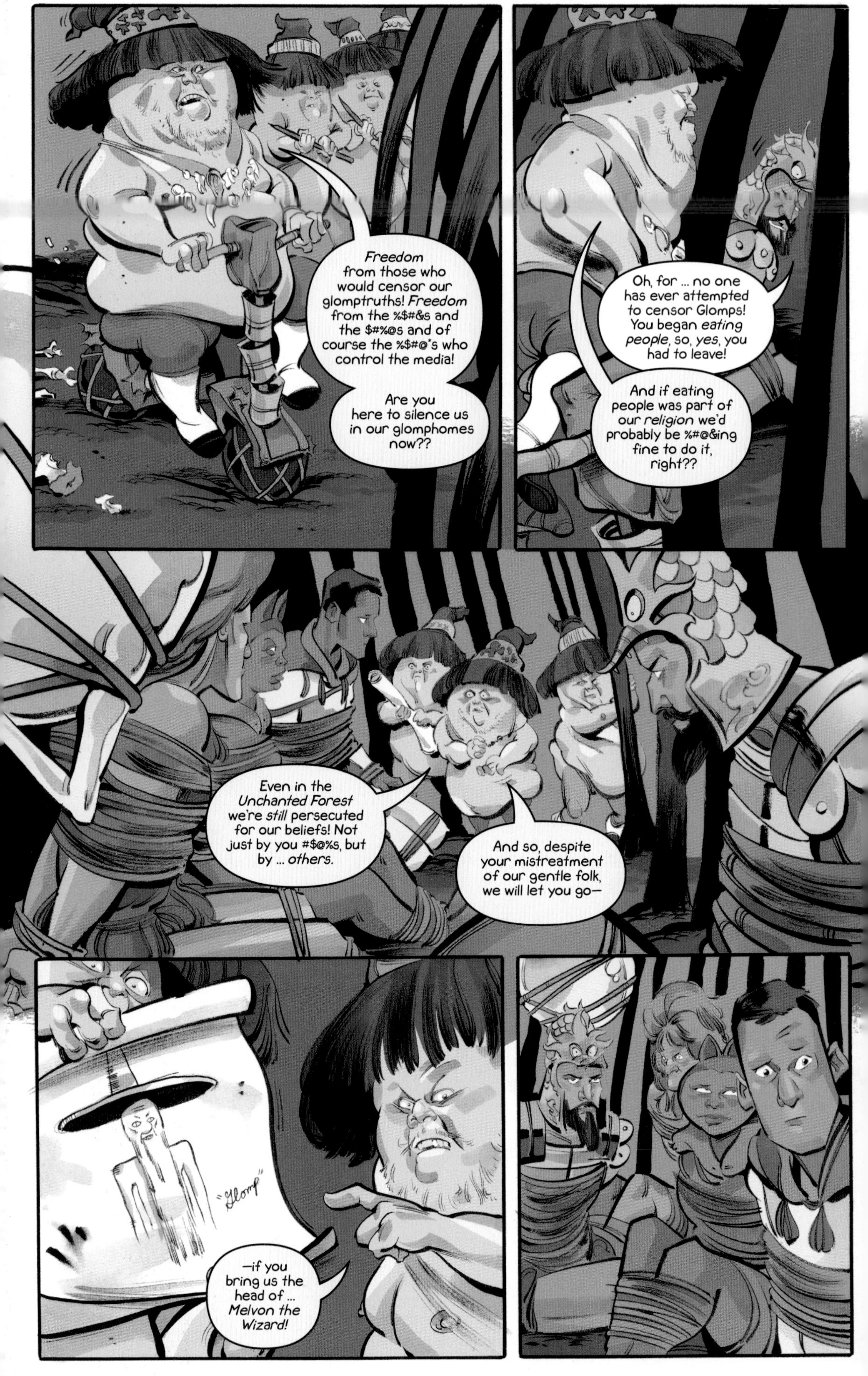
Freedom from those who would censor our glomptruths! *Freedom* from the %$#&s and the $#%@s and of course the %$#@*s who control the media!
Are you here to silence us in our glomphomes now??
Oh, for ... no one has ever attempted to censor Glomps! You began *eating people*, so, *yes*, you had to leave!
And if eating people was part of our *religion* we'd probably be %#@&ing fine to do it, right??
Even in the *Unchanted Forest* we're *still* persecuted for our beliefs! Not just by you #$@%s, but by ... *others*.
And so, despite your mistreatment of our gentle folk, we will let you go—
"Glomp"
—if you bring us the head of ... *Melvon the Wizard!*

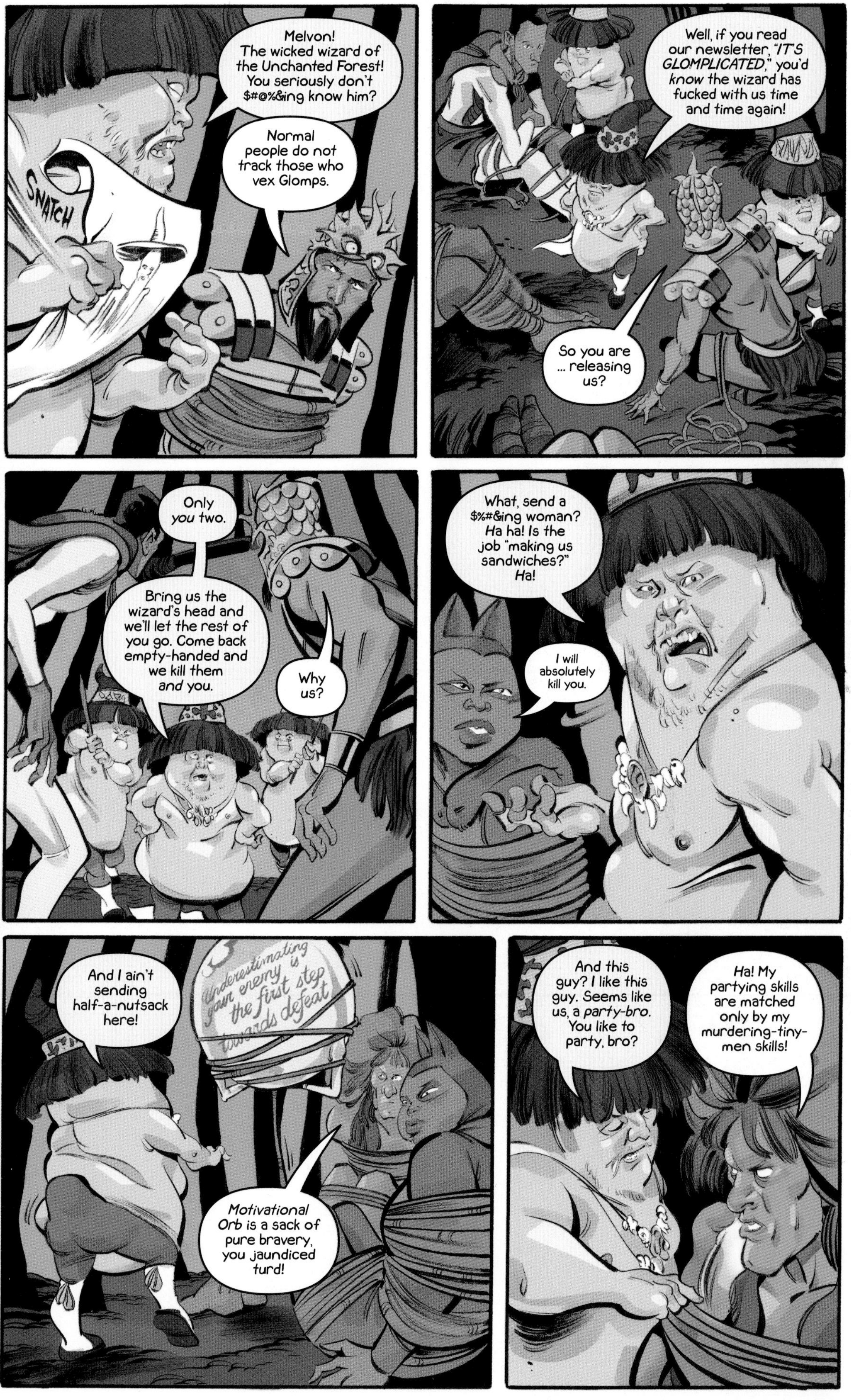
Melvon! The wicked wizard of the Unchanted Forest! You seriously don't $#@%&ing know him?
SNATCH
Normal people do not track those who vex Glomps.
Well, if you read our newsletter, *"IT'S GLOMPLICATED,"* you'd *know* the wizard has fucked with us time and time again!
So you are ... releasing us?
Only *you two.*
Bring us the wizard's head and we'll let the rest of you go. Come back empty-handed and we kill them *and* you.
Why us?
What, send a $%#&ing woman? *Ha* ha! Is the job "making us sandwiches?" *Ha!*
I will absolutely kill you.
And I ain't sending half-a-nutsack here!
Underestimating your enemy is the first step towards defeat
Motivational Orb is a sack of pure bravery, you jaundiced turd!
And this guy? I like this guy. Seems like us, a *party-bro.* You like to party, bro?
Ha! My partying skills are matched only by my murdering-tiny-men skills!

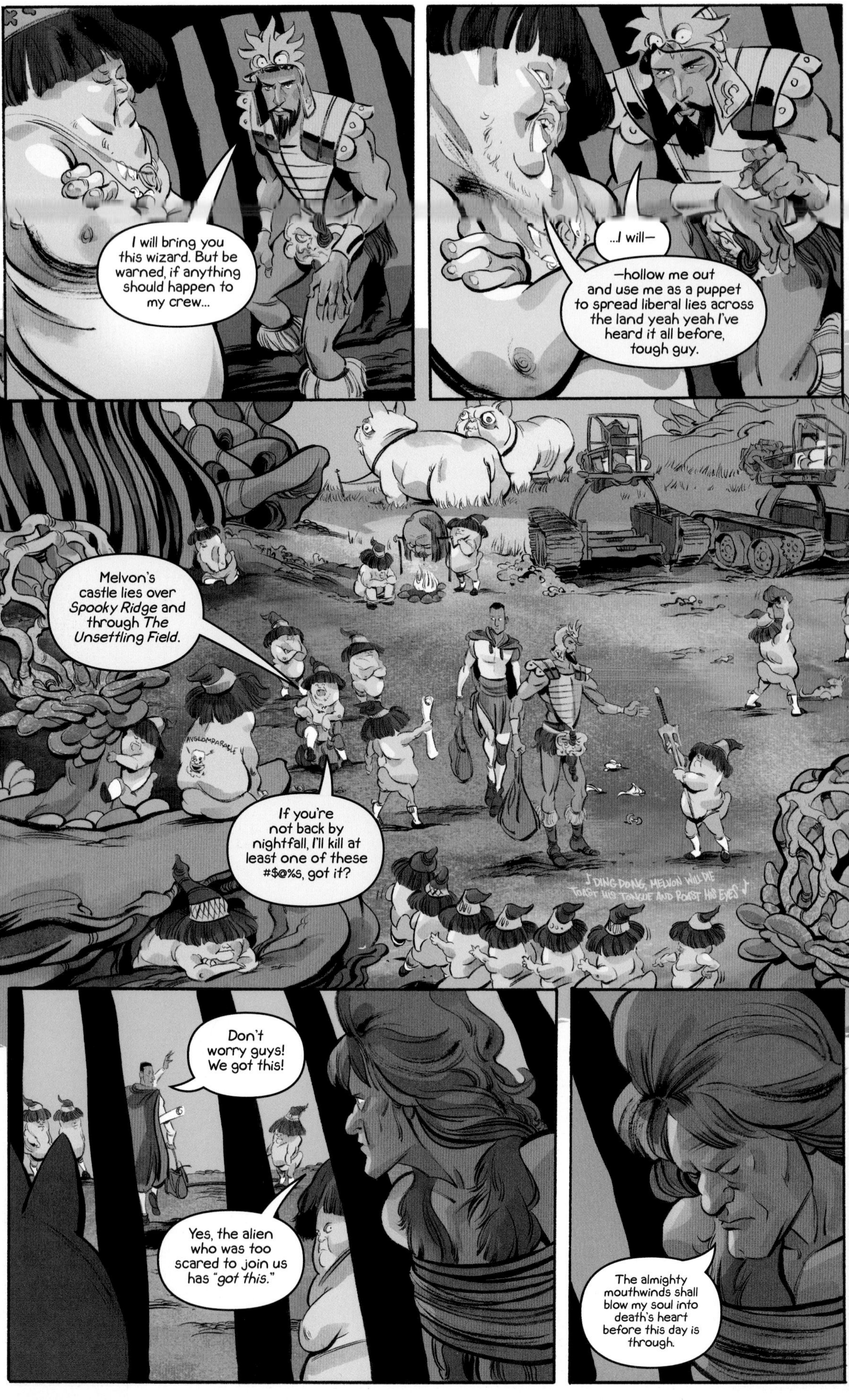
I will bring you this wizard. But be warned, if anything should happen to my crew...
...I will—
—hollow me out and use me as a puppet to spread liberal lies across the land yeah yeah I've heard it all before, tough guy.
Melvon's castle lies over *Spooky Ridge* and through *The Unsettling Field*.
INCLOMPARABLE
If you're not back by nightfall, I'll kill at least one of these #$@%s, got it?
♩ DING DONG, MELVON WILL DIE
TOAST HIS TONGUE AND ROAST HIS EYES ♩
Don't worry guys! We got this!
Yes, the alien who was too scared to join us has *"got this."*
The almighty mouthwinds shall blow my soul into death's heart before this day is through.

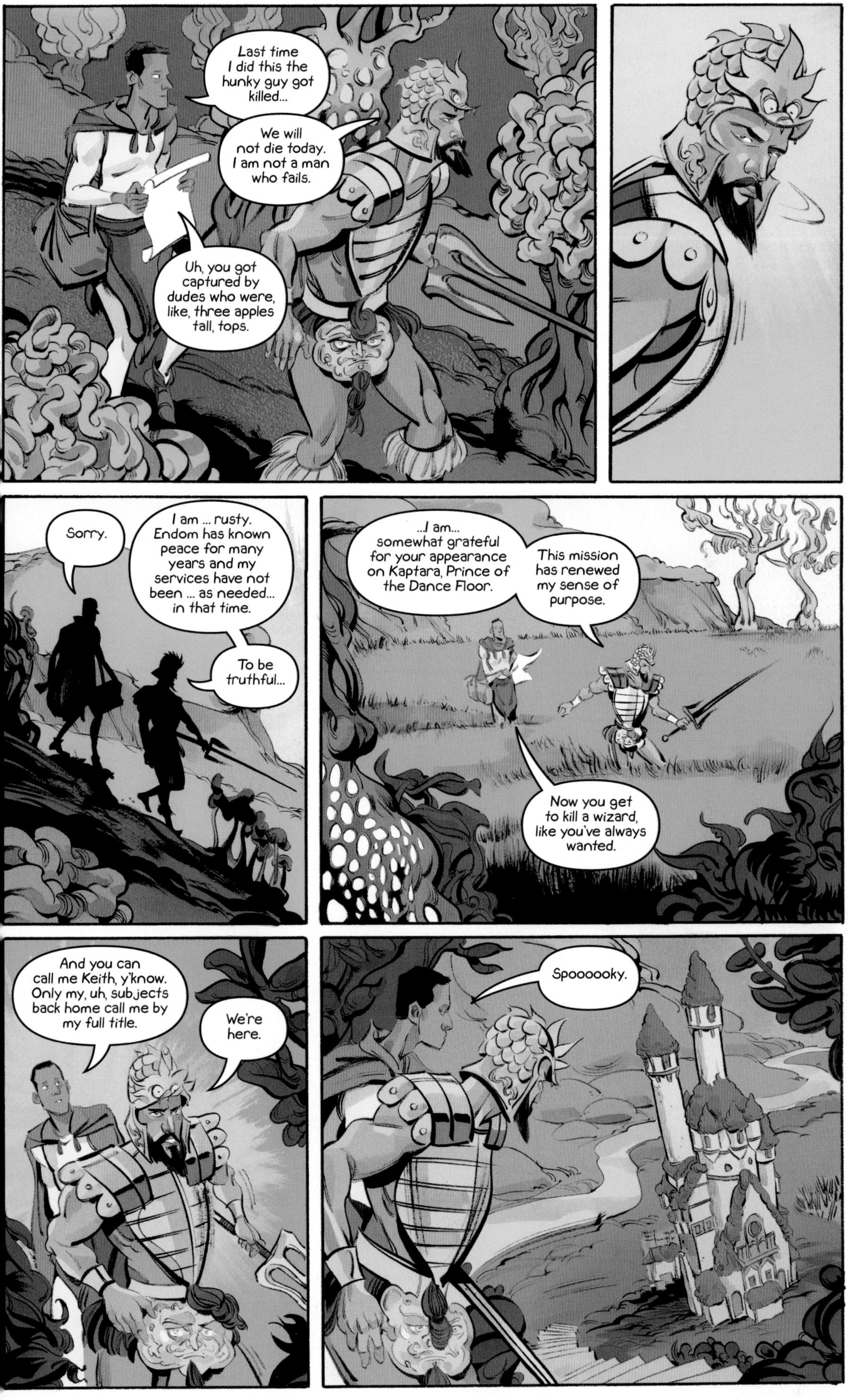
Last time I did this the hunky guy got killed...
We will not die today. I am not a man who fails.
Uh, you got captured by dudes who were, like, three apples tall, tops.
Sorry.
I am ... rusty. Endom has known peace for many years and my services have not been ... as needed... in that time.
To be truthful...
...I am... somewhat grateful for your appearance on Kaptara, Prince of the Dance Floor.
This mission has renewed my sense of purpose.
Now you get to kill a wizard, like you've always wanted.
And you can call me Keith, y'know. Only my, uh, subjects back home call me by my full title.
We're here.
Spoooooky.

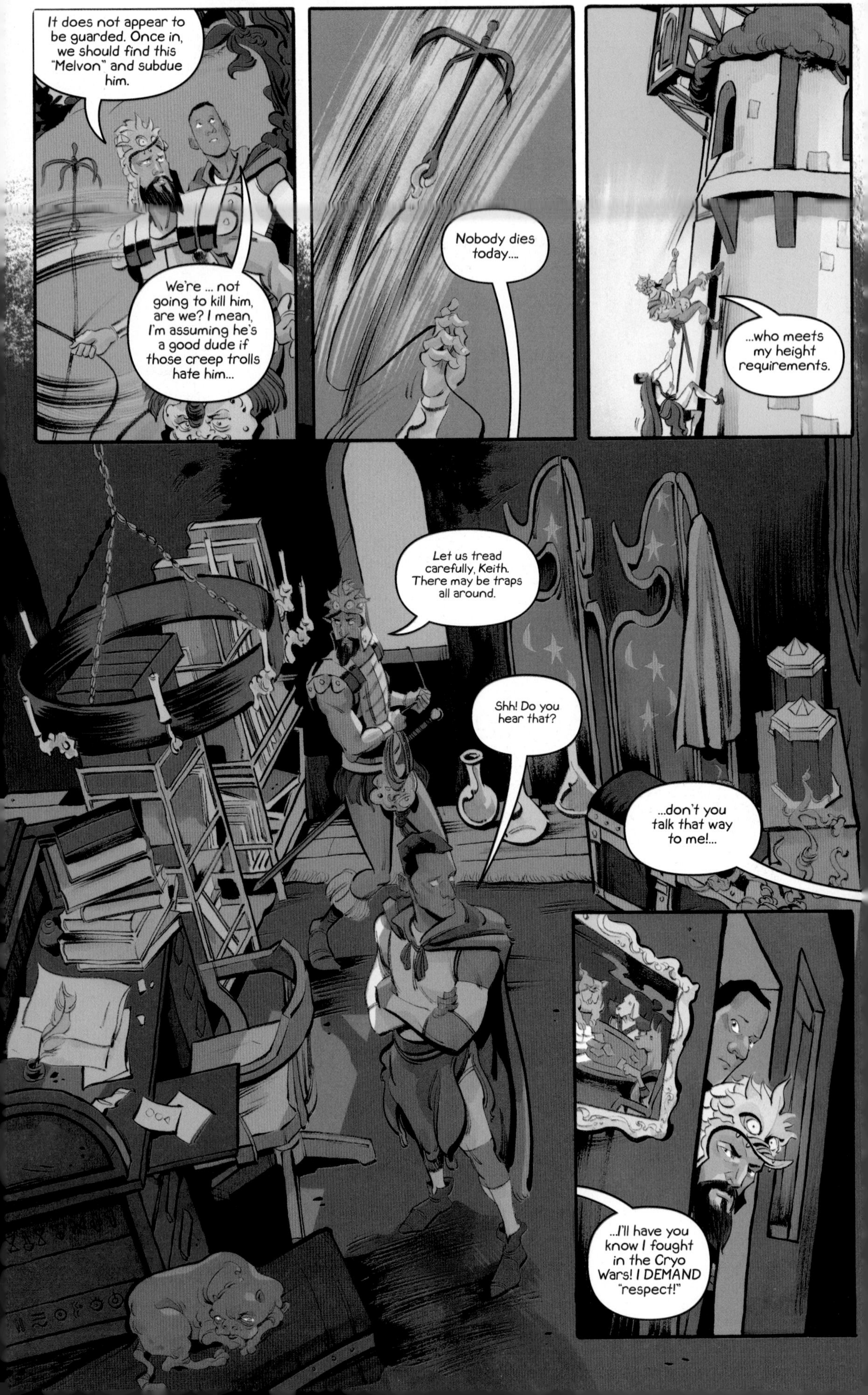
It does not appear to be guarded. Once in, we should find this "Melvon" and subdue him.
We're ... not going to kill him, are we? I mean, I'm assuming he's a good dude if those creep trolls hate him...
Nobody dies today....
...who meets my height requirements.
Let us tread carefully, Keith. There may be traps all around.
Shh! Do you hear that?
...don't you talk that way to me!...
...I'll have you know I fought in the Cryo Wars! I DEMAND "respect!"

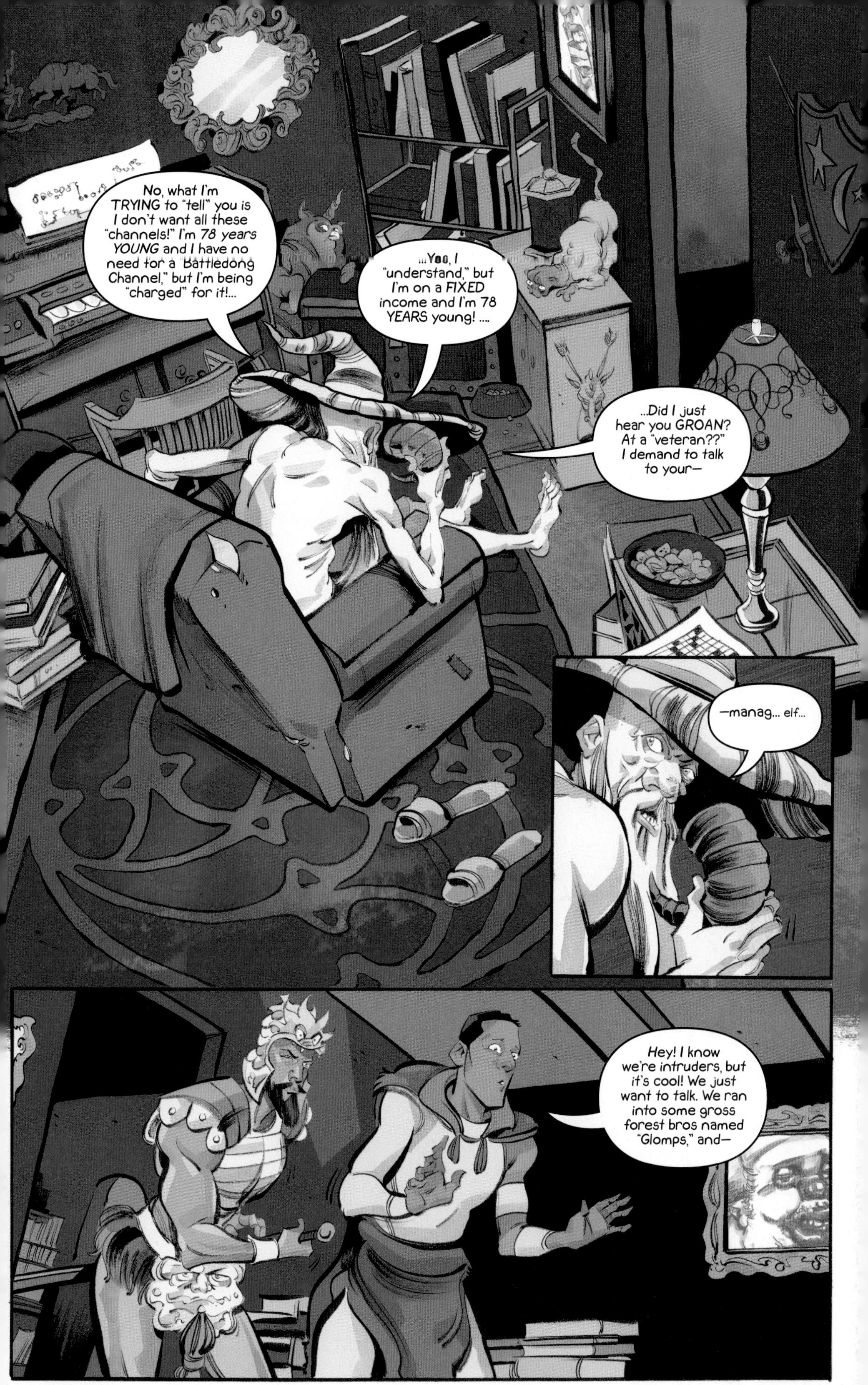
No, what I'm TRYING to "tell" you is I don't want all these "channels!" I'm 78 years YOUNG and I have no need for a "Battledong Channel," but I'm being "charged" for it!...
...Yes, I "understand," but I'm on a FIXED income and I'm 78 YEARS young! ....
...Did I just hear you GROAN? At a "veteran??" I demand to talk to your—
—manag... elf...
Hey! I know we're intruders, but it's cool! We just want to talk. We ran into some gross forest bros named "Glomps," and—

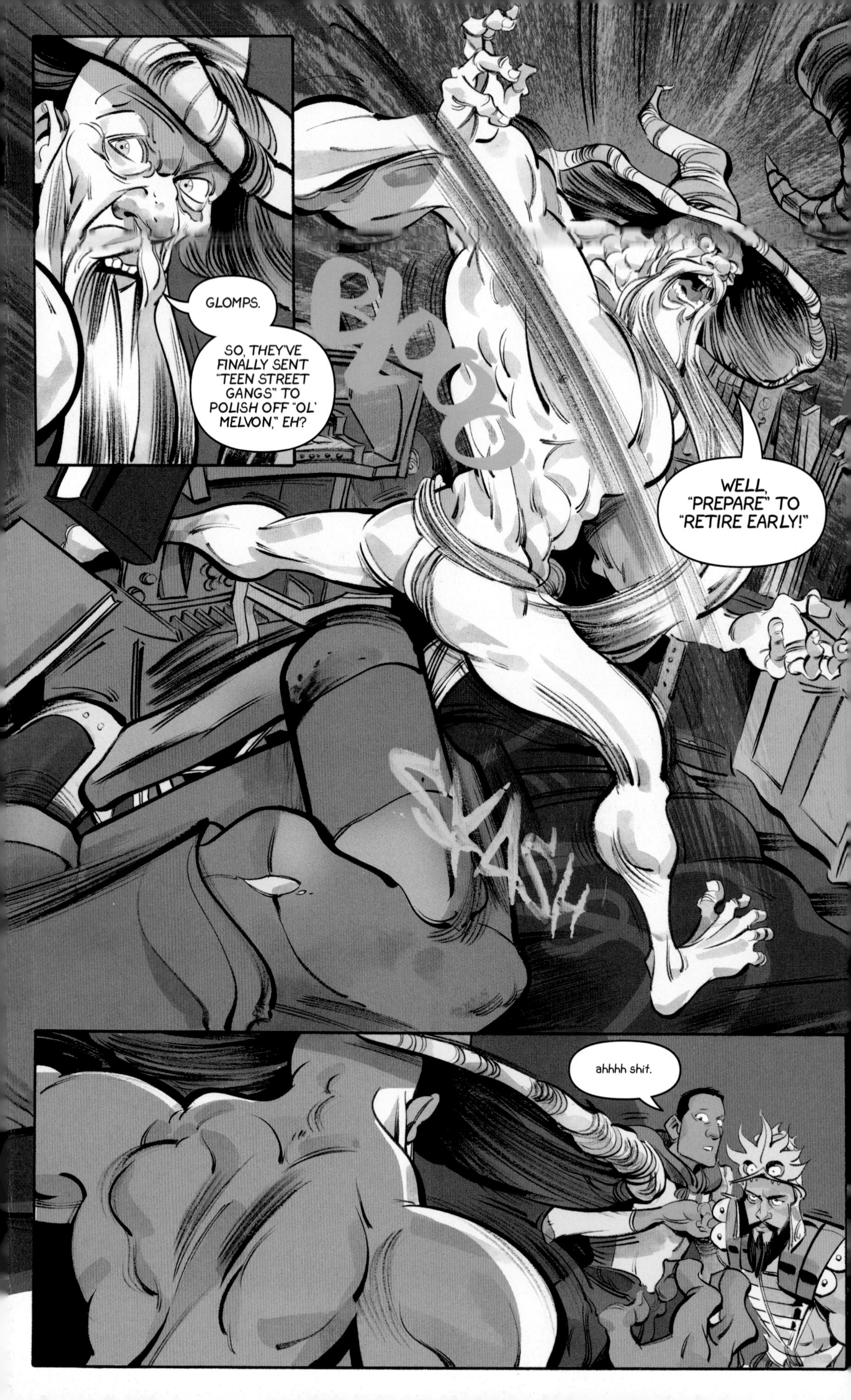
GLOMPS.
SO, THEY'VE FINALLY SENT "TEEN STREET GANGS" TO POLISH OFF "OL' MELVON," EH?
BLOOG
WELL, "PREPARE" TO "RETIRE EARLY!"
SMASH
ahhhh shit.

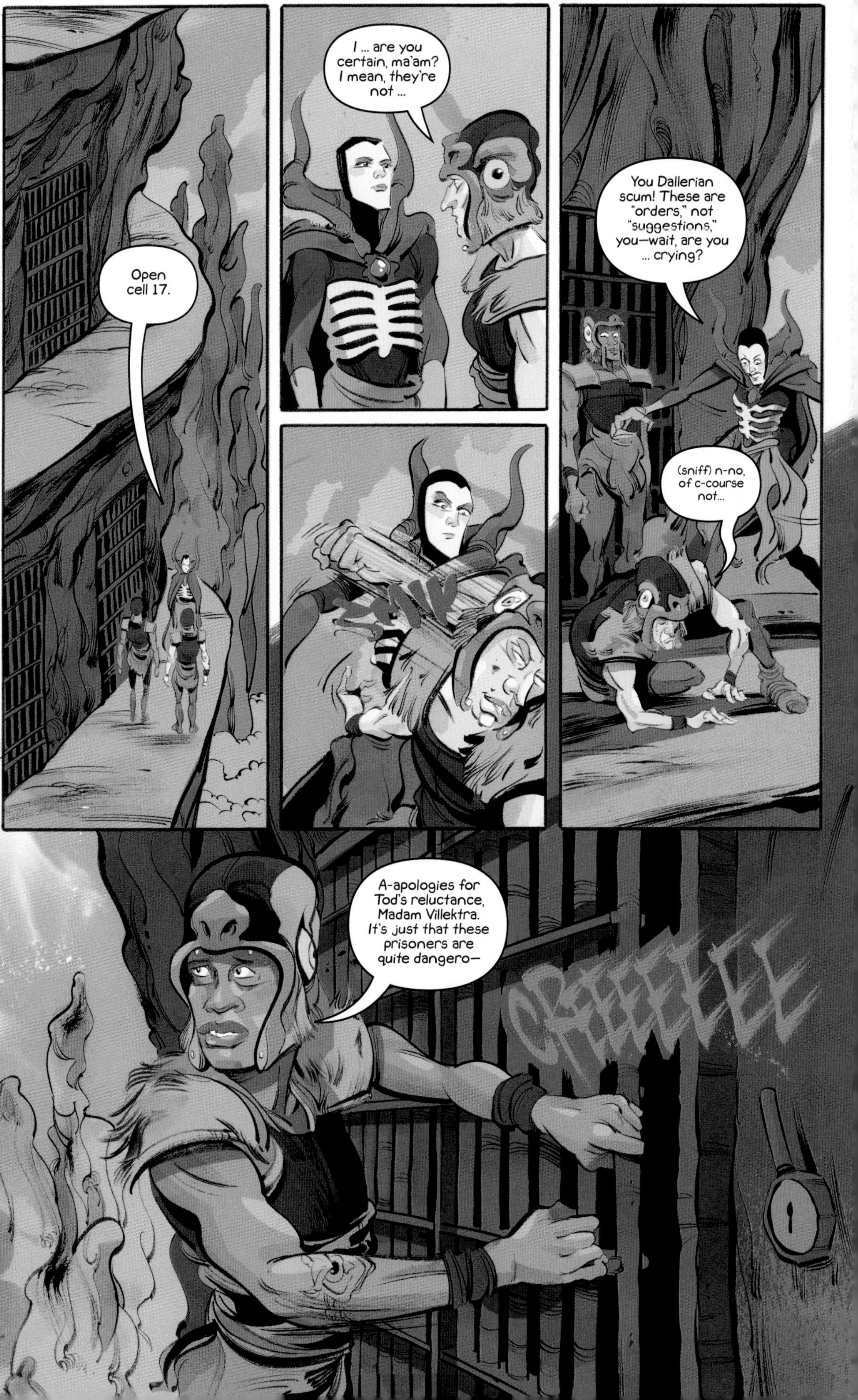
Open cell 17.
I ... are you certain, ma'am? I mean, they're not ...
You Dallerian scum! These are "orders," not "suggestions," you—wait, are you ... crying?
(sniff) n-no, of c-course not...
A-apologies for Tod's reluctance, Madam Villektra. It's just that these prisoners are quite dangero—
CREEEEEEE

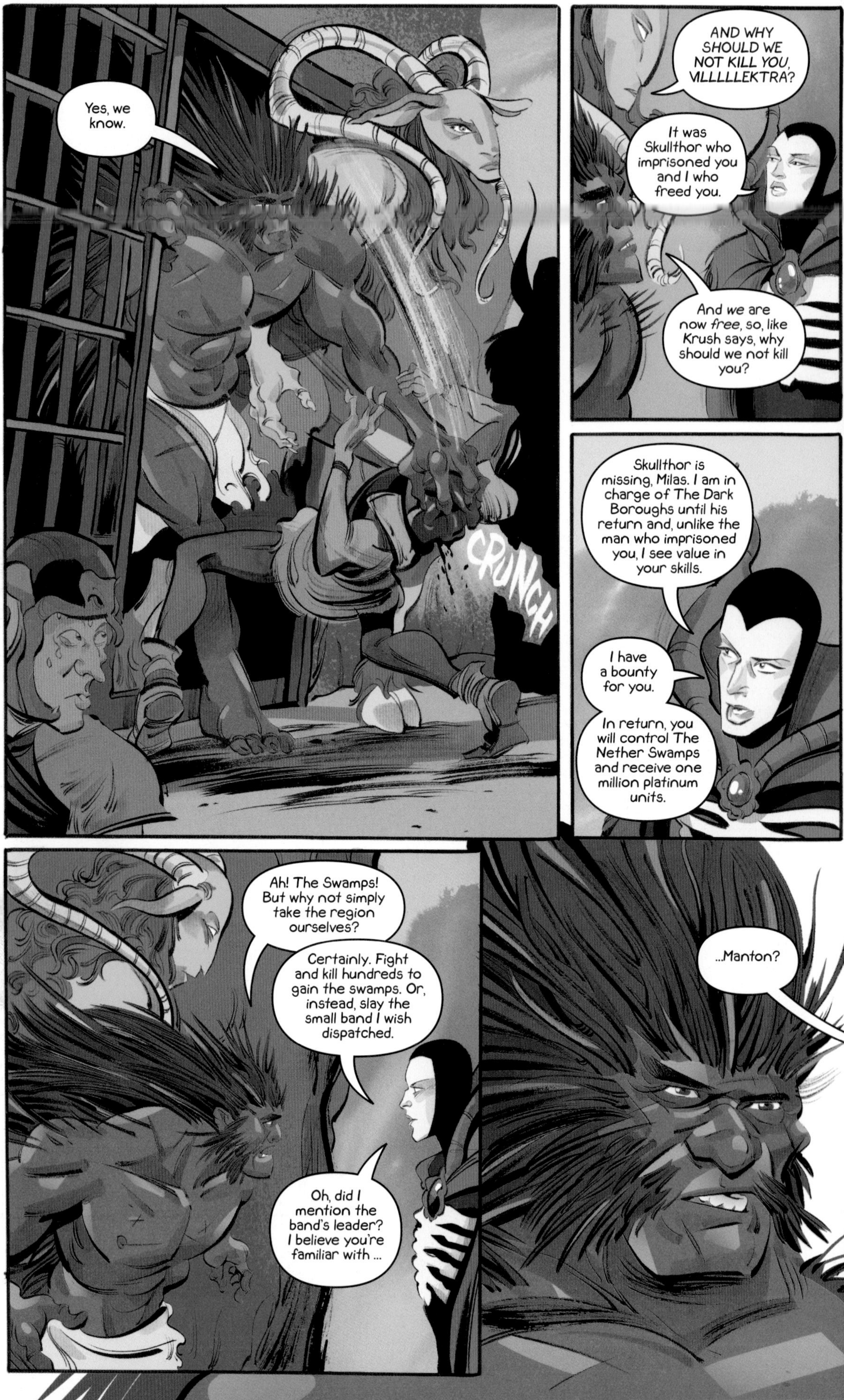
Yes, we know.
CRUNCH
AND WHY SHOULD WE NOT KILL YOU, VILLLLLLEKTRA?
It was Skullthor who imprisoned you and I who freed you.
And we are now free, so, like Krush says, why should we not kill you?
Skullthor is missing, Milas. I am in charge of The Dark Boroughs until his return and, unlike the man who imprisoned you, I see value in your skills.
I have a bounty for you.
In return, you will control The Nether Swamps and receive one million platinum units.
Ah! The Swamps! But why not simply take the region ourselves?
Certainly. Fight and kill hundreds to gain the swamps. Or, instead, slay the small band I wish dispatched.
Oh, did I mention the band's leader? I believe you're familiar with ...
...Manton?

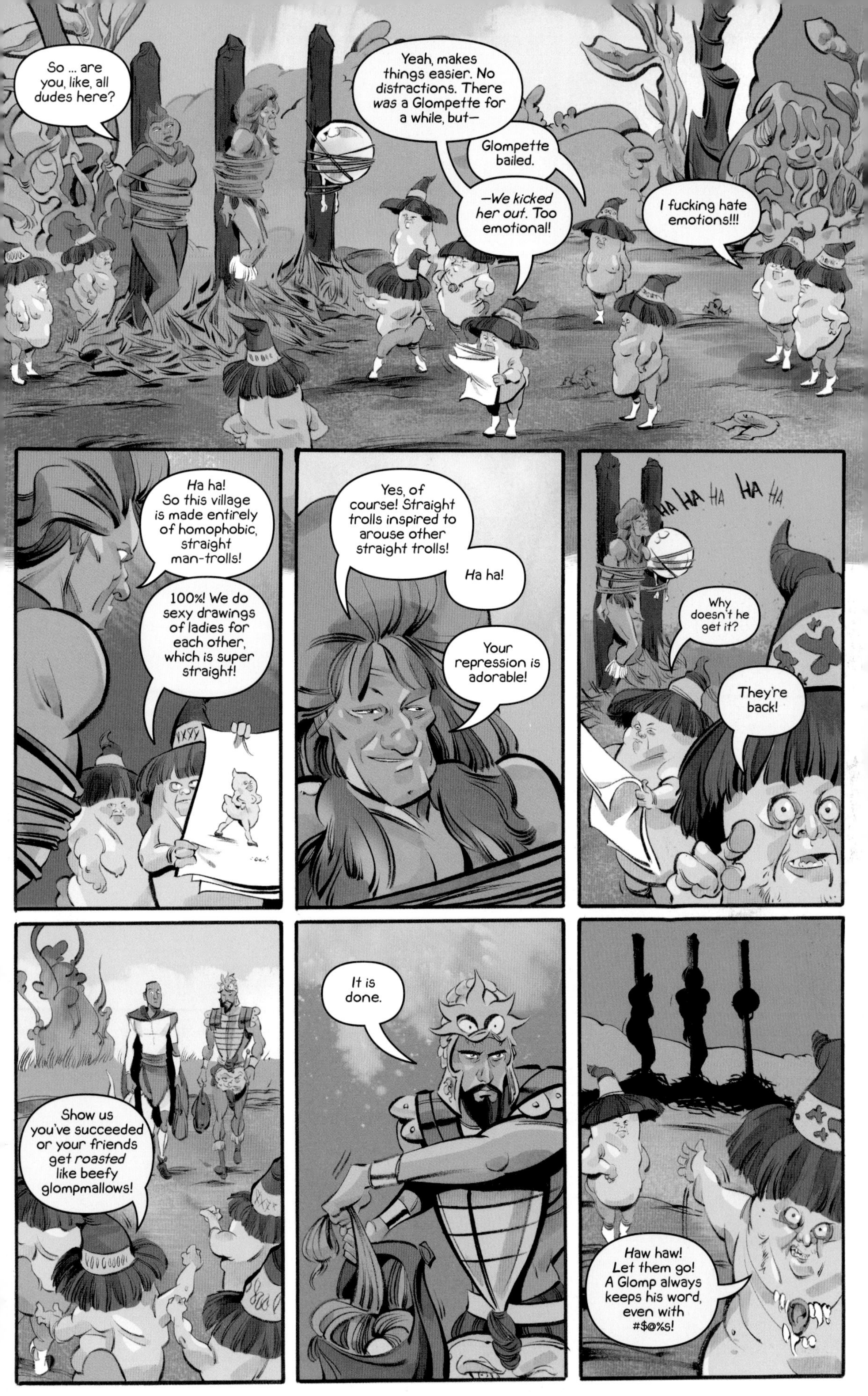
So ... are you, like, all dudes here?
Yeah, makes things easier. No distractions. There *was* a Glompette for a while, but—
Glompette bailed.
—We kicked her out. Too emotional!
I fucking hate emotions!!!
Ha ha! So this village is made entirely of homophobic, straight man-trolls!
100%! We do sexy drawings of ladies for each other, which is super straight!
Yes, of course! Straight trolls inspired to arouse other straight trolls!
Ha ha!
Your repression is adorable!
HA HA HA HA HA
Why doesn't he get it?
They're back!
Show us you've succeeded or your friends get *roasted* like beefy glompmallows!
It is done.
Haw haw! Let them go! A Glomp always keeps his word, even with #$@%s!

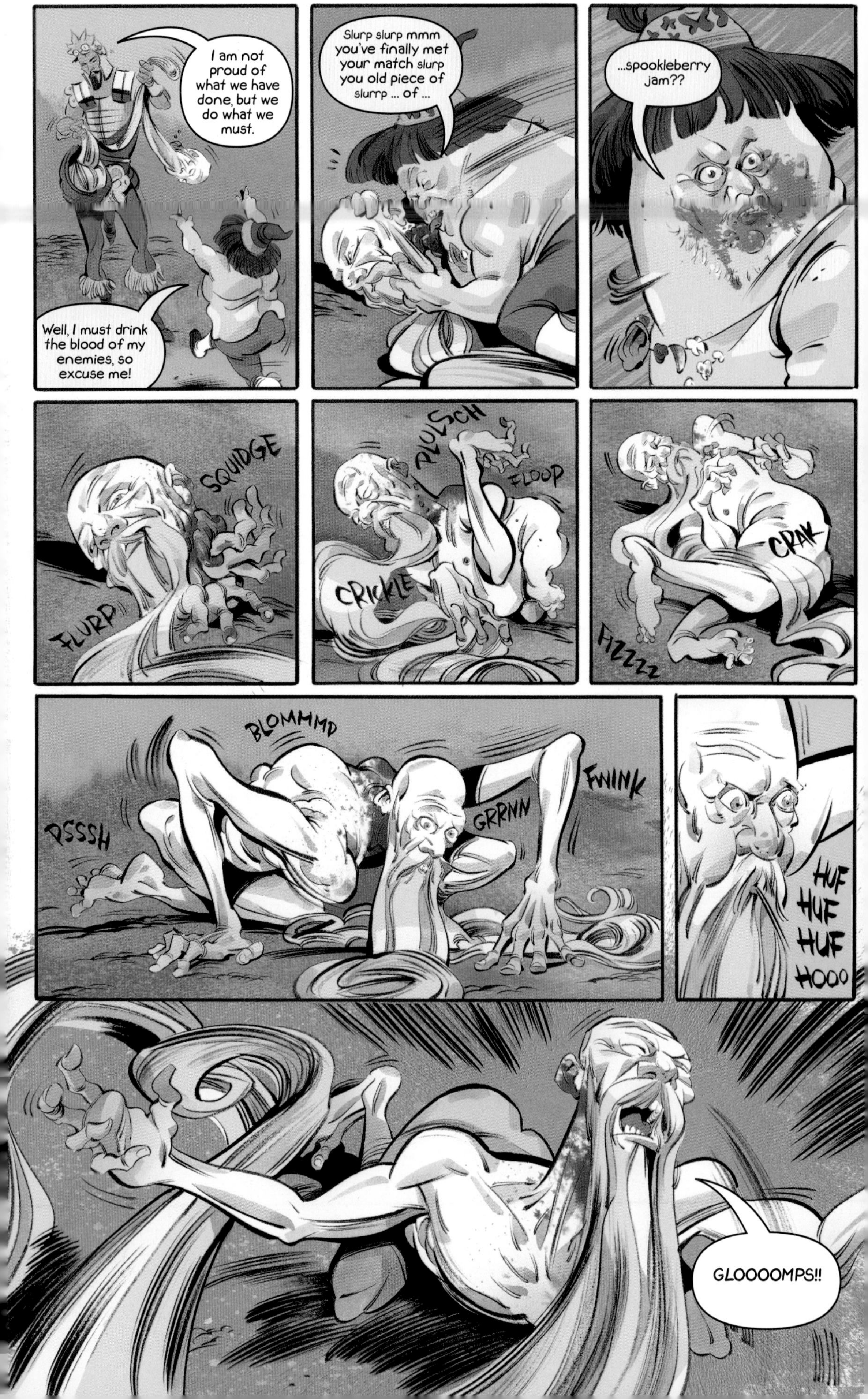
I am not proud of what we have done, but we do what we must.
Well, I must drink the blood of my enemies, so excuse me!
Slurp slurp mmm you've finally met your match slurp you old piece of slurrp ... of ...
...spookleberry jam??
SQUIDGE
FLURP
PLULSCH
FLOOP
CRICKLE
CRAK
FIZZZZ
BLOMMMP
FWINK
GRRNN
PSSSH
HUF
HUF
HUF
HOOO
GLOOOOMPS!!

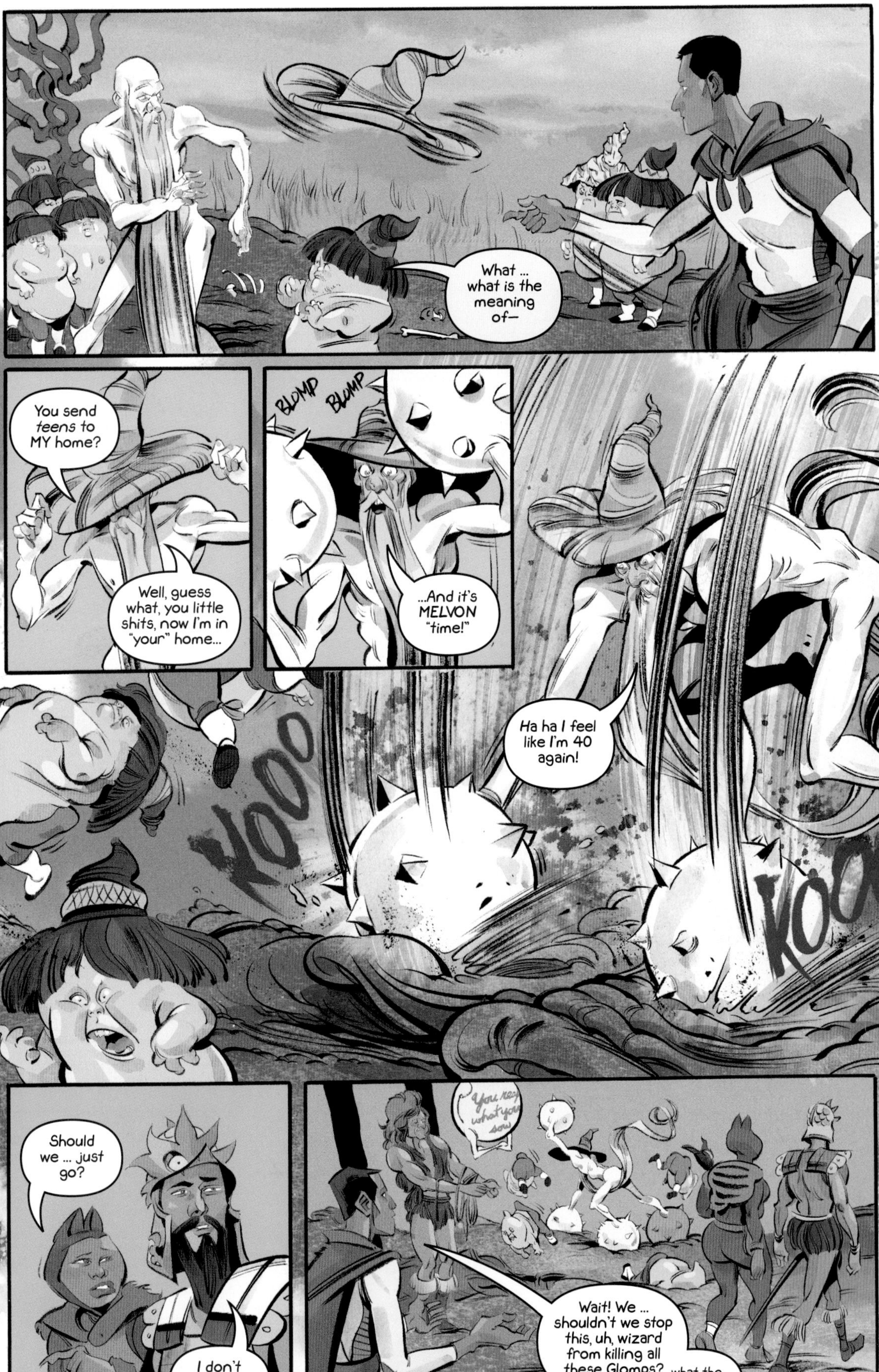
What ... what is the meaning of—
You send *teens* to MY home?
Well, guess what, you little shits, now I'm in "your" home...
BLOMP
BLOMP
...And it's MELVON "time!"
Ha ha I feel like I'm 40 again!
KOOOO
KOOO
Should we ... just go?
I don't see why not.
Wait! We ... shouldn't we stop this, uh, wizard from killing all these Glomps?
what the hell is my life now?

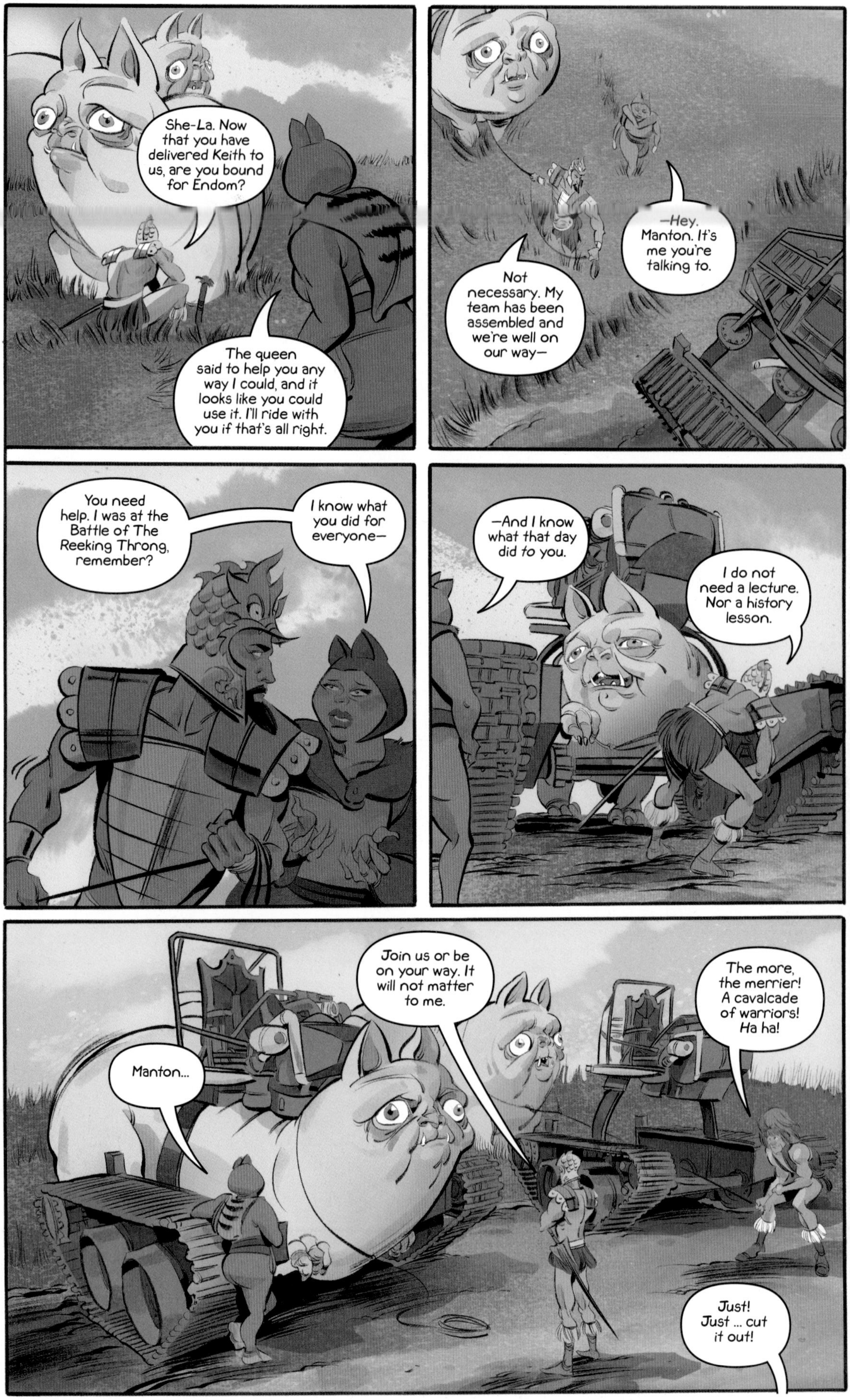
She-La. Now that you have delivered Keith to us, are you bound for Endom?
The queen said to help you any way I could, and it looks like you could use it. I'll ride with you if that's all right.
Not necessary. My team has been assembled and we're well on our way—
—Hey. Manton. It's me you're talking to.
You need help. I was at the Battle of The Reeking Throng, remember?
I know what you did for everyone—
—And I know what that day did *to* you.
I do not need a lecture. Nor a history lesson.
Manton...
Join us or be on your way. It will not matter to me.
The more, the merrier! A cavalcade of warriors! Ha ha!
Just! Just ... cut it out!

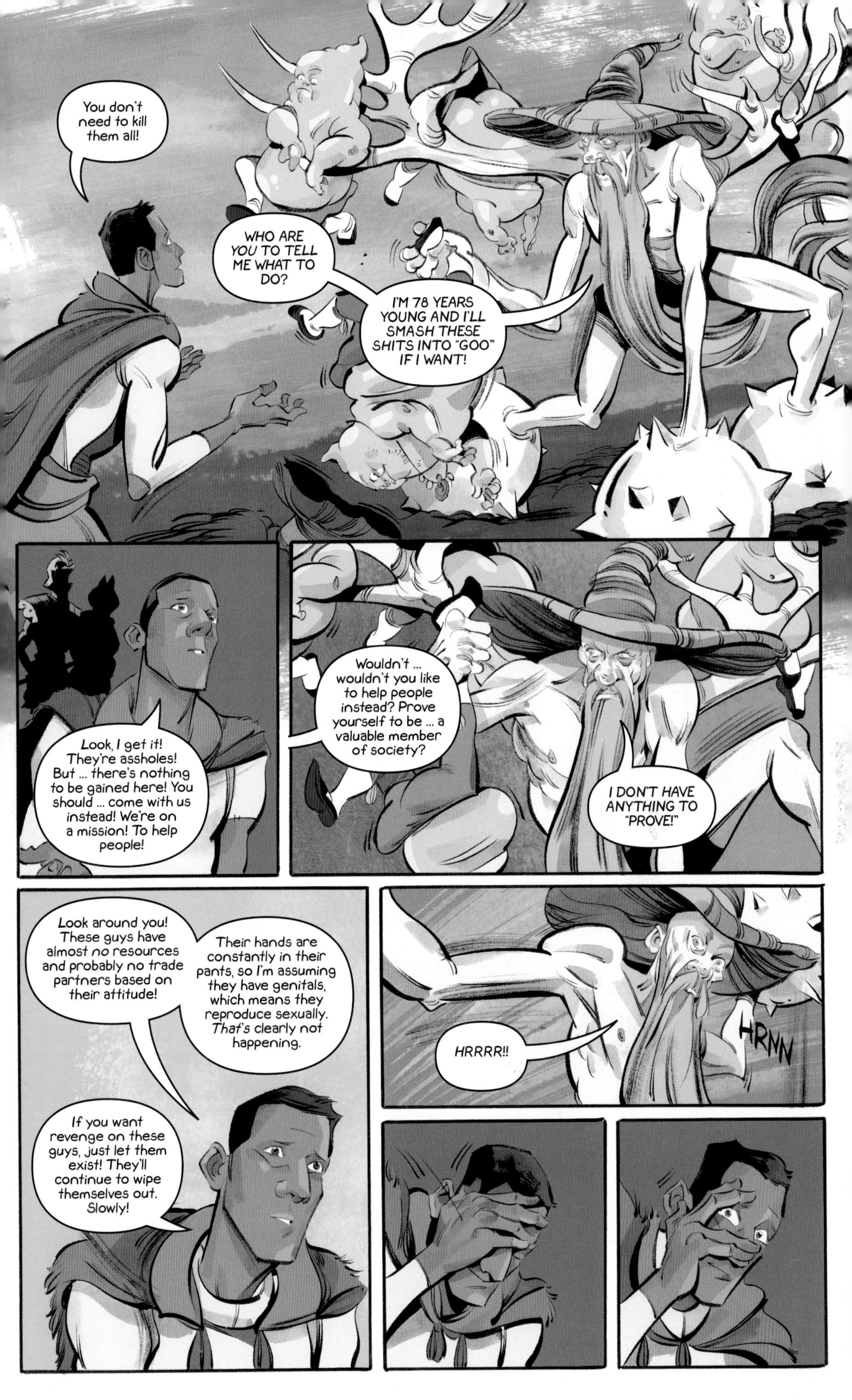
You don't need to kill them all!
WHO ARE YOU TO TELL ME WHAT TO DO?
I'M 78 YEARS YOUNG AND I'LL SMASH THESE SHITS INTO "GOO" IF I WANT!
Look, I get it! They're assholes! But ... there's nothing to be gained here! You should ... come with us instead! We're on a mission! To help people!
Wouldn't ... wouldn't you like to help people instead? Prove yourself to be ... a valuable member of society?
I DON'T HAVE ANYTHING TO "PROVE!"
Look around you! These guys have almost no resources and probably no trade partners based on their attitude!
Their hands are constantly in their pants, so I'm assuming they have genitals, which means they reproduce sexually. That's clearly not happening.
If you want revenge on these guys, just let them exist! They'll continue to wipe themselves out. Slowly!
HRRRR!!
HRNN

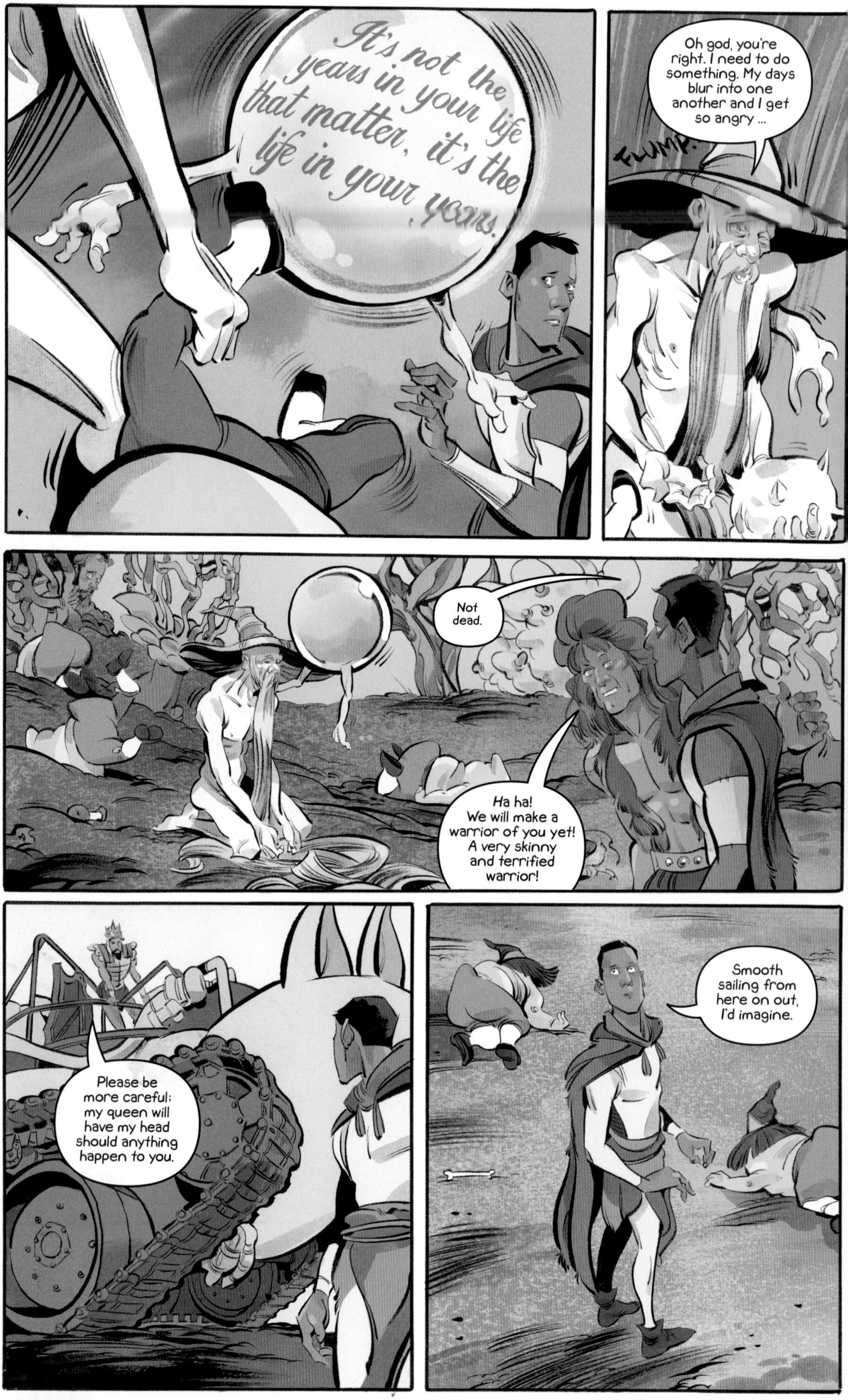
It's not the years in your life that matter, it's the life in your years.
Oh god, you're right. I need to do something. My days blur into one another and I get so angry ...
FLUMP.
Not dead.
Ha ha! We will make a warrior of you yet! A very skinny and terrified warrior!
Please be more careful; my queen will have my head should anything happen to you.
Smooth sailing from here on out, I'd imagine.

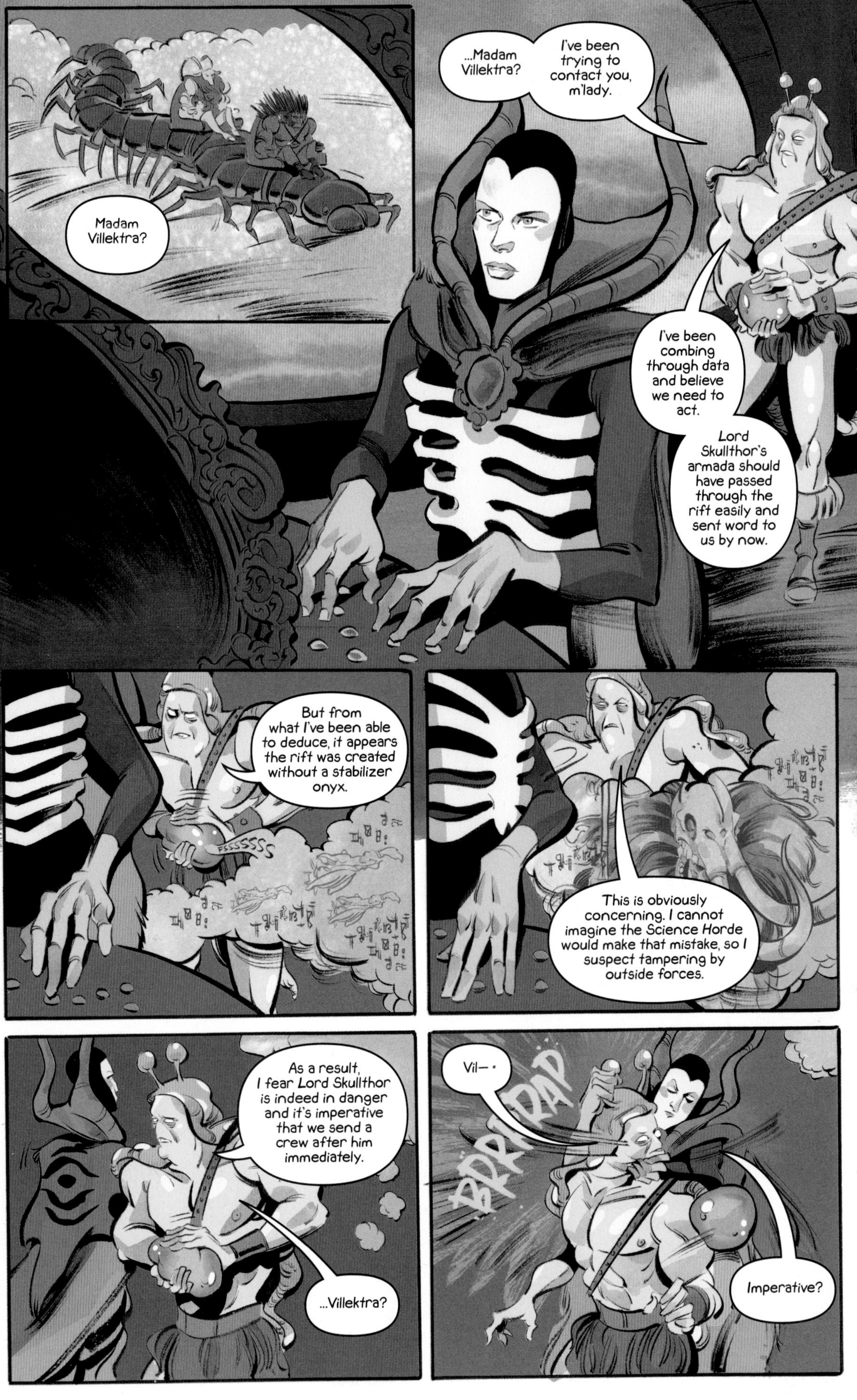
Madam Villektra?
...Madam Villektra?
I've been trying to contact you, m'lady.
I've been combing through data and believe we need to act.
Lord Skullthor's armada should have passed through the rift easily and sent word to us by now.
But from what I've been able to deduce, it appears the rift was created without a stabilizer onyx.
FSSSSSSS
This is obviously concerning. I cannot imagine the Science Horde would make that mistake, so I suspect tampering by outside forces.
As a result, I fear Lord Skullthor is indeed in danger and it's imperative that we send a crew after him immediately.
...Villektra?
Vil—
BRRRAP
Imperative?

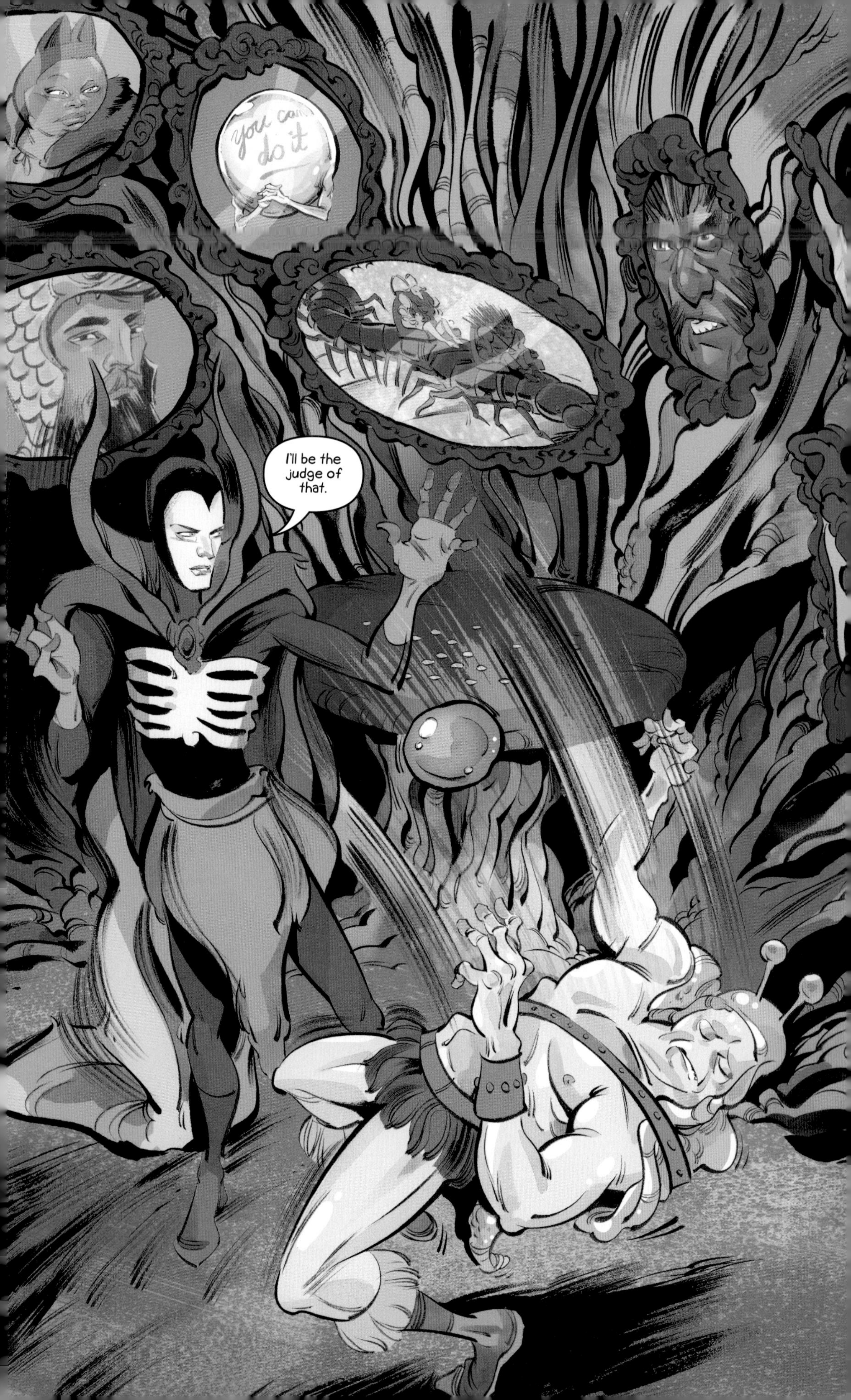
you can do it
I'll be the judge of that.

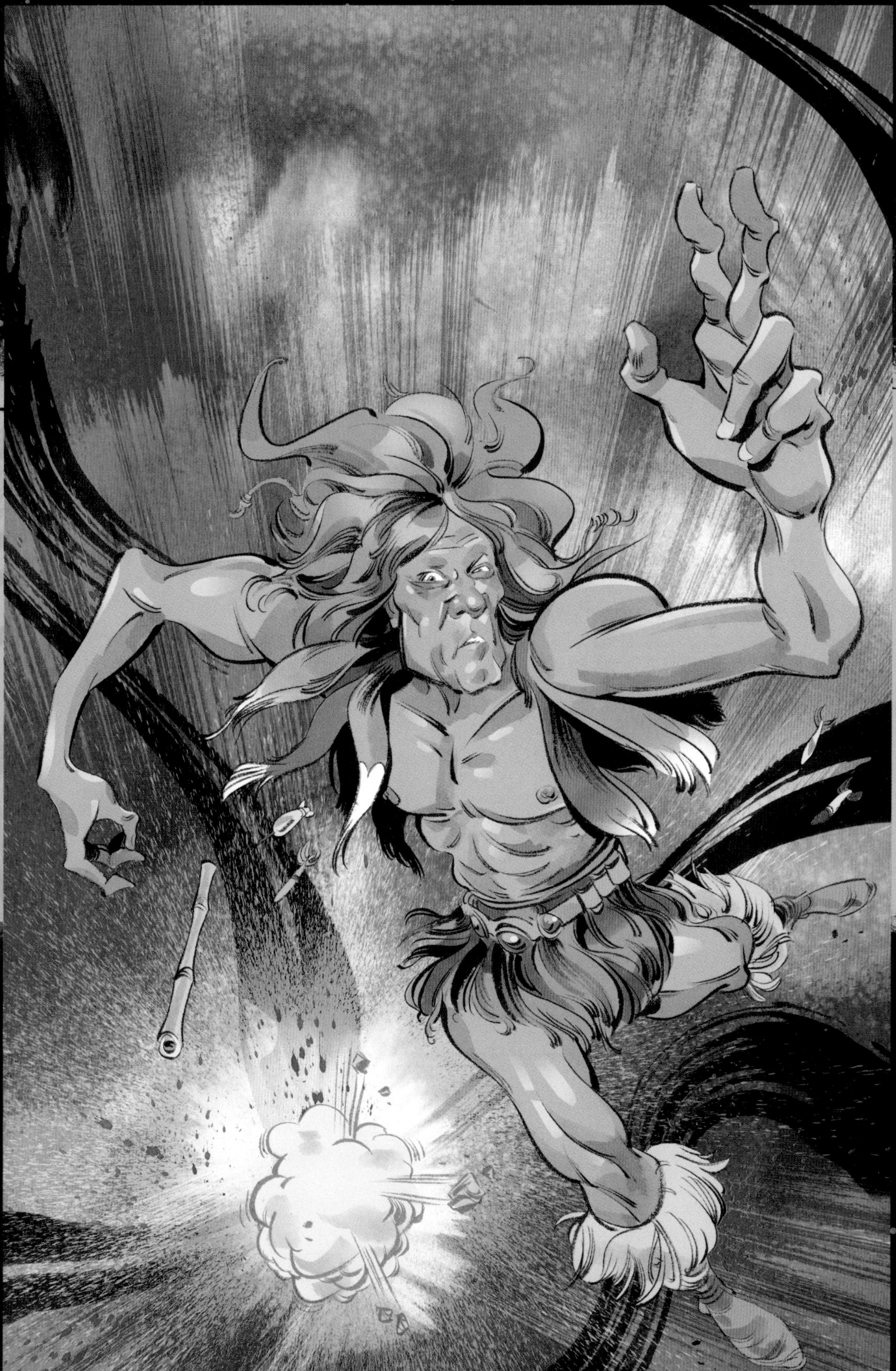

CHAPTER FOUR

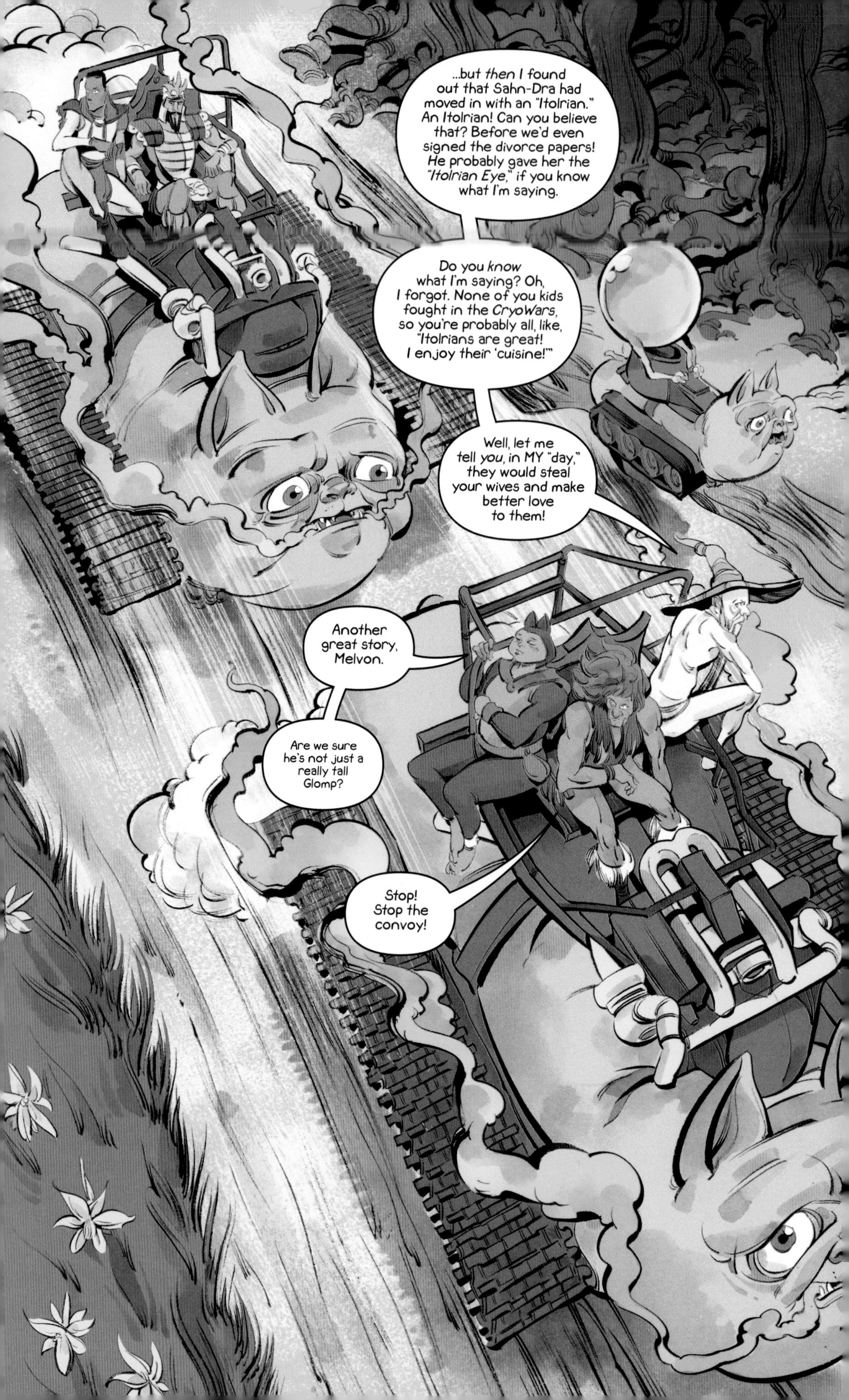
...but *then* I found out that Sahn-Dra had moved in with an "Itolrian." An Itolrian! Can you believe that? Before we'd even signed the divorce papers! He probably gave her the *"Itolrian Eye,"* if you know what I'm saying.
Do you *know* what I'm saying? Oh, I forgot. None of you kids fought in the *CryoWars*, so you're probably all, like, "Itolrians are great! I enjoy their 'cuisine!'"
Well, let me tell *you*, in MY "day," they would steal your wives and make better love to them!
Another great story, Melvon.
Are we sure he's not just a really tall Glomp?
Stop! Stop the convoy!

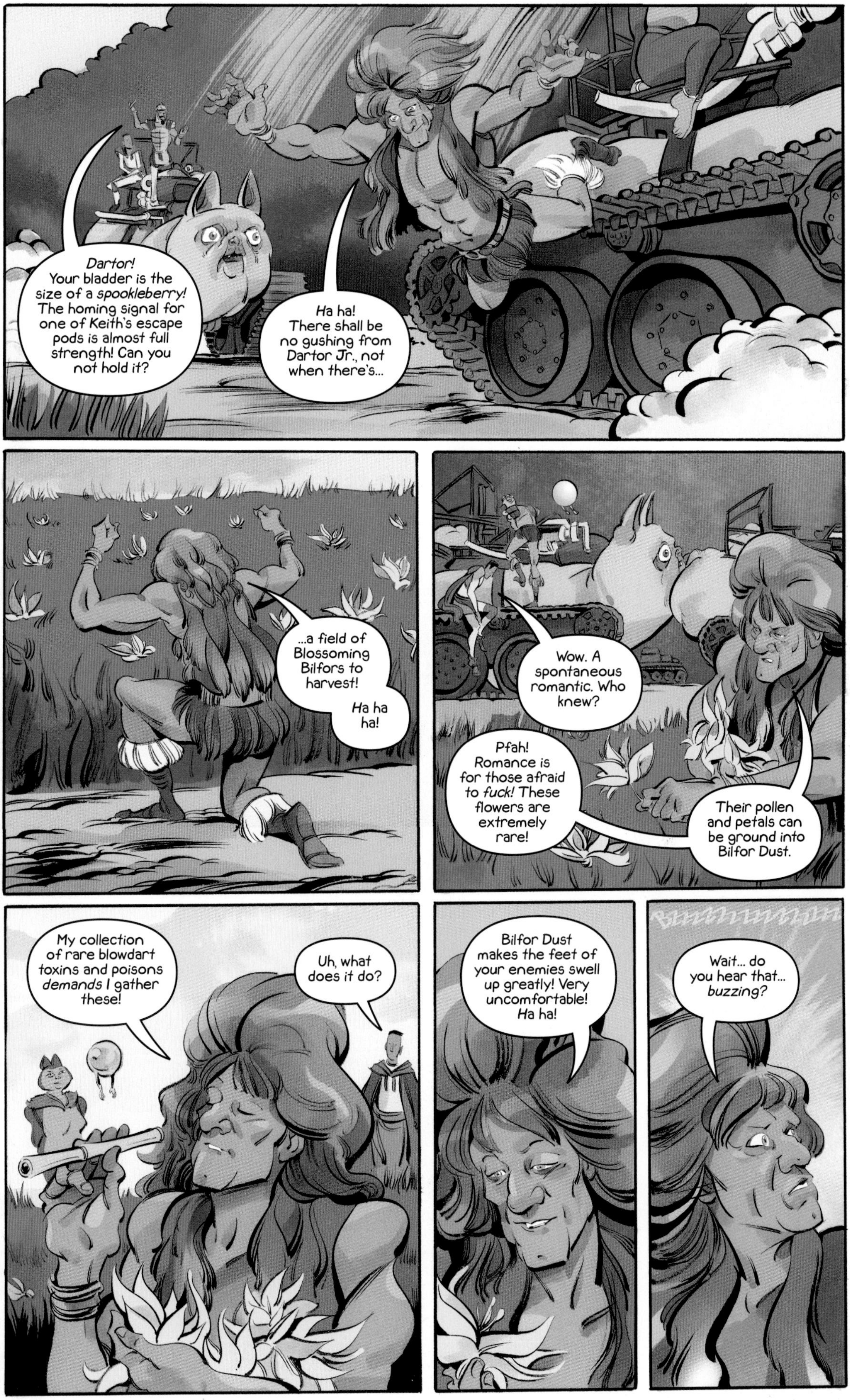

Dartor! Your bladder is the size of a *spookleberry!* The homing signal for one of Keith's escape pods is almost full strength! Can you not hold it?
Ha ha! There shall be no gushing from Dartor Jr., not when there's...
...a field of Blossoming Bilfors to harvest!
Ha ha ha!
Wow. A spontaneous romantic. Who knew?
Pfah! Romance is for those afraid to *fuck!* These flowers are extremely rare!
Their pollen and petals can be ground into Bilfor Dust.
My collection of rare blowdart toxins and poisons *demands* I gather these!
Uh, what does it do?
Bilfor Dust makes the feet of your enemies swell up greatly! Very uncomfortable! Ha ha!
BZZZZZZZZZZZZZ
Wait... do you hear that... *buzzing*?

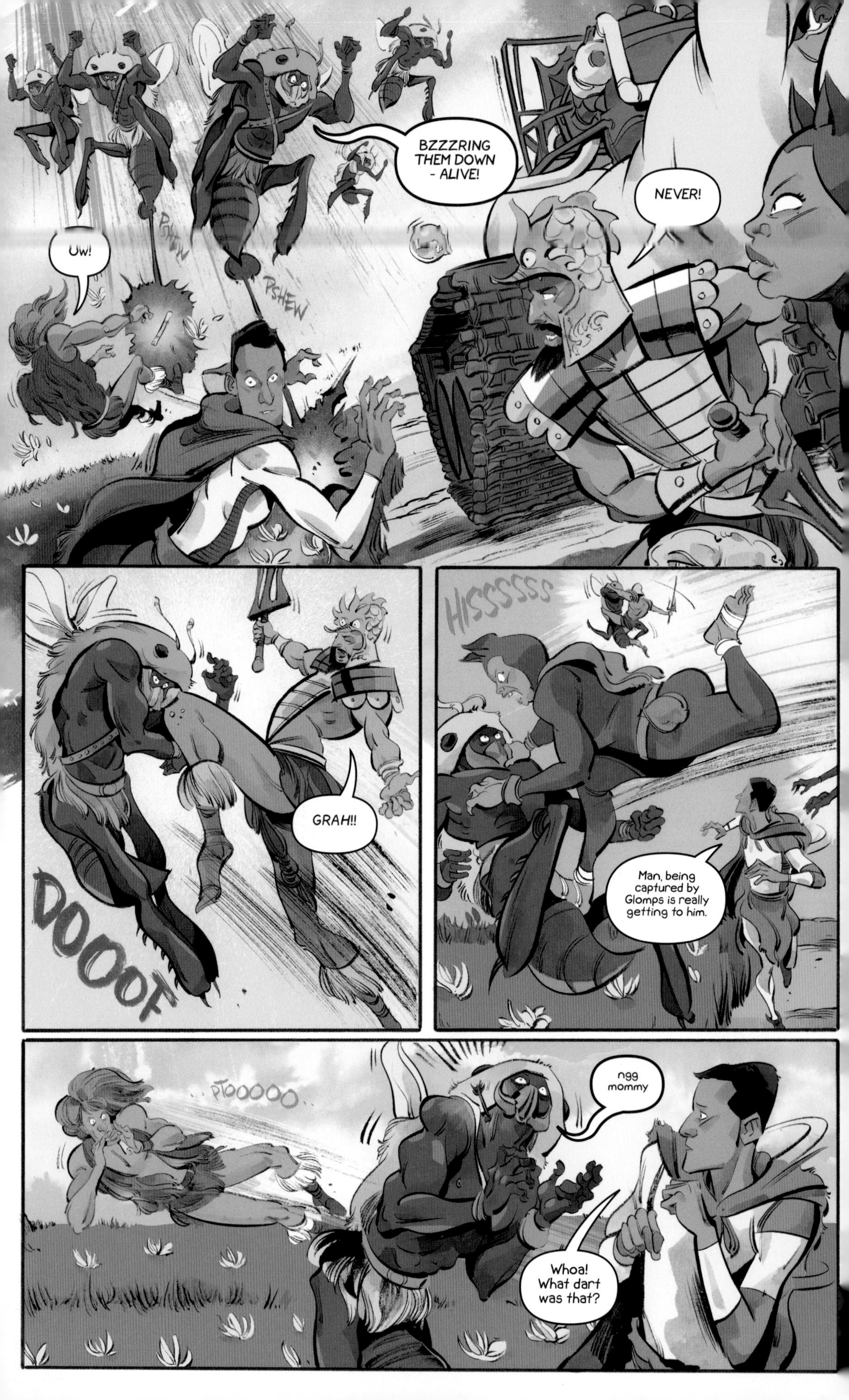
BZZZRING THEM DOWN - ALIVE!
NEVER!
Uw!
PSHEW
PSHEW
GRAH!!
DOOOOF
HISSSSSS
Man, being captured by Glomps is really getting to him.
PTOOOOO
ngg mommy
Whoa! What dart was that?

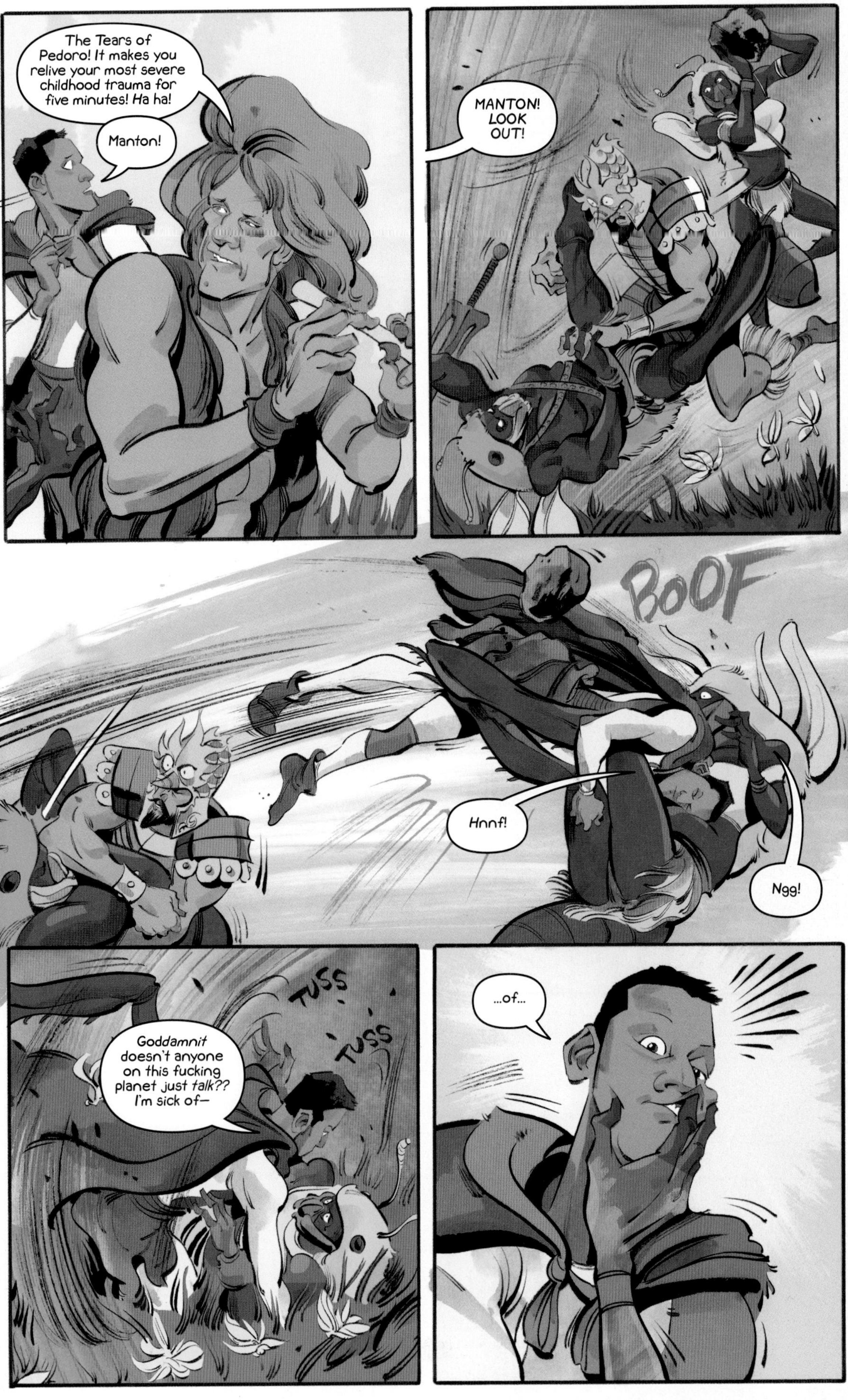
The Tears of Pedoro! It makes you relive your most severe childhood trauma for five minutes! Ha ha!
Manton!
MANTON! LOOK OUT!
BOOF
Hnnf!
Ngg!
TUSS
TUSS
Goddamnit doesn't anyone on this fucking planet just *talk*?? I'm sick of—
...of...

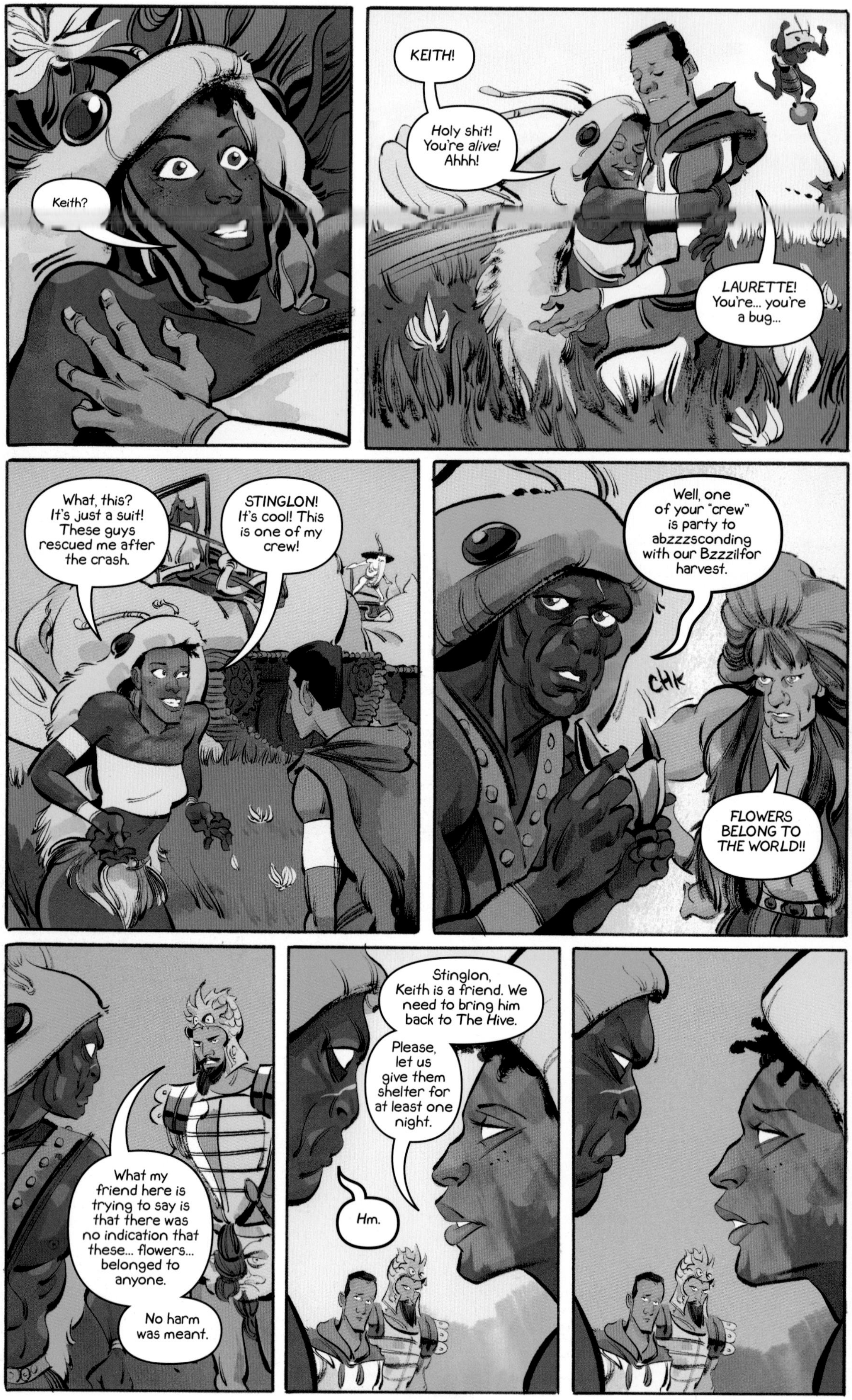
Keith?
KEITH!
Holy shit! You're alive! Ahhh!
LAURETTE! You're... you're a bug...
What, this? It's just a suit! These guys rescued me after the crash.
STINGLON! It's cool! This is one of my crew!
Well, one of your "crew" is party to abzzzsconding with our Bzzzilfor harvest.
CHK
FLOWERS BELONG TO THE WORLD!!
What my friend here is trying to say is that there was no indication that these... flowers... belonged to anyone.
No harm was meant.
Stinglon, Keith is a friend. We need to bring him back to The Hive.
Please, let us give them shelter for at least one night.
Hm.

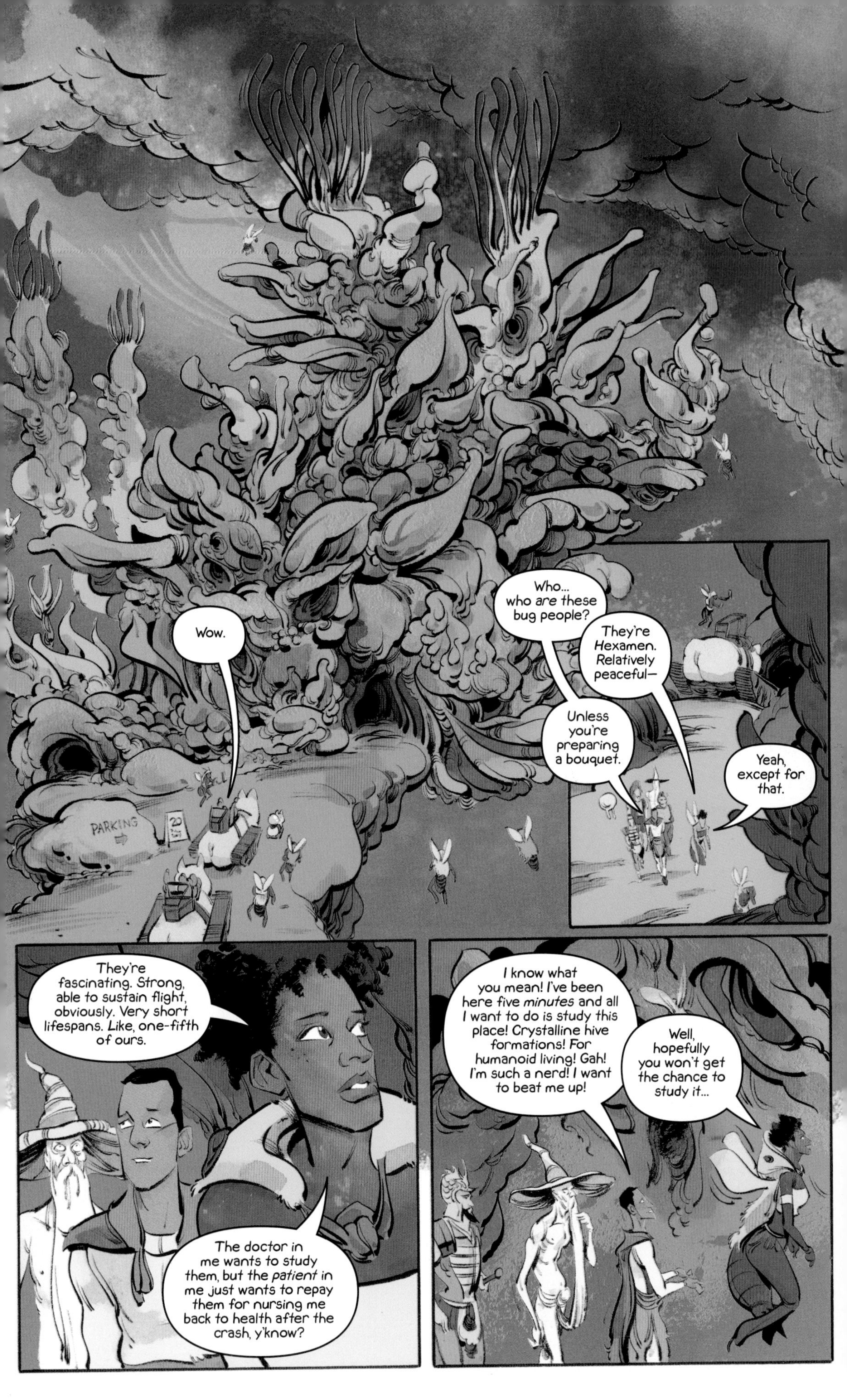
Wow.
PARKING
Who... who *are* these bug people?
They're Hexamen. Relatively peaceful—
Unless you're preparing a bouquet.
Yeah, except for that.
They're fascinating. Strong, able to sustain flight, obviously. Very short lifespans. Like, one-fifth of ours.
The doctor in me wants to study them, but the *patient* in me just wants to repay them for nursing me back to health after the crash, y'know?
I know what you mean! I've been here five *minutes* and all I want to do is study this place! Crystalline hive formations! For humanoid living! Gah! I'm such a nerd! I want to beat me up!
Well, hopefully you won't get the chance to study it...

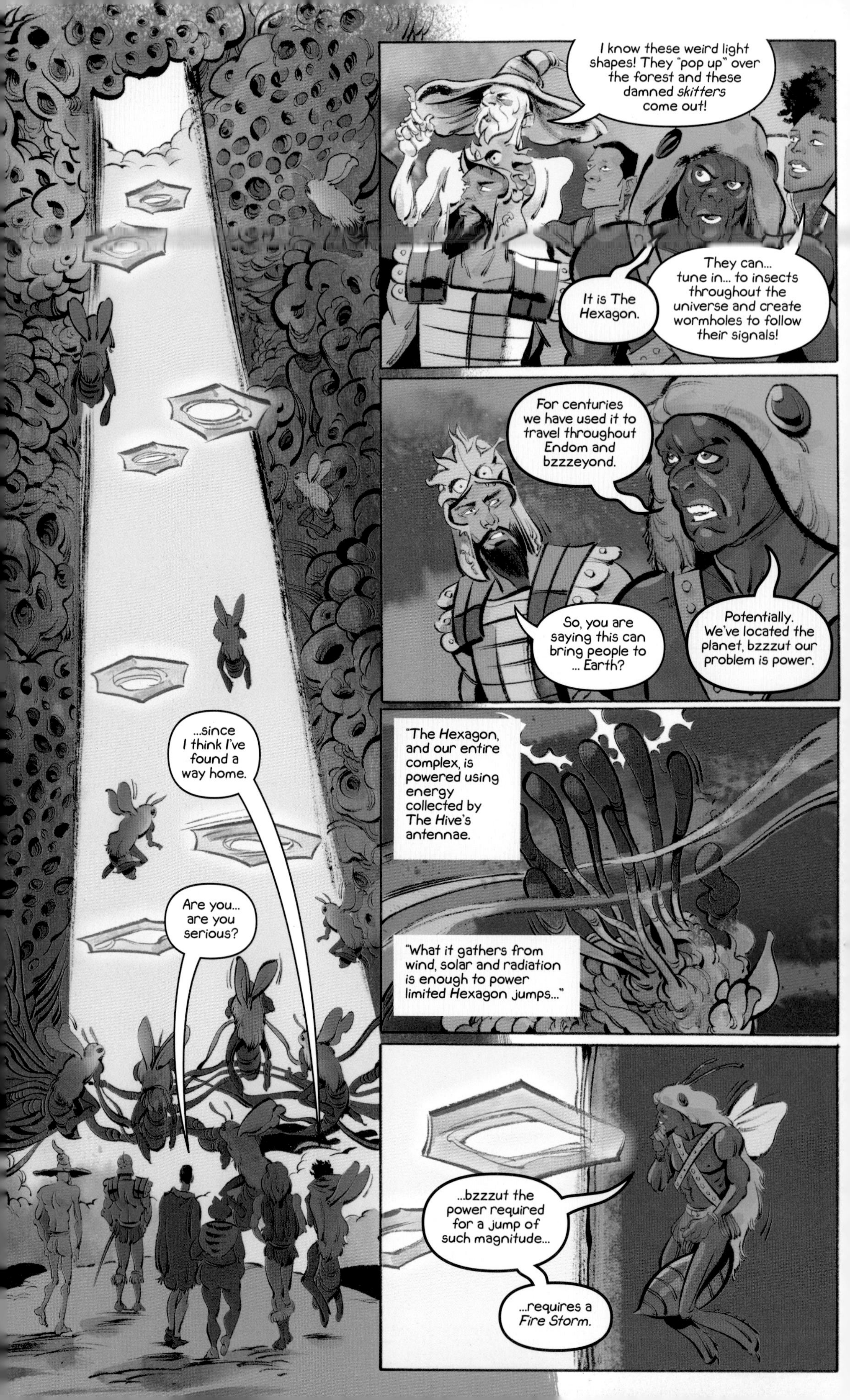
...since I think I've found a way home.
Are you... are you serious?
I know these weird light shapes! They "pop up" over the forest and these damned *skitters* come out!
It is The Hexagon.
They can... tune in... to insects throughout the universe and create wormholes to follow their signals!
For centuries we have used it to travel throughout Endom and bzzzeyond.
So, you are saying this can bring people to ... Earth?
Potentially. We've located the planet, bzzzut our problem is power.
"The *Hexagon*, and our entire complex, is powered using energy collected by *The Hive's* antennae.
"What it gathers from wind, solar and radiation is enough to power limited *Hexagon* jumps..."
...bzzzut the power required for a jump of such magnitude...
...requires a *Fire Storm.*

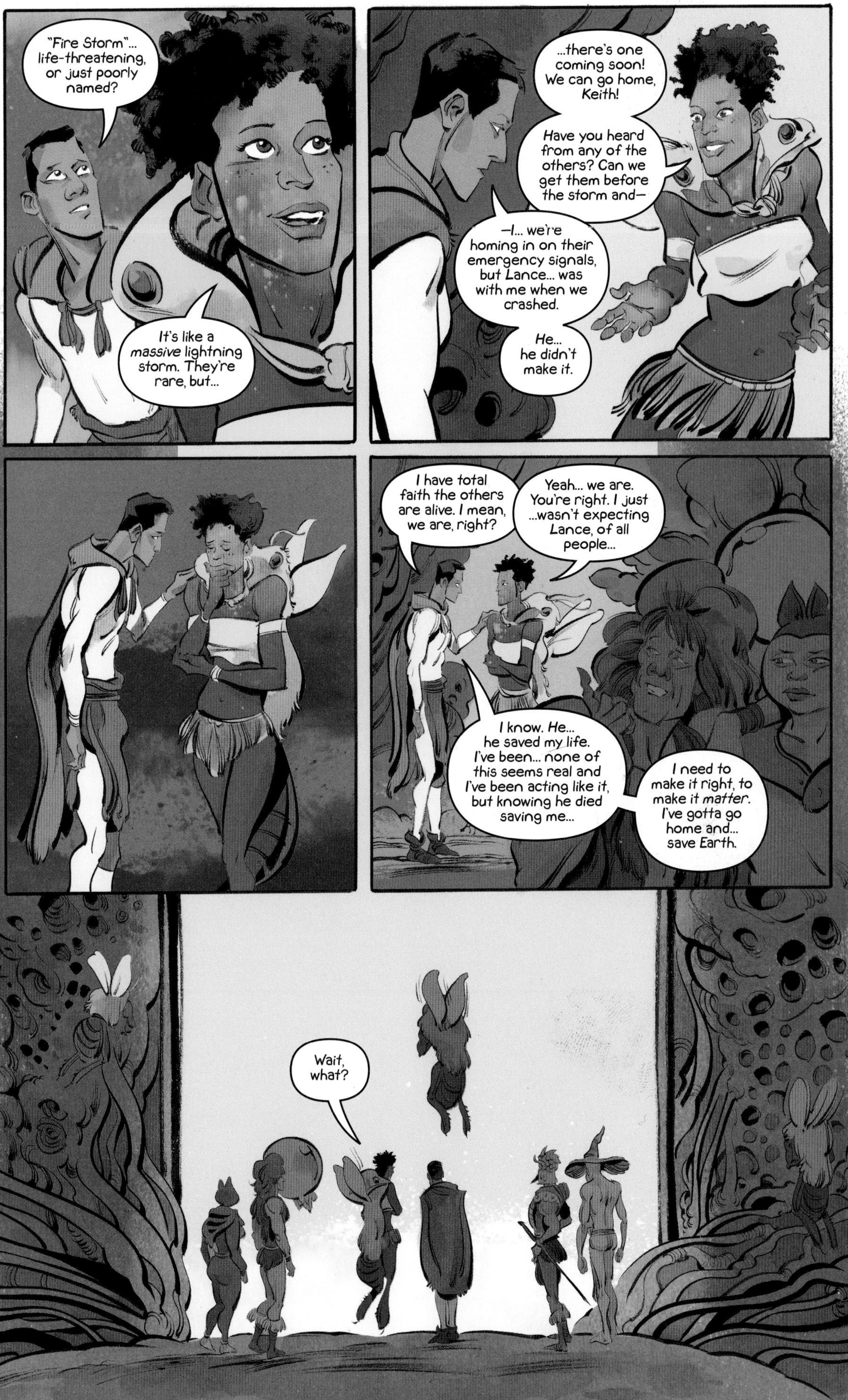
"Fire Storm"... life-threatening, or just poorly named?
It's like a *massive* lightning storm. They're rare, but...
...there's one coming soon! We can go home, Keith!
Have you heard from any of the others? Can we get them before the storm and—
—I... we're homing in on their emergency signals, but Lance... was with me when we crashed.
He... he didn't make it.
I have total faith the others are alive. I mean, we are, right?
Yeah... we are. You're right. I just ...wasn't expecting Lance, of all people...
I know. He... he saved my life. I've been... none of this seems real and I've been acting like it, but knowing he died saving me...
I need to make it right, to make *it matter*. I've gotta go home and... save Earth.
Wait, what?

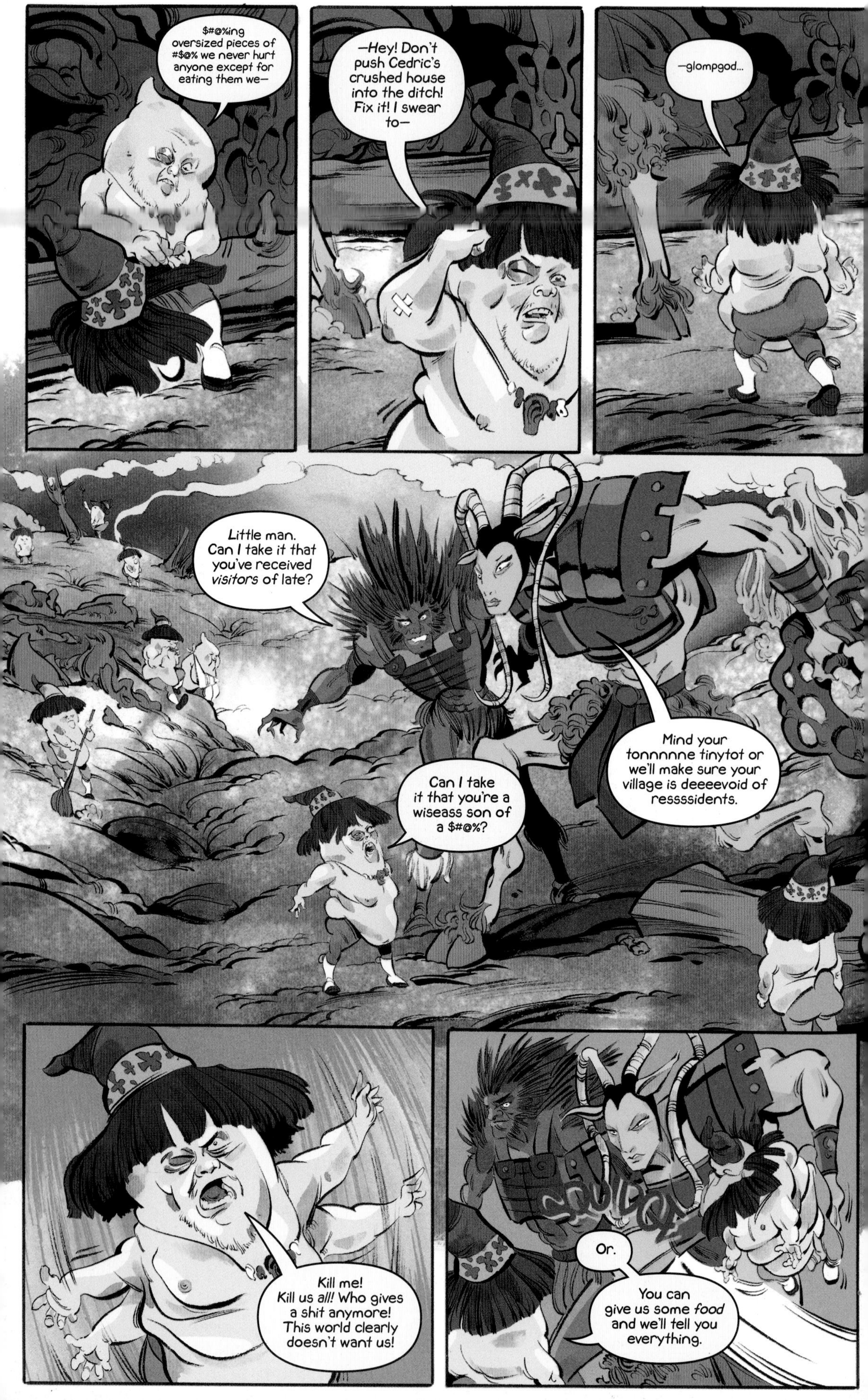
$#@%ing oversized pieces of #$@% we never hurt anyone except for eating them we—
—Hey! Don't push Cedric's crushed house into the ditch! Fix it! I swear to—
—glompgod...
Little man. Can I take it that you've received *visitors* of late?
Mind your tonnnnne tinytot or we'll make sure your village is deeeevoid of ressssidents.
Can I take it that you're a wiseass son of a $#@%?
Kill me! Kill us *all!* Who gives a shit anymore! This world clearly doesn't want us!
Or.
You can give us some *food* and we'll tell you everything.

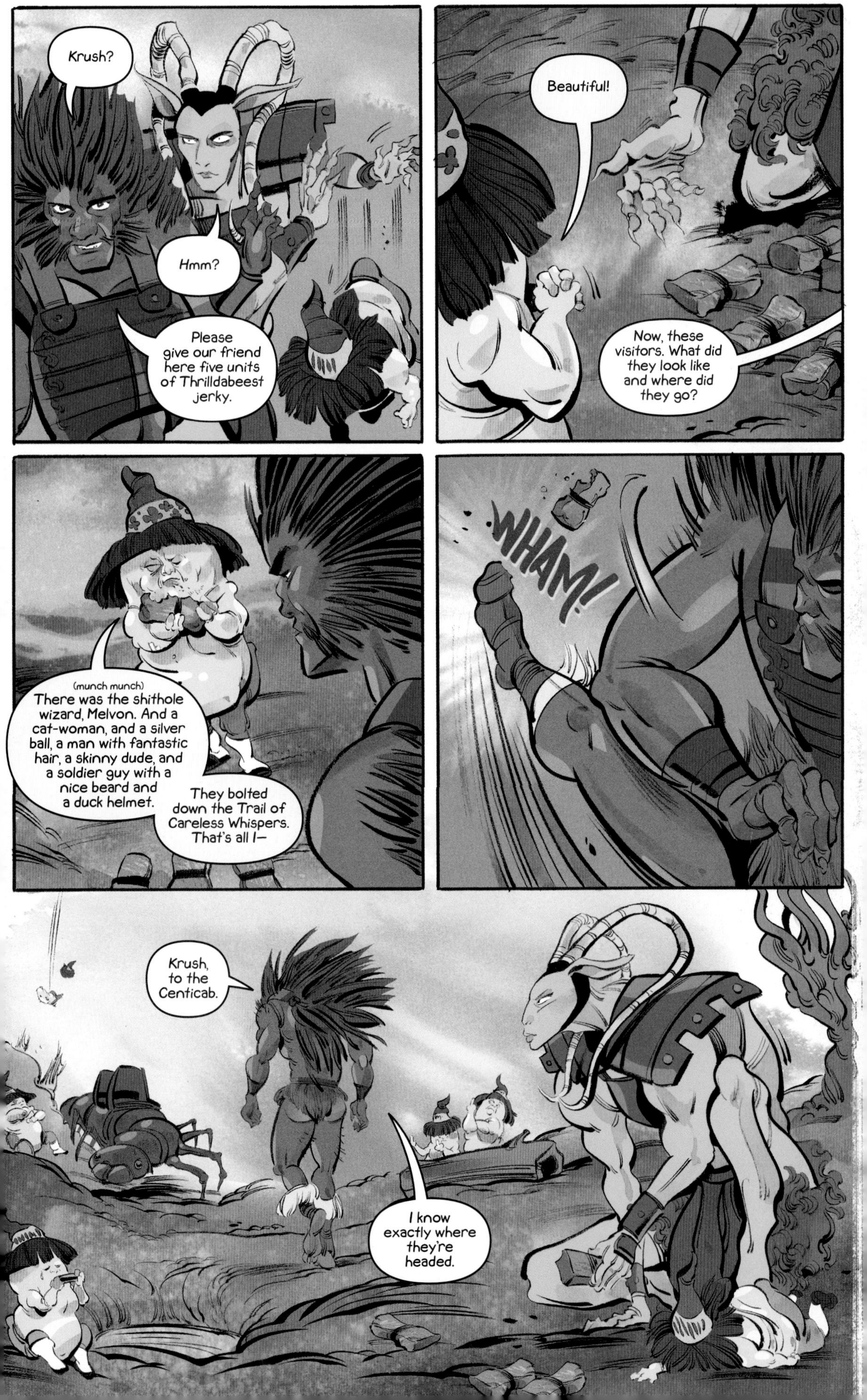
Krush?
Hmm?
Please give our friend here five units of Thrilldabeest jerky.
Beautiful!
Now, these visitors. What did they look like and where did they go?
(munch munch)
There was the shithole wizard, Melvon. And a cat-woman, and a silver ball, a man with fantastic hair, a skinny dude, and a soldier guy with a nice beard and a duck helmet.
They bolted down the Trail of Careless Whispers. That's all I—
WHAM!
Krush, to the Centicab.
I know exactly where they're headed.

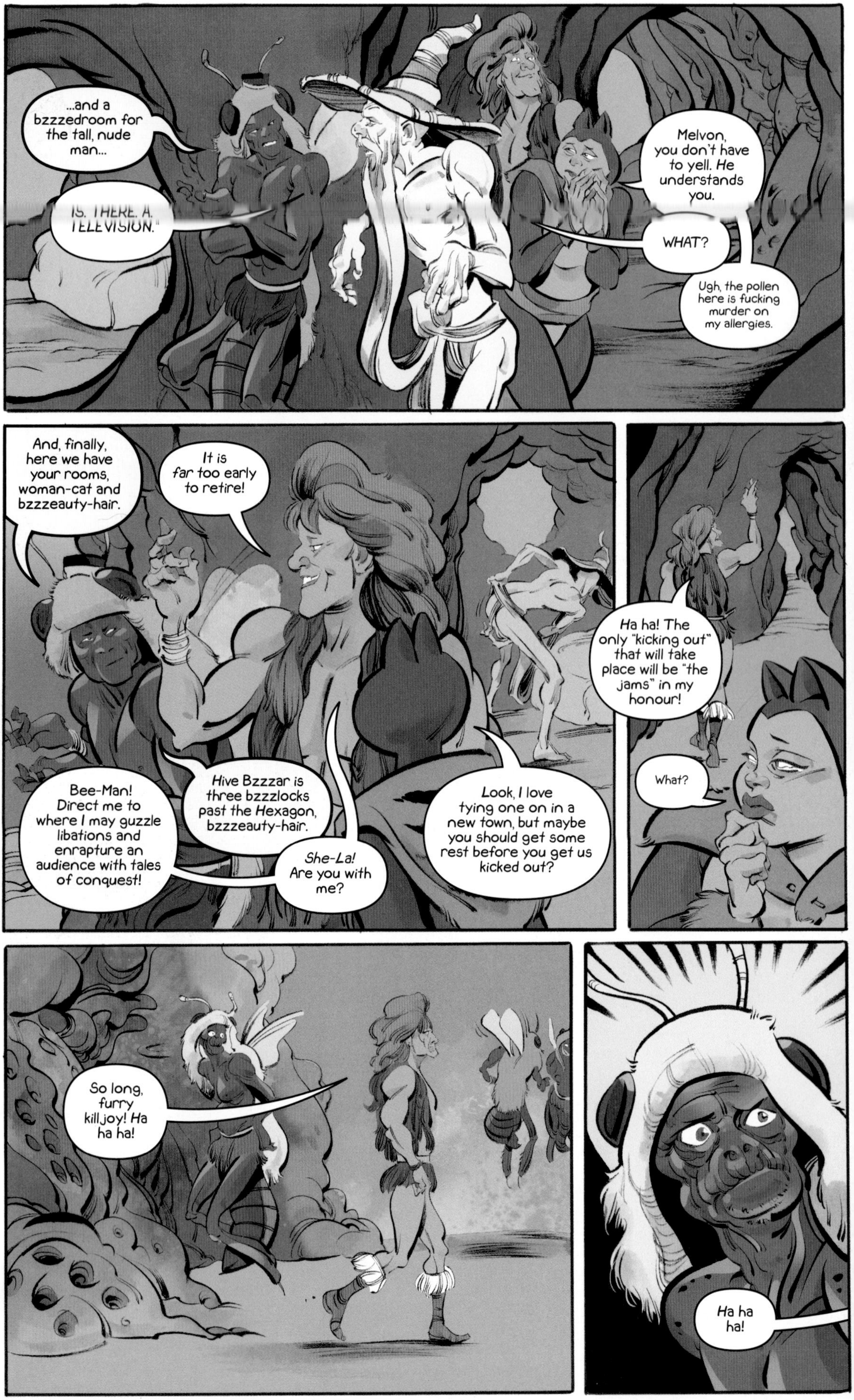
...and a bzzzedroom for the tall, nude man...
IS. THERE. A. TELEVISION."
Melvon, you don't have to yell. He understands you.
WHAT?
Ugh, the pollen here is fucking murder on my allergies.
And, finally, here we have your rooms, woman-cat and bzzzeauty-hair.
It is *far* too early to retire!
Bee-Man! Direct me to where *I* may guzzle libations and enrapture an audience with tales of conquest!
Hive Bzzzar is three bzzzlocks past the *Hexagon*, bzzzeauty-hair.
She-La! Are you with me?
Look, I love tying one on in a new town, but maybe you should get some rest before you get us kicked out?
Ha ha! The only "kicking out" that will take place will be "the jams" in my honour!
What?
So long, furry killjoy! *Ha* ha ha!
Ha ha ha!

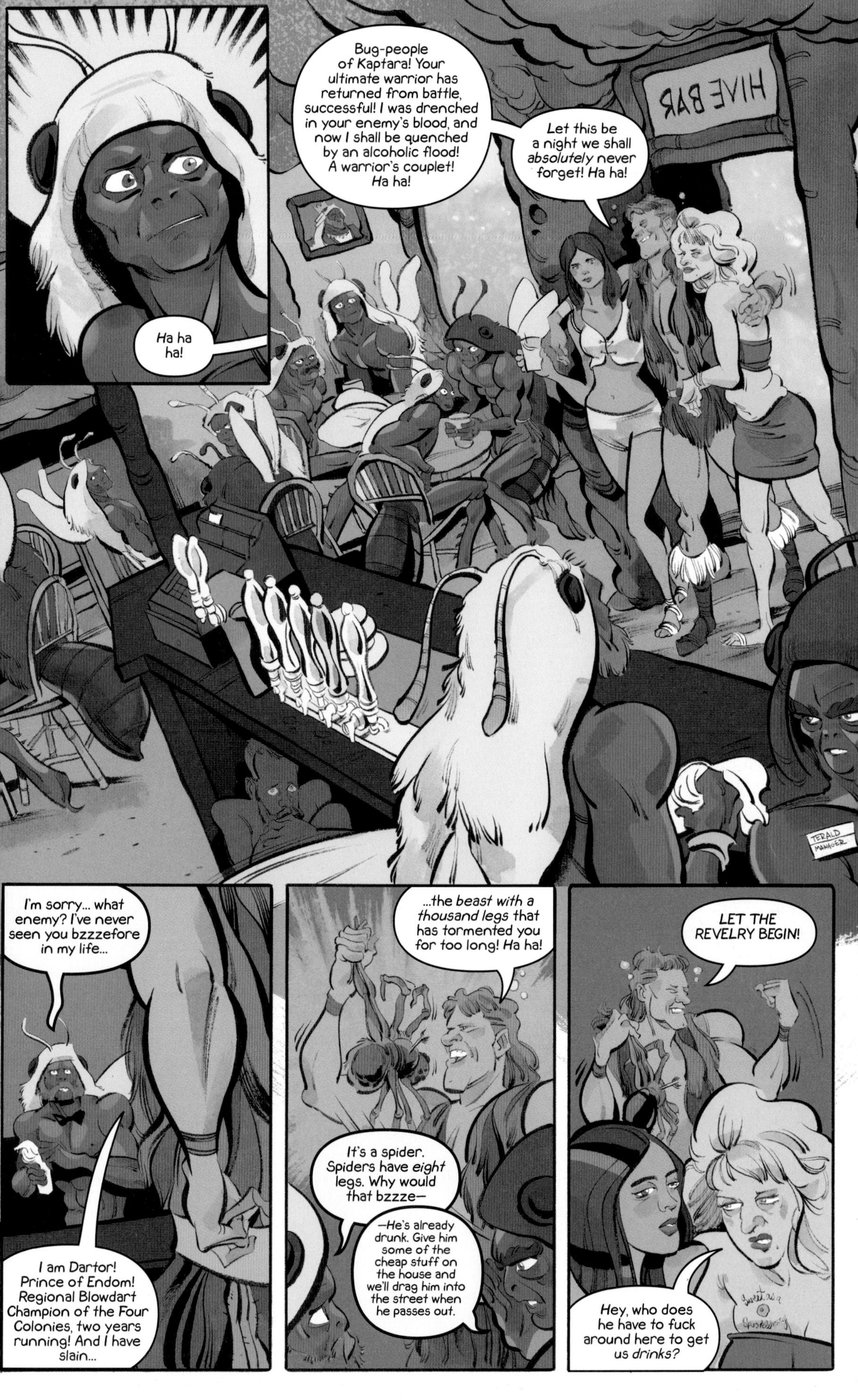

Bug-people of Kaptara! Your ultimate warrior has returned from battle, successful! I was drenched in your enemy's blood, and now I shall be quenched by an alcoholic flood! A warrior's couplet! *Ha ha!*
Let this be a night we shall *absolutely* never forget! Ha ha!
Ha ha ha!
HIVE BAR
TERALD MANAGER
I'm sorry... what enemy? I've never seen you bzzzefore in my life...
I am Dartor! Prince of Endom! Regional Blowdart Champion of the Four Colonies, two years running! And I have slain...
...the *beast with a thousand legs* that has tormented you for too long! *Ha ha!*
It's a spider. Spiders have *eight* legs. Why would that bzzze—
—He's already drunk. Give him some of the cheap stuff on the house and we'll drag him into the street when he passes out.
LET THE REVELRY BEGIN!
Hey, who does he have to fuck around here to get us *drinks?*

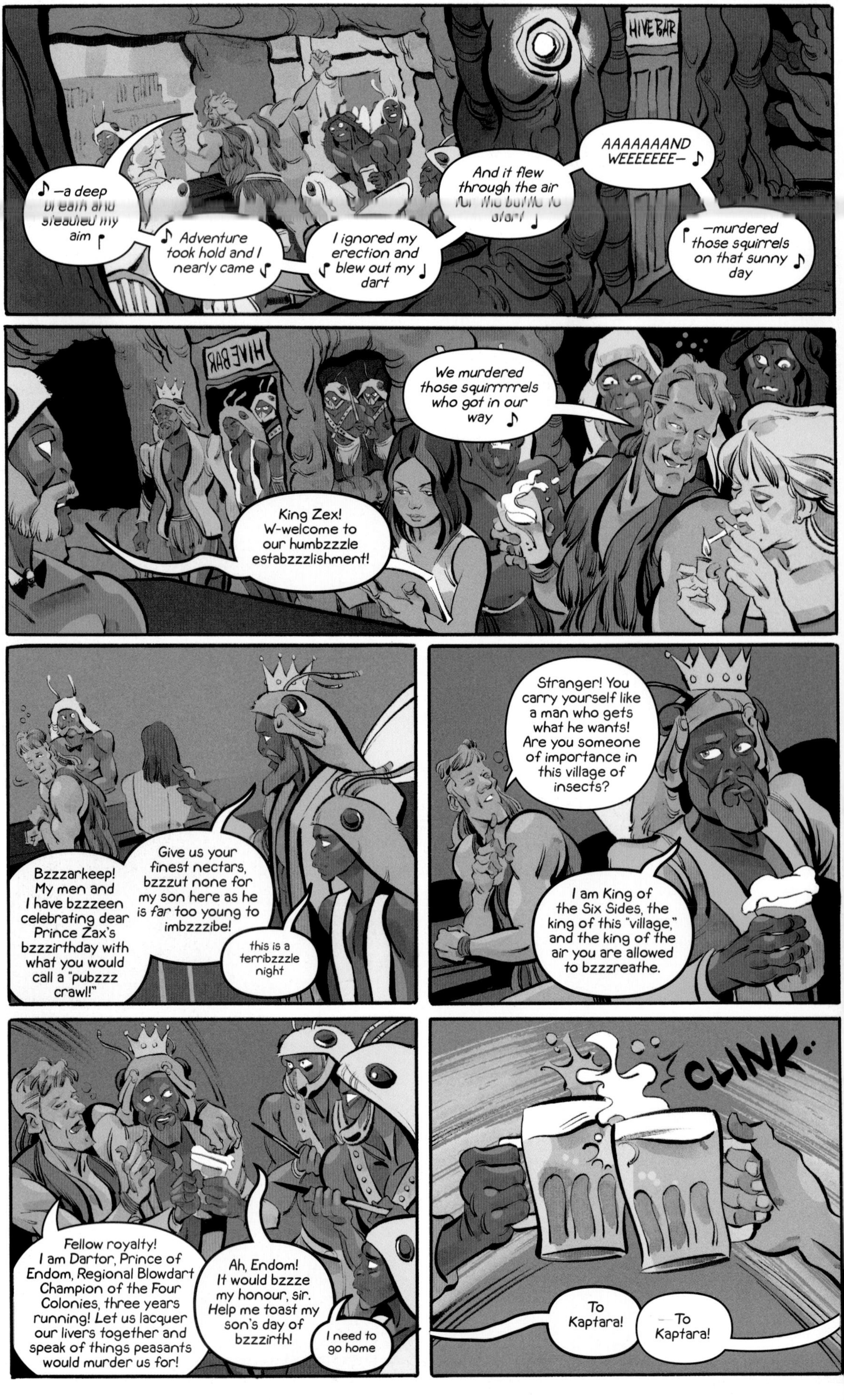
HIVE BAR
♪ —a deep breath and steadied my aim ♪
♪ Adventure took hold and I nearly came ♪
I ignored my erection and ♪ blew out my ♪ dart
And it flew through the air for the battle to start ♪
AAAAAAAND WEEEEEEE— ♪
♪ —murdered those squirrels on that sunny ♪ day
HIVE BAR
We murdered those squirrrrrels who got in our way ♪
King Zex! W-welcome to our humbzzzle estabzzzlishment!
Bzzzarkeep! My men and I have bzzzeen celebrating dear Prince Zax's bzzzirthday with what you would call a "pubzzz crawl!"
Give us your finest nectars, bzzzut none for my son here as he is far too young to imbzzzibe!
this is a terribzzzle night
Stranger! You carry yourself like a man who gets what he wants! Are you someone of importance in this village of insects?
I am King of the Six Sides, the king of this "village," and the king of the air you are allowed to bzzzreathe.
Fellow royalty! I am Dartor, Prince of Endom, Regional Blowdart Champion of the Four Colonies, three years running! Let us lacquer our livers together and speak of things peasants would murder us for!
Ah, Endom! It would bzzze my honour, sir. Help me toast my son's day of bzzzirth!
I need to go home
CLINK
To Kaptara!
—To Kaptara!

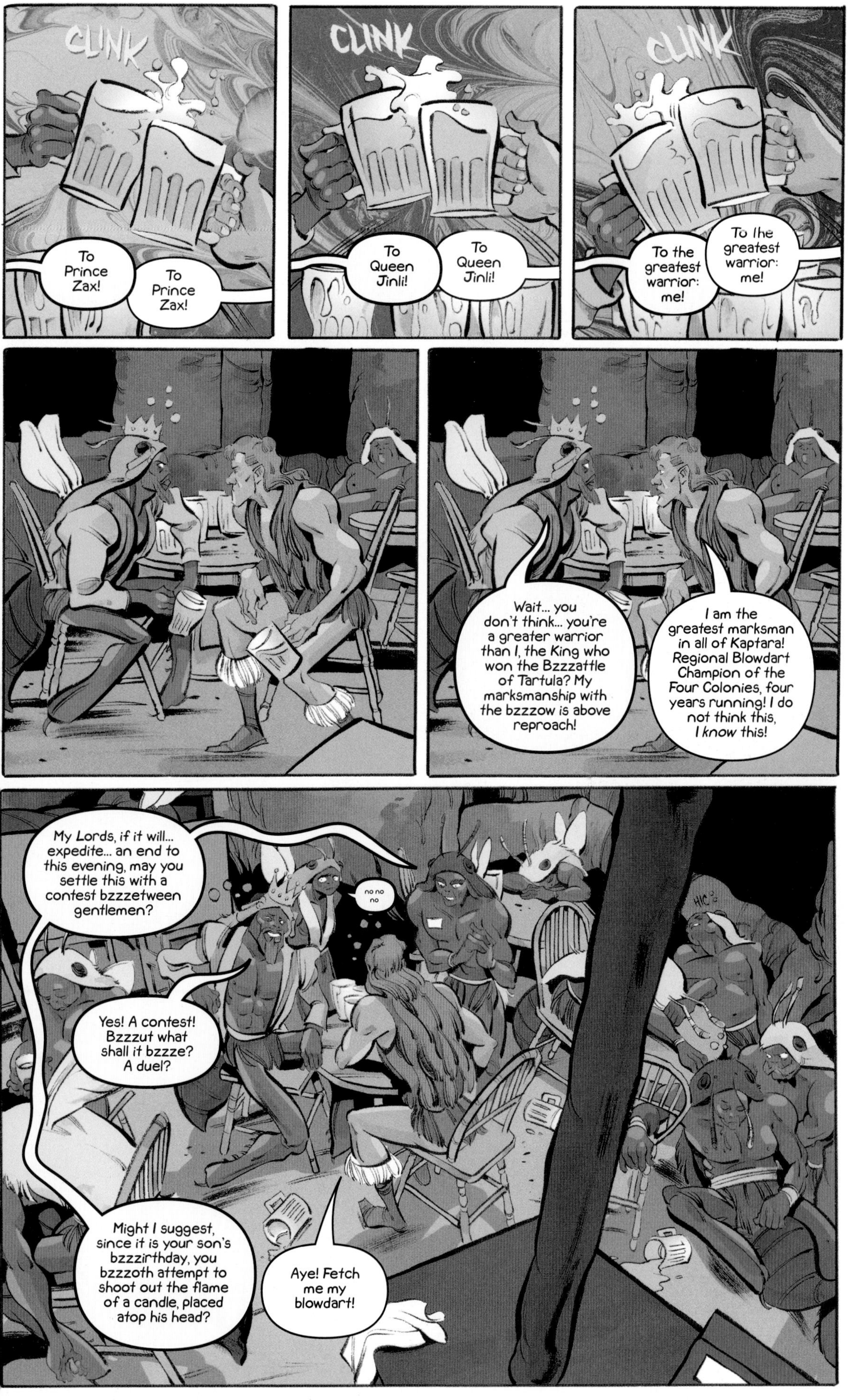
CLINK
To Prince Zax!
To Prince Zax!
CLINK
To Queen Jinli!
To Queen Jinli!
CLINK
To the greatest warrior: me!
To the greatest warrior: me!
Wait... you don't think... you're a greater warrior than I, the King who won the Bzzzattle of Tartula? My marksmanship with the bzzzow is above reproach!
I am the greatest marksman in all of Kaptara! Regional Blowdart Champion of the Four Colonies, four years running! I do not think this, *I know this*!
My Lords, if it will... expedite... an end to this evening, may you settle this with a contest bzzzetween gentlemen?
no no no
HIC
Yes! A contest! Bzzzut what shall it bzzze? A duel?
Might I suggest, since it is your son's bzzzirthday, you bzzzoth attempt to shoot out the flame of a candle, placed atop his head?
Aye! Fetch me my blowdart!

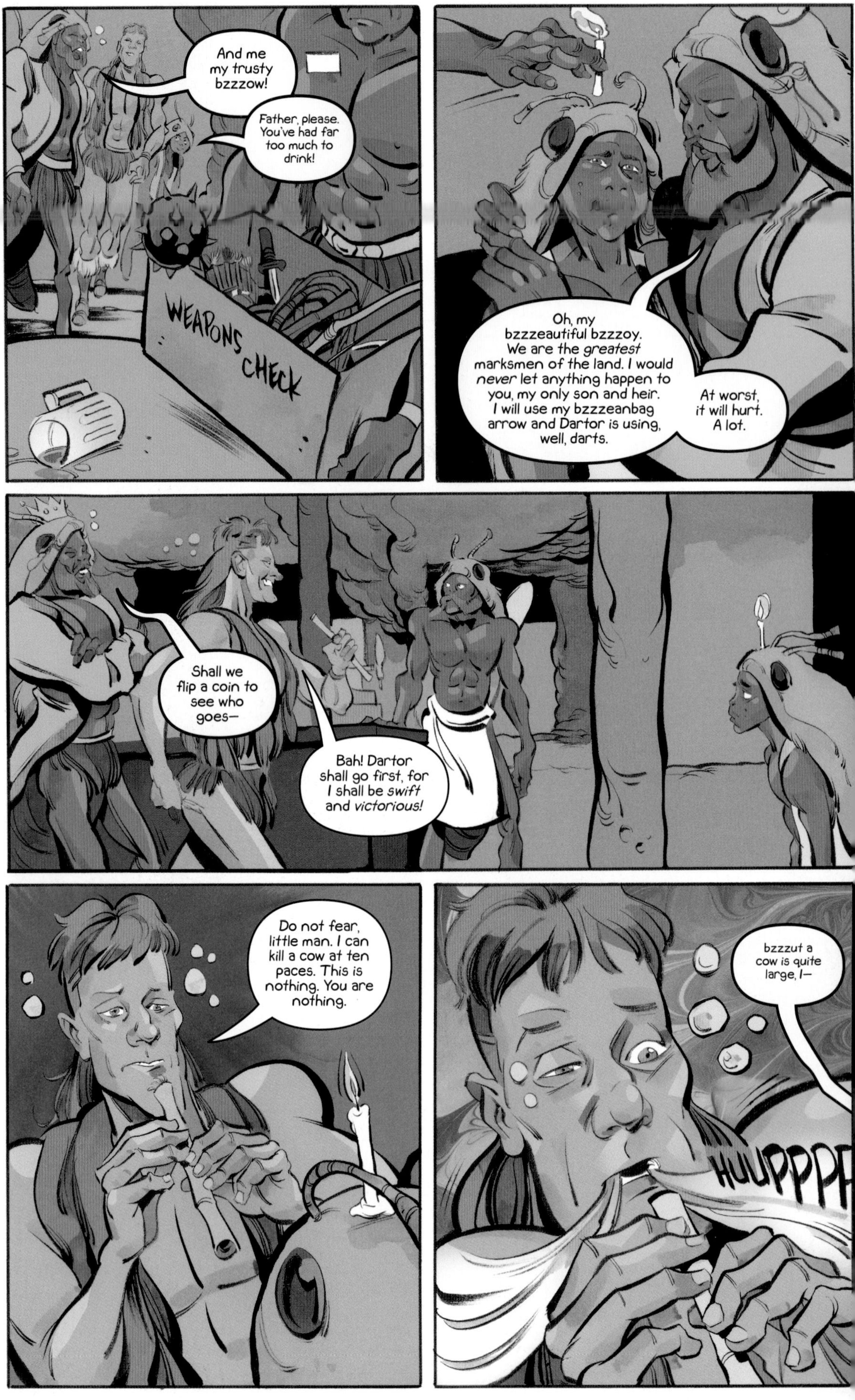
And me my trusty bzzzow!
Father, please. You've had far too much to drink!
WEAPONS CHECK
Oh, my bzzzeautiful bzzzoy. We are the *greatest* marksmen of the land. I would *never* let anything happen to you, my only son and heir. I will use my bzzzeanbag arrow and Dartor is using, well, darts.
At worst, it will hurt. A lot.
Shall we flip a coin to see who goes—
Bah! Dartor shall go first, for I shall be *swift* and *victorious!*
Do not fear, little man. I can kill a cow at ten paces. This is nothing. You are nothing.
bzzzut a cow is quite large, I—
HUUPPPF

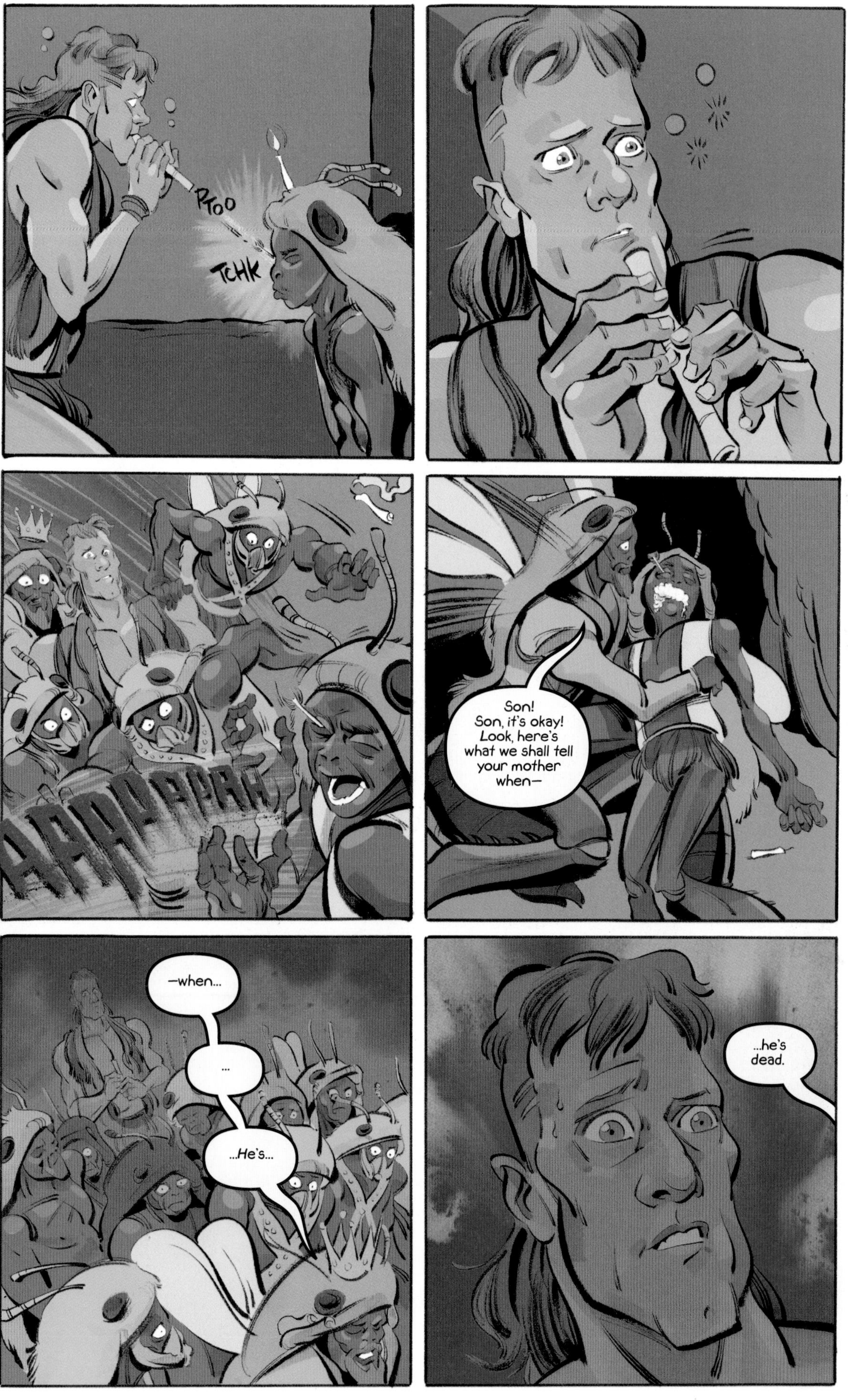
PTOO
TCHK
AAAAAAAA
Son! Son, it's okay! Look, here's what we shall tell your mother when—
—when...
...
...He's...
...he's dead.

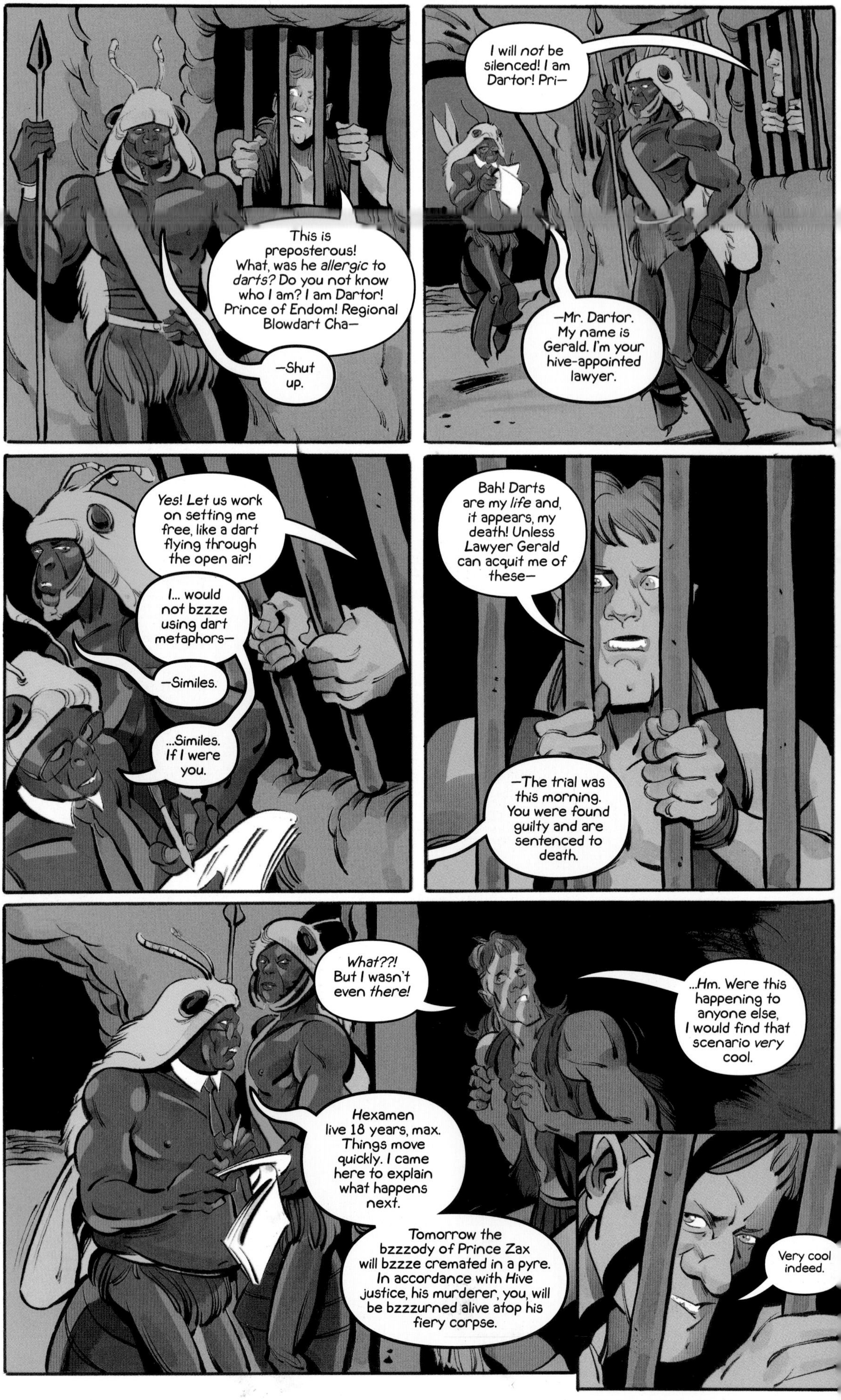
This is preposterous! What, was he *allergic* to *darts?* Do you not know who I am? I am Dartor! Prince of Endom! Regional Blowdart Cha—
—Shut up.
I will *not* be silenced! I am Dartor! Pri—
—Mr. Dartor. My name is Gerald. I'm your hive-appointed lawyer.
Yes! Let us work on setting me free, like a dart flying through the open air!
I... would not bzzze using dart metaphors—
—Similes.
...Similes. If I were you.
Bah! Darts are my *life* and, it appears, my death! Unless Lawyer Gerald can acquit me of these—
—The trial was this morning. You were found guilty and are sentenced to death.
What??! But I wasn't even *there!*
Hexamen live 18 years, max. Things move quickly. I came here to explain what happens next.
Tomorrow the bzzzody of Prince Zax will bzzze cremated in a pyre. In accordance with *Hive* justice, his murderer, you, will be bzzzurned alive atop his fiery corpse.
...*Hm.* Were this happening to anyone else, I would find that scenario *very* cool.
Very cool indeed.

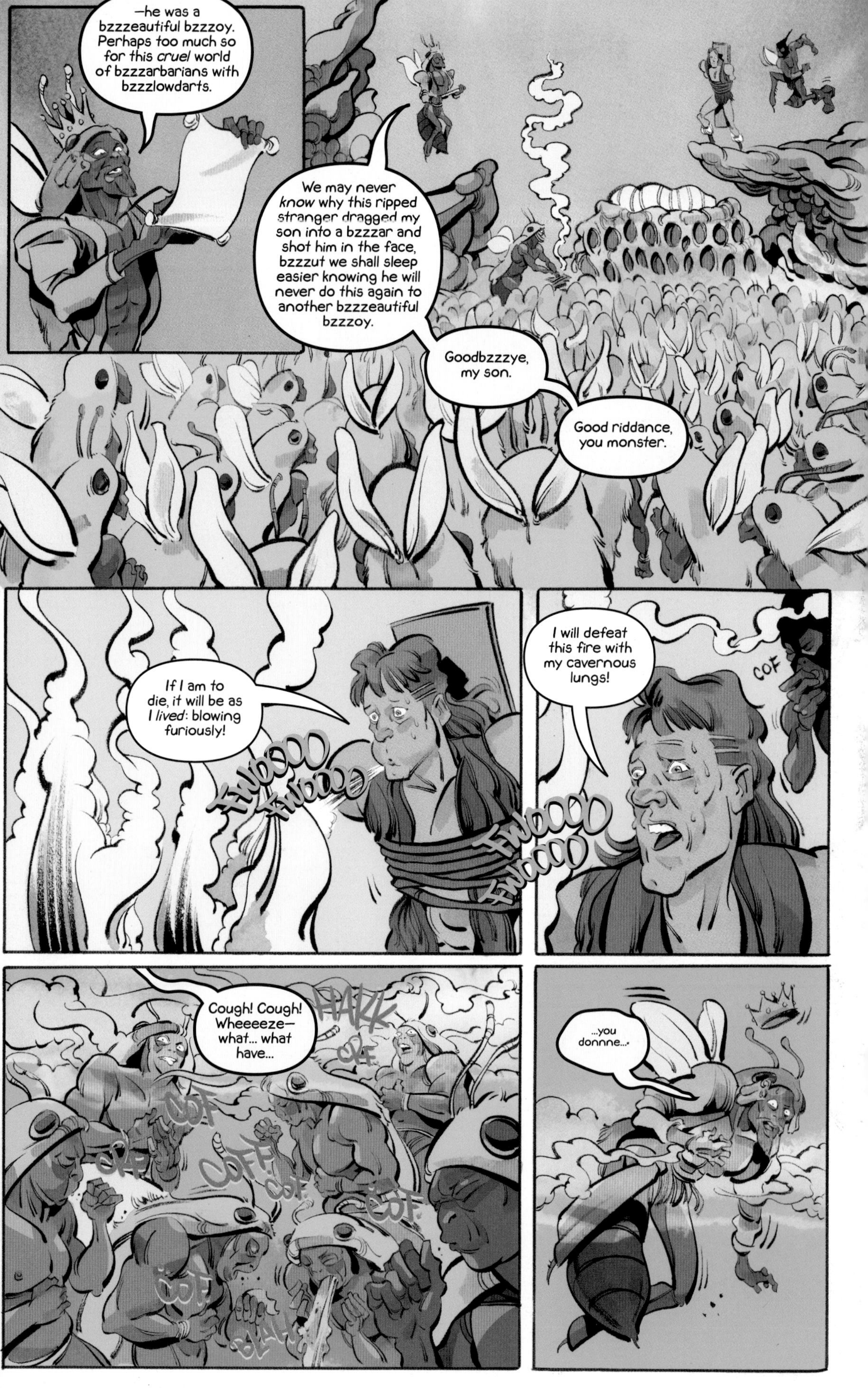
—he was a bzzzeautiful bzzzoy. Perhaps too much so for this *cruel* world of bzzzarbarians with bzzzlowdarts.
We may never *know* why this ripped stranger dragged my son into a bzzzar and shot him in the face, bzzzut we shall sleep easier knowing he will never do this again to another bzzzeautiful bzzzoy.
Goodbzzzye, my son.
Good riddance, you monster.
If I am to die, it will be as I *lived*: blowing furiously!
FWOOOO FWOOOO
I will defeat this fire with my cavernous lungs!
COF
FWOOOO FWOOOO
Cough! Cough! Wheeeeze— what... what have...
HAKK
COFF!
...you donnne...

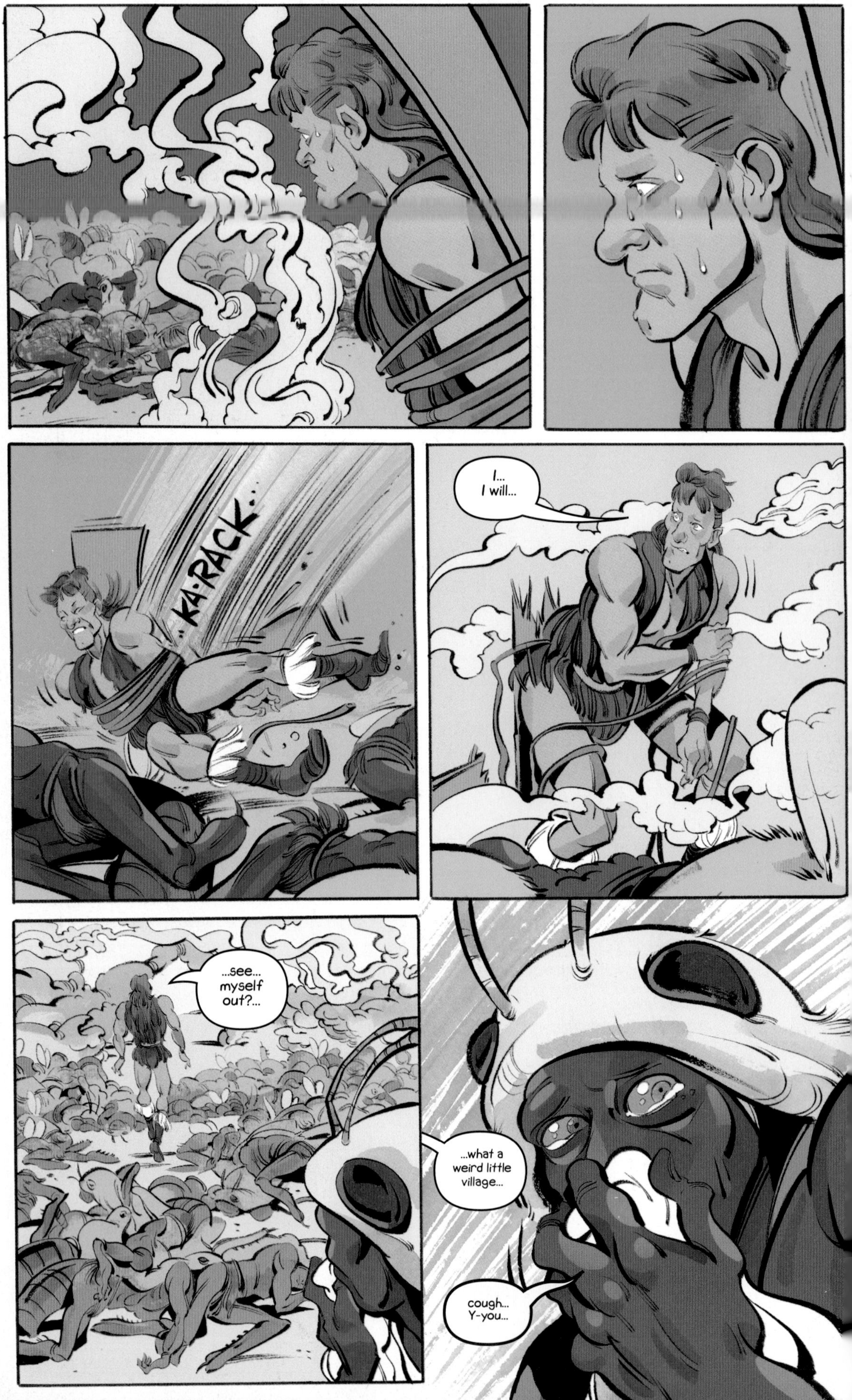
KA-RACK
I...
I will...
...see...
myself
out?...
...what a
weird little
village...
cough...
Y-you...

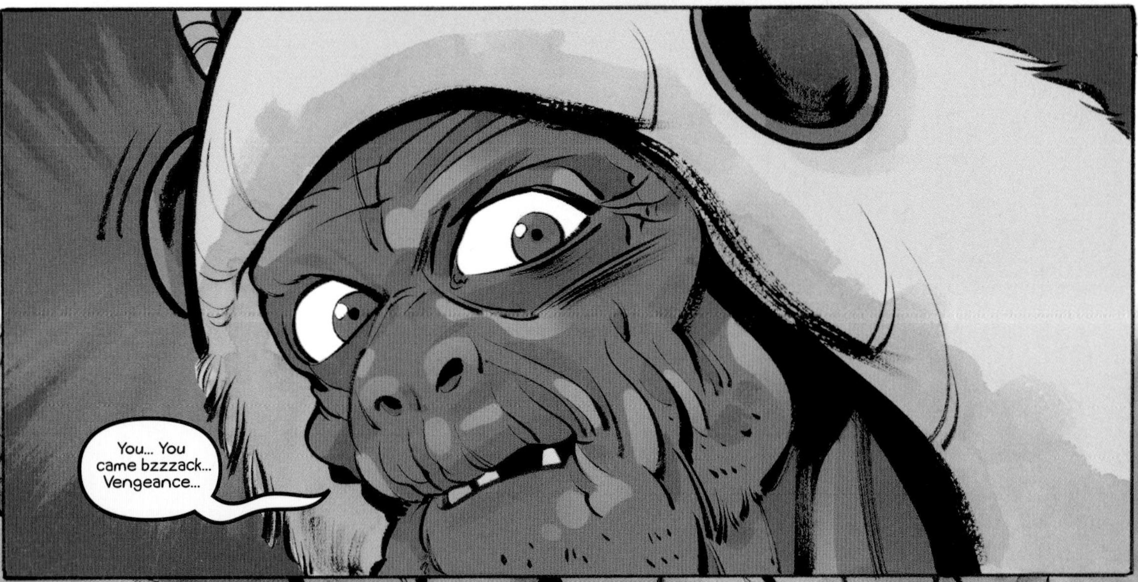
You... You came bzzzack... Vengeance...

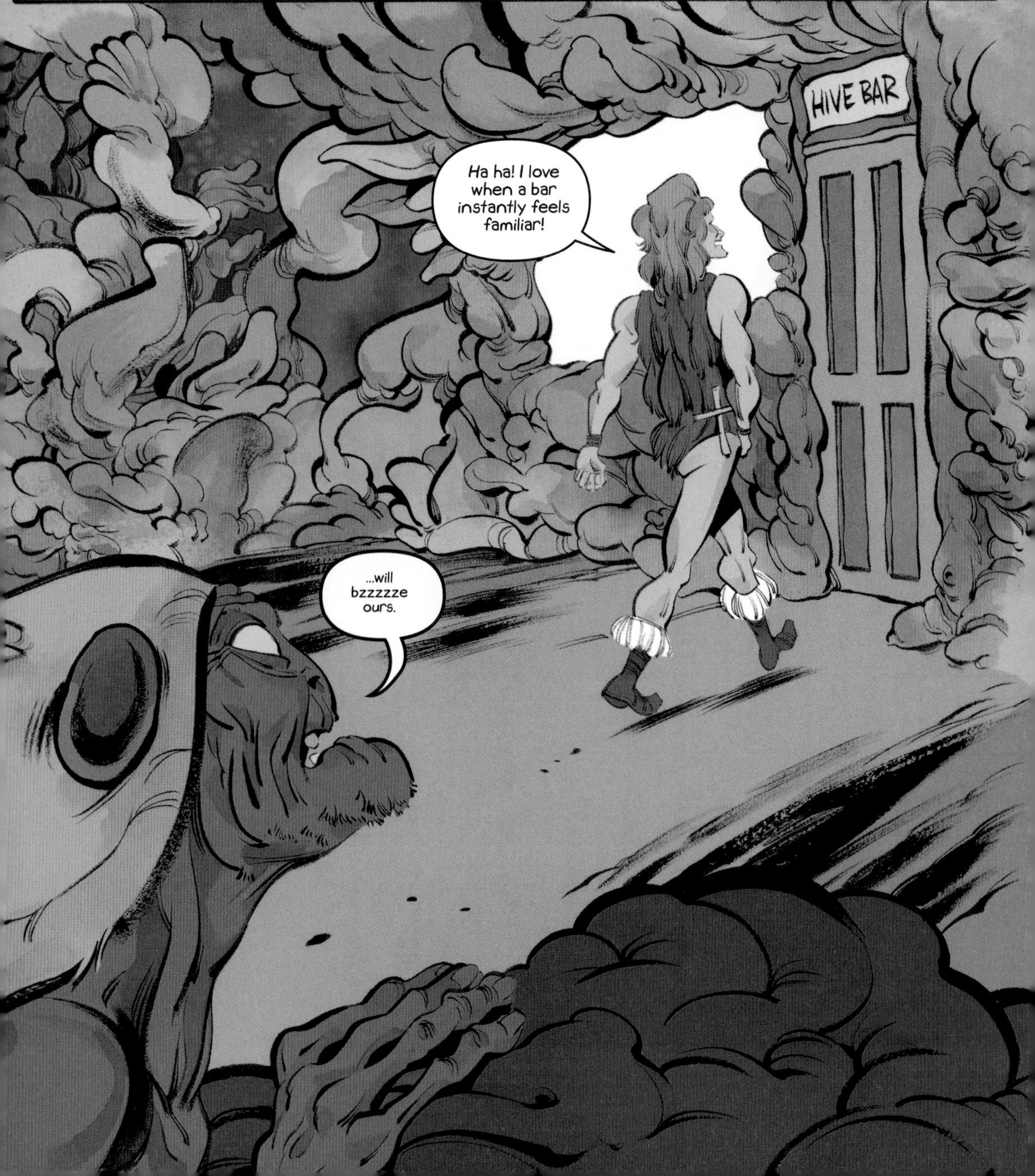
HIVE BAR
Ha ha! I love when a bar instantly feels familiar!
...will bzzzzze ours.

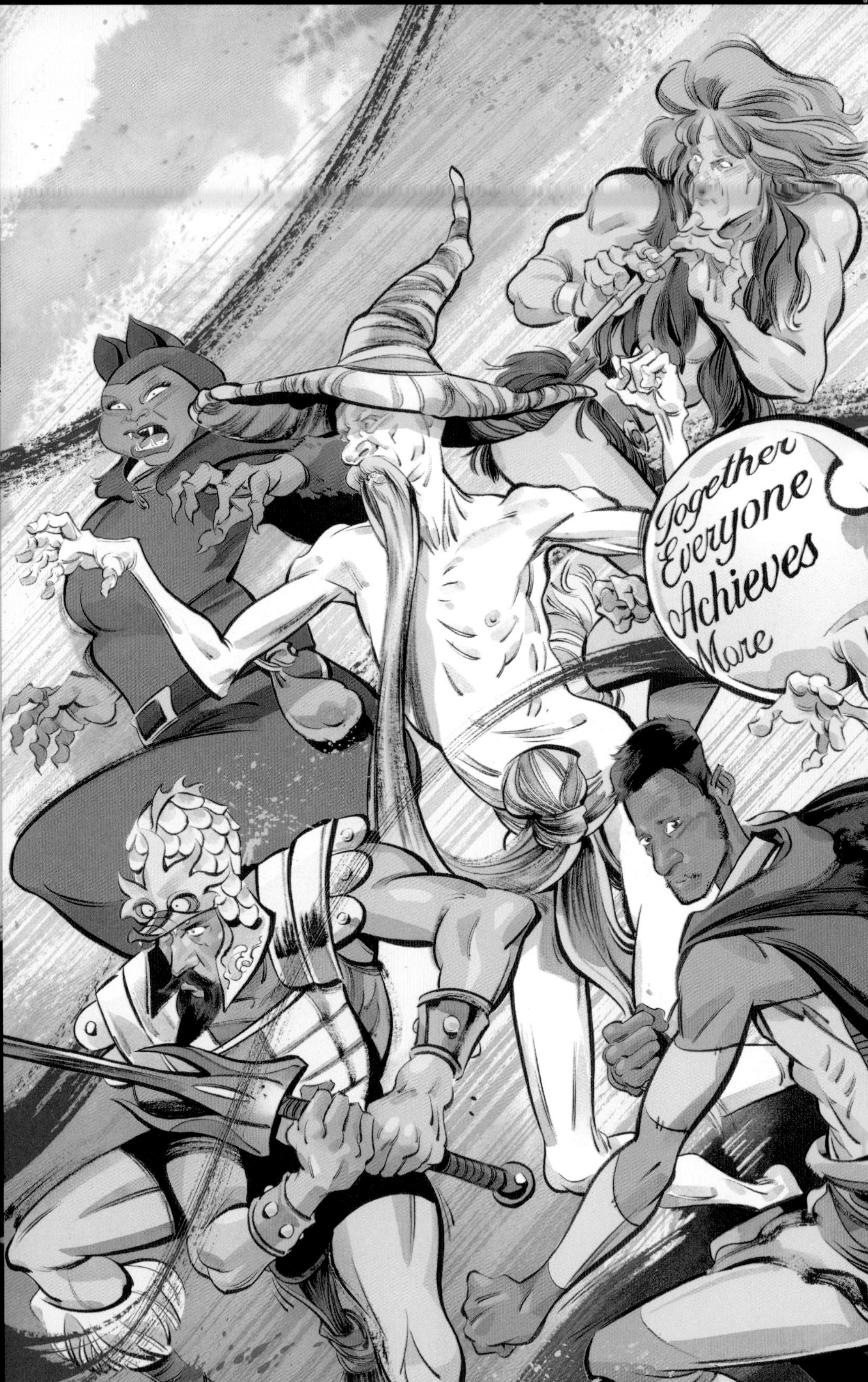
Together Everyone Achieves More

CHAPTER FIVE

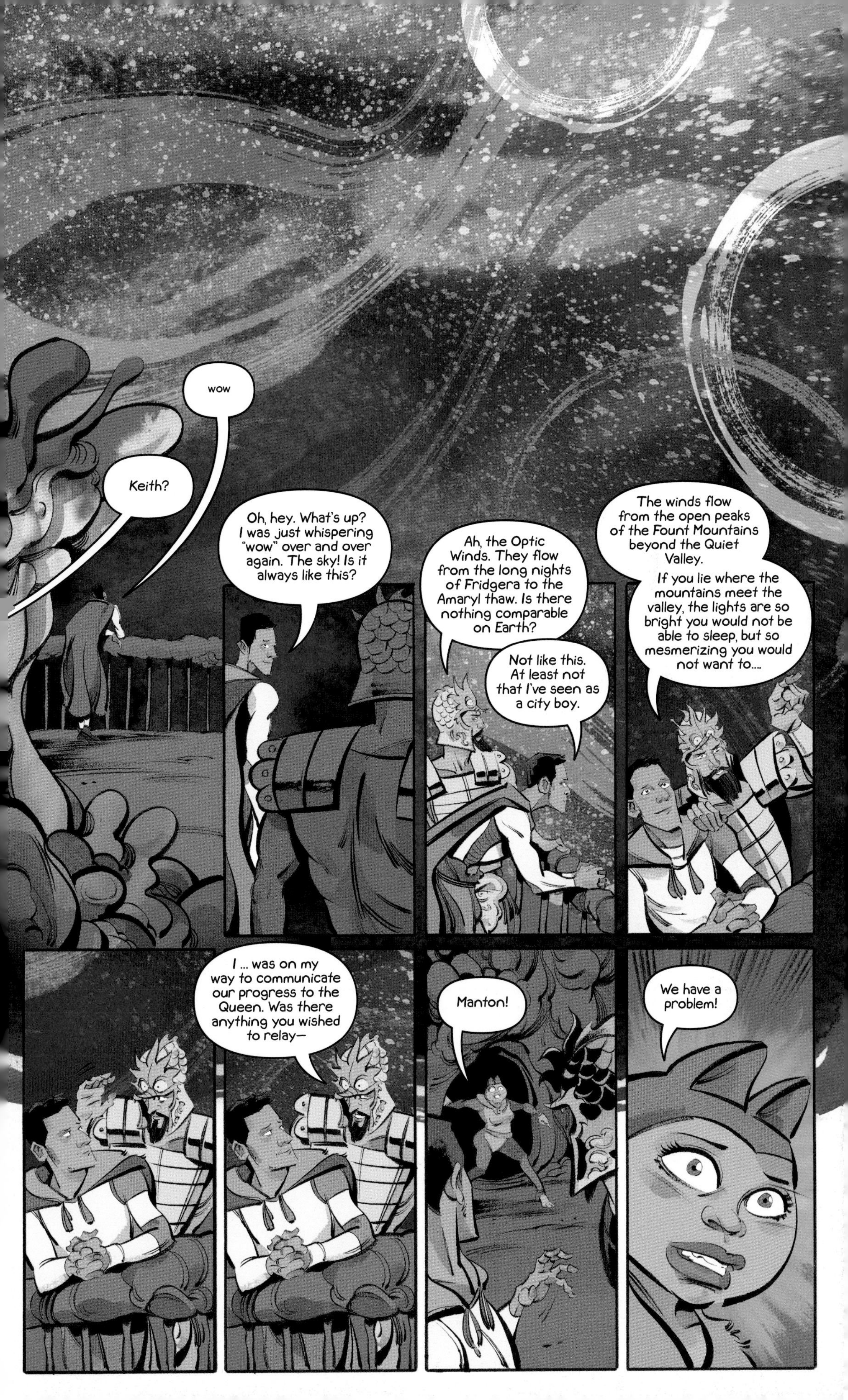
wow
Keith?
Oh, hey. What's up? I was just whispering "wow" over and over again. The sky! Is it always like this?
Ah, the Optic Winds. They flow from the long nights of Fridgera to the Amaryl thaw. Is there nothing comparable on Earth?
Not like this. At least not that I've seen as a city boy.
The winds flow from the open peaks of the Fount Mountains beyond the Quiet Valley.
If you lie where the mountains meet the valley, the lights are so bright you would not be able to sleep, but so mesmerizing you would not want to....
I ... was on my way to communicate our progress to the Queen. Was there anything you wished to relay—
Manton!
We have a problem!

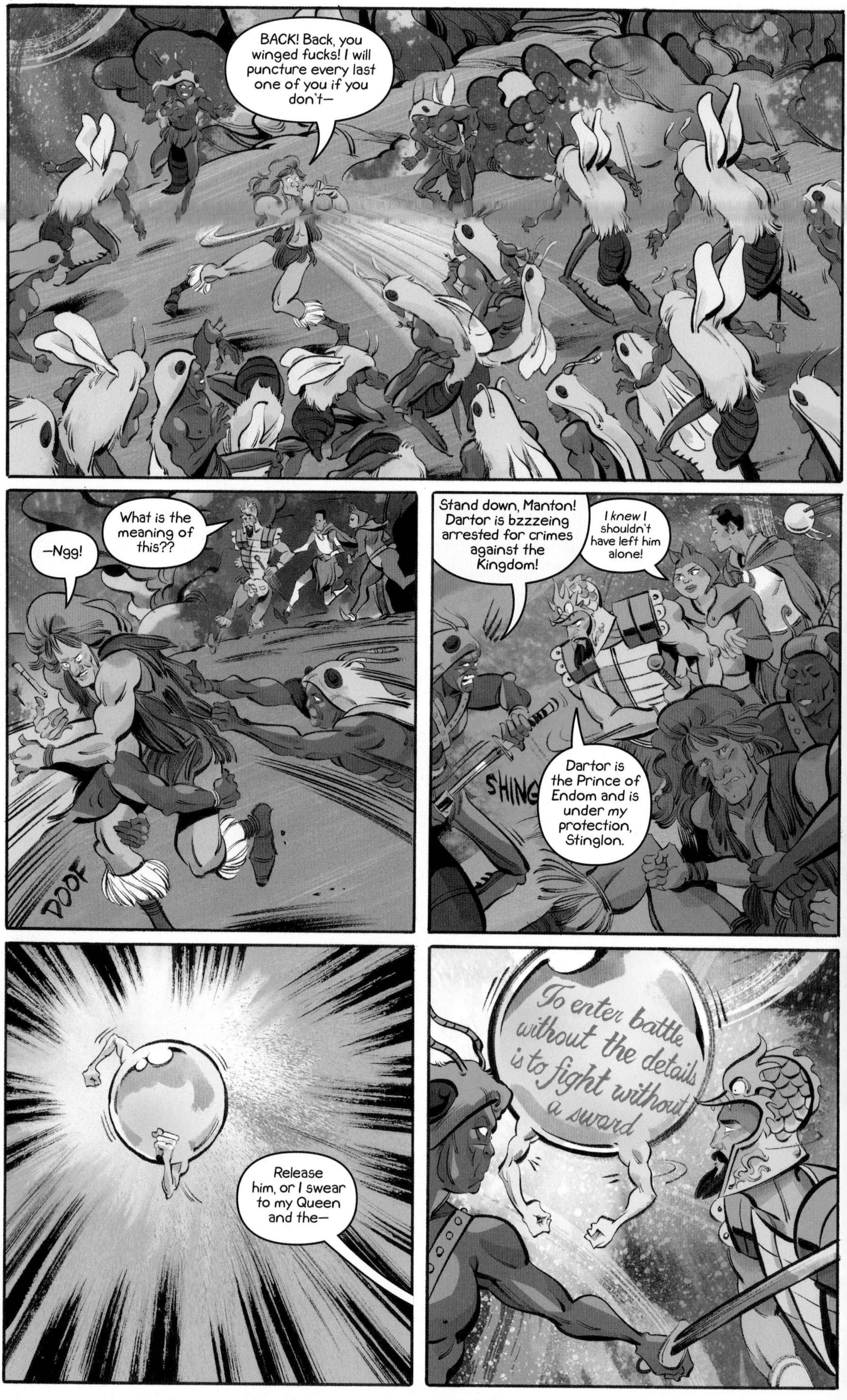
BACK! Back, you winged fucks! I will puncture every last one of you if you don't—
What is the meaning of this??
—Ngg!
DOOF
Stand down, Manton! Dartor is bzzzeing arrested for crimes against the Kingdom!
I knew I shouldn't have left him alone!
SHING
Dartor is the Prince of Endom and is under my protection, Stinglon.
Release him, or I swear to my Queen and the—
To enter battle without the details is to fight without a sword

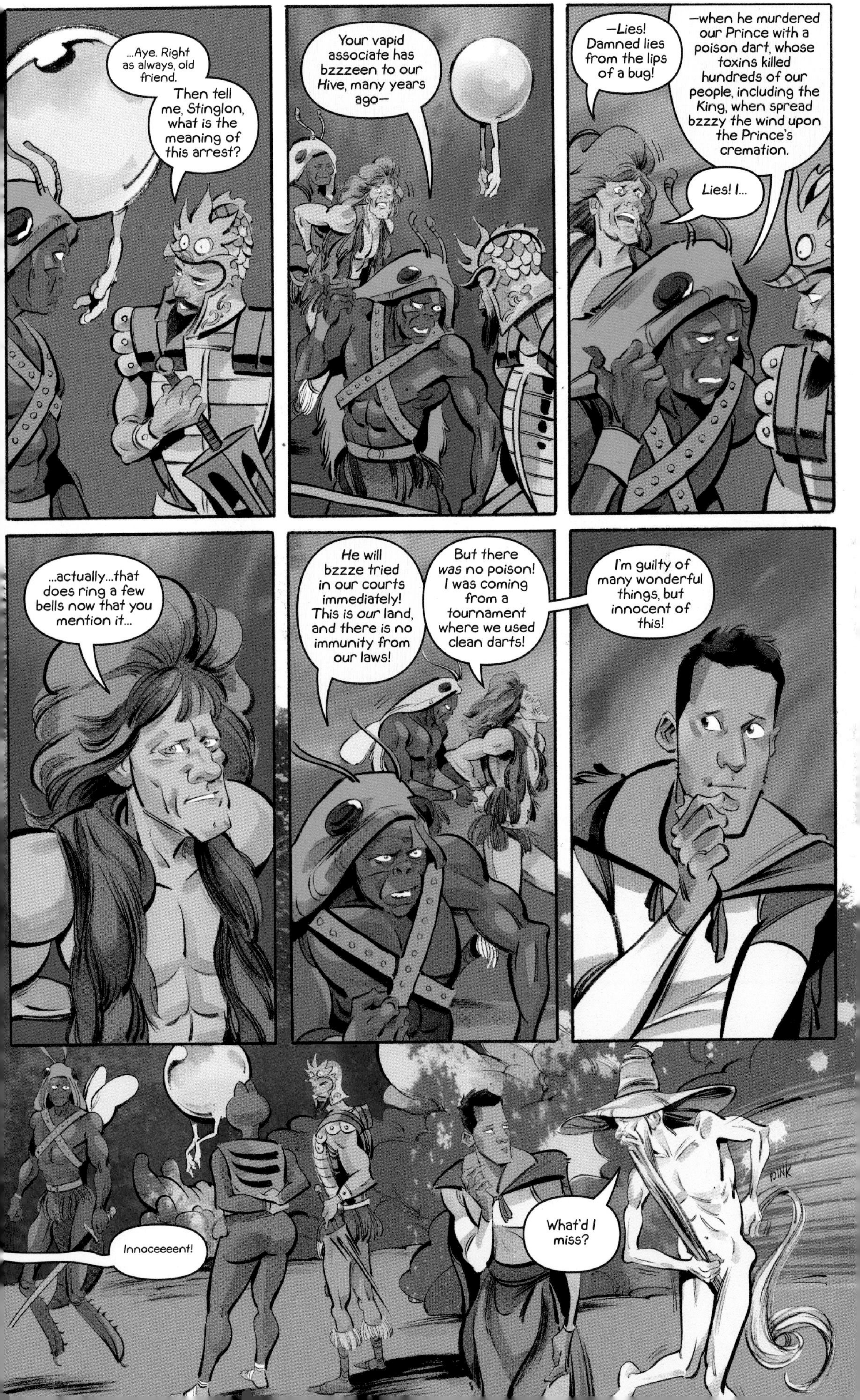
...Aye. Right as always, old friend.
Then tell me, Stinglon, what is the meaning of this arrest?
Your vapid associate has bzzzeen to our Hive, many years ago—
—Lies! Damned lies from the lips of a bug!
—when he murdered our Prince with a poison dart, whose toxins killed hundreds of our people, including the King, when spread bzzzy the wind upon the Prince's cremation.
Lies! I...
...actually...that does ring a few bells now that you mention it...
He will bzzze tried in our courts immediately! This is our land, and there is no immunity from our laws!
But there was no poison! I was coming from a tournament where we used clean darts!
I'm guilty of many wonderful things, but innocent of this!
Innoceeeent!
What'd I miss?
YOINK

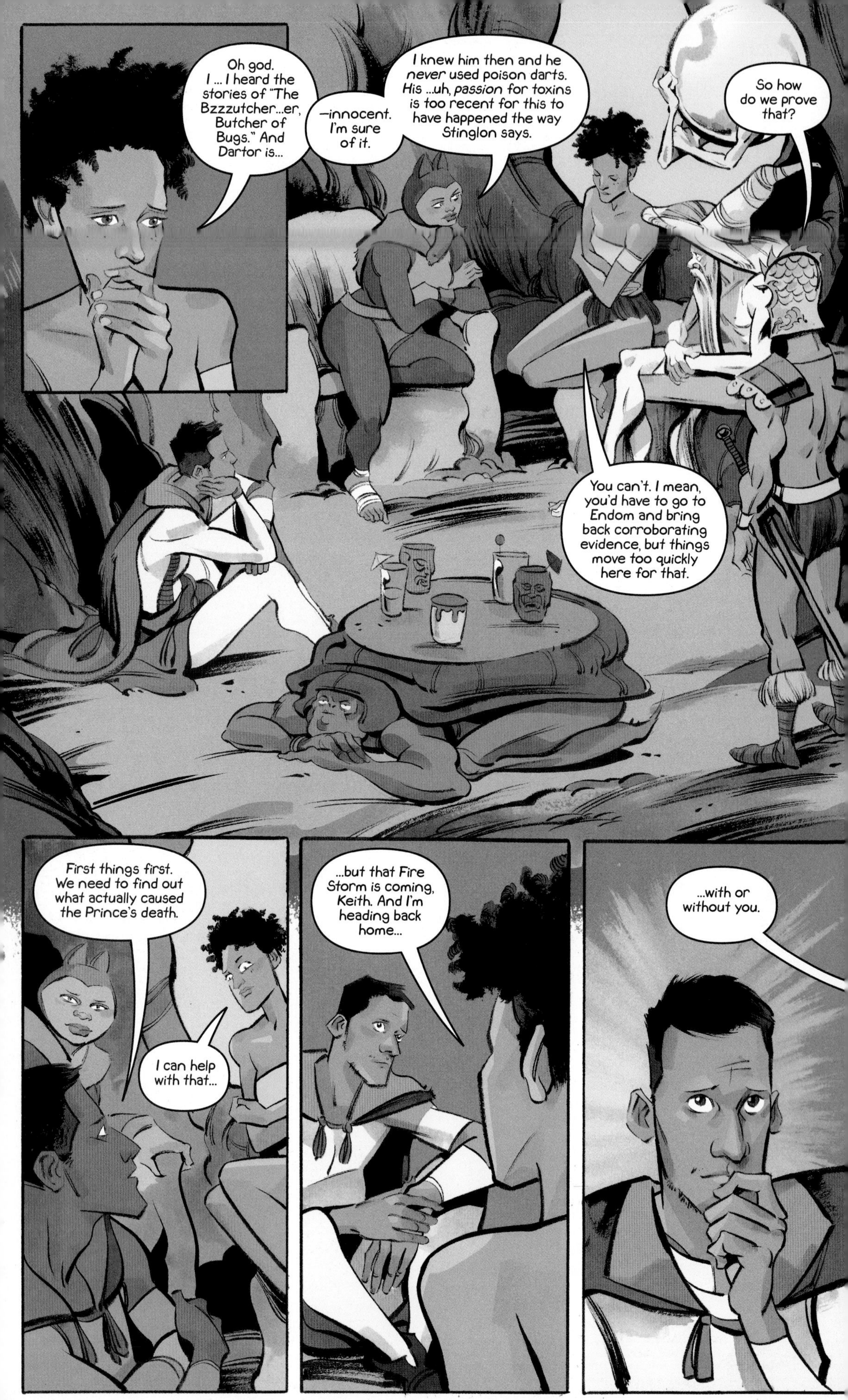

Oh god. I ... I heard the stories of "The Bzzzutcher...er, Butcher of Bugs." And Dartor is...
—innocent. I'm sure of it.
I knew him then and he *never* used poison darts. His ...uh, *passion* for toxins is too recent for this to have happened the way Stinglon says.
So how do we prove that?
You can't. I mean, you'd have to go to Endom and bring back corroborating evidence, but things move too quickly here for that.
First things first. We need to find out what actually caused the Prince's death.
I can help with that...
...but that Fire Storm is coming, Keith. And I'm heading back home...
...with or without you.

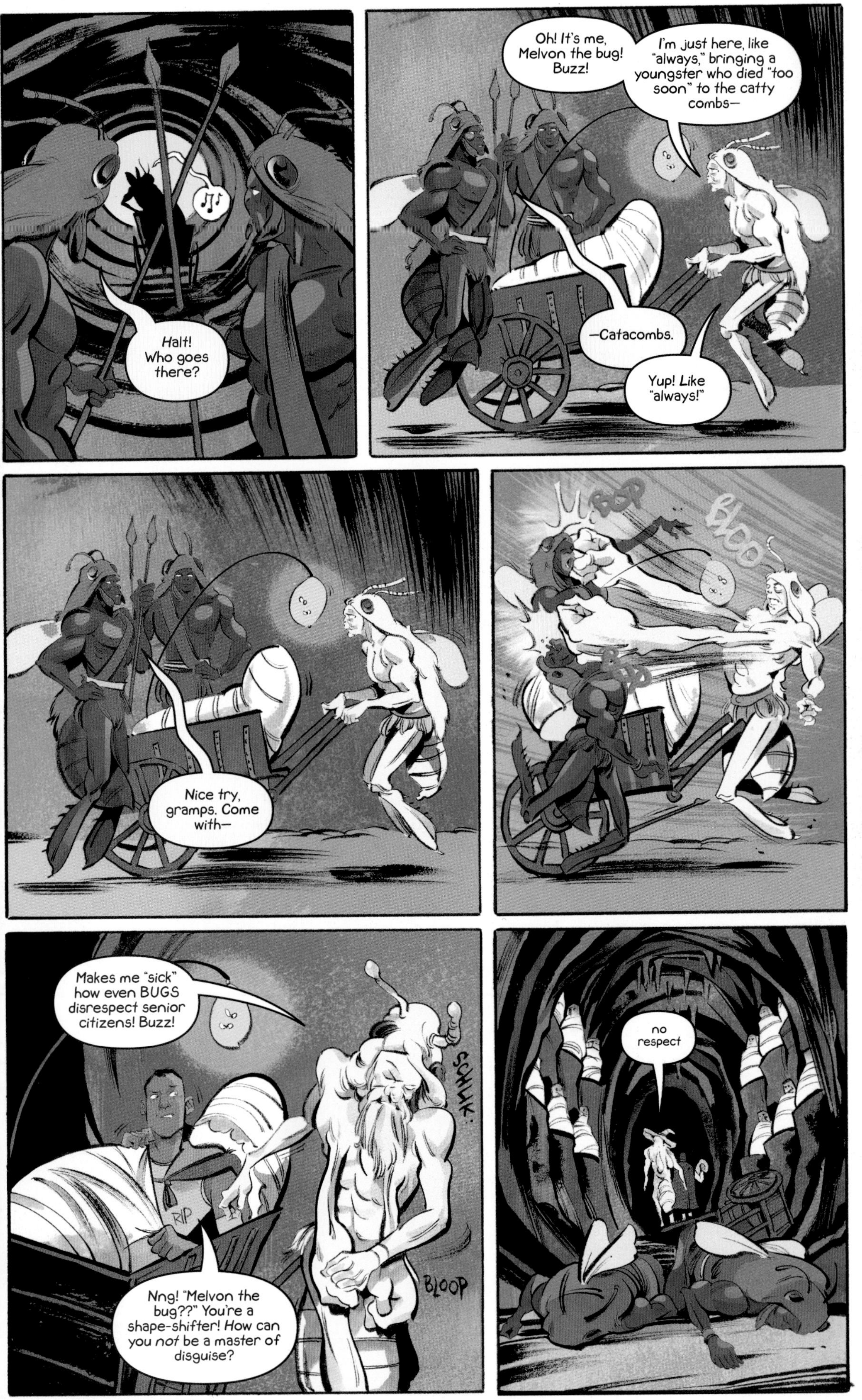

Halt! Who goes there?
Oh! It's me, Melvon the bug! Buzz!
I'm just here, like "always," bringing a youngster who died "too soon" to the catty combs—
—Catacombs.
Yup! Like "always!"
Nice try, gramps. Come with—
BLOO
BOP
Makes me "sick" how even BUGS disrespect senior citizens! Buzz!
SCHLK
RIP
BLOOP
Nng! "Melvon the bug??" You're a shape-shifter! How can you *not* be a master of disguise?
no respect

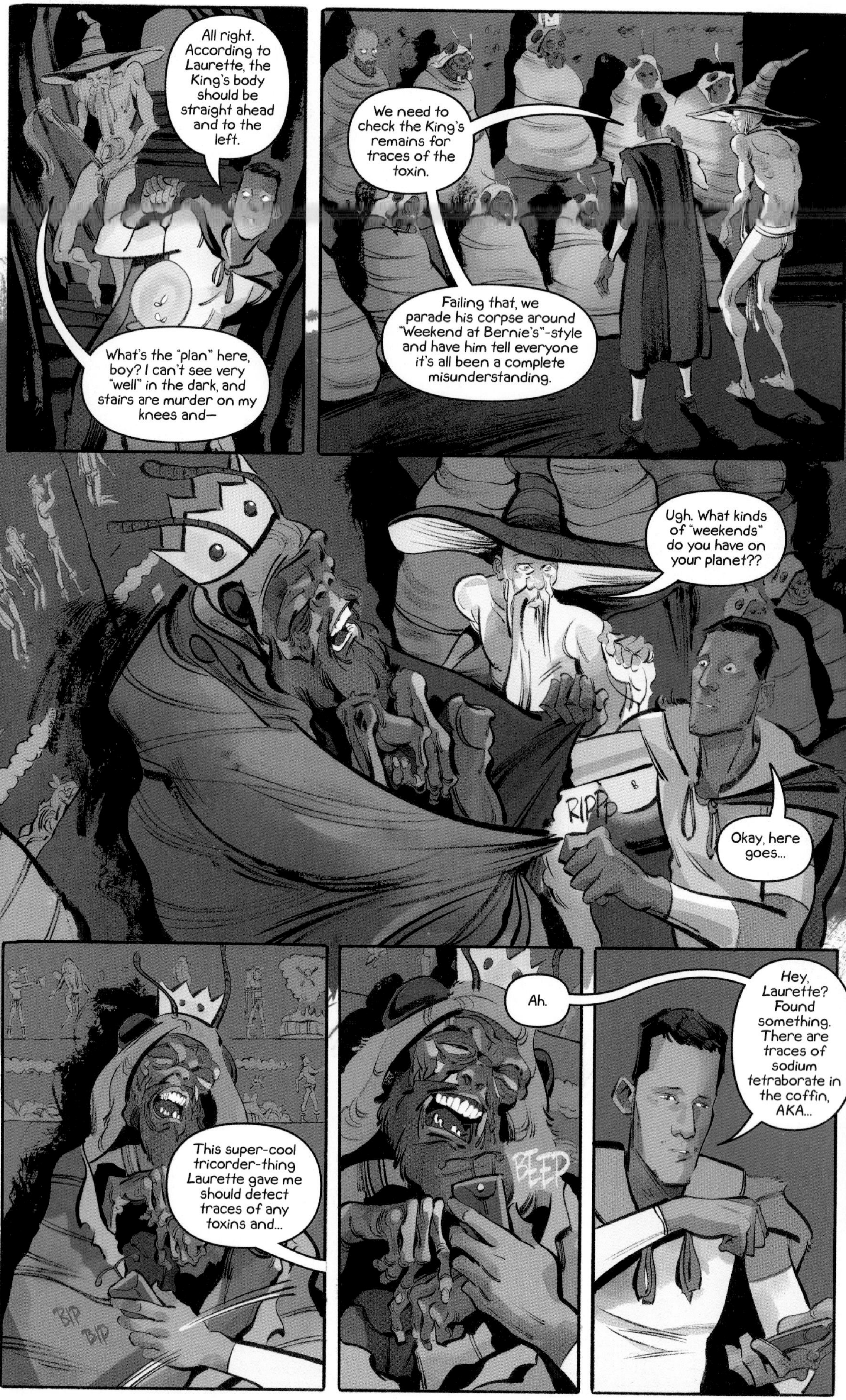
All right. According to Laurette, the King's body should be straight ahead and to the left.
What's the "plan" here, boy? I can't see very "well" in the dark, and stairs are murder on my knees and—
We need to check the King's remains for traces of the toxin.
Failing that, we parade his corpse around "Weekend at Bernie's"-style and have him tell everyone it's all been a complete misunderstanding.
Ugh. What kinds of "weekends" do you have on your planet??
RIPP
Okay, here goes...
This super-cool tricorder-thing Laurette gave me should detect traces of any toxins and...
BIP BIP
Ah.
BEEP
Hey, Laurette? Found something. There are traces of sodium tetraborate in the coffin, AKA...

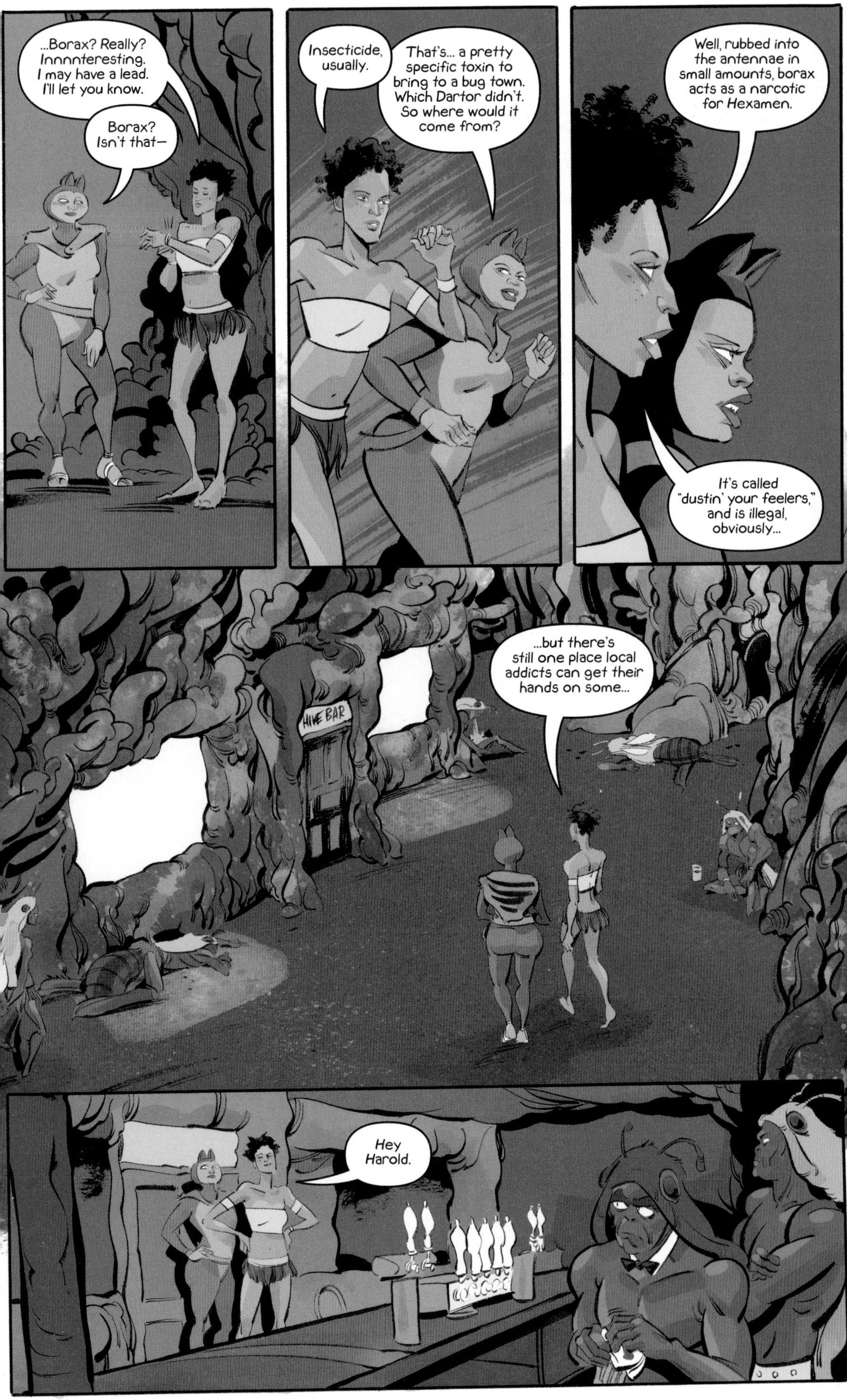
...Borax? Really? Innnnteresting. I may have a lead. I'll let you know.
Borax? Isn't that—
Insecticide, usually.
That's... a pretty specific toxin to bring to a bug town. Which Dartor didn't. So where would it come from?
Well, rubbed into the antennae in small amounts, borax acts as a narcotic for Hexamen.
It's called "dustin' your feelers," and is illegal, obviously...
...but there's still one place local addicts can get their hands on some...
HIVE BAR
Hey Harold.

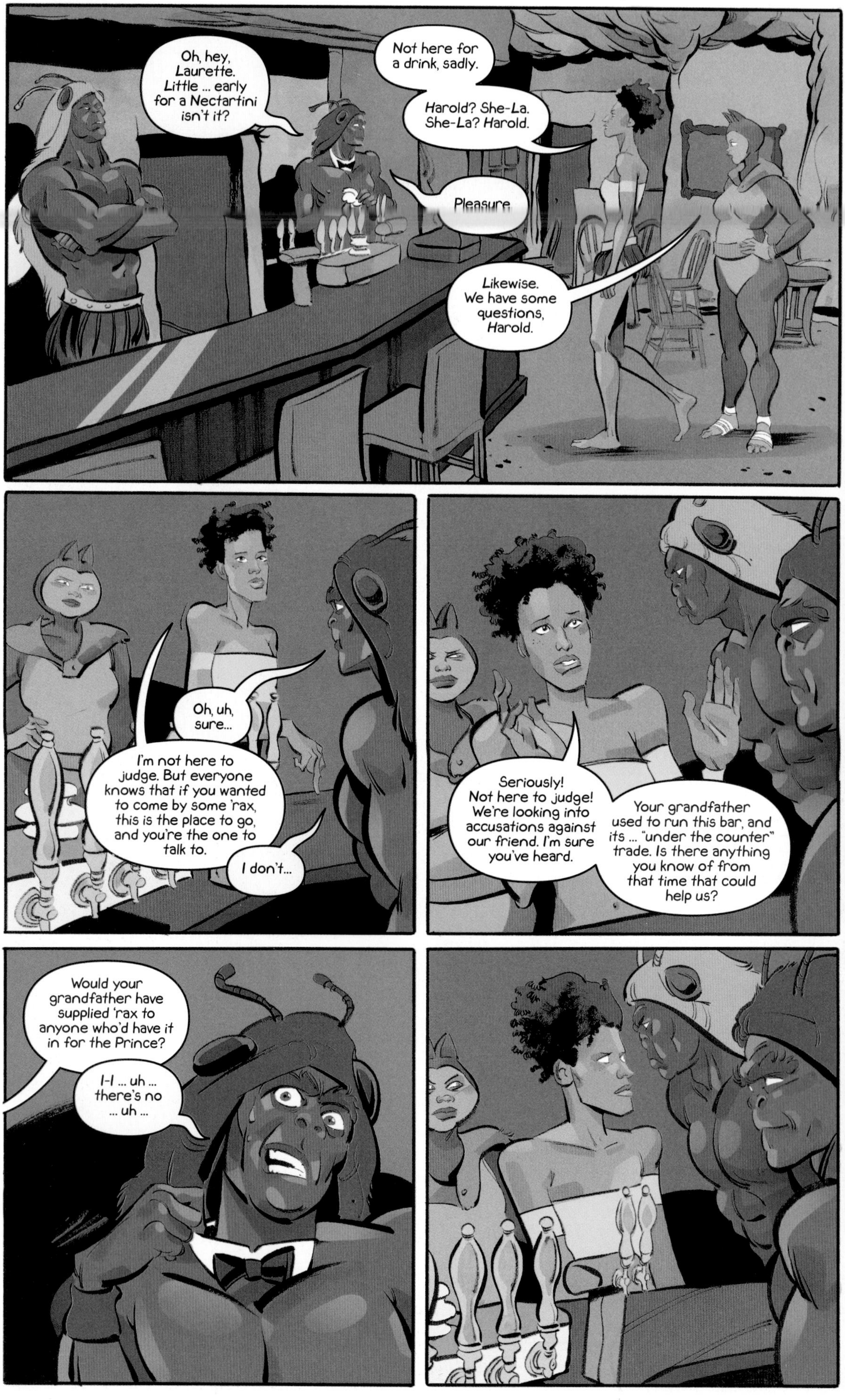
Oh, hey, Laurette. Little ... early for a Nectartini isn't it?
Not here for a drink, sadly.
Harold? She-La. She-La? Harold.
Pleasure.
Likewise. We have some questions, Harold.
Oh, uh, sure...
I'm not here to judge. But everyone knows that if you wanted to come by some 'rax, this is the place to go, and you're the one to talk to.
I don't...
Seriously! Not here to judge! We're looking into accusations against our friend. I'm sure you've heard.
Your grandfather used to run this bar, and its ... "under the counter" trade. Is there anything you know of from that time that could help us?
Would your grandfather have supplied 'rax to anyone who'd have it in for the Prince?
I-I ... uh ... there's no ... uh ...

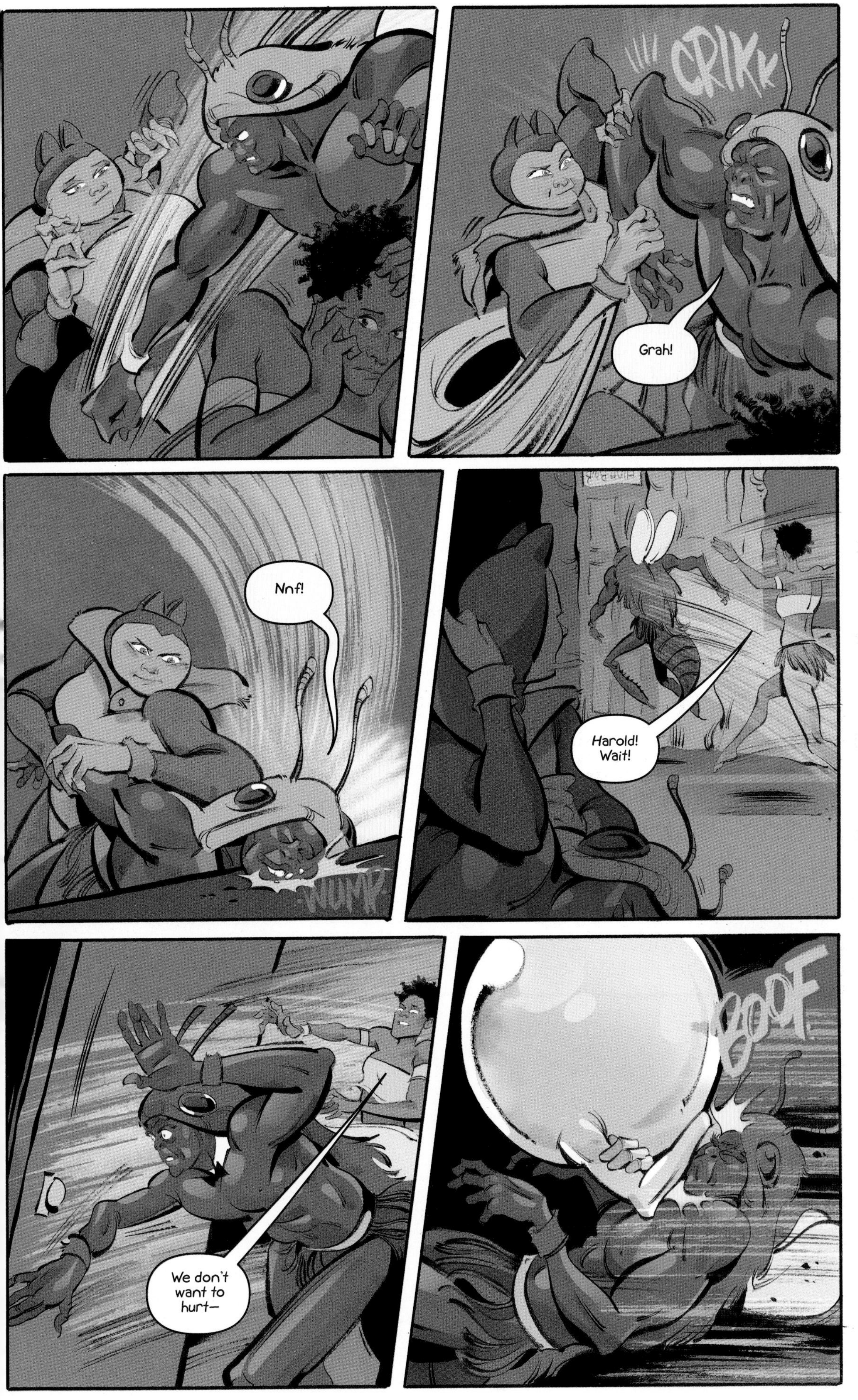
CRIKK
Grah!
Nnf!
WUMP
Harold! Wait!
We don't want to hurt—
BOOF

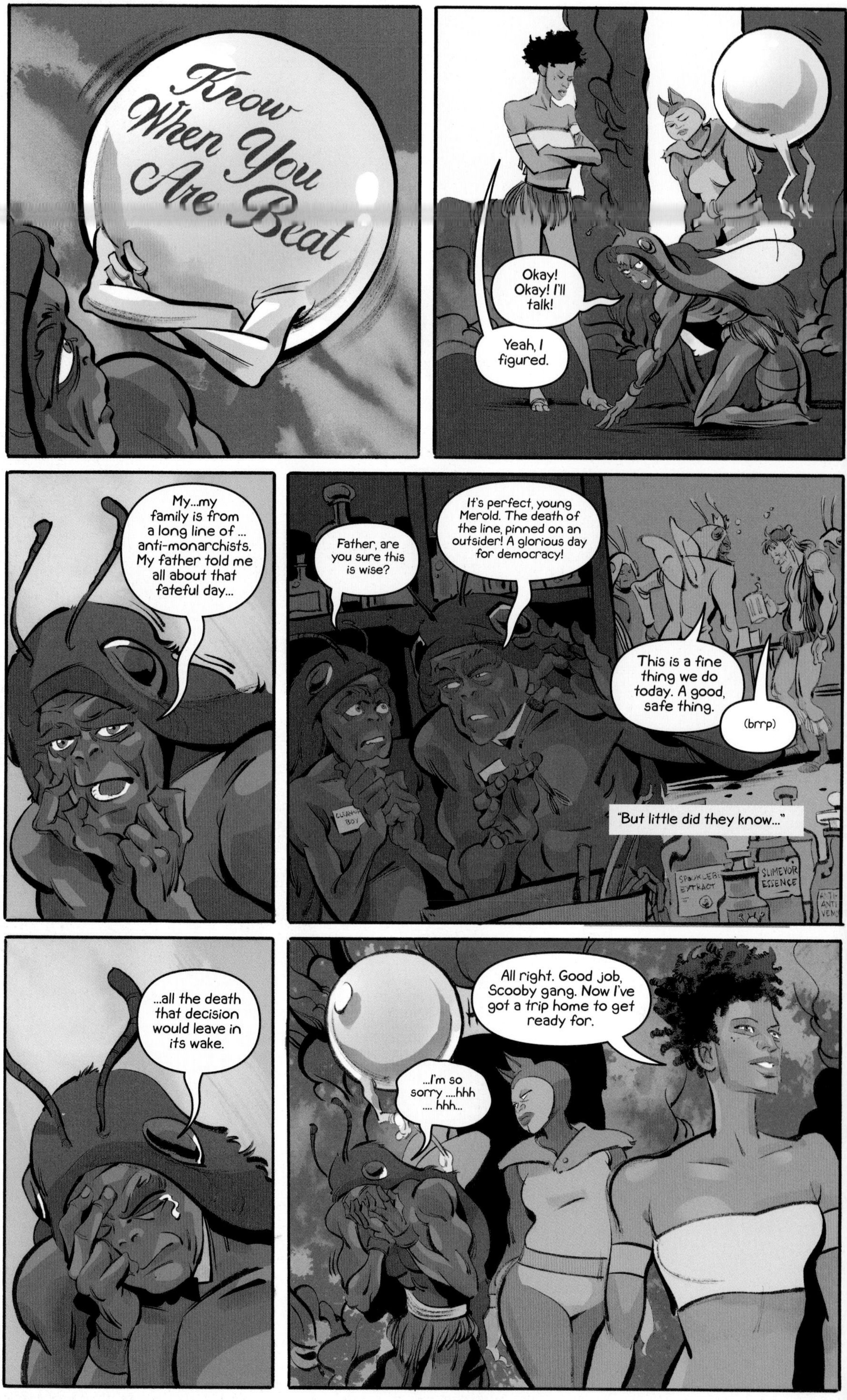

Know When You Are Beat
Okay! Okay! I'll talk!
Yeah, I figured.
My...my family is from a long line of ... anti-monarchists. My father told me all about that fateful day...
Father, are you sure this is wise?
It's perfect, young Merold. The death of the line, pinned on an outsider! A glorious day for democracy!
This is a fine thing we do today. A good, safe thing.
(brrp)
"But little did they know..."
SLIMEVOR ESSENCE
...all the death that decision would leave in its wake.
All right. Good job, Scooby gang. Now I've got a trip home to get ready for.
...I'm so sorry ....hhh .... hhh...

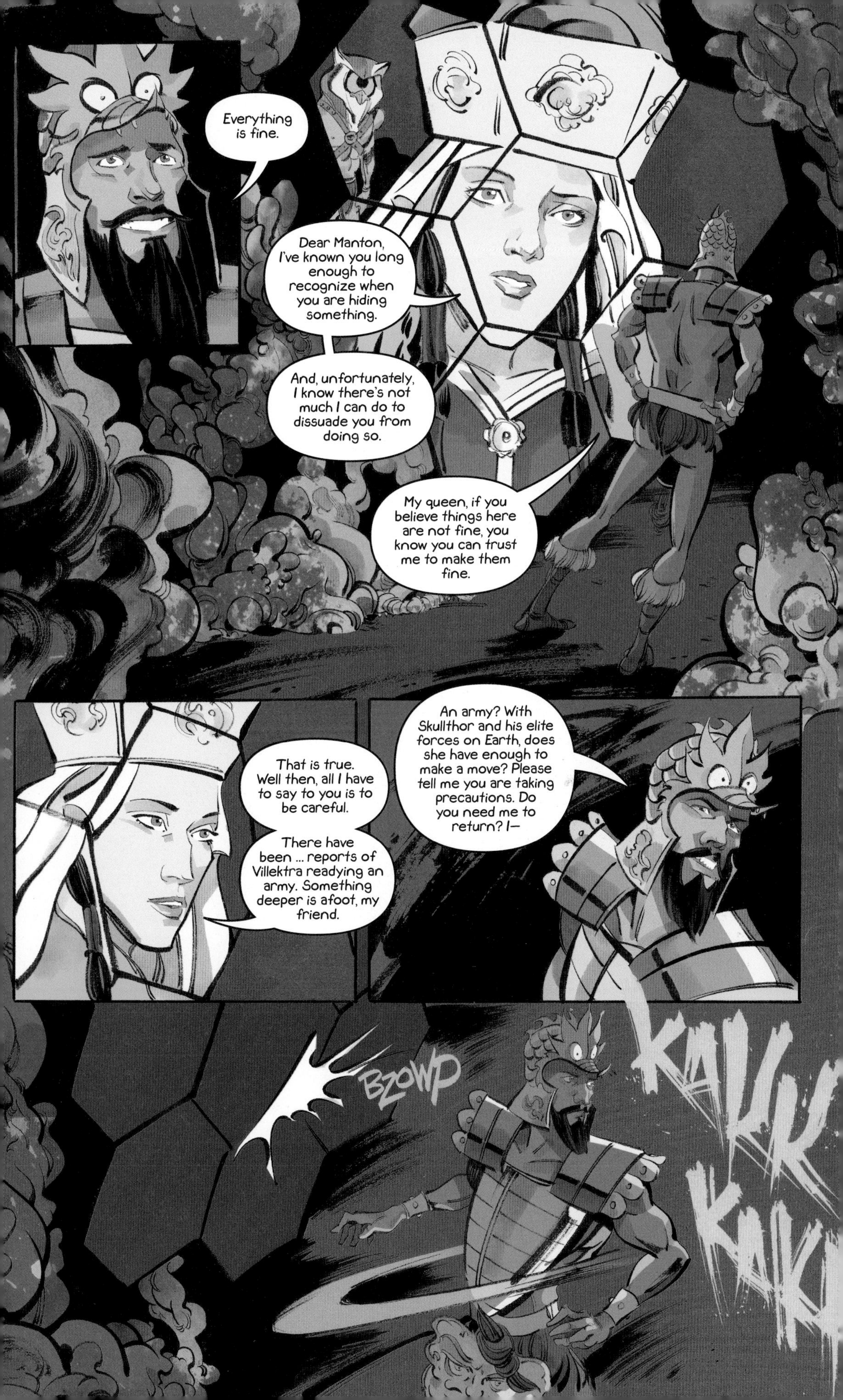

Everything is fine.
Dear Manton, I've known you long enough to recognize when you are hiding something.
And, unfortunately, I know there's not much I can do to dissuade you from doing so.
My queen, if you believe things here are not fine, you know you can trust me to make them fine.
That is true. Well then, all I have to say to you is to be careful.
There have been ... reports of Villektra readying an army. Something deeper is afoot, my friend.
An army? With Skullthor and his elite forces on Earth, does she have enough to make a move? Please tell me you are taking precautions. Do you need me to return? I—
BZOWP

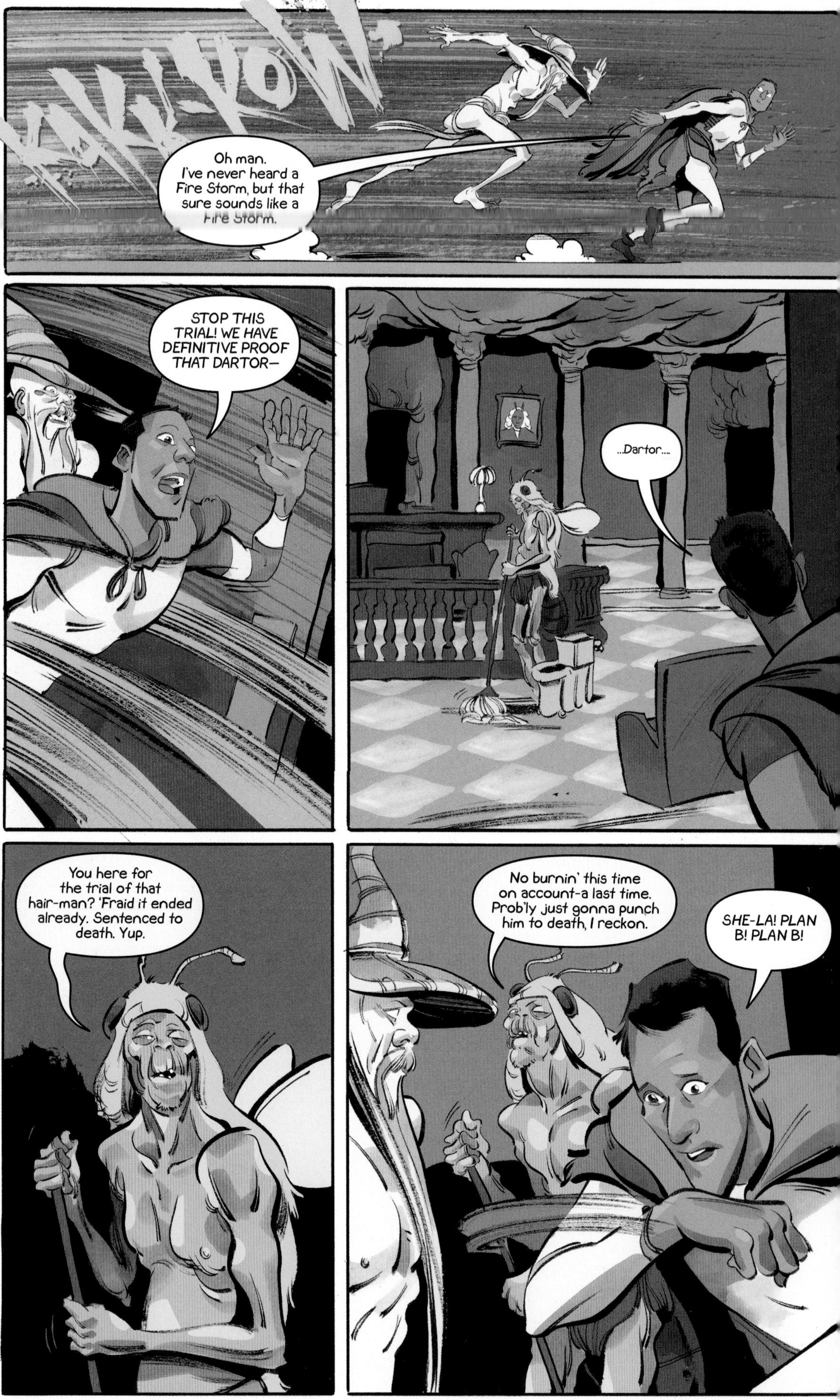
KAK-KOW!
Oh man. I've never heard a Fire Storm, but that sure sounds like a Fire Storm.
STOP THIS TRIAL! WE HAVE DEFINITIVE PROOF THAT DARTOR—
...Dartor....
You here for the trial of that hair-man? 'Fraid it ended already. Sentenced to death. Yup.
No burnin' this time on account-a last time. Prob'ly just gonna punch him to death, I reckon.
SHE-LA! PLAN B! PLAN B!

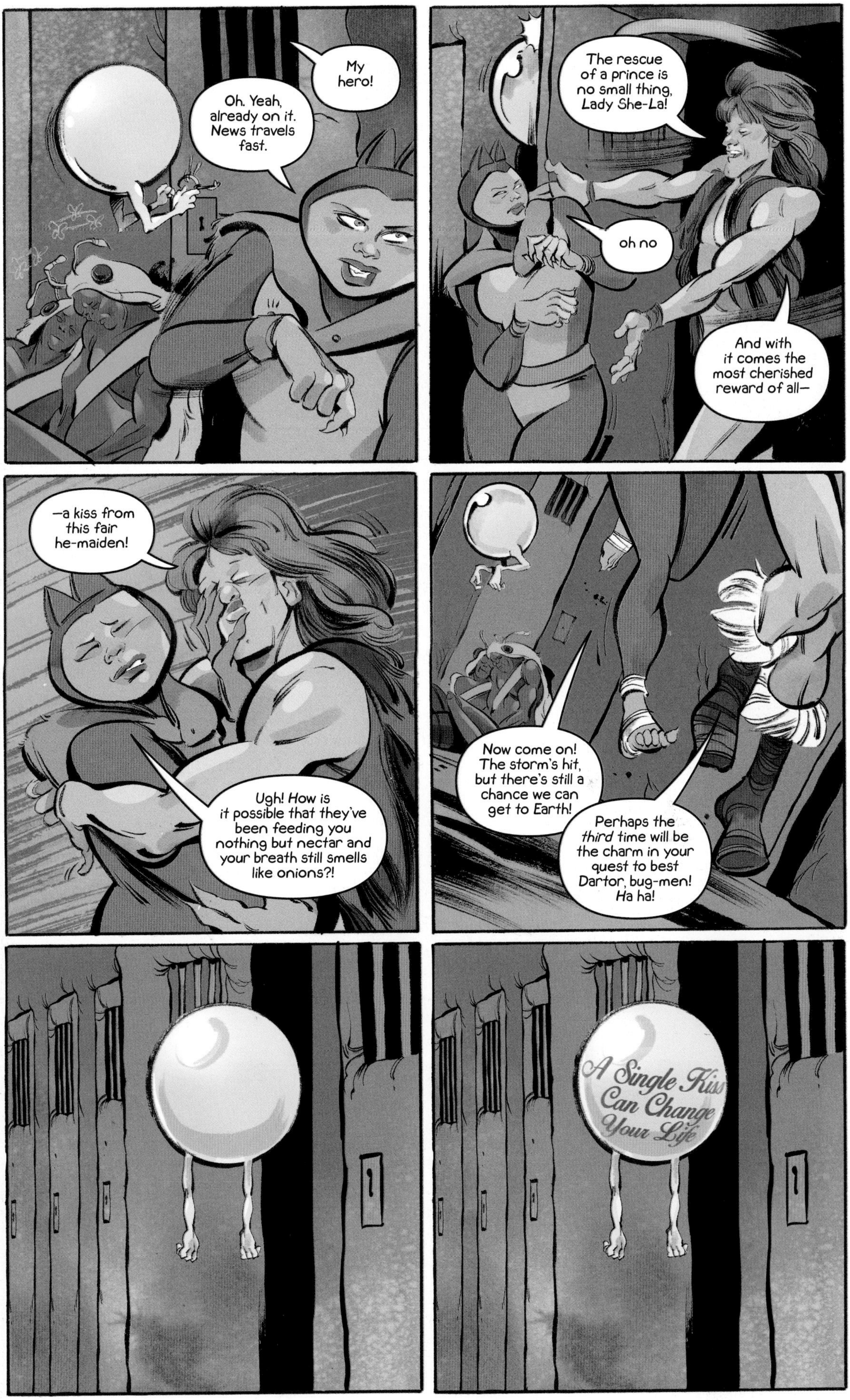

My hero!
Oh. Yeah, already on it. News travels fast.
The rescue of a prince is no small thing, Lady She-La!
oh no
And with it comes the most cherished reward of all—
—a kiss from this fair he-maiden!
Ugh! How is it possible that they've been feeding you nothing but nectar and your breath still smells like onions?!
Now come on! The storm's hit, but there's still a chance we can get to Earth!
Perhaps the third time will be the charm in your quest to best Dartor, bug-men! Ha ha!
A Single Kiss Can Change Your Life

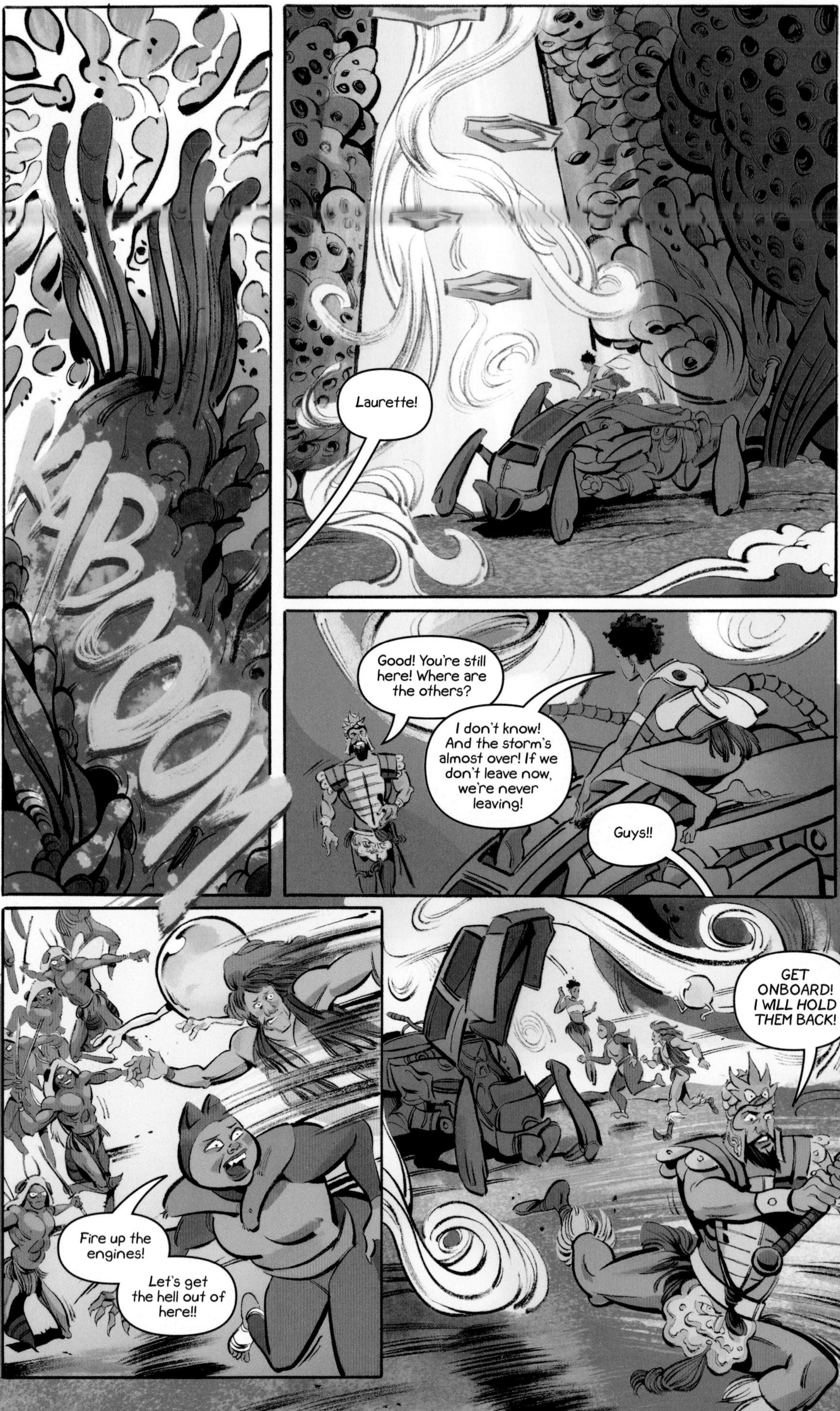
KABOOOOM
Laurette!
Good! You're still here! Where are the others?
I don't know! And the storm's almost over! If we don't leave now, we're never leaving!
Guys!!
Fire up the engines!
Let's get the hell out of here!!
GET ONBOARD! I WILL HOLD THEM BACK!

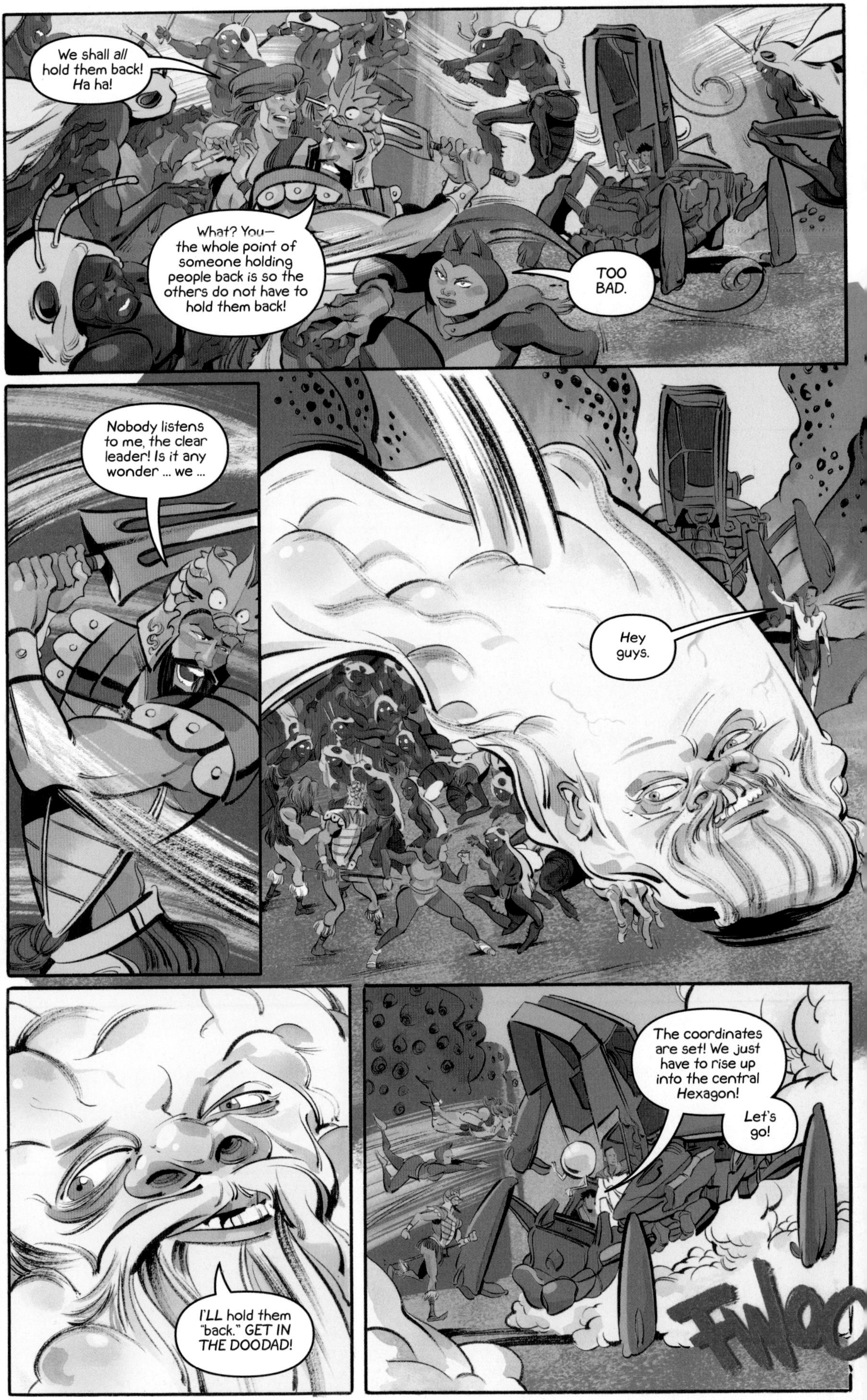
We shall *all* hold them back! *Ha ha!*
What? You— the whole point of someone holding people back is so the others do not have to hold them back!
TOO BAD.
Nobody listens to me, the clear leader! Is it any wonder ... we ...
Hey guys.
I'LL hold them "back." GET IN THE DOODAD!
The coordinates are set! We just have to rise up into the central Hexagon!
Let's go!
FWOO

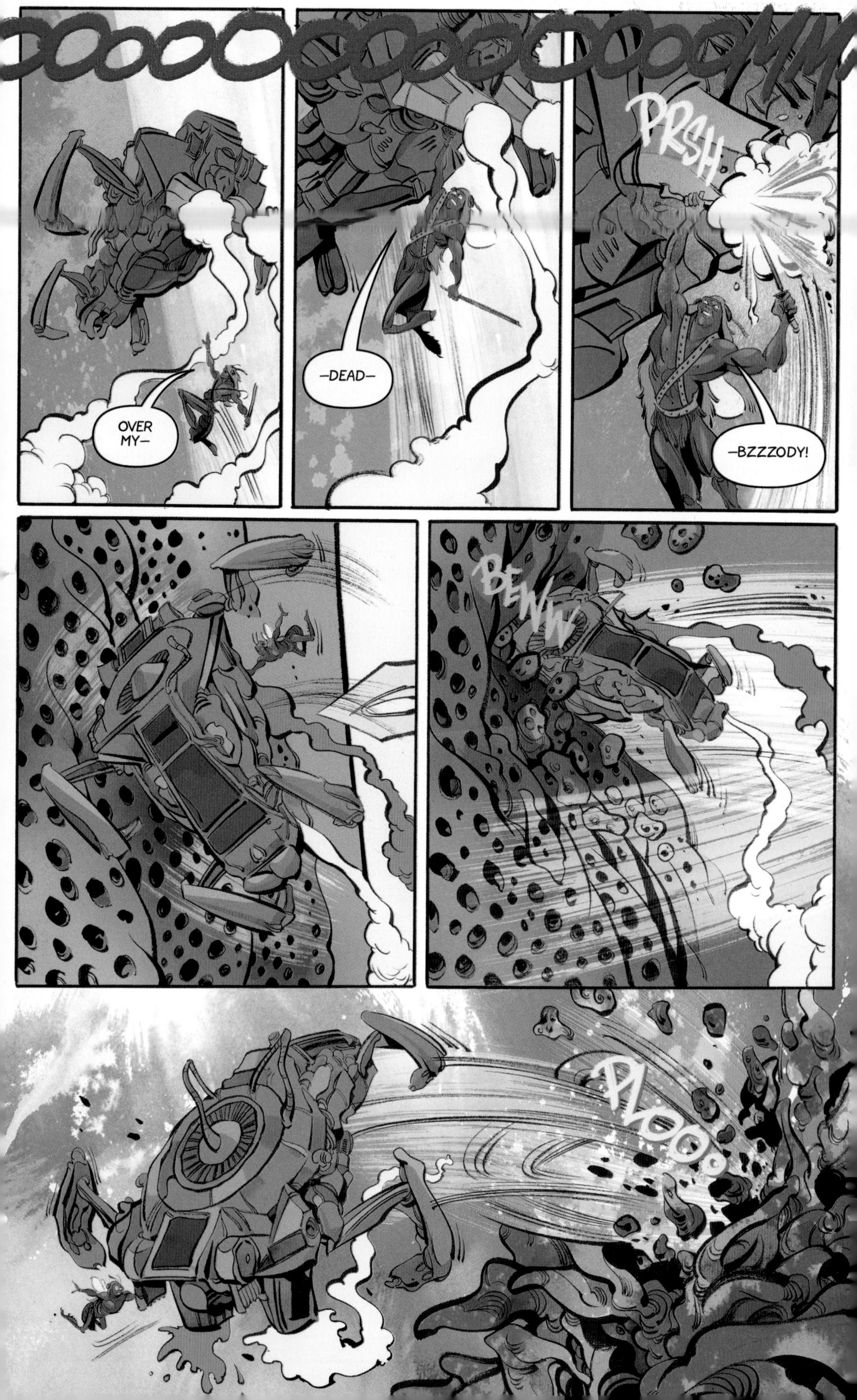
OVER MY—
—DEAD—
PRSH
—BZZZODY!

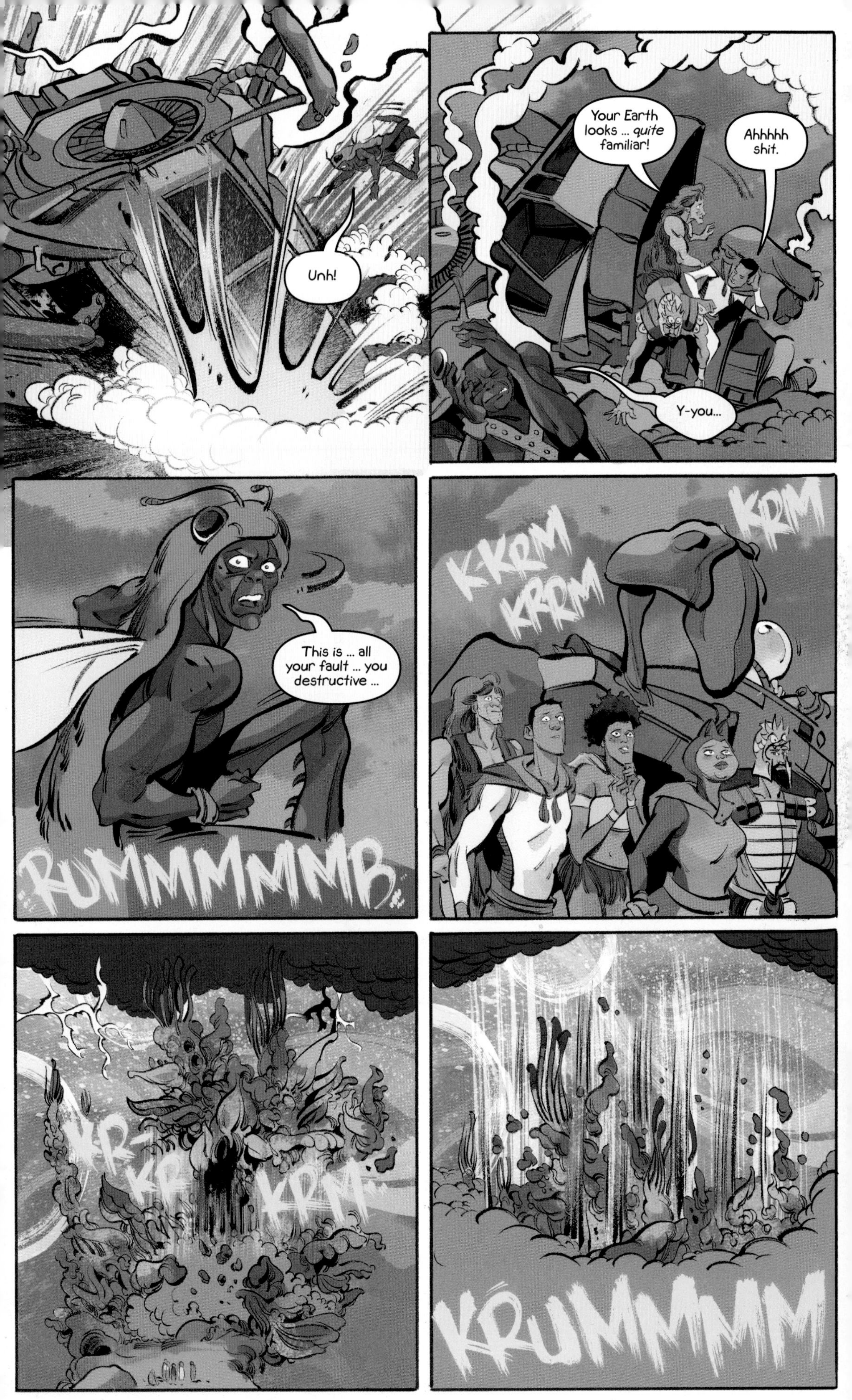
Unh!
Your Earth looks ... *quite* familiar!
Ahhhhh shit.
Y-you...
This is ... all your fault ... you destructive ...
RUMMMMMB
K-KRM KRRM
KRM
KR-KR KRM
KRUMMMM

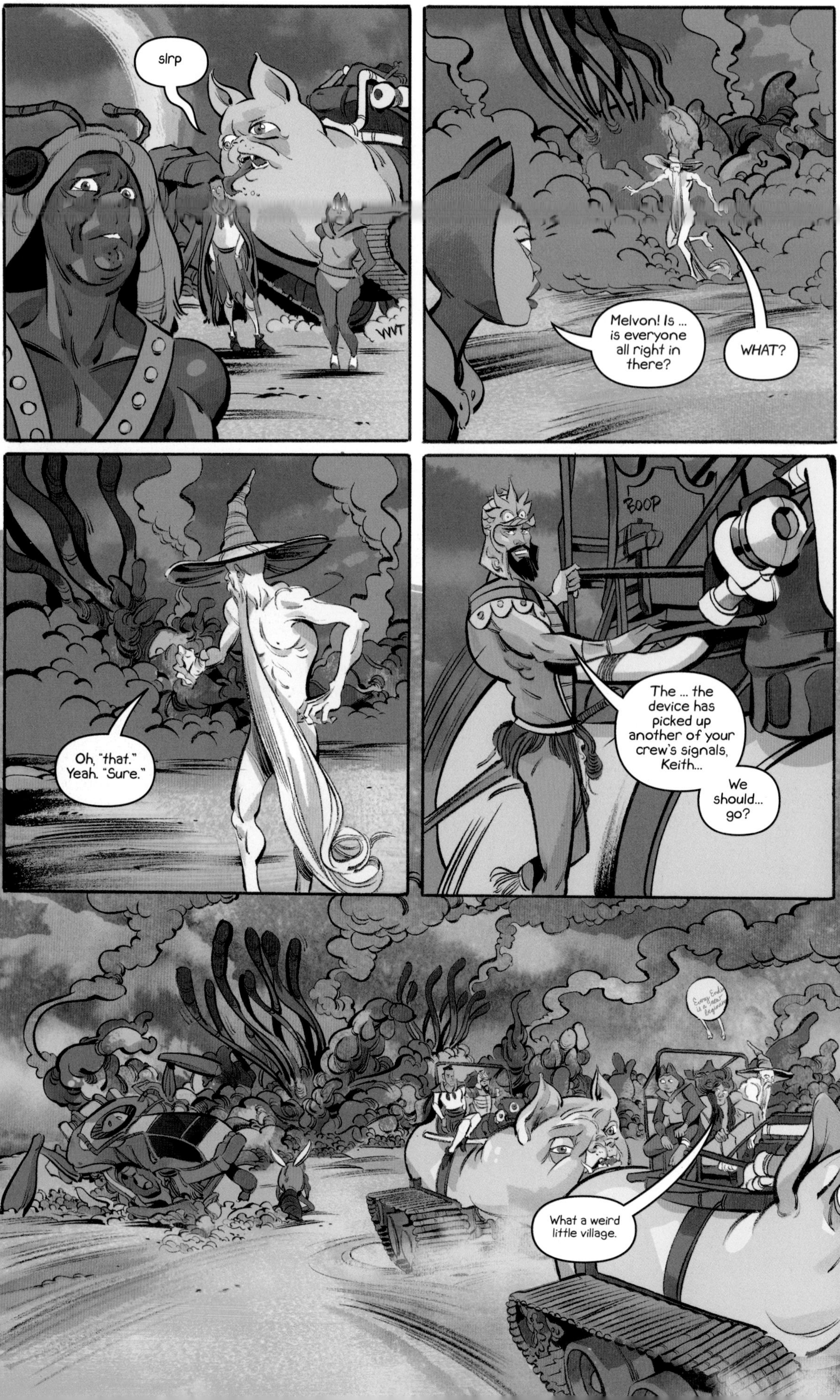
slrp
WVT
Melvon! Is ... is everyone all right in there?
WHAT?
Oh, "that." Yeah. "Sure."
BOOP
The ... the device has picked up another of your crew's signals, Keith...
We should... go?
What a weird little village.

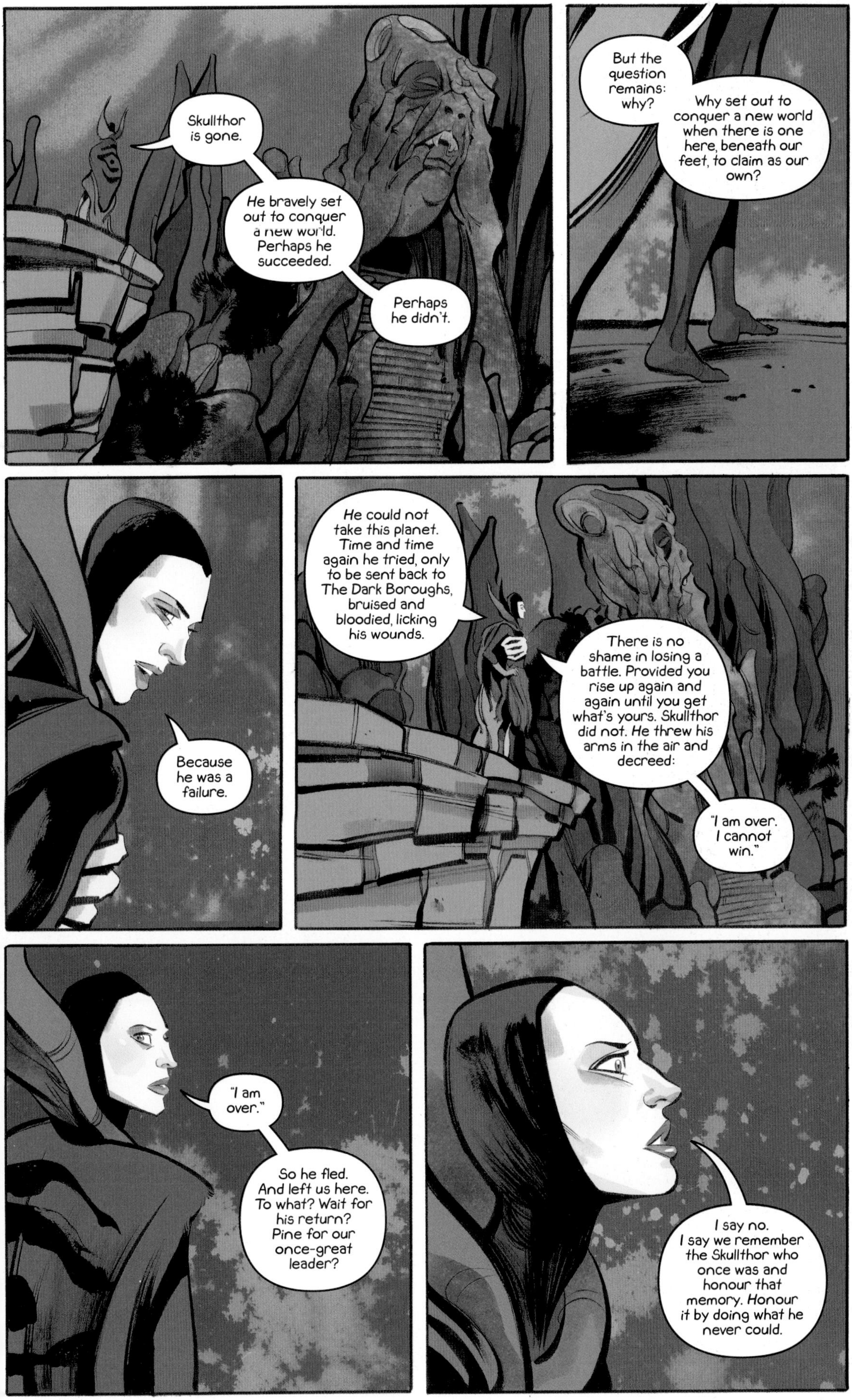

Skullthor is gone.
He bravely set out to conquer a new world. Perhaps he succeeded.
Perhaps he didn't.
But the question remains: why?
Why set out to conquer a new world when there is one here, beneath our feet, to claim as our own?
Because he was a failure.
He could not take this planet. Time and time again he tried, only to be sent back to The Dark Boroughs, bruised and bloodied, licking his wounds.
There is no shame in losing a battle. Provided you rise up again and again until you get what's yours. Skullthor did not. He threw his arms in the air and decreed:
"I am over. I cannot win."
"I am over."
So he fled. And left us here. To what? Wait for his return? Pine for our once-great leader?
I say no. I say we remember the Skullthor who once was and honour that memory. Honour it by doing what he never could.

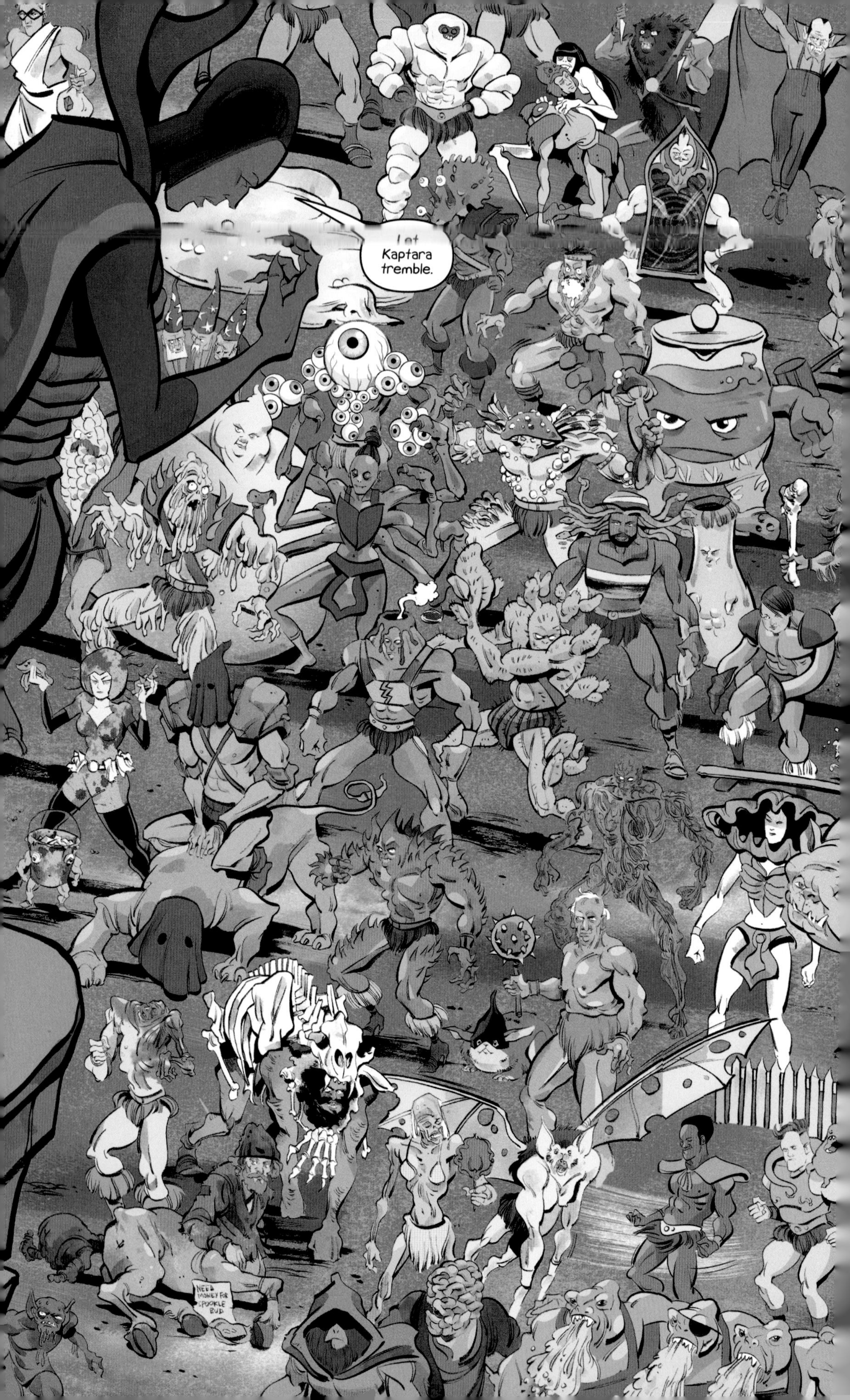
Let Kaptara tremble.
NEED MONEY FOR SPOOKLE BUD

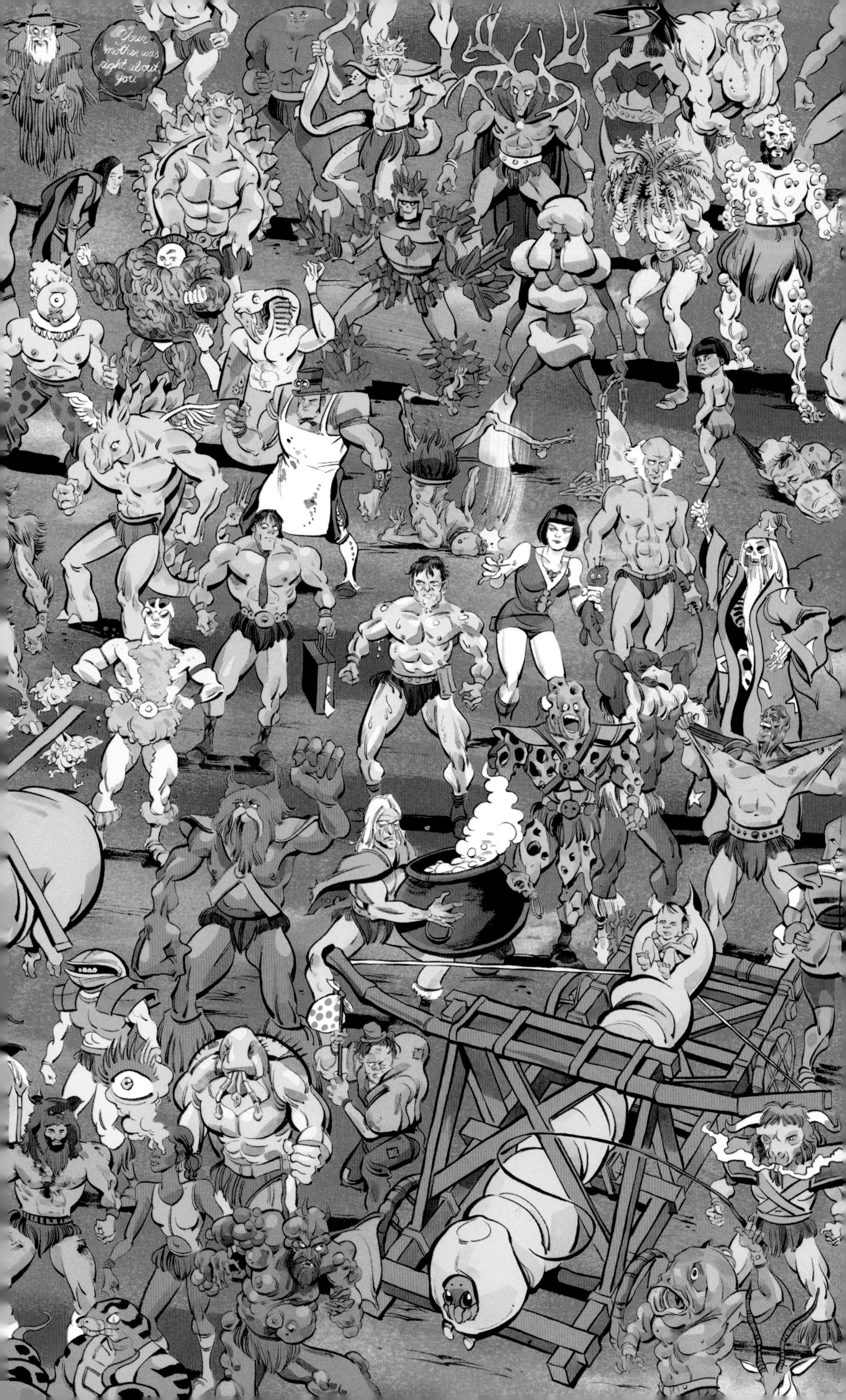
Your mother was right about you

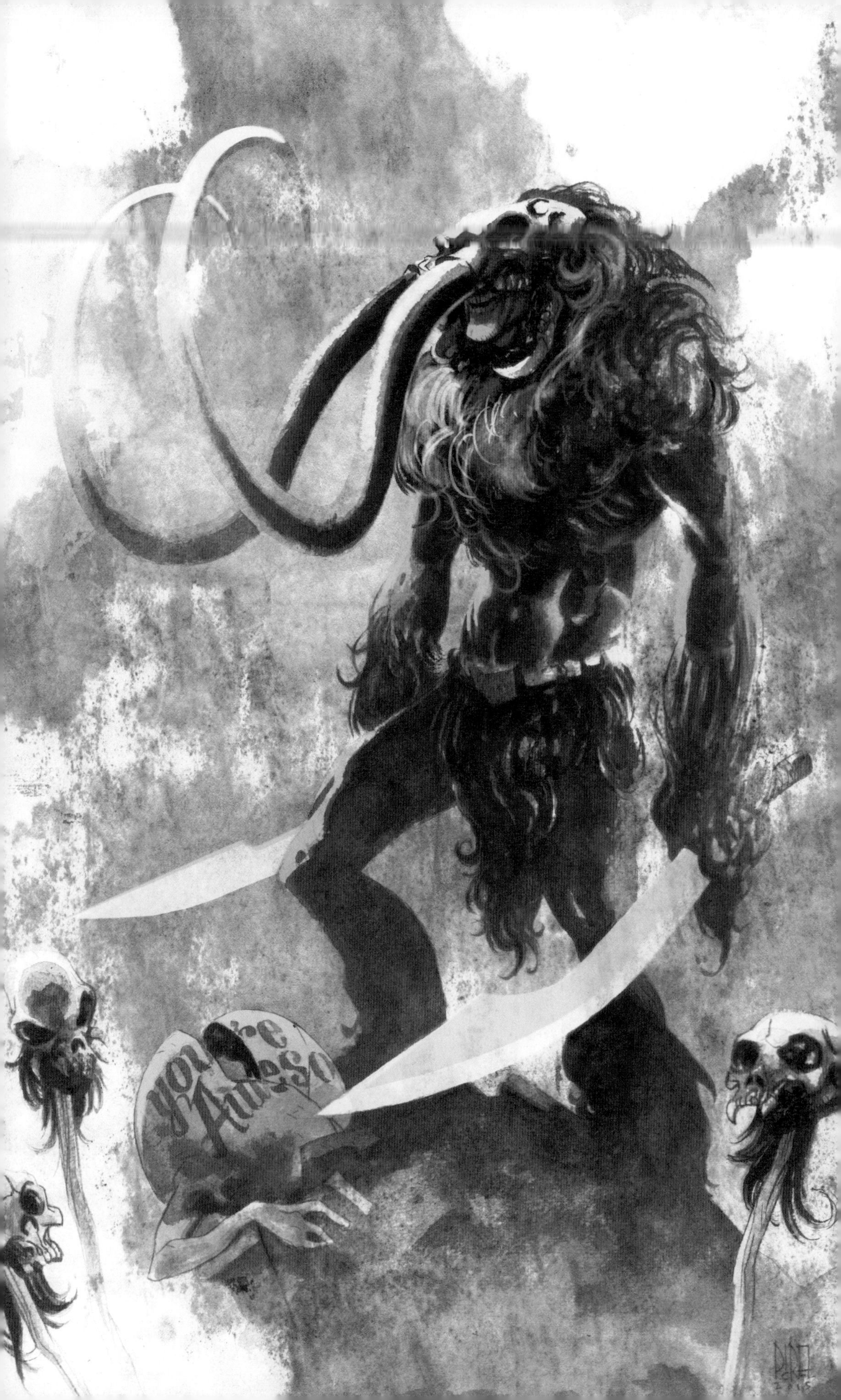

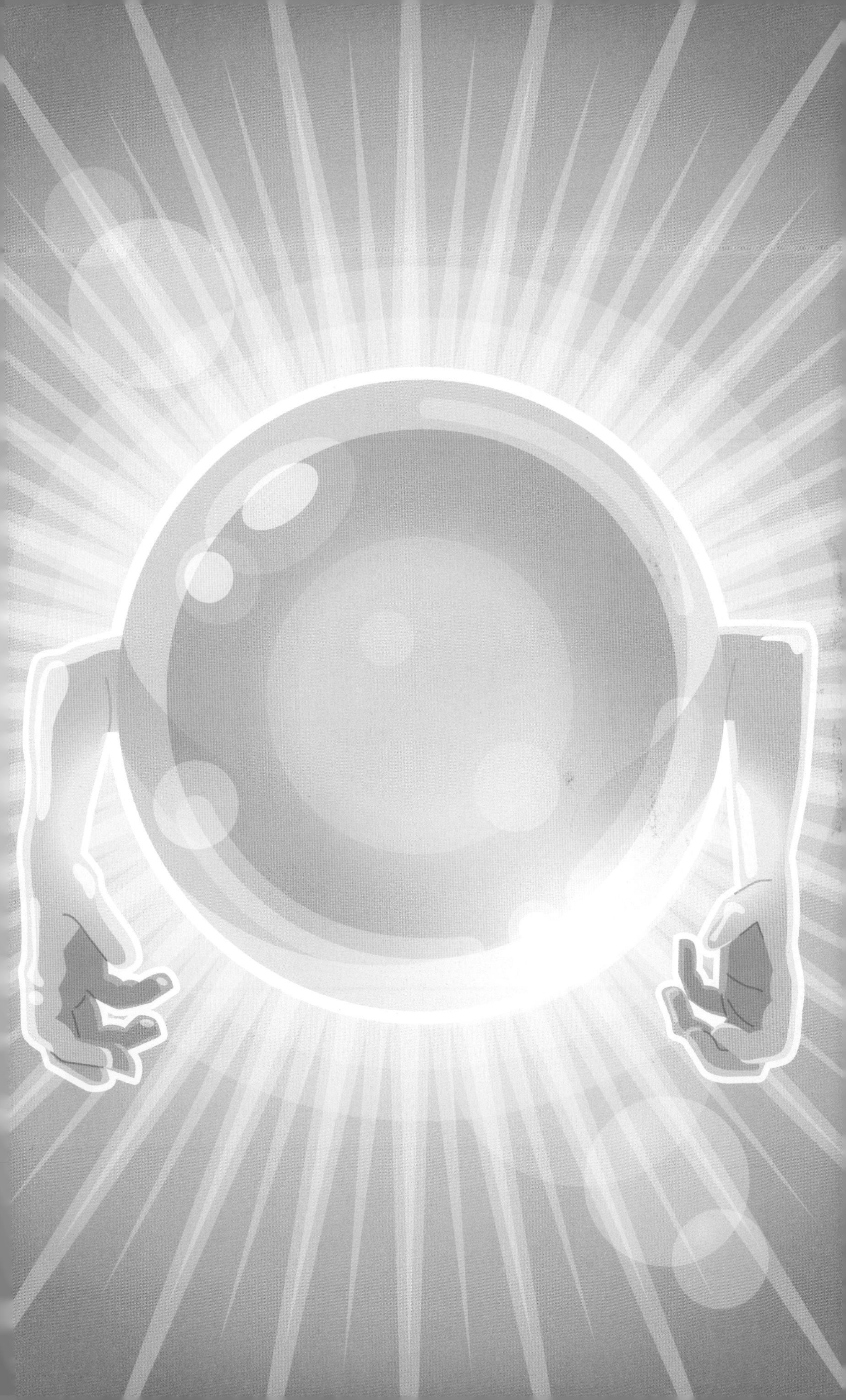

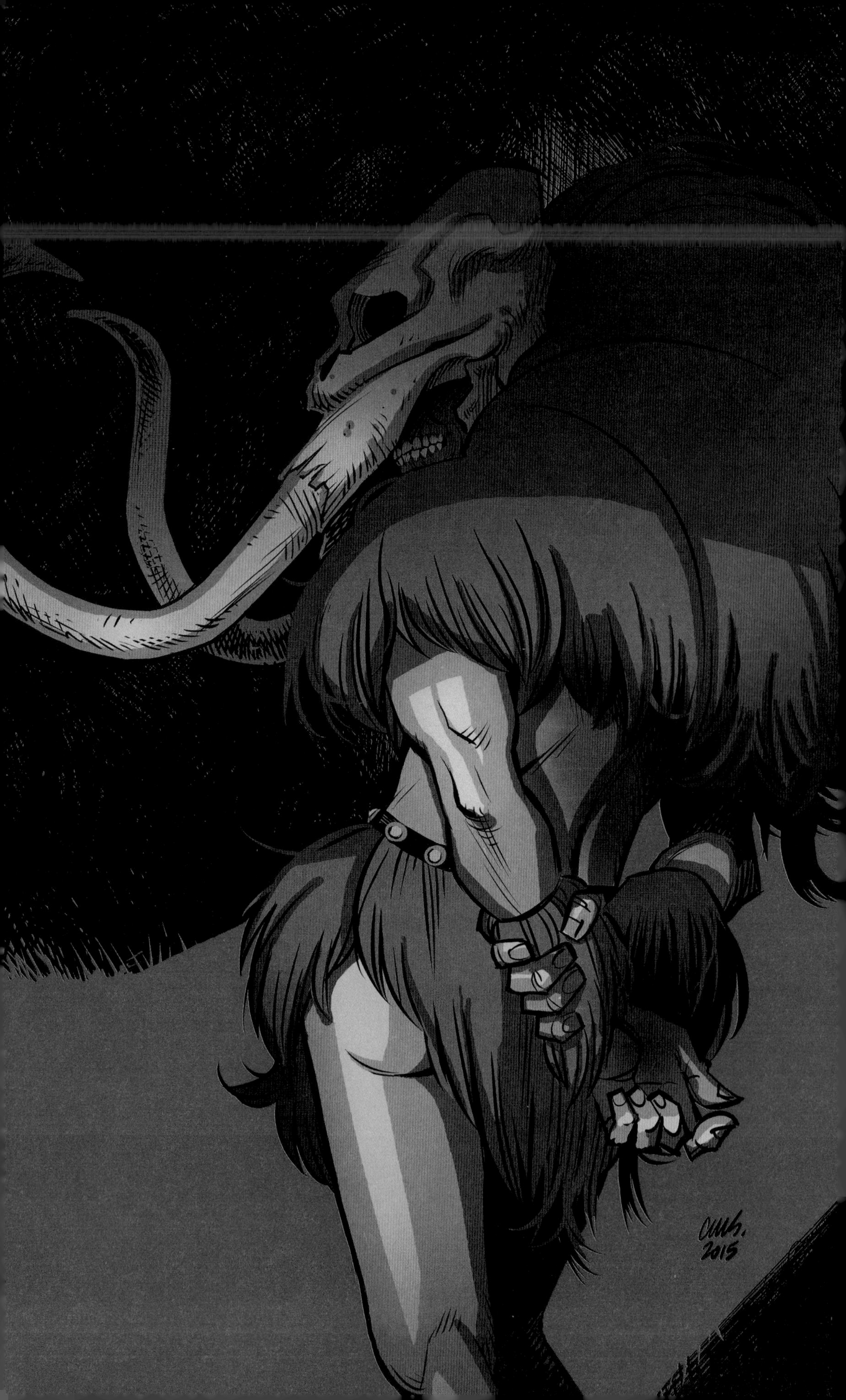
2015

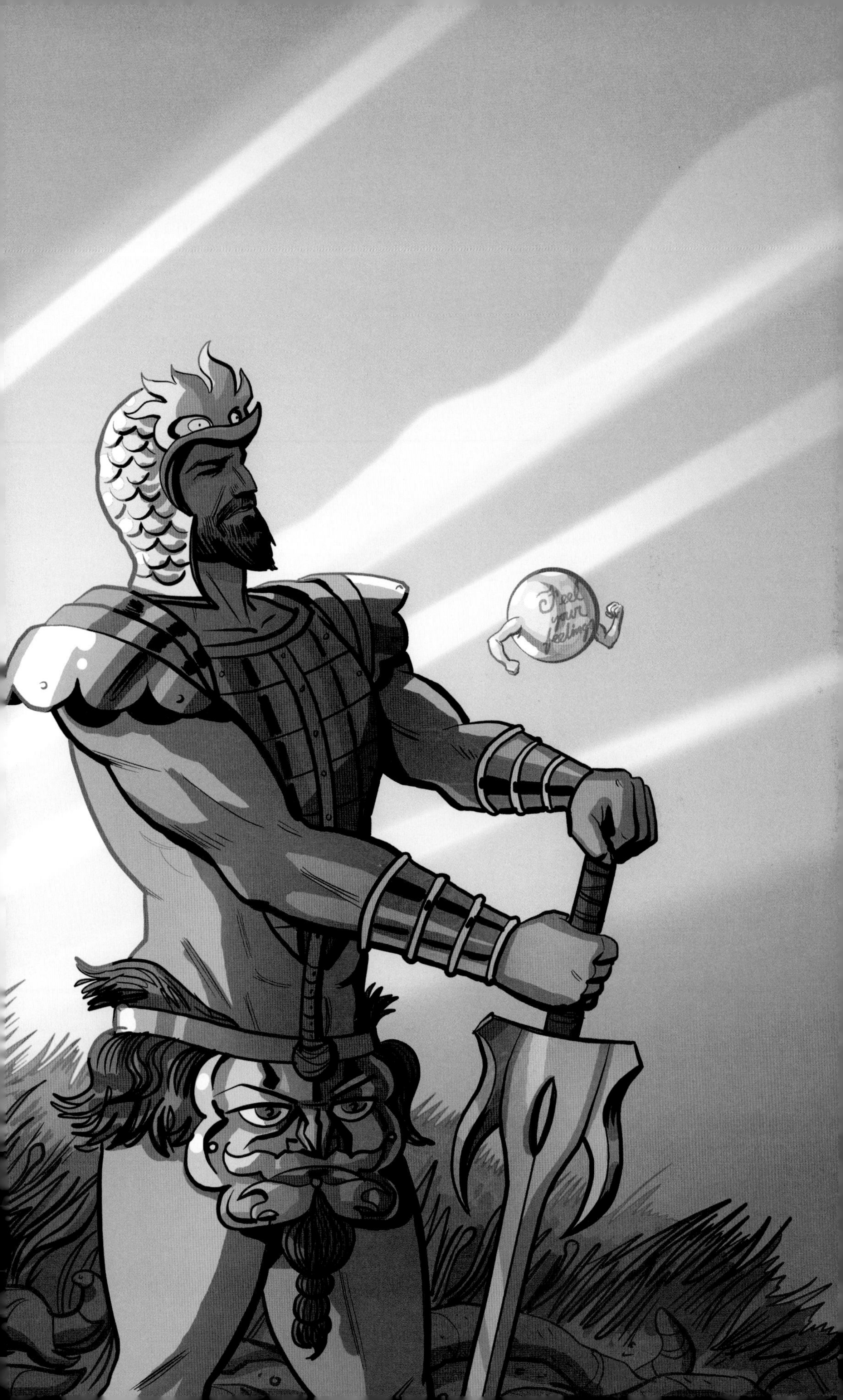
Feel your feelings

A HORDE TOUR

Bone up on barbaric brutes with this Kaptaran rogues' gallery

Villektra has gathered the most nefarious evil warriors in the land! But what's their deal? What are their hopes and dreams? How much can they bench press? We can only scratch their terrible surfaces here, but I think you'll agree: They're scary!

JEWELIUS SEIZURE
CLASSIFICATION: Classical Thief

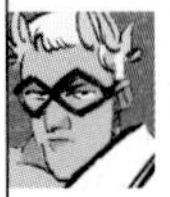

Protect your pockets! This ne'er-do-well is known for stealing all the treasure from your chest, including your heart! Literally! He collects human hearts.

MUSCULARVA
CLASSIFICATION: Shredded Grub

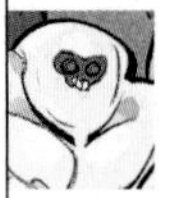

Every time Muscularva flexes, BRAND NEW MUSCULARVAS emerge from his larva muscles! But they are only babies and very useless and needy on the battlefield.

TORMENTULA
CLASSIFICATION: Spousicidal Seductress

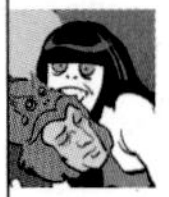

Known for public displays of arachnid affection, Tormentula shrugs off repulsed passersby as strait-laced prudes. Then she tears off her lover's head and eats it.

TARANTULORD
CLASSIFICATION: Arachnoid Patsy

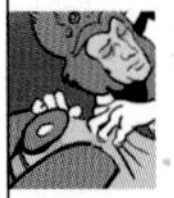

Drawn into Tormentula's web of seduction, unsuspecting Kaptaran men are convinced to don the sacred garb of the Tarantulord, only to meet their fates during eerie mating rituals.

STABBIN' WOLF
CLASSIFICATION: Lupine Knife Enthusiast

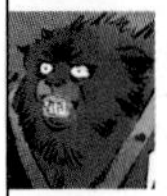

Born with a degenerative disease which turned his fangs into floppy jelly. Stabbin' Wolf trained for years to become a ninth-level master of stabbing!

BOSSFERATU
CLASSIFICATION: Doddering Bloodsucker

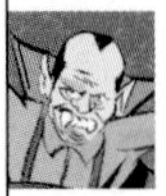

A local senior-citizen mafia leader who was bitten by another mafia leader (who happened to be a vampire). Bossferatu now controls Kaptara's garbage disposal business ... at night!

PROSPECTRE
CLASSIFICATION: Incorporeal Mountain Man

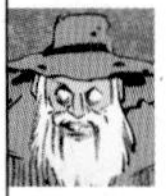

A grizzled and ghastly apparition with a thirst for precious metals, Prospectre will gut you with a pan (since he once heard that some people have "hearts of gold").

VICIOUS CIRCLE
CLASSIFICATION: Discouraging Globule

Your mother was right about you

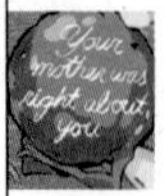

Motivational Orb's arch-enemy, Vicious Circle will highlight your greatest disappointments like a real jerk. Hot-blooded, cold-hearted, heavy-handed, no-legged.

JUGGERNECK
CLASSIFICATION: Headless Humanoid

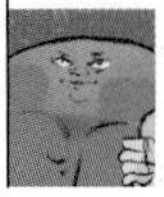

With no head to worry about, Juggerneck focuses on his body! He prides himself on never having to decide whether to get an earring, or to duck when passing through a low doorway.

SLIZZARD
CLASSIFICATION: Reptilian Phlebotomizer

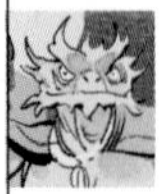

A wild, slippery contortionist, it would be almost impossible to grab Slizzard if it wasn't for his 8-foot-long, weak and dry tail. It's incredibly cumbersome! Though it has razors.

MANTLER
CLASSIFICATION: Cervoid Tyrant

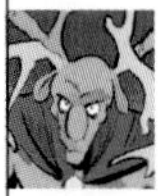

When you see Mantler charging at you with his sharp and massive antlers, you'd better pray you're on the other side of a doorway because he is NO good at navigating those.

STARK RAVEN
CLASSIFICATION: Avian Lunatic

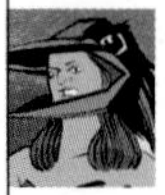

A formidable fighter, Stark Raven has been known to screech high-pitched whines at her enemies just before shitting on them in battle!

GROTESTICLEEZ
CLASSIFICATION: Amorphodermic Grappler

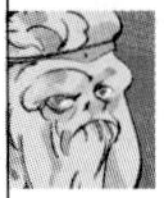

Anyone who ends up face to face with Grotesticleez usually runs away in terror! But if you can overcome that, just the lightest tap will force this monster to collapse in pain!

S.P.U.M.E
CLASSIFICATION: Unstoppable Mucoid Entity

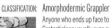

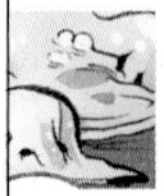

Created in one of Kaptara's seedy underground laboratories, S.P.U.M.E. stands for Science Project: Unstoppable Mucoid Entity*. 'Nuff said.

* Created by Mike Faille

TRICERACLOPS
CLASSIFICATION: Trinocular Chasmosaur

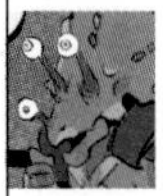

A powerful warrior who has three eyes instead of the usual two! What can he do with the third eye? Nobody knows, but SOME say it does very little.

BERZERKULES
CLASSIFICATION: Rabid Muscleman

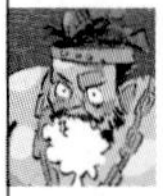

One of the strongest villains in the land, Berzerkules is wildly unpredictable! Will he punch you to death? Do your taxes? Fall asleep? Impossible to know!

DEFENESTRATOR
CLASSIFICATION: Aggressive Window

A human window, Defenestrator will grab his enemies and smash them through the regenerating glass of his portal-torso! His catchprase? "Bring the pane!"

TRAUMADERY
CLASSIFICATION: Intense Ungulate

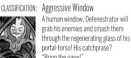

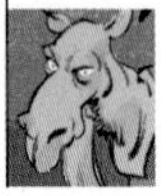

His mantra? "Hump and thump." His other mantra? "I can survive almost seven months without water by extracting energy from the fat reserves in my noticeable hump."

TEEN FIEND
CLASSIFICATION: Sullen Scoundrel

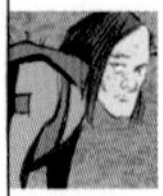

ugh who cares

PREDATORTOISE
CLASSIFICATION: Carnivorous Testudine

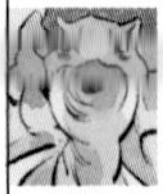

He's over 400 years old and ready to kick ass! And how does he do that? By retreating into his terrifying, impenetrable shell and waiting for you to die!

AMEFYST
CLASSIFICATION: Crystalline Pugilist

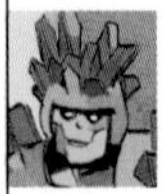

Amefyst shoots beautiful, rare crystals from his massive fists! Will you fight him? Or collect those crystals and pay off your mortgage? While you decide, Amefyst strikes!

BRUTLE
CLASSIFICATION: Elegant Barbarian Dog-Woman

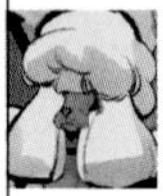

She's vicious! She's fast! She poops everywhere! A runway model turned prize fighter, Brutle will trick you with her elegance and then bite down. Hard. Watch out for her Groomstick™.

FERNUS
CLASSIFICATION: Ornamental Spy

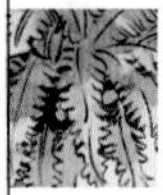

Provided your enemies are holding secret talks where ferns are present, Fernus is the perfect camouflaged intelligence agent. Ever loyal, in-group treachery makes his fiddleheads unfurl.

MUMP
CLASSIFICATION: Contagious Wrestler

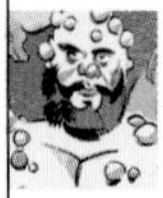

Mump's trademark mumps are highly contagious! But they also give him muscle pain, fever, headaches and lethargy, so it's not too hard to stay ahead of him.

SORCERBERUS
CLASSIFICATION: Three-Headed Wizard

Three heads are better than one, so beware the magical spells of Sorcerberus! Except ONE of the heads does all the work and the other two are inept! Strike wisely!

THREATINA
CLASSIFICATION: All-Seeing Gal

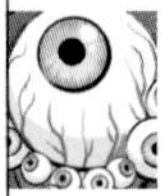

Threatina sees all! And it has driven her MAD! She really can't cope with it all, so she lashes out in a not-so-blind fury at the drop of a hat! Often stands close to Thornicus to cause general unease.

BUNGUS
CLASSIFICATION: Fungal Bungler

This cool "fun guy" sprouts up anywhere things seem to going really well and promptly bungs it all up. He has an air of superiority, as well as hallucinogenic pungence .

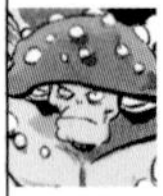

BRUTE PUNCH
CLASSIFICATION: Combative Pitcher of "Juice"

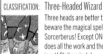

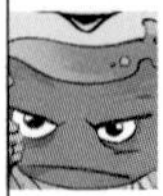

He's a good father, a devoted husband, and a jug filled with burning-acid blood! Known for bursting through the walls of death cult meetings.

CYCLOWN
CLASSIFICATION: Kaptara's Monocular Funnyman

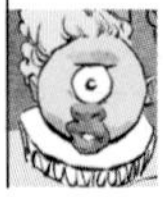

Why so serious? Is it because Cyclown is telling his trademark "jokes," which are quite bad? Well, you'd better laugh or he'll kill you. Also, he has one eye!

BEEFMASTER
CLASSIFICATION: Man Meat

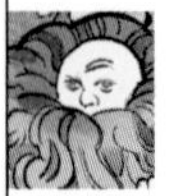

Born with the ability to control fresh, unliving beef, Beefmaster travels everywhere with choice ground chuck which he can hurl at enemies using th power of his MIND.

HYSSSTERIOR
CLASSIFICATION: Delirious Serpent

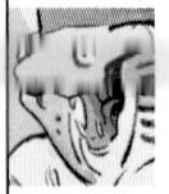

You want Hyssterior to calm down? Good luck! Once he plunges into a fit, fangs fly and scales swirl at the cente of a toxic cloud of venom mist. On Kaptara's no-fly list.

DECAPITOT
CLASSIFICATION: Infant Executioner

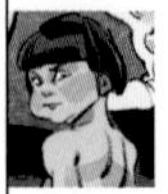

Someone's been a baaaad boy! Sorry, that seems a little flippant sinc Decapitot has taken the heads of over 200 people. No one knows why because no one has survived asking.

COLONEL COBULUS
CLASSIFICATION: CLASSIFIED

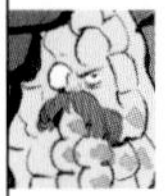

A military mind like no other, Col. Cobulus is highly decorated (and highly decorative in the fall). He can feed his infantry from his own beautiful, replenishable corn body.

SLIMEVOR
CLASSIFICATION: Ceaseless Secreter

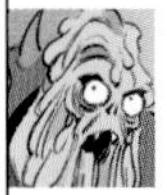

Working for Villektra as part of what calls "the Secretion Service," Slimev once wronged by Dartor, spends his time plotting assassinations in a poo of his muculent discharge.

FLABBERGHOST
CLASSIFICATION: Morbidly at Peace

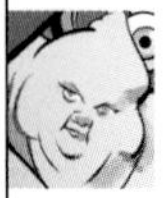

He's the ghost with the most... body mass, that is! Flabberghost has eate hundreds of ghosts, and now has moved on to pre-ghosts, AKA huma beings!

SPYDRA
CLASSIFICATION: Arachnid Madam

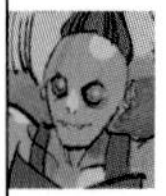

Eight arms, but no opposable thumb Spydra can't even hold a fork. But c one of her limbs and another grows place, keeping her amply equipped hurt or tickle you in up to eight place

DREDUSA
CLASSIFICATION: Rasta Rattler

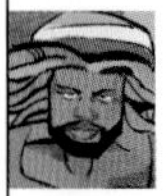

If you catch the eye of Dredusa's sn dreads, beware! But don't worry ab him, as he's been bitten so many tin by his hair he can barely move!

MANNON THE HUMAN CANNON
CLASSIFICATION: Long-Distance Relationships

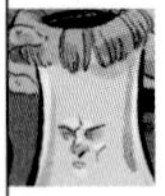

Fill him with balls and watch him explode! Unfortunately, Mannon's t arms are useless when it comes to ball-filling, so he needs a friend with ramrod in battle or he'll surely die.

MANGIAC
CLASSIFICATION: Feral Canine Man

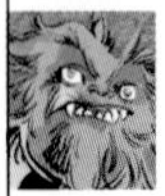

It's not the breed of Mangiac, it's th way he was raised. And he was raise really, really poorly, so watch out. P he's had all his shots... of fermente fusciabeast milk (he's drunk).

STEGASUS
CLASSIFICATION: Winged Dino-Man

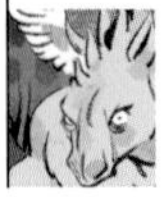

What's that down there?
Just a dinosaur. Can't get us up he
WAIT, HE HAS WINGS.
...
Oh no.

THE STEAMLAND CLEAVER

CLASSIFICATION: Steam-Powered Butcher

The only thing more dangerous than a cleaver is a STEAM-POWERED cleaver! I mean, I guess there are other things more dangerous than that, but The Steamland Cleaver doesn't think so.

NECROFAIL

CLASSIFICATION: Blundering Cadaver

Wildly clumsy in life, Necrofail couldn't even die right, so now he roams Kaptara, fumbling about and menacing citizens. He is also their top-grossing movie star for the past three years.

UNCLE SCOURGE

CLASSIFICATION: Stingy Sadist

If you try to steal his gold, he'll pin you to his Ouchie Table! And if you cry "Uncle" he'll only hurt you worse! And his greatest secret? He has no brothers or sisters.

ELVIRAL

CLASSIFICATION: Mistress of Rags

Elviral does battle using germ-covered rags, supplied by her sidekick, Pump Pail. You may win the battle, but in two weeks you'll be in rough shape unless you hit the Vitamin C, bro.

BOULDERGEIST

CLASSIFICATION: Rock of Faces?

There's no visible reason he's called "Bouldergeist," so people assume he has a rock-encrusted face under his hood. Why wouldn't he just show us so we can get past this name confusion?

PHANTICORE

CLASSIFICATION: Bouldergeist Buddy

Bouldergeist rides this beast, who also has a hood for some reason. His body's hideous, so is his face very beautiful? Trying to figure it out will drive you mad, and THAT'S when they kill you.

LAVALANCHE

CLASSIFICATION: Top Blower

This guy's a real hothead! Ha ha ha! Interesting fact: The lava Lavalanche produces is actually white, but he treats it with red dye because he thinks it just looks better.

SMACKTUS

CLASSIFICATION: Cacti Guy

Half man, half cactus, all Smacktus! This nefarious brute is filled with a thick, viscous liquid which could save your life in the desert, but fat chance of convincing him to give it up!

MR. KISSES

CLASSIFICATION: Lip Lash

His hands are lips! And when they come together and pucker up they become a powerful battering ram! Also, they have a mild case of herpes.

PHLEGMLINS

CLASSIFICATION: Hobgoblins of hork

Story has it these beasts were coughed up by a Dry Dragon after an encounter with Elviral! Another story insists they're actually made of delicious, sweet gelatin! Only one way to find out!

SPORDAK

CLASSIFICATION: Spore loser

While his body produces traditionally asexual spores which can suffocate his enemies, Spordak insists he is VERY sexual, like he has something to prove?

BRIEFCAKE

CLASSIFICATION: Musclebound Businessman

Briefcake was a simple barbarian until bitten by a businessman during a sexual encounter. He insists the bite gave him business powers, but really he just killed the guy and stole his briefcase.

GREASEDMASTER

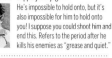

CLASSIFICATION: Slippery Subjugator

He's impossible to hold onto, but it's also impossible for him to hold onto you! I suppose you could shoot him and end this. Refers to the period after he kills his enemies as "grease and quiet."

HEXUS

CLASSIFICATION: Cursing Queen

Bad things will befall you if you go up against Hexus! Or maybe it's just coincidence! Guess it depends whether you believe in that stuff or not.

SPELLETON

CLASSIFICATION: Bone Wizard

A great magician, Spelleton can do almost anything, except make his crystal-clear skin, organs and blood visible! His wife almost leaves him every single day!

THORNICUS

CLASSIFICATION: Barbedbarian

Every rose has its thorn, and it's true for Thornicus. His wife, Morosebud, is a super lady who really keeps him grounded, especially since she has to stay in one place for her entire life.

VEINIAC

CLASSIFICATION: So Vein

Don't let Veiniac sink his veins into you! He drains blood with them to feed his large heart! That heart is literal AND metaphorical as he donates his free time to the local children's hospital!

CLAMAZON

CLASSIFICATION: Clammy Ma'am

Her face is made of beautiful pearl and is priceless, but good luck getting past her clam! Once it shuts it's closed for about three hours, forcing her to fumble about blind in a panic!

HELI-KITTY

CLASSIFICATION: Apocalypse Meow

A cat tank with trust issues, Heli-Kitty took to the skies instead, to avoid helping others. He is known to expel fiery defecations onto an unsuspecting populace.

FISTOPHELES

CLASSIFICATION: Feline Fighter

Due to an allergic reaction to his own fur, Fistopheles' hands swelled to ten times their normal size! And what do you do with large hands? You punch people for money, of course!

SCALDRON

CLASSIFICATION: Thermogenic Warlock

A master of scalding liquids, Scaldron insists his superpower is the ability to hold very hot items, but the look on his face as he carries his battle cauldron indicates that's surely not the case.

AGHASTEROID

CLASSIFICATION: Awestruck Spacerock

Crash landed on Kaptara years ago, Aghasteroid is constantly stunned at the behaviour of the planet's denizens, despite his own boorish conduct.

RAZZAMATAZZARD

CLASSIFICATION: Birdy Dancer

Due to a mixup at the orphanage, this buff buzzard was raised by exotic dancers instead of exotic birds. His dance abilities dazzle his enemies moments before he goes in for the kill!

FLAYTALITY

CLASSIFICATION: Next of Skin

Cursed with skin that explodes every 15 minutes, Flaytality needs to constantly skin himself or he'll die! But don't feel bad for him; he usually tosses his exploding skin at orphanages!

THE SHRIVELLER

CLASSIFICATION: Raisin Hell

The Shriveller can shrink to the size of two or three spookleberries! But he does it by eliminating all water in his body, making it hard for him to accomplish much. Drink more water, guys!

OSTEO FEROCIOUS

CLASSIFICATION: Bony Pony

It appears that Osteo Ferocious is a caveman wearing animal bones, but he's actually animal bones riding a caveman! The bones are a symbiote that controls him! VERY cool!

CARCASSIST

CLASSIFICATION: Conceited Corpse

Even though she's been dead for twenty years, Carcassist insists she's the most beautiful person in Kaptara. What's weird though? She is! Because beauty's in the eye of the beholder.

EXECUTIE

CLASSIFICATION: Hangman Hamster

She was Endom's executioner due to the calming effect she had on those about to die. But everyone committed crimes so they could be killed by her! She was fired and now freelances.

BENJAMIN BLUDGEON

CLASSIFICATION: Killing Time

Believing he has the ability to age backwards with every person he kills, Benjamin Bludgeon has taken many lives! But he actually ages normally, so we're not sure how that idea started.

WIFFLE BAT

CLASSIFICATION: Bad Bat Man

This holy winged creature of the night is a poor flier, so he overcompensated by getting super jacked. He is a very strong bat.

THRUST GUST

CLASSIFICATION: Windy warrior

With his powerful pelvic thrusts, Thrust Gust can create strong winds. Where do the winds come from? Let's not think about it too much, okay?

THE PICKET WITCH OF THE FENCE

CLASSIFICATION: Advice Agitator

The Picket Witch seems friendly, offering up neighbourly advice; but if you listen to her, a series of events will unfold, killing everyone you love!

LAW AND OGRE

CLASSIFICATION: Fanatic Duo

Law is an ex-cop, looking to make some money; Ogre is just a weird thing. Together they take on any assignment, no matter how shady!

VITRIO

CLASSIFICATION: Venomous Triplets

Kaptara's version of a barbershop quartet, but with three members and spewing acid in lieu of beautiful harmonies. If any one of them is out of sync, the others start sulking and refuse to spew for at least a day.

CRABSENT

CLASSIFICATION: Sneaky Crustacean

Where's Crabsent? Probably burrowing underneath you, about to strike. Unless you're standing on rock, of course. So stand on rock.

VAPOR EYES

CLASSIFICATION: Killer Looks

Emitting an all-seeing mist, Vapor Eyes can spy almost anywhere! But while she does that, she can't see where she's going, and her mortal enemy, Staircase, takes full advantage!

CATASTROFLEA

CLASSIFICATION: Ingratiating Insect

A powerful enemy with a ferocious bite, the worst thing about Catastroflea is that it's nearly impossible to get rid of him! He'll literally move into your home if you can't defeat him!

QUASIHOBO

CLASSIFICATION: Shady Hump

Deemed too unattractive to hang with the supermodel homeless of Kaptara, Quasihobo roams the land looking for lodgings and opportunities to use his bindle full of nails.

CATERPILLARPULT

CLASSIFICATION: Larval Siege Weapon

This sentient catapult is ideal for large battles, as she's continually birthing rock-hard babies to be flung at enemies!

INCINERATAUR

CLASSIFICATION: Fire-Breathing Minotaur

Minotaurs are pretty scary as is, so one who breathes fire is terrifying! He can't even breathe out regular air, so he's never been kissed! Hard to be mad at him, really.

HEMOGOBLIN

CLASSIFICATION: Blood Imp

He's made of O-type blood, so if you're hurt in battle, hold him to your open wound and he'll enter you, healing you quickly! But he will also control you, so there's that.

CENTAUR FOR THE HOMELESS

CLASSIFICATION: Selfless Tramp

This "selfless" centaur helps fellow homeless with awareness seminars. But they're actually pyramid schemes! Call him on it and he'll hit you with his signature move: The Tramp Stamp!

BEELZEBULBOUS

CLASSIFICATION: Diseased Devil

This demon appears to be covered in goiters, but they're actually air pockets! And if you pop them during battle, the released air will whisper a devastating truth about you!

WHIPPERSNAPPER

CLASSIFICATION: Fish & Whips

Whippersnapper spends 95% of his time underwater! Which makes it incredibly hard to practice his whipping skills, so he tends to do a lot of it while on land! TO INNOCENT PEOPLE.

WHERE THE WINDS BLEW

THE AUTOBIOGRAPHY OF DARTOR, PRINCE OF ENDOM

An excerpt

I had never intended to go to The City of Lunges, but my best friend, Johnny Fists, refused to believe I was dating a girl there. Yet the fair maiden Mel-Lissa was no imaginary woman-friend! Far from it! She was as real as the many hickeys which adorned my princely neck like bruise jewelry! Johnny Fists laughed at my proof of good times, noting that the dark marks looked like something my roommate, Trunk Hunk, could deliver with ease.

"No one calls Prince Dartor a liar!" I deeply squealed, and punched Johnny Fists in the throat. But, as the old adage goes, "never start a fist fight with a man who has 'fist' in his name." Johnny clocked me but good in my attractive nose, breaking it once again. After our scuffle it was agreed: I must supply definitive proof of Mel-Lissa's existence and interest in me.

She had visited me in Endom a week prior, but had made no plans to return soon, citing the fact that she "had a lot on her plate" and was "going through some stuff." Perhaps a surprise visit from the "Prince of Makeouts" would be just the thing to pick her spirits up! Ha ha!

I left the next day, riding Samuel, my trusty cat-tank, and accompanied by a fine acquaintance, Photo Bomb, who could capture proof of Mel-Lissa and me making love using his built-in torso camera. Could I have simply taken a regular camera on my quest? Of course, but friendship on a long journey is important and I enjoy people watching me make love. I am a giver!

Samuel caught a cold on day two, so I had to put him down on the side of the road. Photo Bomb left a note on his bloated body apologizing for our not burying him, and explaining that we were late for a grand fucking. I dare you to find a single person alive who would not empathize with such a note!

Photo Bomb was a husky man-camera, so I rode him for most of the journey's remainder. At least until he started sniffling. He was a good man and will be missed, but I was not about to give Mel-Lissa a cold on top of what she surely acquired on our first evening of love-making!

So, alone, I strolled Bloodletting Trail, my mind reeling from thoughts of all the wonderful sex I was to have in three days time. Oh, Mel-Lissa! With your correct number of teeth and interesting body! Soon you would be mine yet again!

As I approached The City of Lunges days later, a man stood on the trail, defiantly in the centre. He was a burly, middle-aged sort with a receding hairline and a very droopy face. He was almost nude, save for much gold jewelry and a fur-covered girdle and manties (man panties). Also, he was covered in blood.

"Hello!" I barked, one hand on my trusty blowgun, the other waving like a child. The man held his sword away from him like a cock presented to a loved one on Freedom Day.

"WHO GOES THERE?" he barked back.

I barked once again. "I am Dartor, Prince of Endom! And I have come to make love to Mel-Lissa, Music Promoter of The City of Lunges! Step aside or feel the sting of my nasty darts!" The road gentleman's muscles tensed and he declaratively barked back, "I AM RED CARL, WARRIOR OF THE LOST LANDS. AND WHOSOEVER BEATS ME IN BATTLE GETS TO BED ME."

Red Carl was not my type, so this unusual offer held no appeal to me, but getting past him and on to Mel-Lissa (and onto Mel-Lissa ha ha) did. "I do not wish to bed you! But I really need to get past you to a very important appointment! Is there any way of—"

Red Carl swung his sword, narrowly missing my powerful chest. I stumbled back and quickly put blowgun to lips. I blew a tight, short burst of air and a level seven intoxication dart flew toward my new nemesis. But Red Carl was faster than he appeared, and knocked the dart to the ground with his blade. His next swing caught my blowgun itself, cutting it in two and rendering it useless. All I had now was my greatest weapon of all: my body.

As Red Carl swung his blade again, I dove to the ground, avoiding its trajectory. Once low, I punched the fiend's left knee quite hard, and he tumbled to the ground in agony. I took that moment to leap atop him, knocking the sword from his grasp. He struggled mightily, but a classic "Dartor-elbow-to-the-face" showed him he was defeated. He looked up at me with fury and sadness.

"You have defeated me. I am yours." Red Carl gestured with his head down to his very average body, dotted with sporadic tufts of hair. Again, he was not my type, but I admired how he swung his blade, so I kissed him. He eagerly returned my affection and we fucked in the road for hours. Later, as we lay off to the side of that dusty trail to finally let the backed-up carriages through, I managed to get him to admit that he does this every day because it is the only way he knows to explore this side of himself while still honouring his marriage to a lovely office administrator that he'd been with since high school.

"I made up this code, which she respects, even though it confuses her. I suppose one day I will just have to talk to her honestly about an open marriage." He grew sad, which, frankly, is a huge turn-off for me, so I left. Did I continue on to meet Mel-Lissa and her expected sex?

Aye, I did.

Kagan McLeod is an illustrator whose work has been published by *Newsweek*, *Sports Illustrated*, *The Wall Street Journal*, and *Entertainment Weekly*. He did a book all by his lonesome called *Infinite Kung Fu* (Top Shelf), which Chip was the first to read.

Chip Zdarsky likes to party. In between parties he writes and/or illustrates comic books, such as *Jughead* (Archie), *Howard the Duck* (Marvel), and the award-winning *Sex Criminals* (Image). So maybe you should invite him to more parties?